Not Death,
But Love

A Quill Gordon Mystery

Michael Wallace

ISBN: 978-0-9903871-1-4

Cover Design: Deborah Karas, Karas Technical Services

Amazon Readers Praise
The Quill Gordon Mysteries

The McHenry Inheritance
Average rating 4.1 out of 5 stars

"I really enjoyed reading this story and getting to know the characters. In a very short time, I found myself caring what happened to them. I am a mystery fan, and this definitely was a fun ride."

—Mountain Mom

"Quill Gordon courts trout, a lady, and justice, and there's a little 'catch and release' applied to all three in this most entertaining murder mystery."

—Edan D. Cassidy

"Well written good story. Ready for next book about these people. Could be a start to a fun set of books."

—Tim Smith

Wash Her Guilt Away
Average rating: 4.7 out of 5 stars

"The characters are so well drawn, each one seemed to be plucked from real life and placed into the story."

—Sentia

"As languid and dark as a quiet trout stream on an overcast day, the second Quill Gordon novel is a pleasure to read ... even the weather has a plot twist."

—Judy Parrish

"The fly-fishing descriptions were amazing. I was thoroughly engaged. I couldn't figure out who dunnit until the very end ... Great story."

—Lovedrama

Also by Michael Wallace

Quill Gordon Mysteries

The McHenry Inheritance
Wash Her Guilt Away

Nonfiction

The Borina Family of Watsonville (California history)

**In the spirit of Anthony Berkeley
and Earl Derr Biggers**

*For Jack McDonald,
Carroll Irwin and Ruth Carruth:
Terrific English teachers*

Table of Contents

I thought once how Theocritus had sung
    Of the sweet years, the dear and wished-for years,
    Who each one in a gracious hand appears
To bear a gift for mortals, old or young:
And, as I mused it in his antique tongue,
    I saw, in gradual vision through my tears,
    The sweet, sad years, the melancholy years,
Those of my own life, who by turns had flung
A shadow across me. Straightway I was 'ware,
    So weeping, how a mystic Shape did move
Behind me, and drew me backward by the hair;
    And a voice said in mastery, while I strove,—
'Guess now who holds thee?'—'Death,' I said. But, there,
    The silver answer rang,—'Not Death, but Love.'

                    — Elizabeth Barrett Browning
                    Sonnets from the Portuguese

The Searcher and the Match

THE INTRUDER WAS ABOUT to leave the house, but decided, out of customary caution, to look through the desk one more time. Missing something now would be no more than a minor problem, but it would be better to have everything in hand.

There was little point in checking the middle drawer again; the owner used it to house the various paraphernalia — pens, pencils, stamps, envelopes, blank pads, paper clips — that one typically uses at a desk.

In the top right drawer was a .38 Smith & Wesson revolver. It was highly unlikely that the owner of the house ever touched it; probably it had belonged to her father and simply remained where he kept it after he died.

The next drawer down was one that called for a special look. It contained the most papers, but nearly all were systematically filed in one of a half-dozen file folders, all labeled with some aspect of the minutiae of daily life. Taking each file out separately, the intruder again flipped through them slowly and carefully. Nothing seemed to be anything other than what it plainly appeared to be. After several minutes of close scrutiny, the files went back into the drawer. However, the business card that had been sitting on the top of the desk, with its unusual name and a San Francisco address, puzzled and troubled the intruder, who decided to hold on to it just in case.

Her journal was in the third and bottom-most drawer, along with an address book, personal stationery and two boxes of thank-you notes. The last journal entry was dated three days ago, and the first entry three months ago. None of the 50 written pages dealt with what the intruder was concerned about. It was actually a bit depressing — the random musings of a seemingly dull life. The intruder began reading the last three pages again just to be sure.

The phone on the desk rang.

Dropping the journal on the floor, the intruder sat up, tensed, relaxed, then retrieved the journal, replaced it in the drawer, and began leaving the room while counting the number of rings.

Four, five, six, seven. Who in God's name, the intruder thought, has the phone ring seven times before letting the machine pick up? The intruder entered the spacious living room, with its massive stone fireplace, comfortable old furniture and large picture windows looking out over the lake. A trace of light remained in the sky behind the mountains, but darkness was fast taking over.

From the living room, it would be easy enough to hear the answering machine in the adjacent kitchen. It clicked on after the greeting, and the volume was clearly turned to the loudest setting. The voice on the other end practically bellowed.

"Hi, it's me — Gina. Hope you haven't forgotten our sherry nightcap. Maybe you're just out getting a new bottle. I'll be there in 30. See you." Click.

The intruder's heart was beating faster now. No time to lose. Stepping over the woman's body on the floor in front of the fireplace and moving to the front door, the intruder looked at the large pile of oily rags in the service area just off the entryway. For a moment, the intruder considered pouring some gasoline from the can in the car onto the hardwood floors but decided against it. The oily rags would take a bit longer to get going, but with any luck, it might look as if they had spontaneously combusted. The intruder took out a book of matches and prepared to light one, turning to the body on the floor and saying:

"So long. I don't know where you put it, but as long as everything burns, it doesn't matter. You should have stuck to gardening and left things alone. No sense in digging up the past. Just leave us to our memories. It was better then."

Striking the match, the intruder threw it on the pile of rags, which burst into flame, then closed the front door, adding:

"And sorry about the sherry."

The intruder walked briskly back to the car and drove off. By the time a neighbor called 911 and the sirens started, the intruder was miles away.

Part I: Trust

"Charlotte did not stay much longer, and Elizabeth was then left to reflect on what she had heard."

— **AUSTEN**, *Pride and Prejudice*

Monday June 17, 1996

QUILL GORDON WAS BEGINNING to tuck into his breakfast of scrambled eggs, sausage and hash browns at the Shotgun Café when he became aware of someone standing over him. Looking up, he saw a handsome woman of about 60, trim and alert, with short gray hair streaked with a bit of black. She was dressed in khaki slacks and a blue-checked gingham shirt, long-sleeved, with the sleeves rolled up in anticipation of a warm day. She had a folio notebook under her arm and a determined look in her steel-gray eyes. Gordon immediately sized her up as a schoolteacher and, minding his manners, stood up.

"May I help you?" he asked.

"You used 'may'; that is an auspicious beginning," she said.

So I was right about the teacher part, he thought.

"I realize this is somewhat unusual," she said, "but you look like an honest man, and I was wondering if I might talk with you for a few minutes."

There was no polite way of saying no, and in any event he was mildly intrigued. "Please sit down," he said, gesturing to an empty chair at the table for four. "My name is Quill Gordon, and this is my friend, Dr. Peter Delaney."

She shook his hand, sat down, and reached across the table to shake Peter's. "Charlotte London," she said. "Please go on with your breakfasts."

"Would you like coffee or something?"

"No thank you," she said. "I've had my two cups for the morning. I'm fine." She set the notebook on the table in front of her. It had a cover of brown leather, worn to a fine patina, and a zipper around three sides of the perimeter. She unzipped it to reveal a letter-sized pad inside under a 9-by-12 manila envelope. She took the envelope out and set it atop the leather after closing the notebook.

"It's the most extraordinary thing, really, and you'll probably think I'm dotty. But I assure you I'm not. I need someone to hold on to this," she lifted the envelope, "for a short time. It would take too long to explain, but no one local will do. May I ask you a few questions?"

"You can always ask."

"Thank you. I assume you're visiting from outside the area?"

"We're up from San Francisco to do some fishing."

"And how long will you be here?"

"Until the middle of next week."

"Excellent. I expect this matter to be resolved by then. Tell me a bit about yourself. Where did you go to school?"

"Cal. Class of '81."

"And what was your major?"

"U.S. history, with a minor in English."

"Better and better. And when you were at school, were you involved in any extracurricular activities?"

"Well, I played on the basketball team."

"That doesn't count," she said. "I meant of an intellectual nature."

Gordon was taken aback, but tried not to show it. At Cal, he had been a starter and was named second-team all-conference his senior year; even today many people meeting him remembered that.

"I was on an athletic scholarship," he said calmly. "It took up most of my time outside the classroom."

"I suppose," she said. "Would you call yourself curious and inquisitive?"

"I'd say so."

"Are you good at analyzing information and reaching conclusions for it?"

"It's what I did for a living," he replied. That was actually a bit of an understatement. After graduation, he had worked at the old-line San Francisco brokerage Howell, Burns & Bledsoe for a dozen years and had made enough of a fortune through his own investments to quit less than three years ago.

She looked into his eyes for several seconds.

"I think you'll do — that is, if you are willing. I assure you there's nothing illicit or illegal about this. It's

6

simply a personal matter where I need a backup copy kept in a safe place. Will you hold this for me — probably for no more than a week?"

"I'm honored that you asked," he said, "but are you sure *you* want to do this? After all, we've only known each other for, what, three minutes?"

She smiled a winning smile. "Mr. Gordon, I taught high school English for more than 30 years. By the end of that time, I could walk into a class on the first day of school and tell you in five minutes who the honor students were and who the hooligans were. I don't know yet if you are an honor student, but you assuredly are no hooligan."

He took a sip of coffee. "All right, Ms. London. I'll do it for you."

"*Miss* London, please. I've never liked the other title."

"Miss London, then. But can you tell me a little more about it."

She looked at her watch. "I haven't the time right now, but you certainly have a right to know more. Could I invite you and Dr. Delaney to be my guests for lunch on Wednesday, the day after tomorrow? I can explain better then."

"Fair enough."

"Thank you so much. It's probably nothing, but it means a great deal to me." She handed the envelope across the table to him. It was sealed and clasped shut. "All I ask is that you keep it in a safe place and don't look at it. Do you have a card?"

He reached into his wallet and took out one of his personal cards, which read simply "Quill Gordon, Investor and Financial Consultant." Underneath in smaller type were his P.O. Box number, the phone number at his San Francisco apartment, and his pager number. He handed it to her, and she held it at arm's length, looking at it studiously.

" 'Getting and spending, we lay waste our powers,' " she said at last.

" 'Little we see in nature that is ours.' You know your Wordsworth, though that's to be expected," he said.

She flashed a big, warm smile. "Yes, this will do just fine. I'm sure of it now. As I said, simply keep the envelope in a safe place, and do *not* open it unless authorized to do so by me or by my attorney, Cameron Winters. Shall we say one o'clock Wednesday at Ike's Lakeside by Woodward Marina?"

"We'll be there."

"Thank you again. I'm probably worrying about nothing, but it's a relief to me that you have this. I'll see you Wednesday Mr. Gordon, doctor."

She stood up, looked around the café to see if anyone was watching her, then walked resolutely to the front door and left.

Gordon returned to his breakfast and dispatched half his plate before turning to Peter.

"You were uncharacteristically quiet."

Peter shrugged. "She had her eye on you," he said. "I wonder what's in that envelope. The way she came up to you out of nowhere was like something out of a 1940s spy movie."

"She'll tell us on Wednesday, and it'll probably be a letdown. But I'm not looking at it. She trusted me — God knows why — so I have to honor that."

"You want to know what I think, Gordon? This may be God's way of telling you it's time to get married. Your groupies are getting older."

Gordon laughed. "She wasn't looking at me that way, Peter. I wonder if she's ever looked at a man that way."

Peter took another bite of his vegetarian omelet and chewed it thoughtfully.

"It pains me to disagree," he finally said, "but I think you might be reading her wrong. A woman who's been single for a long time can become the most hot-blooded romantic there is. No, it wouldn't surprise me at all if our Miss London turned out to have a reservoir of passion inside her that makes Lake Año Nuevo look like a backyard fish pond by comparison."

Gordon took another sip of coffee.

"Not that we'll ever know," he said.

"Actually," Peter continued, "I'm more surprised that she was so easily won over when you dished

Wordsworth back at her. After all, the world is full of villains who can quote poetry."

THEY EMERGED FROM THE CAFÉ just before nine o'clock into a lovely June morning. The temperature was 55 degrees, but warmer in the sunlight; the air was redolent with the smell of pine needles; and the sky was a rich, clear blue with one small, puffy white cloud on the southern horizon.

"Where are we fishing, boss?" said Peter as they got into Gordon's silver Cherokee. "I'm sure you have it figured out."

"I have a boat booked for us at the marina for the second half of the day," Gordon said. "Three p.m. to sunset. If you can't wait to get started, there are a couple of places we could try this morning, but …"

"You'd rather do something else?"

Gordon looked around. They were parked perpendicular to the café, just off the shoulder of the state highway that ran through the town of Arthur, located at the northwest edge of Lake Año Nuevo, 4,944 feet above sea level in the Cascade Mountains in northeastern California. The traffic was light enough that Gordon could have closed his eyes and backed onto the highway, heading in either direction, with a 90 percent chance of not hitting anything.

"It's been 15 years since I was here," he said. "I'd like to spend the morning driving around and checking it out, if you're okay with that."

"I'm easy. But can we go back to the inn for a second? I don't have my sunglasses."

Gordon backed onto the road after checking carefully in all directions and headed north toward the edge of town, where he and Peter had rooms at Stanhope House.

"By the way," Peter said, as they started up the highway, "thanks for not leaving the city until the afternoon yesterday."

"How did it go?"

"A bit uneasy, as you might expect. But overall, better than I would have hoped. My little girl is turning into a beautiful young woman."

"Was it your first Father's Day with her?"

Peter nodded. "First since she was a toddler, anyway. As you know, my second wife and I don't get along very well, even now. Heather's grown up hearing a lot of bad things about me." He paused. "Some of them might even be true."

"But *she* called *you,* right?"

"Out of the blue. And I don't think she told her mother. She said she wanted to take me to brunch for Father's Day. She just finished her freshman year at UC-Santa Cruz, so we met at a place in Los Gatos." His voice was beginning to shake a bit, and he turned to look out the window. Gordon said nothing and slowed down. "She asked a lot of questions, and I answered the best I could. I'm still processing it. How about you? Do anything special for the day?"

"Actually, it worked out well for me, too. I took the judge out for brunch, just the two of us. My sisters were going to take him and mom out for dinner last night. He got a bit of a double-dip."

"My dad died 15 years ago," Peter said. "All the time I was growing up, I never saw him without a cigarette in his mouth. At age 54, he keeled over from a heart attack at work and was gone by the time the ambulance arrived. He hadn't been seeing a doctor, so they did an autopsy. Turned out he had stage three lung cancer, too."

"That's tough."

"In hindsight, the heart attack may have been a blessing. But it left us with some unsettled business that'll never be resolved." He sighed. "How do you and your dad get along?"

"Reasonably well, all things considered. But I guess we still have some things to clear up, too."

Peter raised his eyebrows.

"What can I say?" Gordon said. "He's my father and I'm his son. We don't always see eye to eye. Here we are."

Stanhope House was a large two-story house, built in the late 1880s, set back from the highway behind about 40 yards of immaculately tended lawn, dotted with pine trees and with a row of aspens marking the northern boundary of the property. There were eight guest rooms in the main house and another six in a renovated carriage house behind it. Gordon stopped on the driveway in front of the main entrance, set a few feet above the ground at the end of a flight of six steps and flanked by a broad porch, shaded by overhang most of the day. The honeymooners in Room 7 were sitting in a rocking bench to the right of the door, holding hands and oblivious to the world.

"I'll be right back," Peter said.

As he started for the house, Gordon looked down and saw Miss London's envelope leaning against the center console.

"Peter!" he shouted, transferring it to his left hand and holding it out the window. "Can you put this in your room for the time being?"

He came back for it and bounded briskly up the stairs. Two minutes later, wearing his sunglasses, he was back in the passenger seat.

"I thought we could drive counterclockwise around the lake," Gordon said. "There's a paved road all around."

"Coriolis effect," said Peter. "Well, we *are* in the Northern Hemisphere."

They turned right from the driveway, heading back into town. Stanhope House was at the northern end of it, at the older part, where the original settlement had been. A hundred feet from the inn they came to the town's entrance sign, with its slogan, "Welcome to Arthur — Your Four Seasons Recreation Area." Below that were the logos of the various clubs in town: Elks, Lions, Masons, and so on. Gordon noted that the Rotary Club, to which his father belonged in San Francisco, met Thursdays at noon. To the right of the welcome sign was another, smaller but clearly distinct. "You're in Cougar Country," it read, and below that, "1962 Northern California Division II Basketball Champions."

"Champions," Peter said. "Men or women, do you suppose?"

"No Title IX then, so it had to be men. And back then, they were called boys."

"I stand corrected. Do you know the story?"

"I could hazard a guess, but it shouldn't be hard to find out. It was probably one of the biggest things that ever happened here, and lots of people would remember. It wouldn't surprise me if half the team's still living here."

The state highway was the main commercial street, and Gordon drove slowly, passing Nelson's Hardware and Sporting Goods, the Forest *Clarion* newspaper office, Proffit's Supermarket, Garbini's Italian Restaurant, the Dew Drop Inn Saloon and Social Club, Fred's Barber Shop, and the Galloping Goose Gift Shop, among other establishments. After a quarter mile they came to the bridge crossing the North Fork of Hawk River, which was running high and fast after the wet winter. To the left on the other side of the bridge, Ponderosa Street ran parallel to the river, passing a park with a large lawn and shaded picnic area.

The part of town on the south side of the bridge was more recently developed, but not necessarily more charming. In short order they passed a post office building with a pinewood front that looked to be ten to 15 years old, a relatively small Safeway, a Rite Aid drugstore, and a Ben Franklin five and dime. Small, locally owned restaurants were mixed in with McDonald's and KFC; there was a Chevron station, a Shell station, and several mini-marts selling non-branded gasoline. Lodging was represented by the Pine Cone, Lakeview (with no lake view), Hawk Valley, Buckhorn and Lumberjack motels.

Just beyond the Shotgun Café, Gordon turned left onto Union Street.

"A detour, so soon?" Peter said.

"This is where the courthouse and high school are."

The courthouse, which they later learned was built in the early 1960s, was a nondescript two-story concrete building. Its architects had made only one concession to style or comfort: large windows all around, allowing the bright mountain light into the building. Across the street from the courthouse was the public library, about the size of a decent branch library in San Francisco. It was a single-story building with the left side ten feet higher than the right, and a channeled steel roof with no gutters connecting the two.

"Probably easier for the snow to melt that way," Gordon said.

They continued down the street. The next two blocks were residential, but the second house down from the courthouse had a shingle over the porch proclaiming it to be the law offices of Cameron A. Winters, Esq. The houses on the street were all one story and of postwar vintage. Many of them had carports, and typically one side of the carport was stacked floor to ceiling with cut firewood.

"You wouldn't think they'd need that wood in the summer," Peter said.

"Ever heard the old joke about life in the mountains?" Gordon said. "They say the weather's nine months of winter and three months of bad skiing. That wood's drying out now so they can start burning it in mid-September."

Union Street dead-ended a quarter mile from the lakeshore, with the high school, out for the summer now, taking up both sides of the last block. On the right side were the administration building, classrooms and auditorium — wood-paneled exteriors with sloping sheet-metal roofs painted crimson, the school color. A sign in front of the building closest to the street announced that summer session would begin next week, and its framing read: "President Arthur High School, Home of the Cougars. Built 1964."

Gordon stopped the car for a minute and they looked.

"Built two years after the basketball team won the championship," Peter said. "I'll bet the school board decided that would be a good time to float a construction bond."

"No bet. I think you're right."

"Since you're the history major, tell me what President Arthur was famous for?"

"Not much. He took over when James Garfield was assassinated in 1881. Probably best known for civil service reform."

Peter nodded. "That explains why the team's called the Cougars. Somehow, the Fighting Bureaucrats wouldn't exactly strike fear into the hearts of opponents."

"Around here it might."

Gordon started the car forward again and turned it around at the loop at the end of the street. Now the athletic facilities opposite the classrooms were on their right. The Gary A. Bowman Gymnasium, a tall rectangular building, came up to the street near the edge of the loop. On the lake side of it was a large parking lot, presumably for games. On the other side was a large open area with four outdoor basketball courts (the nets made with metal chain to better handle the elements) and two tennis courts enclosed by a chain-link fence. Four young men were playing a two-on-two basketball game (skins and shirts) on one of the courts.

"Want to go show them how it's done?" Peter asked.

"No thanks. I'm getting to the age where *they* might show *me*."

Behind the basketball courts, they could see the aluminum bleachers, marked-off football field, and scoreboard of what a prominent sign identified as Leonard Iverson Field.

"If you're going to ask me who Gary A. Bowman and Leonard Iverson were," Gordon said, "the answer is I don't know. But the smart money would be they were coaches."

He drove back to the state highway and turned left, heading out of town. After a half mile they were at the outskirts. Two miles beyond that, on the right side of the road, was the Forest County Airport, a single concrete strip long enough to land a smokejumper or small private jet, with a small administration building that looked like a large mobile home and shared quarters with a small coffee shop. It looked as if it had been put up temporarily a quarter century ago and never replaced with a permanent building. They were driving away from the lake at this point, but just past the airport they turned left on to another state highway heading south, more or less following the west shore of the lake.

They drove south for ten miles. On the right side, every so often, roads, most of them dirt, headed off into the mountains from the valley. Gordon pointed out two: The Bull Meadow road, which led to Copper Creek, one of California's wild trout streams, and the road to Bottom Lake, a reservoir he thought they might check out during their stay.

On their left the landscape continuously changed. At some places they had a clear view to the lake. At others there was dense pine forest through which nothing could be seen. At one point, the highway climbed more than a hundred feet up the side of a cliff, before descending again. Some of the area was developed: two campgrounds and two subdivisions of vacation and permanent homes, set back from the highway and nestled among the pines well enough to be largely invisible to passing motorists.

Eventually, they came to a sign pointing left to County Road A22, labeled "Año Nuevo Dam Road/The Peninsulas." Gordon turned onto it. It was two lanes, paved (but poorly) with no shoulder. They followed it through a dense forest for a quarter-mile, then up a slight rise, at the top of which it became apparent they were about to cross the top of the dam. There was a turnout, large enough for two or three cars, just before the dam and Gordon pulled into it and turned off the engine. Even with the windows closed, they could hear the sound of cascading water.

"Let's check the spillway," Gordon said.

It was after ten a.m. now, and the temperature had risen into the mid-60s, with the faintest of breezes wafting a bouquet of pine needles and campfire smoke through the air. The road across the dam had a waist-high guardrail on either side and an elevated sidewalk two feet wide — just enough to accommodate, if not encourage, pedestrians. They walked about 50 yards to where the road crossed a 60-foot notch in the dam; it was the overflow spillway to release extra runoff early in the season. Stopping in the center of the notch, they looked down to see a fast and deep torrent of water washing under them, then down a steeply angled channel where it frothed, all white, to a riverbed about 150 feet below. The noise was so loud they had to shout to be heard over it.

"This is what happens after a wet winter," Gordon yelled.

Peter nodded. "I'm getting vertigo. Let's go back." He turned back toward the Cherokee, and Gordon followed him.

Crossing the dam, they passed one car coming the other direction. On the other side, they went through a section of forest, during which they crossed Año Nuevo Creek, only ten feet wide during spring runoff. Then there was a stretch of about a mile and a half where there were homes on either side of the road, facing the lake, followed by a rise and drop through a brief forest stretch in which they crossed Trout Creek, slightly smaller than Año Nuevo. As they got back near lake level, Gordon began looking more closely at the left side of the road. He soon saw a log arch rising 15 feet above a driveway and turned under it into Shore Acres Resort.

Almost immediately they were on a gravel road that veered right through a glade and emerged into a large, well-tended lawn on the left, with volleyball and badminton nets, a swing set, a carousel, and several picnic tables. The tables were empty, but a half dozen children, occasionally watched by two mothers talking to each other, were using the swings and carousel, their shrieks of delight carrying across the lawn. On the right side of the road, facing the lawn, were eight rustic pinewood cabins, each with a deck and parking space. The railings on most of the decks were draped with drying swimsuits and beach towels. Gordon stopped in front of one.

"Juniper," he said. "That's where we stayed."

"You were here 15 years ago?" Peter said.

Gordon nodded. "Right about this time of year."

"Any particular reason?"

"I'd just graduated from Cal and was at a turning point. I had three options, really. "My father wanted me to go to law school, and as a gesture to that, and to keep my options open, I applied to Santa Clara and McGeorge. Santa Clara accepted me, but I didn't really want to go. I also had an offer to play basketball for a team in Germany."

"But you didn't?"

"The money wasn't great, and I would have been tenth or 11th man on the roster. It wasn't what you call a growth opportunity. Still, I thought about doing it for a year, just to buy time. Then, a week before graduation, I got a call from Howell, Burns & Bledsoe asking if I'd like to interview for an associate broker position.

"How did they find you?"

"Burns and Bledsoe, it turns out, were big Cal sports fans."

"But not Howell?"

"Dead, I'm afraid. Though in some of the crowds at our games, no one would have noticed. Anyway, they thought I might be able to bring in some athletes as clients. They made a good offer, and I was ready to take it. The judge wasn't happy, and when he was coming up here for a week, I agreed to go with him so we could talk things out."

"How did that go?"

"We agreed to disagree, but only because he had no choice. I was legally an adult and had the law on my side. It was the only argument he understood."

"Any reason for coming here specifically?"

"He was trying case too hot for the locals. An attorney shot his wife during an argument. Didn't kill her, but it was still attempted murder. Judge Fletcher — I wonder if he's still around? — took himself off it because he knew the lawyer so well. The district attorney's office wanted nothing to do with it, either, so the state attorney general's office handled the prosecution." He paused and looked down at the pier. "Judge Fletcher took me fishing a couple of times, though. I'm going to get a bottle of water."

He drove to the far side of the lawn where there was a log building that hosted the office, store and a small café. It sat at the top of a road leading downhill to the right toward a pier and boat launch. He stopped in front of the building, turned off the engine, went up three steps to the store and was back in two minutes. Peter asked how the trial turned out.

"He was acquitted," Gordon said. "I know. I was surprised, too. It seemed like an open-and-shut case, and his defense — that the gun went off when he was trying to take it away from her — was pretty lame and didn't match the other evidence. I asked the judge about it."

"Judge Fletcher or your dad?"

"Number two. He gave me that tight-lipped smile of his and said, 'Hometown verdict, son. He was guilty, but he grew up here, while his wife was from the Bay Area. To the jury, she was an outsider.' That's all he said."

"Frontier justice," Peter said. "But I wonder if your schoolteacher friend was thinking of something like that when she gave you the envelope. You know, that people here hang together so much she couldn't trust anyone she knew with it."

"Could be. We'll know more when we have lunch with her, but let's not let it interfere with our fishing."

He turned left on the county road and continued driving more or less north along the east shore of the lake, past lakefront homes, a couple of older resorts, a campground, and stretches of mostly empty forest. At a sign reading "East Peninsula," they turned left again, and after driving through more forest and a small meadow, came to an area with a golf course on the right and a tract of homes, all 20 years old or less, on the left. The golf course was doing a brisk business, judging from the number of players in shorts and polo shirts, and at one point they drove by a driveway to the clubhouse. Then the road dipped downhill and came to a commercial area consisting of small strip malls on either side of the road. Between them they held a medium-sized grocery store, a Bank of America, a small hardware store, a tiny post office, a pizza parlor and hamburger joint and a couple of gift shops. The strip mall on the left was called London Center.

"Any connection to our friend from this morning?" asked Peter.

"I don't know, but it's not that common a name, so probably."

He turned right at the shopping area and took a road that followed the western shore of the peninsula. There were more lakeside homes and another small resort.

"Lot more built up since the last time I was here," Gordon said.

The road looped around the peninsula, back past the shopping center again, then out to the county road, which they followed again for two miles before turning on to the West Peninsula.

"There were two creeks," Gordon said, "that used to flow into the north fork of the Hawk River before it was dammed. The reservoir filled up the creek beds, but the ridges on either side were above water and became two peninsulas jutting out into the lake. A lot of summer homes here now, plus some places where the better-off locals live."

The lake's primary marina was at the eastern tip of the West Peninsula, along with a small commercial complex that included Ike's Lakeside, a white-tablecloth establishment built partly on pilings jutting out into the water. It was past 11 a.m. now, and the temperature was in the mid-70s. The waterskiing crowd was beginning to go out, and the marina walkways were crowded with parents in shorts and short-sleeved tops leading processions of life-jacket-clad youngsters to powerful motorboats.

Gordon was scanning the surroundings. "It's still here," he said.

"What?"

He gestured to a hamburger stand at the edge of the marina. "The Chainsaw. Best burgers and frosties in town."

"I'm still full from breakfast."

"Have a frosty, anyway. My treat. We can come back in a couple of hours for a burger before we head out fishing."

They walked to the stand and got in line behind three families with indecisive children. When they finally reached the window they were greeted by a young woman of high-school age. She was still trying to master the finer points of eye makeup and fingernail polish but was brimming with positive attitude. She quickly presented them with their cones and they moved to one of the plastic tables, shaded by an umbrella.

"What a hoot," said Peter, licking his frosty. "I haven't had one of these in 25 years. I'd forgotten they even existed."

"Savor the moment, Peter. We're here for ten days of fun and relaxation. Nothing is going to keep us from taking it easy. It'll be like being a kid again."

AT HALF PAST TWO they returned to the Chainsaw for hamburgers and a basket of fries. The burgers, exquisitely seasoned with 20 years' accumulation of grease on the grill, required no condiments, and the fries glistened with residue of the boiling oil from which they had just been plucked. Afterward, they picked up their boat, a small aluminum craft with tattered cushions and a motor capable of speeds up to 15 mph — with the wind at its back. Gordon sat at the stern by the motor and guided the boat onto the lake.

The temperature had risen to the mid-80s, but with the dry mountain air the heat was not uncomfortable. A bank of cumulus clouds was forming over the mountains to the west, but not enough to suggest rain. Gordon took a course that led them past the tip of the East Peninsula, then followed the eastern shoreline of the lake, keeping about 200 feet from land most of the time. By hugging the shore, they stayed out of the way of the water-skiers, speedboaters and jet-skiers, who stayed toward the middle of the lake where they had sufficient room to maneuver and go as fast as they wanted. Gordon's eyes moved constantly, taking in all the surroundings, but focusing primarily on the water between the boat and land.

"Looking for anything in particular?" Peter asked.

"Several things. Coves; shallow areas with weeds that produce insects; and streams running into the lake. They're all promising." He looked behind at the sun, still high in the sky. "Probably a bit early for the good fishing, but you never know. If the sun goes behind those clouds, it might pick up a bit, but the real activity most likely won't get going until around 6:30."

"How do we fish it?"

"Underneath the surface, unless we see fish rising. We could work a nymph under an indicator or try a Woolly Bugger [a large, sinking fly that imitates a leech or minnow] with a short, jerky retrieve. I don't know. We might get an insect hatch later on and be able to fish dry flies. That'd be fun."

They came to a spot along the shore where a small stream, no more than four feet wide, entered the lake. Peter opted to fish a gold-ribbed Hare's Ear Nymph eight or nine feet under an indicator, and Gordon tied on an olive Woolly Bugger. On the second cast, Peter caught, landed and released a 12-inch Rainbow Trout, and on his third cast, Gordon caught an 11-inch Rainbow. Several more casts with no action suggested the two fish were outliers, so they moved south along the shore, heading toward the dam. From time to time, Gordon stopped the boat and they tried their luck. If no fish took their flies after a half-dozen casts, they moved on. If one or both of them caught a fish, which happened sporadically, they kept working the area until they had each made six casts without a fish — at which point they moved on. At one point, Peter asked Gordon why he was leaving an area after six unproductive casts.

"Simple," he replied. "We know from the fact we're catching some fish that there's nothing wrong with our flies or technique. So when we aren't catching them, it probably means they're not there. It's still early, so most of the fish aren't coming out to feed yet. What we're doing at this point is moving from one small group of fish, or the occasional lone wolf, to the next."

At 6:45 they reached Año Nuevo Creek. They were not far from the dam now, and there was a rope with floating buoys stretched across the lake to keep boats from drifting too close to the dam, or, more dangerously, being sucked toward the spillway. The creek bounded down a hill in a series of short cascades and pools shaded by trees and other riparian vegetation. At lake level it ran across a strip of gravel beach no more than 20 feet wide before emptying into the reservoir. The sun was mostly behind the clouds in the west and the light was less bright and more diffuse than earlier in the afternoon.

As predicted, it was the time of day when the fish were beginning to feed in earnest, and for the next hour they rarely went more than a few casts without hooking a fish. Most were Rainbows, ten to 13 inches, but Peter landed one that was 16 inches, and Gordon caught and released a 15-inch Brown Trout. At 7:45, insects began appearing in consistent numbers on the surface of the water, and the trout rose to feed on them. They switched to dry flies and caught several nice fish, then at 8:30, the insects vanished and the surface feeding stopped.

The sun had dropped behind the western mountains, and its waning light turned the cloudy sky into a palette of pink, orange, gray, white and blue. What wind there had been died down, and on the shore a cricket concerto was underway. Gordon looked around with a smile on his face.

"As good as it gets, Peter. As good as it gets." He looked at his watch. "We could keep fishing under the surface and catch more, but it's a good 45 minutes to the marina. You all right with heading back?"

"I've caught enough to be happy. Let's go."

They started back. For half an hour, the western sky put on its light show, but it was nearly dark as they approached the East Peninsula. Moving slowly across the lake, they saw ducks, the occasional rising trout, a couple of other boats heading for the marina, and the houses along the shore with their lights on.

Then there was a noise that was jarringly out of place.

It was faint at first, but quickly recognizable as a siren that grew in volume, followed by another and a third. In the still, quiet air of a mountain evening, the siren sound carried and resonated, beginning to echo from the surrounding mountains. Passing the tip of the East Peninsula, they saw, just a few hundred yards away, the reason for the sirens.

A handsome, modern-looking house, probably not much more than 20 years old, was on fire, the tops of the flames licking the branches of surrounding trees. The firelight was reflected in the lake and lit up Gordon's and Peter's faces. The first fire truck pulled up as they watched, and the crew raced to get its hoses out, but it was clear that not much of the house could be saved, and that the firefighters would be concentrating on keeping the flames from spreading to the trees and any nearby houses. A second and third engine pulled up within a minute.

"Aw, jeez. You hate to see that," Gordon said somberly.

"I know. The only good thing about it is that it's still early. Anybody who was in there probably wasn't sleeping and got out all right."

"There may not have been anyone in there. A lot of those are vacation homes. Still, too bad."

They cruised silently to the marina, tied up their boat, collected their gear, and trudged to Gordon's Cherokee in the parking lot. By the time they reached it, the firefighters had made good work of the burning house, which was now merely glowing and flickering. A light breeze had come up from the east and was blowing smoke in their direction. They could smell it as they got into the car, and, driving with the windows down, for several minutes afterward.

Tuesday June 18

THEY ROSE AT FIRST LIGHT, dressed quickly, and left Stanhope House shortly before six. Breakfast was included with the room but was not served until eight, and it was imperative, Gordon said, that they be on the water well before then. With apologies to their hostess, Emma Crisp, they skipped the meal for the second day in a row.

A mile south of Stanhope House, well past the bridge over Hawk River, Gordon turned into a small strip mall with six storefronts, two of them vacant. At least one of the other four businesses, The Hellwithit Bakery, was doing well, judging from the half-dozen people waiting outside. The door swung open exactly at six, and the customers streamed in as Gordon parked in front of it. Once inside, they inhaled the aroma of freshly baked cinnamon rolls until their turn came. Each man got a croissant and muffin (bran for Gordon, blueberry for Peter) and filled a travel mug with coffee. Gordon asked the sales clerk to add a liter thermos of coffee to the tab and came back to get it filled it after paying.

On the road again, they drove with the windows down, enjoying the damp, piney smell of the early morning air. In ten minutes they reached the road heading west to Bull Meadow, and took it. The pavement ended a quarter mile from the state highway, but it was a good dirt road and they had it to themselves. They drove through stands of dense pine forest, traversed a meadow with a six-foot-wide creek running through it, crossed the creek on a one-lane wooden bridge, and eventually entered the woods again.

"This is the forest primeval," Peter quoted, sighing. "Was that Whittier?"

"Longfellow."

A short distance into the new stretch of forest, the road forked, with the left fork, which Gordon took, veering sharply uphill. The dirt road narrowed slightly, and with the sun still low in the east, the forest was semi-dark. Several deer appeared at various times alongside the road or on it, and the birds were in full morning song. After a mile and a half, they reached a summit, with a road bisecting theirs and following the ridgeline. From there, the main road went sharply downhill, through such dense forest they couldn't see where it was headed. After another mile and a half, and three hairpin switchbacks, the vista opened up onto a large meadow.

Nourished by the past winter's heavy rains, the grass was bright green and lush, with several hundred head of cattle grazing contentedly on it. The east side of the meadow, where they entered it, was still in shade, the sun not having yet climbed over the mountain in that direction, but the other side of the meadow and the hills flanking it were in light. Copper Creek, averaging 15 to 20 feet in width, meandered through the meadow, gently and with little visible current. Fifty feet from its banks on either side were crosshatched wood fences, zig-zagging in a direction that generally followed the flow of the water. Shortly they came to a dirt parking area, where a gray 1991 Ford Ranger was the only vehicle in sight. Gordon parked across and down from it, facing the creek. In the shadow of the mountain, the air was notably cooler than it had been in Arthur. They ate their pastries and finished their coffee unhurriedly, looking out over the meadow. In answer to Peter's question, Gordon explained that Pacific Crest Hydro owned the meadow, leased it for grazing to a cattle rancher, and had worked with the state Department of Fish and Game to restore the creek to Wild Trout status.

"This would be worth the trip if we turned around and went back now," Peter said.

"But we're not going to. It's a little creek, but there are a ton of bugs and a lot of nice fish in it. There are some Brown Trout that are two feet long or more, but they hang under the banks and are hard to catch."

"How do we fish it?"

"If nothing's feeding on the surface, we work nymphs along the weed beds and along the banks where we can. If there's an insect hatch, we switch to dries. We can fish it from the banks, but stay low and back so you don't spook the fish."

They got out of the Cherokee and assembled their rods. Whoever had come in the Ranger was nowhere to be seen, so they had the meadow to themselves. They stepped through an opening in the fence at the edge of the parking lot and headed upstream, looking for likely spots to fish on the way back. They trudged for 20 minutes, covering perhaps two-thirds of a mile. The sun was just coming over the mountain when they stopped.

"You want to start here or go up or downstream?" Gordon asked.

"Take this for yourself. I'm going to try that little hole we just passed."

Approaching the creek cautiously, and kneeling at the edge of the bank to minimize their shadows, they began fishing, moving downstream when they felt they had exhausted the potential of any one place. They each caught and released three fish (all Rainbows) running between 12 and 16 inches; had a couple of strikes where they didn't set the hook fast enough; and hooked a few other fish briefly before losing them. They also lost several flies in the weeds, but it was a good morning overall.

At 8:45 the sun was well over the mountain and the air began to fill with fluttering mayflies, who, when they landed on the water, were apt to become breakfast for a hungry trout. Gordon and Peter switched to dry flies and each caught and released a few more fish in the next hour. Then the insect hatch began to taper off, and by ten o'clock there were hardly any insects visible, and no fish rising to the surface. They tried working nymphs under the surface, but when their flies had received no attention for 45 minutes, Gordon said it was time to quit.

"I think they're done feeding until this evening. Early lunch at the Shotgun is looking good to me."

"I've more than worked off my croissant," Peter said.

With the sun beating down on the meadow, the temperature was quickly ascending from warm to hot. At the parking area, the Cherokee and Ranger had been joined by a Jimmy, the occupants of which seemed to be fishing a hundred yards downstream from the parking area. Gordon and Peter were back in town, parked in front of the café, by 11:40.

The Shotgun Café had been a local institution when Gordon was last in the area 15 years earlier and was still going strong. Coming through the front door, a visitor found himself even with the middle of a long counter, with red upholstered stools. The opening between the kitchen and dining area cut through the back wall, behind the counter. On either side of the front door, along the outside wall, were four tables for four, formica-topped and laid out with flatware, paper napkins, and coffee cups turned upside down in their saucers. To the left of the counter, the building dog-legged slightly inward to a back room, with rectangular tables hugging the walls on three sides and two small round tables, set for four, in the center area. The wall on the street side had two large windows, affording a fine view of the vehicles parked in front. The opposite wall had faux-wood wainscoting to waist level, giving way to whitewashed drywall above. Its decorations consisted of the stuffed head of an eight-point buck and a stuffed bobcat in reactive mode, protruding from the wall. On the back wall was a large painting of a mountain scene consisting of a creek running past a cabin with smoking chimney and a waterfall in the distant background. It was done in a literal, but not realistic, style, with over-bright colors. The morning before, they had been sitting at one of the rectangular tables, directly under the bobcat, when Miss London approached, but today the hostess-waitress put them at one of the round ones in the center.

When they arrived, the lunch crowd was just beginning to trickle in, but by the time they ordered (a patty melt for Gordon and a hot turkey sandwich for Peter), two-thirds of the tables in the back room were occupied, and the sound of voices talking to old friends had filled the low-ceilinged room, creating a mid-level din that made it hard to hear more than a few words of any nearby conversation. Between the short night and the morning's exertions, they were tired and mostly sat silently, collecting their thoughts. From the snatches of conversation he could hear from time to time, Gordon became aware that the fire they had seen on the way back to the marina the previous night was the big news of the day.

"Both fire stations sent every truck they had. Jordy says … "

" … rags in the service porch. It took off so fast … "

" … a complete loss, but they kept the building from collapsing … "

"They say she died of smoke inhalation … "

"I sure hope so. That would be more merciful … "

"She was a great teacher. Nobody'll deny that."

At that line, which came from the table directly to his left, Gordon snapped to attention. He looked at the table, where three men were sitting. They were in their late thirties to early fifties, all wearing jeans and faded checked flannel shirts. Two of them had on caps and the third, a well-worn gray Stetson. A tourist might try to emulate the look (and some did), but there was no mistaking the fact they were locals. Gordon leaned slightly in their direction to see if he could pick up more of their conversation, but just then the waitress — attractive, in her late twenties, and wearing a large diamond ring — came up to refill their coffee cups. It took a minute because she and the men chaffed each other in a good-natured way before she moved on to the next table. Afraid that the thread of the conversation might be lost, Gordon decided to put a foot forward.

"Excuse me," he said. "I couldn't help overhearing that you just said something about a great teacher. Do you mind …?" His voice trailed off.

They looked at him with curiosity but no animus. Seeing what was up, Peter shifted in his chair toward the conversation. The oldest of the three men, the one in the Stetson and with stubble on his face that suggested he shaved and showered after work, rather than before, finally spoke.

"There was a fire last night. House on the East Peninsula burned down."

"We saw it," said Peter. "We were bringing our boat back to the marina."

"Then you can probably guess how bad it was. It was Miss London's house. They found her body inside once the fire was out." He shook his head and paused.

"She was Ned London's daughter." The last sentence was spoken with a gravitas and certainty that came from an assumption that nearly everyone in town knew who Ned London was and what it meant to be his daughter.

"I'm sorry," Gordon said.

"She taught English for 35 years at President Arthur High," the man in the Stetson continued. "Books were never my strong point, but I learned more from her than almost anyone else. My son and daughter had her, too. Almost everybody in town took a class from her or had a kid who did. You wouldn't know her, of course, but it's a real loss for the community."

Gordon nodded sympathetically and spoke softly.

"Thank you for filling me in," he said. "Again, I'm sorry."

He turned to Peter, and as they exchanged a meaningful look, the waitress arrived and set down their meals.

"I guess I have to pay a visit to the sheriff," Gordon said. "I wonder who's the sheriff now?"

Twenty minutes later, they were back at Stanhope House, where they had booked separate rooms because cardiac-care nurse Stella Savoy, who had been tending to Peter's heart (in a non-medical way), had been making vague utterances that she might join him later in the week. Gordon stopped the Cherokee in front of the inn, and they walked briskly up the steps, past the unoccupied reception desk, and up the flight of stairs toward their second-floor rooms. Peter reached his room first and began to let himself in. Gordon kept going to the next room, and as he reached it, noticed that the door was open a crack. He frowned. Had he really been in that much of a hurry to go fishing that morning?

When he pushed the door open, he saw it was worse than that. The room, which he had left neat that morning, looked as if a pair of giant hands had turned it upside down and shaken it. The sheets were off the mattress; the mattress was off the bed; the suitcase was open and its contents scattered helter-skelter on the floor; and every drawer in the chest was pulled out.

He walked several feet to where the contents of his suitcase were scattered on the floor. Lifting a T-shirt at random, he saw his backup travel wallet under it and was surprised, on opening it up, to find that the 300 dollars in twenties and two credit cards he had placed in it before leaving San Francisco, were still there. Either this was no robbery, or the robber was singularly incompetent. Looking around at the devastation of the room, he felt his bile rising as a sense of violation began to take hold. The spell was quickly broken by the sound of a long whistle coming from the door, where Peter was standing, Charlotte London's manila envelope in his left hand. Peter had put it in his own room the morning before, and Gordon had forgotten to reclaim it.

Peter held the envelope out toward Gordon.

"Do you suppose they were looking for this?"

SHERIFF GENE BALLOU had been in a bad mood for precisely two weeks. The citizens of Forest County, in their infinite wisdom, had given him 48.6 percent of the vote in the June 4 primary election for his fourth term, forcing him into the bother, expense and uncertainty of a November runoff election against a former deputy, who now worked for the Highway Patrol. He had just returned from lunch, and was sitting at his desk, beginning to stew once more in the injustice of the electoral insult, when his secretary appeared at the door to tell him that there was a Mr. Quill Gordon at the counter, who said he had some information about the death of Charlotte London. Ballou's first inclination was to have his secretary direct Mr. Gordon to the fire department. But he checked himself, figuring that sorting out a problem — even if it wasn't really *his* problem — was better than nursing his resentment.

"Send him in," he said.

Gordon knew none of this as he walked into the office and sized up its occupant. Ballou was wearing khaki slacks, a navy blazer with gold buttons, a blue dress shirt, a string tie with a Northwest totem symbol as its clasp, and, even indoors, an off-white Stetson, immaculately shaped, with a ridge at its top, flanked by a sharp parallel crease on either side. As the sheriff stood to shake hands, Gordon saw that he was seven or eight inches shorter than Gordon's six-four-plus — small for a lawman these days — with a compact, but not wiry, frame. His handshake was firm, but the eyes lacked the penetrating glare Gordon had often noticed in veterans of law enforcement. Later in the interview, it occurred to him that Ballou had the eyes of prey, not predator. His face was round, pleasant and nondescript, with blue eyes behind wire-rimmed glasses and a crisply trimmed sandy-colored mustache. Following introductions, Gordon presented one of his cards. Ballou gave it a quick look and set it down on his clean desk pad, motioning Gordon to a chair on the other side of the desk. In a firm tenor voice he said:

"Pleased to make your acquaintance, Mr. Gordon. To what do I owe the pleasure?"

"Thank you for your time." He took a deep breath. "I have some information that may be relevant to the death of Charlotte London.

Ballou gave a nod so slight as to be almost imperceptible, picked up a freshly sharpened pencil to the right of the desk pad, and set it down next to Gordon's card.

"Very civic minded of you, I'm sure." He picked the pencil up and set it down again two inches farther from the card. "But do you mind if I ask why you're coming here? She died in a fire, which was a tragedy, but we have no evidence of a crime at this point, so the fire department is handling the investigation.

"Aren't you the coroner?"

"In name only. The actual medical work is contracted out to Dr. Brantley in Adams [a town about 30 miles to the south] and the lab is associated with the community college there. He's promised a report by Friday, and unless there's a surprise in it, the case stays with the fire department."

He picked up Gordon's card again, looked at it more carefully, looked at Gordon for several seconds, and set the card back on the desk pad.

"The name just rang a bell," he said. "Gordon from San Francisco. Are you by chance related to Judge Gordon?"

"My father."

"A good man. Good judge, too. He came in here years ago to handle the John Boline trial. The attorney who shot his wife. He ran it fast and fair, and I have no argument with his performance, even though we lost." He picked up the pencil and contemplated its eraser for several seconds. "Hometown verdict."

"So I hear." They sat in silence for the better part of a minute, Gordon controlling his impatience and waiting to see if the sheriff's knowing his father gave him any kind of edge. Finally Ballou spoke.

"Well, I can't promise it'll lead to anything, but let's hear what you have."

Gordon exhaled, then began describing, in as much detail as he could remember, his encounter with Charlotte London at the Shotgun Café and the burglary at his room, discovered less than an hour ago. Ballou listened without asking any questions, nodding from time to time. When Gordon finished, the sheriff picked up the pencil and tapped it on the desk pad several times.

"I can certainly understand your being suspicious under the circumstances, but there might be a simple explanation. We've had several motel break-ins since the summer season started, and we're pretty sure we know who's behind it. It's just a matter of catching them in the act or with the loot. Now if you'll give me a list of what was taken … "

"But that's the whole point," Gordon interrupted. "Nothing was taken."

"Then we probably won't be able to pin this one on them, but we will catch them sooner or later. Do you have this envelope Miss London gave you?"

Not without misgivings, Gordon handed it across the desk.

"Have you looked at it?"

"Not at all. I brought it straight here."

"That was the right thing." Ballou reached for the pencil cup on his desk and extracted from it a letter opener with a handle bearing the logo of the 1993 California Sheriffs' Association annual convention. He slid the blade under the seal at the top of the manila envelope and began to slit it open. Halfway into the process, the blade caught and ended up ripping the top of the envelope and opening a tear that ran six inches down the front.

Inspector Clouseau, Gordon thought, biting down hard on his lower lip as he tried to suppress the image in his mind.

Nonplussed, the sheriff took two 8½ -by-11 pieces of paper and a floppy disk from what remained of the envelope. The paper was covered with type from a computer printer, and he looked at it briefly before adding it to the collection of items on the desk pad and holding up the disk.

"Mind if I take a look?"

"That's why I brought it."

Ballou turned to the left of his desk, where there was an IBM PC, probably about five years old, with a heavy wire leading from it to a printer on a counter against the back wall of the office. He turned on the computer, which gave the impression of being little used, albeit with an impressive collection of coffee stains on its keyboard. As they waited for it to warm up, Gordon checked out the artwork on the walls (which consisted mostly of black and white photographs of the sheriff with other lawmen and politicians) and wondered if he'd ever see the disk again once it went into the computer.

Finally the computer was ready, and after checking the disk to make sure which end went first, Ballou put it in the slot. Gordon leaned back and tried to breathe regularly as Ballou scanned its contents on the screen. In less than half a minute, a frown began to cloud the sheriff's face, and the frown gained in intensity and severity as he kept looking. Finally, he turned to Gordon.

"I hate to say this, but I think Miss London was pulling your leg."

"What?"

"There's nothing here but gibberish. Random letters, numbers and symbols. Here, see for yourself."

Gordon got up and leaned over the desk so he could see the screen. Ballou was right. Gordon sat down again.

"That makes no sense."

"I agree, but we're both seeing the same thing, right?

He ejected the disk, set it on the desk pad, and looked at the adhesive label on it.

"It says 'Family History,' and these pages look like a short chapter outline, so it probably goes together." He put the disk and papers back in the remains of the shredded envelope. "You know, I have a theory that if you have a deep, dark secret that you want to be sure nobody ever hears about, the thing to do with it is put it into a family history. Put it anywhere after about page 20, and no one will ever know."

He stood to indicate the interview was over, extending the torn envelope with his left hand. When Gordon took the envelope, the sheriff extended his right hand, and Gordon had no choice but to rise and shake it.

"You did the right thing, Mr. Gordon, and I appreciate your coming in. A lot of people wouldn't. Still, at the end of the day, it doesn't look as if we have anything here. I have your card, and if anything new comes up, I'll be sure to give you a call."

He gave a jerky nod of his head and flashed a slightly crooked smile.

"Thanks for coming in, and have a nice day."

WALKING OUT OF THE COURTHOUSE into the bright afternoon sun, Gordon knew the rest of the day would be anything but nice. He was convinced that Charlotte London wasn't playing a practical joke on him, and that the floppy disk was important. Yet he was at a loss to explain the digital mess that had come up on the sheriff's computer screen.

The Cherokee was parked by the curb, under a large shade tree in front of the library, and when he got to it, he looked around to check if he was being observed. Seeing nothing suspicious, he opened the driver's side door, lifted the floor mat, and slid the envelope and its contents under it before climbing in.

Peter had expressed a desire to take a nap, so Gordon decided not to go back to the inn yet. After a moment's thought he concluded that exercise might help him clear his head, and with that in mind, he drove to the high school, turned around in the loop, and parked in front of the outdoor basketball and tennis courts. Reaching behind him, he grabbed a pair of shorts from the back seat and changed into them while sitting at the wheel of the car, a skill he had acquired from going to City League basketball games immediately after work in San Francisco.

Stepping out of the Cherokee, he removed his long-sleeved shirt and tossed it on the front seat, leaving himself clad in shorts, T-shirt and athletic shoes. He opened the rear driver's side door, took a basketball from behind the front seat, bounced it on the pavement twice to satisfy himself that it was properly inflated, and locked the door. Dribbling the ball with his left hand, he strode purposefully onto the courts, heading for the far basket, where his back would be to the sun. As he reached the three-point line on that court, he stopped, and in one fluid motion, leaped a foot and a half into the air, switched the ball from his left to his right hand, and launched a shot that arced upward to a height of 13 feet, then dropped cleanly through the hoop, clanking noisily against the chain-metal net.

Gordon was under the basket to grab the ball on the first bounce and throw up a left-handed reverse layup. He put too much spin on it, and the ball came out over the front of the rim, where he tapped it back through with his right hand. He took it back to the three-point line and began shooting his way around it, moving a few feet to one side or the other after each shot. He did that several times and had just amassed a streak of five straight baskets when he heard a voice at his right.

"Pretty easy when no one's guarding you. Want to play a little one-on-one?"

He turned so see a boy in his late teens, six-three, muscular, with a crewcut and a chiseled face lightly touched with acne. Probably a player on the high school team, Gordon thought.

"Sure. You need to warm up a bit?"

"Just give me a couple of minutes." The kid put out his hand. "Jack Henry."

"Quill Gordon."

The kid blinked. "Like the trout fly?" he asked. Gordon nodded. "Good to meet you, Mr. Gordon."

"Just call me Gordon. My friends do."

After three or four minutes doing layups and outside shots, Jack declared himself ready. They agreed to play to 12 baskets, with the winner needing to beat the loser by two. Gordon won the free-throw contest for first possession and started by doing a head fake from the free throw line and driving for a layup. The second time, he took the shot instead of faking, and hit it. Before long, he had taken a 9-4 lead. By that time, they had been playing 20 minutes, and the hot sun, reflecting mercilessly from the asphalt, was combining with the mile-high altitude to tire him out.

Younger and more accustomed to the altitude, Jack was fresher, and he was beginning to figure out and better defend Gordon's moves. The next time the kid got the ball, he dribbled it around the court for two minutes, forcing a tired Gordon to chase him around, then drove past Gordon, when he let up a bit, for a layup. Jack did that twice, and when Gordon decided to leave him alone outside the three-point line, he sank an outside shot, forcing Gordon back into coverage. Gordon made only one more basket, and Jack finally passed him for a 12-10 win. The kid had the mind-set of an assassin, and Gordon was impressed by the maturity and tenacity of his play.

"Good game," he said, gasping, when it was over. "I have some soda and water in the cooler. Can I get you something?"

"Thank you. You have Coke?"

Gordon nodded and walked slowly to the Cherokee, returning with a Coke and 7-Up. They sat down on the steps to the gymnasium, now in shade.

"I'm guessing you play for the team," Gordon said.

"Small forward, occasionally guard if somebody gets into foul trouble. I'll be a senior this year."

"You played a smart game just now."

"Actually, I remembered what Coach says whenever a team comes up from the Valley to play us. He says they're used to playing at 500 feet elevation, not 5,000, so if we're within 12 points at the end of the third quarter, we can usually wear 'em down in the fourth and win it."

"Smart coach," Gordon said.

"How about you? You look like you played high school, maybe even college ball."

"Don Bosco High in San Francisco, then Cal."

"Scholarship?"

Gordon nodded.

"Figures. You were probably a good three-point shot."

"They didn't have the three when I played. Even a half-court shot was two points."

"Wow." Gordon felt he had inadvertently placed himself among the dinosaurs.

Gordon took another pull of his 7-Up. "Can I ask you something? My friend and I noticed on the sign as you come into town that the team won a state championship in 1962. Before your time, obviously, but do you know the story?"

Jack nodded. "They show a film and tell us about it each year on the first day of practice. It was a big deal in this town. The only big deal in a long time."

"I'm guessing you had a couple of pretty good players that year."

"One for sure. Gary Bowman. He was six-nine, fast and strong. Nobody could take a rebound away from him, and nobody could defend him one-on-one. If they tried, he scored at least 30 points. If they played zone or double-teamed him, he'd pass to another guy for an open shot or a layup. They tried guarding him one-on-one in the championship game. He scored 38 points, and we won, 62-57."

"And they named the new gym after him for that?"

"Not for that," Jack said, and he became more serious. "Gary got a scholarship at Oregon State and was a starter sophomore and junior years. After a Saturday afternoon home game junior year, he and another player were driving through Corvallis during a really bad storm — wind and rain. There was a car at the side of the road with its hazard lights on, and Gary told the other guy, who was driving, to pull over so they could go help." He paused. "That's what you're taught to do when you grow up in a small town, where everybody looks out for everybody else.

"They parked about a hundred feet away and started walking back toward the car. It was dark and rainy, and their faces were wet. A live power line had come down and was hanging six and a half feet above the street, practically invisible. Gary walked into it with his wet forehead and was electrocuted. Six weeks before his 21st birthday."

There was a long silence as Gordon absorbed the story.

"That's the stuff of legend," he finally said.

"Sure is. The funny thing — well, not funny, really, but you know what I mean — is that the other player was walking ahead of Gary to that car. But he was only six-three and went under that live wire without even knowing it was there. It kind of makes you wonder whether there's any rhyme or reason to things."

"That it does," Gordon said quietly.

Jack drained the last of his Coke and crushed the can in his powerful right hand.

"You up for one more?"

Gordon shook his head. "I've seen enough. Thanks for the game, and good luck to you and the team this year."

They stood up and shook hands. The kid started back up Union Street toward the courthouse, dribbling his basketball as he went, switching from left hand to right and back again. As he watched him go, Gordon was thinking.

Thinking about Gary Bowman, the kid who never lived long enough to be anything but a basketball player. Who didn't have the chance to make a life for himself after the playing days were over, in the way Gordon had done — or tried to. Who died helping someone in trouble because it was the right thing to do — so instinctive you didn't even think about it. Charlotte London had asked Gordon for help, had trusted him with something she felt was important, and hadn't lived a day after doing so. Whatever she'd given him, he had an obligation to follow through on it. That was the right thing to do.

He looked at his watch. It was 4:15, and the courthouse would be open another three quarters of an hour. He walked back to the car, put the long-sleeved shirt back on, changed out of his shorts, and started the engine.

GOING BACK INTO THE COURTHOUSE, Gordon remembered immediately that the judges' chambers were down the hall to the right. When he reached them, he was pleased to see that Louis T. Fletcher was still Superior Court Judge.

"Gordon, my boy, what a pleasure and surprise," the judge said in his booming and high-pitched voice, emerging from his office after being told who wanted to see him. They shook hands.

"The pleasure's mine, your honor. Glad to see you're still working."

"The voters haven't gotten wise to me yet," he said with a wink. "Do come in. We have a lot to catch up on."

Gordon followed him into chambers. There was a medium-sized window on the outside wall, looking out over the lawn behind the courthouse, and the connecting door to the courtroom was on the left as they entered, only a few steps from the judge's desk. The desk itself held several freestanding photos of Judge Fletcher's family, and about it were scattered two piles of file folders containing case information, a yellow writing pad, several pens sitting where they had last been set down, and in the center, a stack of white paper, filled with words seeking justice (or at least vindication) for a client, painstakingly written at a three-figure hourly rate. It looked like the desk of someone who was working and concentrating on the work. The room itself was dark, with dark wood walls and a deep burgundy carpet. Hung on the walls were the judge's law degree (Stanford '55) and a number of prints of outdoor scenes and drawings of plants native to the area. Gordon recalled that when Judge Fletcher had taken him fishing 15 years ago, he was always stopping to point out and discourse upon some plant or other.

The judge slapped the pile of legal papers on his desk and motioned Gordon to a chair opposite the desk.

"An indigestible legal brief," he said. "You've done a public service by taking me away from reading it."

"But isn't justice delayed justice denied?"

"Generally, yes. But not in this case. This property line dispute," he lifted the brief and dropped it with a thud on the desk, "has been dragging on for three-and-a-half years. It threatens to become Forest County's version of *Jarndyce v. Jarndyce*. One day more could hardly matter."

Gordon smiled. The judge's appearance had changed in 15 years. His hair, salt-and-pepper back then, was all white now, and Gordon had noticed a slight stoop when following him into chambers. But he still looked a fit five-nine and his sharp mind was clearly in evidence.

"So how have you been? No — first tell me how Judge Gordon is doing."

"The judge is fine. I had breakfast with him on Sunday and he shows no sign of letting up."

"He struck me as being one of the ones who would keep working to the end and die with his boots on. Let's hope that's not for a long time. And you? You must be married and a father by now."

"I'm afraid that's still a 'yet' for me."

"Haven't found the right girl? Well, don't wait too long. A man's not complete without a family." He picked up a photo on the desk, looked at it affectionately, and set it down. "Now the last time you were here, things were up in the air, as I recall. Your father wanted you to go to law school, but you had other ideas."

"It didn't seem right, and I had an offer to go to work for an old-line brokerage in San Francisco. I thought I'd give it a try."

"Maybe for the best," the judge said after a pause. "Your father cast a long shadow in the legal profession. Some of the cases he litigated before becoming a judge are still talked about. I could see his son wanting to take a different path. I trust it worked out."

"Pretty well, actually. It turned out I had a flair for reading the stock market and seeing where things might go."

"You're still with the brokerage, then?"

"Not anymore. I made enough money on my own investments that I don't have to work, so I left the brokerage at the end of '93."

"You have me a bit worried now. No job and no family. So what *are* you doing?"

"This and that. Actually, I have a little project going locally right now. You must have known Charlotte London?"

"Good heavens, yes. Everyone did. A real tragedy what happened to her. She did so much for the young people in this town. My son, Joe, said that what he learned from her about how to write — how to think, actually — got him top grades in law school. And my daughter, Maggie, went on to become a teacher because of Miss London's influence." He picked up another photograph from the desk. "Though her career is temporarily on hold because of the two lovely granddaughters she's given us. But how do you know Miss London?"

"Do you have a few minutes, and can I count on your complete discretion?" When Judge Fletcher nodded, Gordon told him about the meeting with Miss London Monday morning, the break-in at his room at Stanhope House, and the sheriff's tepid response to his information. Knowing the judge's legal mind, he tried to make the presentation as precise, succinct and thorough as possible. But then, Gordon was used to arguing with his father.

"It doesn't make sense," Gordon concluded. "She was highly respected, and she could have gone to almost anybody in town for help, yet she came up to me, a total stranger, in a coffee shop and gave me a floppy disk that turned into fairy dust when the sheriff put it in his computer. She didn't show it at the time, but she had to be afraid of something."

The judge had been sitting back in his chair and listening with an air of seeming distraction, cultivated during years on the bench. He sat up now and leaned forward slightly.

"Based on the evidence, I'd have to agree with you. And I must say I'm disappointed, though not surprised, by our sheriff's reaction. Gene Ballou is a politician and a bureaucrat. Don't get me wrong — he knows his business more or less. But he's too concerned with appearances and terrified of looking bad or failing. Someone once said Ballou wouldn't investigate a murder unless there were already five witnesses who saw a suspect standing over the body with a smoking gun in his hand. And being in a runoff for his job this fall probably hasn't done much for his courage."

"I take it he won't be getting your vote?"

Judge Fletcher frowned. "His opponent's worse. What can I say? In a county this small, the pool of political talent isn't always as deep as the discriminating voter would like. But some people probably say that about me. Can you keep a secret, Gordon? My term ends in two years, and I've decided to finish it out but not run for re-election. That means my replacement will be elected by the people, the way I was 22 years ago, and not appointed by the governor like most judges. It'll be a crowded election. I expect at least 15 people to run."

"Fifteen? That must be half the attorneys in the county."

"Pretty close. But you see, the job pays over a hundred thousand a year. That may not be much in San Francisco, but it's a kingly salary around here. I dare say there are few attorneys in this county who make a hundred thousand in the best year of their career. Not to mention the pension. As a student of human nature, I look forward to seeing what they'll do to get it."

Gordon had nothing to say and simply shook his head.

"But back to your problem. If I were the sheriff, I'd be more suspicious simply because of the burglary in your room where nothing was taken. I'm not the sheriff, however, and I have no way of making him do anything. As for Miss London coming to you, I can only hazard a guess."

"Which is?"

"How can I put this? We're a small community, and everybody knows everybody else. A lot of families have been here for generations. In a situation like that, you get to know people pretty well, or at least think you do. She was writing a family history, was she not? Well, sometimes when you dig into the past, you find out something discreditable that someone else thought was buried and forgotten. If you had that knowledge about another person and were afraid of the consequences, to whom could you turn? Miss London had Gene Ballou as a student early in her career, so I doubt she had any illusions on that score. Anyone else in town would probably know the person you're worried about and might be inclined to give him or her the benefit of the doubt if anything happened. That's when someone like Charlotte London, who's a good judge of people, might be inclined to take a leap of faith and trust a stranger — especially one with an honest and trustworthy face like yours."

"Channeling my inner Boy Scout again," Gordon murmured.

There was a tap on the door, and it swung open to reveal the legal clerk who had greeted Gordon at the counter.

"Excuse me, judge," she said. "It's five o'clock. Do you need anything before we leave?"

He waved his hand. "I'm fine, Carla. Have a nice evening."

The door closed, and they were alone again. The lawn outside the window was deeper in shade than it had been earlier, and the room seemed slightly darker.

"I really don't know what to tell you, Gordon. It's a tough situation. If I knew a secret that someone in town would kill to keep quiet, I'm not sure who *I'd* trust"

Gordon thought that over.

"Still," he finally said, "this helps me some. You've validated my idea that I'm onto something and have to be careful. That's a start." He looked at his watch. "I hadn't realized it was so late, and my friend's probably wondering where I am. I should probably be going."

"Friend? Male or female?"

"Just a fishing buddy. Nothing to get excited about."

He stood, and so did the judge.

"Sorry I couldn't be more help, but maybe something will come to me. Check in again if you get the chance. And thank you for keeping me from reading this brief. I'll be a few minutes more, but you can let yourself out. Just push the door all the way shut behind you, and it'll lock automatically."

"It's been good seeing you again."

He walked to the chamber door and opened it. As he began to step through, the judge called his name, and he backed into the chamber again.

"I just thought of something. I don't know if it's the answer, but we have a lively little weekly newspaper here, and the editor's fairly new to town. Only been here 20 years, and sort of an aging hippie, but not afraid to ruffle a few feathers. It's a possibility, anyway."

Gordon nodded. "That doesn't seem right yet, but it's something I'll think about if things heat up. And I'll definitely be back in touch."

On the way out, he double-checked to make sure the office door was locked after he closed it.

FIVE MILES SOUTH OF ARTHUR, the state highway veers away from the lake to skirt a heavily forested area known as Año Nuevo Pines. A single, discreetly marked road leads from the highway into the woods, which, out of sight of the main road, turn out to hold about 200 homes (the majority second homes and vacation rentals) and a resort, also known as Año Nuevo Pines, consisting of two dozen cabins, 40 campsites, a general store, a laundromat and a lakeside restaurant. Gordon and Peter arrived just in time to snag one of the few remaining tables on the outdoor deck.

It was just past six o'clock, and the west side of the lake (including the restaurant's deck) was in shadow. The temperature had dropped just below 80, and from time to time a gentle breeze tried to pick up, then died again as quickly as it had started. It was the beginning of an evening of enchantment and promise, and the vacationers (they were mostly vacationers at the restaurant) were trying to enjoy it to the utmost.

Not Gordon. The conversations with Judge Fletcher and Sheriff Ballou had left him unsettled and on edge. He was growing increasingly worried about the possibility of losing what Charlotte London had given him before its secret could be divined, and therefore unwilling to risk leaving it in his car. He had put her envelope into his messenger bag, brought it to the restaurant with him, and set it down on an empty chair at their table for four. Only then was he able to relax enough to tell Peter about the afternoon.

Refreshed from his nap, Peter listened attentively and asked good questions, but they were questions, not answers. They were both inclined to conclude that Judge Fletcher was correct in his surmise that Miss London had come across something damaging to someone in the community — something she could trust only to an outsider despite the leap of faith involved in doing that. But that left them in the dark on such critical issues as what they were dealing with and whom they should be worried about.

The food arrived, and they fell to eating in silence. Gordon had ordered the trout — breaded, pan-fried, and served with lemon sauce and capers. He rarely ate the fish he caught anymore but held fond memories of trout cooked over a campfire on family vacations when he was young. The restaurant's version was more subtle and complex, but the flaky white meat of the fish was more than enough to bring back those memories. Peter had chicken kebabs over rice, with steamed vegetables. They were more than halfway through the meal when the conversation resumed.

"It seems to me," Peter said, "that job one is to clean up that garbage on the floppy disk and see what's really there. I assume we're agreed that there *is* something there if we can only get to it."

Gordon nodded and swallowed. "From our brief meeting with her, and from everything else I've heard afterward, there has to be. It would have been out of character for her to forget to load the disk or to be playing a practical joke."

"I was thinking just now. I know the guy who manages the computers at Presbyterian Hospital. I should be able to pick his brain tomorrow by phone, but I'd have to be able to describe what we're seeing on the screen."

"I'm impressed. I didn't realize surgeons fraternized with the computer techs at the hospital."

"Actually, he was a patient, too." Peter took a sip of iced tea. "Emergency appendectomy. He owes me one."

They continued eating in silence and cleaned their plates. Mindful of his performance on the basketball court that afternoon, Gordon had planned on skipping dessert that night, but Peter ordered the cherry pie, and it sounded too good to pass on. In for a dime, in for a dollar, Gordon let the waitress talk him into adding a scoop of vanilla ice cream to it. He was on vacation, after all.

Most of the lake was in shadow by now, though the mountains behind the eastern shore were still topped with sunlight. The temperature had dropped to the mid-70s. Fish were rising far out on the lake, and several swallows had gone into business, swooping around the water and gobbling insects. It was a perfect evening. Even the small children on the deck were well behaved. Gordon wished he could enjoy it more, but his entire body was tense, and every few seconds he put his hand on the computer case to make sure it was still there.

Peter broke the silence. "They have a computer and printer at Stanhope House, don't they?"

Gordon nodded. "There's a little alcove on one end of the Fireside Room with a computer, printer and fax. They call it the Business Center — though I'm not sure how many people come there to do business."

"Then let's check it out as soon as we get back. Wait a minute. Did you bring your laptop on this trip?"

"Gordon nodded.

"Where is it?"

"Right here." He tapped the messenger bag.

"Take it out, and let's look now, while we're waiting for dessert."

Gordon set the case on the table and unzipped it, removing a Macintosh PowerBook computer he had bought in January.

"I've been thinking of getting one of those myself," Peter said, "but I'm not sure I'd really use it that much, and it's a lot of money."

Gordon opened the top of the device and pressed the power button.

"Go ahead and buy it," he said. "You'll be surprised how much you use it. "

Peter couldn't take his eyes off it. "How much hard drive does this baby have?"

"A hundred twenty eight megabytes."

Peter shook his head. "More than you'll ever need."

"I know, but better safe than sorry."

Gordon slipped Miss London's disk into the portal on its right side. It fell into place with a loud snap, then whirred and sputtered for several seconds, finally producing an image of the disk, labeled CLDisk, on the desktop. He double-clicked on it, and a new window opened to reveal a Word document labeled History. He double-clicked on the document.

Instead of the gibberish he'd seen on the sheriff's computer screen, the document opened on what was clearly the title page of a book. It read:

**A History of the London Family
of Forest County, California**

By Charlotte London

**Copyright © 1996, Charlotte A. London
All Rights Reserved**

Gordon began scrolling down. Everything that followed was perfectly formatted and intelligible prose. He scrolled back to the title page.

"Well?" said Peter. "What have we got?"

"See for yourself."

He turned the computer around so Peter could see the screen.

"Well I'll be damned," Peter said. "The old darling was using a Mac. No wonder the sheriff couldn't get it on his IBM."

"Well, it looks like I have some reading to do tonight," Gordon said.

He ejected the disk, turned off the computer, and put everything back in the case just as the waitress arrived with their pie. He ate it with pleasure, feeling, for the first time since learning of Charlotte London's death, that he was moving in the right direction.

EMMA CRISP AND HER HUSBAND, Phil, owned Stanhope House, but Emma was in charge of the operation. Within a year of buying it, they realized that the income it generated was erratic enough that one of them should have a job. So Phil worked about 30 hours a week at Nelson's Hardware and Sporting Goods. That provided enough of an income to cover most of the monthly essentials, plus a substantial discount on hardware and building supplies, two commodities Stanhope House consumed like a lumberjack at a breakfast buffet.

When Gordon caught her at the front desk, she was still out of sorts over the burglary of his room. Ordinarily a calm and level-headed woman, she nonetheless realized that having a guest's room ransacked while he was out fishing was the kind of PR the Stanhope could ill afford. She greeted Gordon and Peter and apologized profusely, for the fifth time that day, for the burglary.

"Please," Gordon said, "there was nothing you could have done about it."

"This has only happened once in 14 years, and the last time, they caught the boys who did it. But they never recovered what was stolen."

"Nothing was stolen here. It was a minor inconvenience." There was an awkward pause. "Would you mind if I connected my laptop to your printer and tried to print on it? I'm afraid it's rather a long document."

"No, no, no. Be my guest. No charge. It's the least we can do after what happened today. I just put 200 sheets of paper in the printer."

"And I have about 100 to print, so we should be fine."

The Business Center was only 20 feet from the front desk. Gordon and Peter were able to connect the laptop to the printer with only minor confusion, and soon it began to print the family history, spitting the pages out to a plastic tray. They cleared the tray every ten pages, and had got the first 30 run off when Emma, who had been at the front desk, came over.

"Sorry to bother you, but I need to get something off my chest." Gordon and Peter looked at her expectantly.

"I'm wondering if I should have told that person who called that you were staying here."

Gordon's poker face nearly crumbled, but he recovered quickly and said, with a slight croak in his voice:

"When was that?"

"This morning. Just before nine o'clock. We were cleaning up breakfast, and the phone rang. When I answered, the voice on the other end asked if Mr. Quill Gordon was staying here. I said yes, but that you were out fishing, and could I take a message. He said he'd call back later and hung up. No one ever called back."

"He?" said Peter. "Are you sure it was a man?"

"I think so. I'm not sure. It was a deep voice, but sort of muffled and hard to make out. I think there was a bad connection."

"Or somebody trying not to be recognized," Gordon said. "Did it sound familiar at all?"

She thought hard. "There was something familiar about it, but I can't tell you what it was. I certainly didn't recognize the caller. Maybe it'll come to me later."

"Let me ask you something," Peter said. "When would somebody have been able to come in here and go into a room without being seen?"

"There are always people around, but checkout is at 11, and I go out and run errands for an hour or two after that. If Phil's at the store, the front desk and front rooms are pretty empty then."

"How many people know you're in the habit of doing that?" Gordon asked.

"Everybody who knows me and maybe some people who don't. I always tell friends not to call between 11 and one because I probably won't be in. I shouldn't have told that person about you, should I?"

"Of course you should have," Gordon said. "It might have been a family emergency or an important business matter. There was no reason to suspect that anyone was planning to rob me. Please don't worry."

"What should I do if I get another call?"

"Easy," Peter said. "Ask who's calling and write it down. Though I suppose a clever villain could make something up on the spot."

The front desk phone rang, and she excused herself to answer it. From her end of the conversation, it sounded as if somebody was calling about booking a room and had detailed questions about the options. They turned back to the printer, which had completed its job, but because the tray had been left unattended, several dozen sheets of paper had fallen on the floor and were scattered about. Peter knelt and began picking them up.

"At least they're numbered," he said. "From what we know about Miss London, it would have been surprising if they weren't."

They were able to assemble the manuscript in a few minutes and headed upstairs. At the door to his room, Gordon asked Peter if he'd like to join him.

"Sit there and watch you reading a manuscript?" he said. "There has to be *something* better on cable." Gordon laughed. "Breakfast here tomorrow, then hit the lower river?"

"You're on," Gordon said.

He stepped into his room, turned on the light, and froze. Methodically noting every detail, his eyes swept the room twice. Nothing seemed amiss, but he realized that for the rest of the trip, he'd be unable to enter the room nonchalantly. Emma had offered to move him to another room, but he had declined. It would be, at some level, letting the burglar win.

The room held a four-poster queen bed, covered with a locally made quilt, an antique armoire where some of his clothes were hanging, and a comfortable easy chair by the window at the far end. To the left of the entry was a nook with a small writing table and a couch for two. A standing lamp stood next the couch, and, figuring it would provide good light for the task ahead, Gordon turned it on and sat under its glow.

He began reading. What Charlotte London's style lacked in the way of verve and elegance, it made up for in simplicity, clarity, precision, and thoughtful, succinct organization. Gordon had not expected to care much for the London family, but within a few pages he found himself getting caught up in the story.

It began with Jeremiah London, a native of Cape Cod, who had signed on for the whaling business but discovered, halfway through the second voyage, that the seafaring life was not for him. He jumped ship in San Francisco in December of 1880, only to discover that the Gold Rush, about which he had heard so much, had ended decades earlier. Working odd jobs and living frugally, he saved enough money to enable him to head for the mountains in May 1882.

He landed in Arthur, which had become a boomtown providing lumber for the railroad being built through the mountains to the south. The Empire Lumber Company happened to need of a bookkeeper at the time. Having a bit of experience in that line (though not as much as he told the superintendent), he got the job and was soon put in charge of all financial operations. Flush with prosperity, he wooed and won Dorothy Manchester, the formidable teacher at the local school. On their wedding day in August 1885, he was 31 and she was 35; she gave him three strapping boys in the next five years.

Their names were, in order, Matthew, Mark and Luke. Luke volunteered for the Army in World War I, went to France, and found a final resting place in one of the large cemeteries resulting from that conflict. Mark moved to San Francisco, never married, and died of tuberculosis at the age of 42. Matthew London, however, remained in Forest County and became one of its leading lights.

He was elected sheriff in 1924 and served six terms before retiring in 1948. By Charlotte's account, he was universally respected, serving on the school board, the library board, the fire board, and anything else anyone could think of to ask him to do. He married Ruby Jensen, daughter of the general store's owner, and they had two children, Edward and Pearl. Edward, known as Ned, was born in 1912, married Lydia Dawson in 1934. They had two children: Charlotte Ann was born in 1935 and Gregory two years later. Ned went into real estate and prospered, especially when the postwar creation of Lake Año Nuevo began to make the area a summer vacation destination.

That took the manuscript to page 65 and the clock to 10:15. So far, Gordon thought, there was nothing remotely scandalous in the document. In fact, in the hands of a less competent writer, it could have been downright boring. The remaining 35 pages seemed to be one long chapter. He decided to take a break, make a cup of herbal tea downstairs, and finish before falling asleep, if he could.

The sun had been down for an hour and a half, and it had cooled off outside. The ancient timbers of Stanhope House, which had expanded with the midday heat, were beginning to contract, resulting in a variety of intermittent squeaks, groans and thumps. An owl hooted from a nearby tree. Through the open second-story window, Gordon could hear something, probably a dog, rustling and shuffling in the yard below. A car drove past on the highway, and he could track its passage by the sound it made. A whisper of wind kicked up, and he could feel the breeze through the window and hear it caressing the leaves of the aspen trees. He stood, stretched, and headed for the door.

When he put his hand on the knob, he paused. After several seconds, he walked back to his computer case, which was on top of the bed, removed Miss London's floppy disk, and stuck it in his side pants pocket. Ordinarily, he would not have locked the door when leaving for a few minutes, but tonight he did. The hallway was well lit, and he enjoyed the feel of its thick carpet against his bare feet. The stairs leading to the ground floor had a landing halfway, and he stopped on it to look and listen. A couple of small table lamps had been left on, leaving the downstairs area in dim, but navigable light. There seemed to be no one stirring, but the owl hooted again.

He walked down the rest of the stairs, through the main sitting room (where tables against the walls were set for tomorrow's breakfast) to the guest pantry, next to the kitchen. It was dark, but he reached out with a long arm and flipped on the light switch just inside the entryway. The light illuminated a small area, with a countertop holding trays of tea, cocoa and fruit, a two-burner stove with a teakettle and saucepan on its burners, a sink and a refrigerator. He drew a pint of tap water into the saucepan and turned on the burner underneath it. Rummaging through the teas, he found a box of Celestial Seasonings Sleepytime and put a bag into a Styrofoam cup. The water came to a boil, and he poured it over the tea bag, leaving it to steep for a few minutes.

The house — at least he assumed it was the house — made a noise unlike any he had heard before.

Gordon couldn't place what was different about the sound — just that something was. He tensed up, all senses heightened. Another car drove by on the highway, and he could hear the sound of its tires on the pavement for a full 20 seconds. He listened, and hearing nothing out of the ordinary for a couple of minutes, concluded his imagination was beginning to run riot. Removing the tea bag from the Styrofoam cup, he squeezed in a half-lemon he'd found in the refrigerator, and started back to his room, turning out the pantry light.

He stopped after doing that, and took a long look at the sitting room. Nothing seemed out of order, but it occurred to him that the lights inside kept him from seeing anything through the windows. Someone could be on the veranda outside, watching his every move. He tried not to think about it as he walked to the stairs and started up, stopping again at the landing to look and listen before continuing to the second floor. He let himself into the room as quickly as possible, and locked the door once inside.

When he turned to survey the room, everything looked as it had when he had left to go downstairs. The manuscript was on the writing table, the read portion turned upside down and the last chapter face up. He picked up that chapter and sat down on the couch, but, before starting reading, looked around the room one more time.

The armoire.

There was enough space in it to conceal someone, and for a moment his mind flashed on the idea of those French bedroom farces, in which various lovers are concealed about the room as others come in. But he wasn't laughing. Now that the idea was in his head, he had to look. Quietly, he moved over to it and yanked the door open. There was nothing in it but his Spartan holiday wardrobe.

At least, he thought, as he sat on the couch again, he would be able to stay awake through the final chapter. In fact, he wondered if he would get to sleep at all that night.

The last chapter turned out to be a departure from the rest of the manuscript, and Gordon found himself drawn into it. It had to do with the development of the Lake Año Nuevo Peninsulas, in which it turned out Charlotte's father had played a leading role.

Before building the dam across Hawk River to create the lake in 1947, Pacific Crest Hydro had bought up the land that would be flooded. This included a near-ghost town called Conkling a couple of miles south of Arthur, whose residents received top dollar for their not-so-valuable land. The company had also bought the land that was now the Peninsulas, with the idea that it might some day add a smaller barrier across the creeks that ran past them.

Two decades later, that was no longer an option, and Pacific Crest Hydro decided to sell the Peninsulas and some adjacent shoreline land. In the summer of 1969 it announced there would be a sealed-bid auction, with bids opened Friday October 24. It was a choice bit of land, expected to command top dollar. Several Bay Area development consortiums were interested, and it was expected one of them would make the winning bid.

But Ned London had other ideas. He joined forces with a fellow real estate man, a friendly competitor named Roger Paris. They formed a limited partnership called the London & Paris Land Company and set to preparing a bid. London's insight, critical to the enterprise, was that as locals they could better assess the development potential of the land and could more likely get a larger project approved by the county's Board of Supervisors. Holding that edge, they might be able to outbid their big-city competitors for the property.

That was what happened. The London & Paris bid was highest by $10,000, and nine months later, in August 1970, they submitted a plan to the county for a 550-home subdivision, a golf course, several commercial areas, two resorts and a marina.

And then the Peninsulas became a campaign issue. When the plan was filed with the county, the Board of Supervisors looked to be in favor of it by a four-to-one margin, with one young supervisor, Bart Sturges, apparently opposed. Two of the board members supporting it were up for re-election in November and were expected to win easily. But the project had begun to divide the community. Some felt it would bring growth and prosperity to the area; others that it would destroy the rustic character of Lake Año Nuevo and make the community too heavily dependent on tourism. The incumbents' challengers sided with the opposition to the project, and both of them narrowly won in November and assumed office Tuesday January 5.

The London & Paris development came before the Board of Supervisors on Tuesday, January 19, 1971, seemingly headed for defeat. The supervisors' chambers were filled to capacity when the public hearing began at 11 a.m., and dozens of people stood outside in a blizzard, waiting for their turn to testify. With breaks for lunch and dinner, the hearing ran until 2:15 a.m. the following day, which was when the last person testified.

At that point, the supervisors stated their reasons for the vote they were about to cast, and after four of them had spoken, the count was 2-2. Bart Sturges was the final speaker, and to the surprise of almost everyone in the audience, he announced that he would vote yes, citing the standing arguments of the growth and prosperity proponents. The development passed on a 3-2 vote, and fights broke out in the chamber, forcing sheriff's deputies to clear the room.

In the paragraph summarizing Sturges' speech, Charlotte London had written at the end, in brackets and italics, *Seems weak. Need to interview.* From what he had read to that point, Gordon was inclined to agree. Something else was tickling the back of his brain — he was sure he had encountered Bart Sturges before. After a minute it came to him. Several years ago, when his father was up for re-election as judge, he faced a challenge for the first time. He won with 78 percent of the vote, but at one of the fund-raisers Gordon attended, he'd met a State Senator named Bart Sturges. It was an uncommon enough name that it almost certainly had to be the same man.

Only a couple of pages remained, and Gordon began reading again:

"But Ned London was not to enjoy his unexpected triumph. On the night of Wednesday January 13, six days before the vote, he was killed when his car skidded off the state highway a little after ten o'clock and tumbled down a hundred-foot embankment, landing on boulders at the edge of the lake. The incident was recorded as an accident arising from an icy roadway, but the accident report, retrieved from Highway Patrol files, contains ambiguities and omissions. [*Add A.D. interview.*] His son, Gregory, and the Paris family (Roger, Robert, Ronald and Richard) represented him at the public hearing."

The remaining couple of pages dealt with her father's legacy in the community and her brother's assuming the family real estate business, which apparently was still a going concern. Gordon set the manuscript down after finishing, his mind racing. It pointed to three possible lines of further inquiry:

• Assuming Ned London's family had inherited his stake in the partnership, Charlotte London was a wealthy woman by the standards of this remote mountain community.

• The source of her wealth was a large and controversial land development that had narrowly been approved when an elected official — now holding a higher and more powerful office — had implausibly changed his vote at the last minute.

• Just before that had happened, Charlotte's father died in circumstances that she now felt were suspicious.

She had clearly felt she was onto something, and whatever it was could have been a motive for killing her. Thinking it over, Gordon realized that he had to share what he had in his possession. Thinking it over further, he didn't want to go back to Sheriff Ballou with it — not now, anyway. He finished the last of the herbal tea, cold by now, and remembered what Judge Fletcher had said about the local newspaper. It might, he thought, be worth talking to the editor to see if some news coverage might pressure the sheriff to investigate Charlotte London's death more aggressively. He suddenly felt tired and decided to sleep on it and act in the morning.

Before turning in, he closed the window and slid the chair from the writing table against the door to the room.

Wednesday June 19

THE BUFFET OPENED AT EIGHT, and Peter and Gordon were the first ones downstairs at 8:01. From a table groaning under toast, muffins, pastries, fruit, bagels, cereal, bread and cheese, they filled their plates in anticipation of an active day's fishing. Gordon had noticed that the library had one dining table and steered them to it so they could speak without being overheard.

With the morning sun streaming through the windows across from them, they ate and drank coffee while Gordon gave a brief précis of the London family history and concluded by saying he wanted to meet with the newspaper editor after breakfast. Peter greeted the news with stoic resignation.

"It seems to me you have some questions at the very least," he said. "And it would probably help to talk to someone who knows the community better — knows where the bodies are buried." He took a swallow of coffee. "Sorry, inappropriate analogy."

"But right, even so. The only question is who I can trust. It looks as if the London family got rich from a project that polarized the town and left some hard feelings. Charlotte seems to think there was more to her father's death than meets the eye, and the fact that her house burned down right after she gave me that envelope would make anybody suspicious."

"Anybody but the sheriff, apparently."

"Which, again, is suspicious."

"How well do you know Judge Fletcher?"

"Well enough to feel he's being straight with me. But I don't know enough about the politics of this place to have a sense of what other issues might be out there."

"Then I'd say you should probably take the judge's advice. If you talk to the newspaper editor, he might be able to tell you what other people in town are saying and who else might have some information. It's a start."

Gordon popped the last bite of a raspberry scone into his mouth and washed it down with coffee.

"The main thing is I have to get this into the hands of somebody who can do something about it — assuming there's anything to be done." He finished the last of the coffee. "But why did she come to me, of all people."

"I can think of two reasons. The first is, as you say, the politics of this place could be touchy, and she didn't feel she could trust anybody in town with it."

"And the second reason?"

Peter finished his cup of coffee and set it on the saucer.

"The second reason is she may have been afraid she was going to die."

AT NINE O'CLOCK, manila envelope in hand, Gordon walked out the front door of Stanhope house, down the front steps, and across the lawn to the state highway. A brisk, cool breeze was blowing, more like early spring than midsummer, and he held the envelope tightly. Looking both ways, he waited for one car to pass, and crossed the road. The sidewalk on the other side took him to the commercial building down the road that housed the offices of the *Forest Clarion*.

The newspaper was in the third of three spaces in a building set perpendicular to the highway, behind the Galloping Goose gift shop and Mountain Cuts hairstyling. The space was not large enough to hold a printing press and housed only the news, advertising and circulation ends of the enterprise. He hoped the editor was in and realized he didn't even have a name, but he figured the paper was small enough that it probably wouldn't matter.

He stepped through the front door into a cramped, low-ceilinged space that nevertheless seemed reassuringly informal. Just inside was a small lobby with four chairs reserved for visitors who might be waiting for someone. It seemed like three chairs too many. The lobby was a 12-by-15-foot area in the shape of a squared-off U, with counters on three sides. The counter a visitor encountered after walking through the door had two large posters — one promoting the upcoming Fourth of July parade and celebration and one showing the basketball schedules for the boys' and girls' teams at

President Arthur High, whose seasons had ended three months ago. There was a low clacking sound made by three people working at computers, and at the back of the classified advertising department, a radio, turned down low, was playing Patsy Cline singing "Crazy for Loving You." The building smelled of ink, old paper, and cigarettes smoked a decade ago.

"Have you been helped?"

Gordon looked to his left and saw a woman who could have been anywhere between 50 and 70 years old with tightly permed grayish-brown hair and large round eyeglasses. She seemed friendly in a bored sort of way that suggested dealing with him was more interesting than whatever she had been doing.

"Not yet." He took a deep breath. "I was wondering if I might have a word with the editor."

The woman stood and nodded.

"Could I say who's calling and what it's about?" The question was asked matter-of-factly with no sense of being protective.

"My name is Quill Gordon and I have some information about Charlotte London that I'd like to share."

"Just a minute, please," she said, with a knowing nod.

She walked to her left, looped behind the counter, and crossed into the right side of the office, stopping at a desk, the entire surface of which was covered with at least six inches of paper, some of it neatly stacked, some scattered. She leaned over and whispered something to a woman who looked to be in her late forties, wearing a snugly fitting burgundy top and a navy blue cap with a ponytail of sandy blond hair pushed through the back of it. The second woman looked up at Gordon and nodded, sending the first woman back to her post, then stood. She was tall, just under six feet, Gordon guessed, and the burgundy top was tucked into tight fitting jeans that showed her long legs and trim figure to good effect. She moved toward him with a stride that exuded languid confidence. A thought crossed his mind. *If John Wayne had been a woman, this is how she would have walked.* As she got closer he noticed an open friendly face, tanned, with freckles, blue eyes, small nose and large mouth, turned up slightly at the corners. At the counter, she extended a long right arm and shook his hand with a good grip that may have included an extra squeeze as she let go.

"Pleased to make your acquaintance, Mr. Gordon. I'm Elke Sundstrom." She paused and sized him up at closer range. "So you have some information about Charlotte London?"

Gordon's college roommate worked at the *San Francisco Chronicle*, and Gordon had learned from him that newspaper offices are magnets for cranks of all stripes. He knew he had to establish his bona fides, so he led with a reference.

"Yes," he said. "I was talking with Judge Fletcher late yesterday, and he suggested I come to you about this." A pause. "So here I am."

She nodded slightly. "Louie's one of the good guys," she said. "I'll hear you out, but can you be to the point? We're on deadline and have to get this week's paper out the door to the printers at noon."

"I'll be concise. But is there someplace a bit more private where we could talk?"

She nodded again, and stepping to her left, pulled open a swinging, waist-high door. He passed through it and followed her to a cubicle at the back corner of the office. Her walk looked as good from behind as it had when she was coming toward him a minute earlier, and when she leaned over her desk on the way to pick up a notebook and pen, it looked like a provocative gesture. There was a small table in the cubicle, with four chairs around it. He pulled out one of the chairs for her, and she did a double-take.

"Whoa," she said. "Haven't seen that move in a while. Now I *know* you're not from around here." She sat down. So did he.

"San Francisco," he said. "My friend and I are here for some fishing."

"You came to the right place. Maybe a little early in the season, but the right place. So how do you know Miss London?"

"It's a strange story." He paused.

"All right," she said. "I'll stop asking questions and let you tell it your way. And I'll take notes, if you don't mind." He nodded. "If you make it interesting enough, I might even follow up on it after we get the paper out this morning. You're on."

Having told the story twice already, Gordon had the organization down pretty well, and he ran through it, including the family history, in under ten minutes. He was encouraged by the fact she was taking copious notes, filling three pages in a spiral-bound notebook. When he finished, he leaned back in his chair, and she set her Bic ballpoint on the notebook, clasped her hands, leaned forward, and said, in a low, husky voice:

"So let me be sure I got this straight. You went to the sheriff with a story about how one of our town's most highly respected citizens came up to you, a total stranger, at a café, handed you something for safekeeping, and died that night in a fire at her nice, up-to-code house — and he didn't think that was worth looking into?"

"I couldn't make that up."

She shook her head. "Even for Gene Ballou, that's pretty clueless. I heard alarm bells going off all over as you were talking."

"So did Judge Fletcher. Can you think of any reason the sheriff is blowing me off?"

"Actually, yes." She looked over his shoulder and lowered her voice. "He's in a tough campaign for re-election this fall. He'll probably win, but if it turns out that Charlotte London's death wasn't accidental, and he can't crack the case — well, we might have ourselves a new sheriff. He has every reason in the world to want to believe it was a tragic accident and the fire department's problem."

"But you're intrigued."

"Very much so. The question is, what to do about it. What do you think?"

"I don't really know. The key part of her family history had to do with the development of the Peninsulas being argued over and approved in 1970-71. Any chance you were here then?"

"Afraid not. I was in the Bay Area back then. But 70 and 71 were pretty good years — at least the half of them I remember."

"What made them good?"

"I was with a really crazy bunch of people, and we did some outrageous things my father wouldn't have approved of. We were all waiting for the Summer of Love to return, but like Vaudeville, it never did."

"You want to get a bit more specific about outrageous?"

"Scouting locations for communes, showing up stoned for protests and being absurd, running naked through fountains at dawn ..."

"Best time to do it." She gave him a sharp look. "Or so I'm told. Why did you run through the fountain?"

"I don't remember that part. Probably because it was there. I think the cold water brought me out of it. I don't suppose you were in San Francisco during the Summer of Love."

"I was only eight years old. I didn't participate."

She gave him a knowing, Cheshire-cat smile. "Well, I suppose we all have to be eight some time."

"Aren't we kind of straying from the point?"

She sighed. "I guess so. But it's a detour down memory lane, and I haven't been there in a while."

Another pause. "So you don't know what went down here in 1970-71?" Gordon said.

"I know the official story. You remember that old black-and-white Western where the newspaper editor says, 'When the legend becomes fact, print the legend?' Well, the legend is pretty well established by now. It's that Ned London and Roger Paris outfoxed the city slickers and saw to it that the Peninsulas got developed locally. It's that they put their balls on the line to do it, and almost got them cut off, but they prevailed. And the fact that Ned London didn't live to see it only added to the mythology."

"Was there any indication that there was something about it that wasn't quite right?"

She thought for a minute. "We took over the paper in 1975, and in 1976, Bart Sturges was running for re-election to the State Assembly. He got elected the first time two years earlier, which was two years after his term on the Board of Supervisors ended. I seem to remember a bit of a whispering campaign that there was a bad odor about his vote to approve the Peninsulas development. But he won the election and kept on winning elections, and the talk went away. I'd forgotten about it until you asked just now."

"How about Ned London's death?"

"Never heard it called anything but a straightforward accident. Ran his car off an icy road and down a hundred-foot embankment. He may have been drinking a bit, but still an accident."

"And a quarter century later, after starting to ask questions about it, his daughter dies in a fire that looks like an accident. That seems like too many accidents in one family."

"Yes it does." She looked at her watch. "Oh, God. We have to wrap this up."

"But you're not going to let it drop?"

"Hell no. At the very least this bears looking into, and if we find something, maybe this newspaper can shame our sheriff into taking it seriously."

"What next, then?"

"Are you free tonight?"

"I can be."

"You know Garbini's?"

"Just down the street?"

"Can you meet me there for a drink at six?"

"Done. Is it OK if I bring my friend? He's pretty sharp and might be able to add something to the discussion."

"Absolutely. And where can I get hold of you if something comes up?"

"We're staying at Stanhope House." He took out his wallet, got one of his cards and handed it to her. "And my pager's on this. But I leave it in the car when I'm fishing, so don't worry if I don't get back to you right away."

"One last thing. Can I get a copy of the family history?"

"You can have this one," he said, handing her his printout. "I have the original on computer and disk, but I'd feel better if there was a copy in other hands."

She took it, stood and extended her hand. Gordon rose and shook it. Again, there seemed to be a bit of a squeeze from her at the end, but it could have been his imagination.

"See you at six, then. Oh, and I may bring someone, too."

He gave her a questioning look.

"Gina Lindsay. She teaches at the high school, too, and says she's Charlotte's best friend. She came by the office yesterday, and she doesn't believe Charlotte's death was an accident. Not at all."

"WELL?" said Peter, when Gordon returned.

"A little bit encouraging, anyway. She seems to be interested."

"She? I thought you said the editor was a man?"

"That was a mistaken assumption."

"You're old enough to know better."

"Don't remind me. In any event, I have an appointment tonight, and you're invited. We're meeting her — Elke Sundstrom is the name — at the bar at Garbini's at six o'clock. She's going to try to have Charlotte London's best friend there."

"No twilight fishing tonight, I take it."

"Sorry, Peter. I have to deal with Charlotte London's envelope."

"The curse of your honest face. But I suppose there are worse things in life than meeting two women at six o'clock."

"That's the team spirit." Gordon looked at his watch. "And we can still get several hours of fishing in before then."

After loading the Cherokee, Gordon started the engine, but at the instant he turned the key, his pager, resting in one of the cup holders, began to beep. He looked at it and switched off the ignition.

"From this area code," he said. "Probably my newspaper friend with something else. Let me call back real quick."

He leaned across the console, opened the glove compartment, and took out the Nokia cell phone he'd bought two months earlier. He had chosen the brand after being told it worked in mountainous areas better than other phones. Quickly, he punched in the number from the pager.

"Law offices," said a female voice on the other end.

He swallowed. "My name is Quill Gordon, and I just got a page from your number."

"Oh, yes. Mr. Winters is expecting your call. Just a minute."

The phone was silent for only a few seconds before a comforting baritone voice came on.

"Cameron Winters here. Mr. Gordon?"

"Speaking."

"Glad I got hold of you. I left two messages yesterday at the number on your card, and decided to try the pager when I didn't hear back. Hope I didn't interrupt you. Are you in San Francisco?"

"Actually, I'm in the parking area at Stanhope House."

"Ah, still here. Good, good. Well, the reason I'm calling is that I am — was — Charlotte London's attorney and am now the executor of her estate. You knew Miss London, I assume, and heard about what happened?"

"Yes. Sad and unexpected."

"That it was. If it hadn't been for this, I'd have expected her to live another 25 or 30 years. But of course, we never know. Be that as it may, she was, as I'm sure you know, a meticulous woman, and had planned for the time, whenever it might have been, in great detail."

Gordon made a sympathetic noise between a grunt and a murmur.

"Actually, that's why I've been trying to get in touch with you. Perhaps you knew already, but if you didn't, you are an interested party in her will."

Gordon was speechless.

"Are you still there? Mr. Gordon?"

"I'm here — just surprised. This comes as news to me."

"I suspected it might. We should probably discuss this face-to-face, instead of over the phone. Are you here for a while?"

"Until the middle of next week."

"Then I'm sure we can arrange something, though given the circumstances, the sooner the better. You'll understand when we talk. What would be convenient for you? My office is right by the county courthouse."

"You said the sooner the better. What's your schedule like today?"

"Pretty flexible. You can come over now if you like. Anything to do with Miss London's affairs moves to the head of the line as far as I'm concerned."

"How long do you think it will take to fill me in on this?"

"Not terribly long. A half hour, 45 minutes at most."

Gordon looked at Peter, who was scowling.

"All right. I'll be there in ten minutes. I look forward to meeting you."

"The pleasure will be mutual, Mr. Gordon. Thank you so much."

Gordon returned the phone to the glove compartment and turned to Peter.

"Sorry. Looks like the fishing is going to have to wait just a bit. That was Charlotte London's attorney."

"Ah."

"Apparently I am a person of interest in her will. I figured I might as well find out what that's about as soon as possible. He said it would only take a half hour to 45 minutes."

Peter laughed. "He's an attorney, Gordon. He charges by the hour. Forty five minutes is what he's hoping for. Make him do it in 15 so we can get some fishing in."

They drove over and parked across the street from the law offices. Gordon bounded up the steps to the front porch two at a time and opened the front door. He was greeted by a plump, fair-haired woman in her early thirties with a cheerful disposition.

"You must be Mr. Gordon," she said. "Mr. Winters asked me to bring you straight in."

She got up and started down the a hallway, pausing at the first door on her left and knocking on it. A voice called to come in, and she opened the door, standing aside to let Gordon in.

Cameron Winters rose from behind his desk. He was about 50, six feet tall with a receding hairline and a crew cut. He wore black dress slacks, a grey herringbone sport coast, button-down blue shirt and a red and gray tie of conservative pattern. His eyes smiled behind glasses with thick black rims.

"So glad you could come on such short notice," he said, shaking Gordon's hand. "Please have a seat."

Gordon sat in a standard-issue cushioned office chair and crossed his legs.

"If you don't mind, Mr. Gordon, I'd like to begin by getting a bit of background." Gordon nodded. "How do you know Miss London?"

Gordon shook his head. "It's the strangest thing. I came up late Sunday for a fishing trip, and Monday morning my friend and I were having breakfast at the Shotgun. She walked up to me out of the blue and said I looked like an honest man."

"You'd never met her before?"

"Not at all. Complete strangers. Anyway, we talked for several minutes, and the upshot of it was that she asked me to hold on to something for safekeeping. An envelope. She said she was in a hurry and would explain later, so we made an appointment to have lunch at Ike's Lakeside today."

"Interesting. And about what time Monday was this?"

"Around 8:30 to 8:45. I wasn't really looking at the time."

"That fits in. Tell me, to the extent you can, did she seem upset or agitated?"

"She seemed preternaturally calm, which in hindsight is kind of surprising. I mean, she made what a lot of people would think was an outrageous request. And yet, she did it so matter-of-factly that I got sucked right into it."

"She had that effect on people."

"She certainly did on me."

"Do you mind if I ask what was in the envelope? You don't have to tell me if you don't want to, but it may be germane to the matter on which I called you here."

Gordon hesitated. Miss London had trusted her envelope to him, a stranger, presumably because she wasn't comfortable giving it to someone she knew. Someone in town. Did that include her attorney and executor? Until he knew more, he didn't want to disclose too much, so he settled on a general answer and a lie of omission.

"It was a floppy disk and a couple of sheets of paper that indicated the disk contained a family history. We tried putting the disk into a computer, but it didn't read."

"All right, then. Things begin to make a bit of sense, anyway. That is, aside from the fact she trusted a total stranger she'd met in a café five minutes earlier. But even that was Charlotte. She was quite proud of her ability to size people up and utterly confident about it. She told me just last year that she'd only been wrong about a person once in her life."

"An impressive record, if true."

"I daresay it was. We gossiped from time to time, and she was spot on about the people we both knew."

"Maybe you could answer a question for me," Gordon said. "This family history — if that's what it was — had she talked about that with you?"

"Some. About a year ago, she talked about it a lot. She had just retired, and this was the big project she was embarking upon. But now that you bring it up, she really hadn't been saying anything about it the past couple of months. That may mean something, or it may mean nothing at all."

"At any rate, that doesn't answer the question of why I'm here."

Winters nodded and leaned over to get something from a leather briefcase on the floor next to him. Gordon looked around the office. There was a large window, offering a view of the house next door and a partial look at the street. Winters' law degree (Santa Clara, '71) was on the wall by the window and next to it a framed copy of the Rotary Four-Way Test. The two side walls were mostly filled with large oil paintings with Western themes. One showed a stagecoach riding through a Monument Valley landscape and the other a gathering of Native Americans. The attorney fished a folder from his briefcase and set it on the desk.

"You say you talked to Charlotte a bit before nine o'clock on Monday. Well, at 9:30, she came here for an appointment, and somewhat to my surprise said she wanted to add a holographic codicil to her will. She wrote it out on this desk, with a bit of help from me, and I called in the usual witnesses — the retired couple next door — to validate it. The original is in my safe, of course, but this is a copy."

From the folder he removed two sheets of paper stapled together and set them on the desk in front of Gordon. His first thought was that the handwriting, crisp clear and confident, must have looked great on a classroom blackboard. It covered the top two thirds of the page, leaving room for the witnesses' signatures, and read:

June 17, 1996

I hereby add and incorporate this handwritten codicil to my last will and testament, dated July 10, 1995. In order to ensure that my family history is carried through to completion, I appoint Mr. Quill Gordon of San Francisco my literary executor. He is to be granted full and complete access to all papers, documents, and relevant computer files in my possession. Any properly documented financial claim made by him upon the estate in connection with the completion of the family history shall be promptly honored by the executor prior to distribution of the residue of the estate.

When he finished reading, Gordon realized he had been holding his breath and exhaled. He lifted the top sheet and saw that the bottom one consisted of a photocopy of the business card he had given Charlotte London Monday morning.

"That seems clear enough," Gordon said. "But why? Why me? Wasn't there someone else she knew who could have done this?"

"She has friends, certainly, and her brother lives here. I believe they're on cordial terms. But I'm afraid I can't answer your question. I won't deny that I was surprised when she asked for this Monday morning, but she was sharp and collected as always, so I went forward. Charlotte was difficult enough to counsel, and arguing with her was out of the question."

"I don't suppose there are any papers left after that fire?"

"Afraid not. I spoke with the assistant fire chief yesterday. He said they were able to save the skeleton of the building, but the fire was so hot that any paper inside the house was burned beyond ashes and any computer equipment was melted beyond saving. She left no papers with me, either. No, Mr. Gordon. It may well be that what she gave you Monday morning is all that's left."

"That's a lot to process."

"Take your time by all means. We'll need awhile to close out the estate. It's easily worth a few million, but a lot of it is tied up in the London & Paris Land Company, and it'll take some time to sort that out. The good news, at least as far as your responsibility goes, is that the land company paid regular dividends, so she had a nice chunk of cash in the bank. If you incur any expenses in relation to your duties, I can get you a check right away."

"Thank you. That's good to know." He stared at the Native American painting, turning things over in his mind. "I don't know if it's appropriate for me to ask, but could you tell me the terms of her will?"

Winters leaned back in his chair, pressed his hands together, and stared at the ceiling for a few seconds.

"I don't see why not. You're an interested party, and when it goes to probate, it'll be a public document. Last-minute codicil aside, it was pretty straightforward. She left cash bequests of $50,000 each to her niece and nephew, and her house jointly to them. They're both grown and out of the area, so I guess it was for vacations and family gatherings. She left $2,000 a year for the next 20 years to the high school library for buying books, and $10,000 to her friend Gina Lindsay, with the direction that it be used to travel abroad. Beyond that, what's left over after expenses is the residue of the estate."

"A few million, you said. And where does that go?"

Winters blinked. "Planned Parenthood of Northern California, with the directive that it be used to expand services in this county."

"Planned Parenthood. Did she say why?"

"She never did, but I think I can hazard a pretty good guess. You see, Mr. Gordon, this is a small town with conservative, traditional values. Everybody who lives here will tell you that. But conservative, traditional values don't always trump young hormones. They didn't when I was growing up, and probably less so now. We have a bear of a teenage pregnancy problem in this county, and working at the high school, she was face to face with it every day. She has told me on a couple of occasions that one of the great frustrations of her job was seeing so many bright young girls who could have gone on to college getting pregnant and marrying straight out of high school. She felt it was a waste of human potential, and I suspect she concluded this was one way she could do something about it."

"Sure. That makes sense."

"Well, Mr. Gordon, I've given you a lot to chew on, and it must have been quite a surprise. Do you have any other questions?"

"Not right now. I'm still taking it all in."

"If you think of something, call. I'll help any way I can. And if anything else comes up, I'll be in touch with you straightaway. How much longer did you say you were going to be here?"

"Until next Wednesday morning You can page me or leave a message at Stanhope House."

"Good enough. Oh, and one more thing. I'd try Charlotte's floppy disk in another computer if I were you. I know that once or twice I've had problems calling up things she did on her computer."

"Will do," Gordon said rising. Winters also stood, and they shook hands. "Thank you for everything, and I'm sure we'll be in touch."

He walked back outside, where it was still windy, crossed the street, and got into the Cherokee. Peter gave him a quizzical look.

"You're not going to believe this," Gordon said, handing him the copy of the codicil.

FROM ARTHUR, they again drove south down the state highway that followed the lake and kept going when they reached the dam. Beyond it, the road dropped steeply through a canyon, after which it traversed a lush, green valley with cattle grazing in the open meadows. They climbed a slight rise, dropped into another valley, then followed the highway through another canyon with a roiling stream tumbling downhill to their left.

"Is that the Hawk?" Peter asked.

"Nope. Hiscox Creek. A tributary. We'll be getting back to Hawk River not too far ahead."

"Who was Hiscox?"

"How the hell would I know? Probably some early settler."

"Something bothering you, Gordon? You're usually quite loquacious when it comes to filling me in on the local lore."

"Yeah, something's bothering me. I'm starting to get more than a little bit of a resentment toward Miss London and her presumptions. I came up here to go fishing, not to spend half the rest of my life finishing a family history. If she wanted me to do that, the least she could have done was ask me beforehand."

"We were supposed to be having lunch with her today. Maybe she was going to ask you then." Gordon made a noise that was a cross between a grunt and a snort. "Probably not her fault that she died first. And grumpy as you are, I'm sure she'd rather be with you at one o'clock today than lying on a slab in the morgue, or wherever she is."

"I know that. And I know I shouldn't be feeling the way I do. I just don't appreciate her trespassing on my good nature."

"At least you have a good nature. Nobody ever said that about me."

"No comment."

"You know, Gordon, I'm beginning to feel this fishing trip start to slip away from us. It's not what I expected, but I'm all right with it. I was there when Miss London approached us in the café, and even at the time, I thought it was an amazing leap of faith for her to trust a complete stranger that much. I don't see that you have any choice but to carry out that trust."

"Neither do I, dammit." He sighed. "I'll get over it, I guess. And I'll probably feel better after we get some fishing in today."

A few miles later they came to a stop at a T intersection. The north-south state highway was meeting up with an east-west state highway. A left turn would have taken them 12 miles to Adams, the second city, such as it was, of Forest County. They turned right onto the highway, which, taken to its end, followed the river 60 miles downstream to the vast Central Valley. Two miles down, they passed a road on the left that crossed a rickety wooden bridge to Steinhart's Lodge and Resort, Est. 1924.

"In a mile or so," said Gordon, feeling better, "there's a dirt road that goes down to a little flat just above the river. This is the Middle Fork of the Hawk, but from the flat we can walk down to where the North Fork joins it." He looked at his watch. "We should have just enough time to fish our way down and back."

The dirt road Gordon spoke of was unmarked, and a casual observer would have missed it. But knowing where it was, he was able to veer sharply to the left, in front of an oncoming pickup. The road was barely wide enough for one car, and went straight downhill at a 30-degree angle for a hundred yards before ending at a flat, gravelly area of about 100-by-150 feet. A red Chevy pickup with license plate guards from an Adams dealership was parked there, but its occupant was nowhere to be seen. Gordon parked parallel to it, 25 feet away, and hopped out of the Cherokee. At the edge of the flat, which commanded a good view of the gorge, he looked downstream, then up, and pointed upstream.

"He's up there," he shouted to Peter. "We stick to the original plan."

They put on vests and waders, grabbed their rods, locked the vehicle, and started down a steep narrow path to the river 20 feet below. The highway was far above them now, and the only noise that could be heard from it was when a large truck shifted gears with a growl. Cut into the canyon walls on the opposite side of the river was a railroad track, and in the time they were fishing, two long trains passed on it. The morning breeze had, if anything, picked up, and the river canyon was serving as a giant wind tunnel. The wind stung their cheeks and threatened to blow away their hats. The noonday sun, almost directly above them, lit the landscape with a burning clarity. Its reflection off the white boulders in the river was only partly mitigated by their polarized sunglasses. The combination of wind and sun was an assault on all their senses.

The river was running high, fast and relatively clear. Gordon stuck a hand in the water, and quickly pulled it out. It had clearly been snow not so long ago. They worked downstream, fishing dry flies in the comparatively slower sections. He caught one fish, a beautifully colored 10-inch Brook Trout, and both of them missed hooking a couple of fish that rose to their flies. The current was so fast and the fish were striking so quickly, there was almost no time to react.

On the way back, Peter kept fishing the moving water with dry flies. With experience, his reflexes improved to the point where he was able to catch and release two Rainbow Trout, 11 and 14 inches. Gordon switched over to nymphs, which he fished below the surface in the larger pools. The fast water was sweeping the flies through the pools before they could sink deep enough, so he clipped a small weight to the line just above them. That got the flies down deep enough to be seen and gobbled by several trout, the best of which was an 18-inch Brown in the pool just before they got back to the flat. The Chevy pickup had vanished, and they had the flat to themselves as they chugged soft drinks from the cooler and removed their waders.

"River's too high for the fishing to be really hot," Gordon said, "but we didn't do too badly under the circumstances." He looked down at the water. "Another four or five weeks, when most of the snow has melted, this should be perfect."

"I'm not complaining. Though I'm kind of zonked from the wind and sun."

"It was pretty intense." He looked at his watch, which said 3:45. "We should be back at Stanhope House by five. That'll give time to shower and change before our cocktail engagement. I'm beginning to look forward to it."

BRUNO GARBINI had come to Forest County in 1947, when they were building the dam that created Año Nuevo Reservoir. There weren't enough local men to do the job, so the construction firm had created a tent city for workers imported for the effort. They had to be fed, and Bruno — 25 years old at the time, with three years of Navy cooking experience behind him — was hired to run the kitchen. When he heard complaints about the sameness of the fare, he wrote to his mother and got her recipe for spaghetti for eight. Multiplying the recipe by a factor of 50, he served mom's spaghetti one Wednesday night, and it immediately became a camp tradition. By the time the dam was finished, he had proposed marriage to the bank teller who deposited his paycheck each week and noticed that Arthur had no Italian restaurant. His eponymous establishment filled that market niche, and for 20 years did a booming business.

As the logging industry declined, so did Garbini's, but by then, Bruno had paid for the building, paid off his house, and had such a low nut it was impossible not to at least break even. So for the past quarter-century, he had preserved it as it was — a 1950s style Italian-American restaurant, with red-checked tablecloths, candles in red glass holders, photographs of Sinatra, Dean Martin and Joe DiMaggio on the wall, and music from their era playing softly over the sound system. Certainly it was true that the wallpaper could stand to be replaced, and that some of the booths had duct tape patching up gashes in the upholstery. But at the same time, the food was good (in an old-school sort of way), the drinks were honest and the prices were reasonable, and that was enough to attract sufficient customers. Every night at five, Bruno took a seat at the bar, close to the front door, ordered the first of two glasses of wine his doctor permitted, and waited to greet the dwindling number of customers he still knew personally.

Gordon and Peter walked through the door exactly at six. Bruno was at his perch, halfway through the first glass and agonizing over whether to take another sip now or hold off a few minutes longer. Two men sat at the bar, desultorily watching a baseball game on TV; a couple in their fifties had just finished their salad at one of the booths; and it was quiet enough that the sound of Dean Martin singing "Houston" filled the air. Gordon was immediately carried back to a summer vacation his family had taken when he was five or six. It had seemed that song was on the radio every 15 minutes, and his father sang along, knowing the words by heart. It had been nearly 30 years now since he'd heard it. Gordon pulled back the cuff of his button-down blue shirt with white pencil stripes and looked at his watch. Bruno stood and moved to greet them.

"You wouldn't, by chance, be the gentlemen meeting El Sundstrom tonight?" he asked.

Gordon nodded.

"Welcome to my place. I'm Bruno Garbini." He shook hands with both of them. "She said if you got here first to put you in the back booth. I guess you have some business to discuss."

He led them to a booth against the far wall. They slipped in facing each other, with Gordon looking toward the front door.

"If you're friends of El, the first drink is on the house. What'll it be?"

Gordon and Peter looked at each other.

"Thanks, but we'll wait for the ladies," Gordon said.

"Suit yourselves, but do have one. I'm only allowed to have two glasses of wine a night, so I have to get my pleasure from watching my customers drink. Damn doctors."

"I know," said Peter sympathetically. "They're terrible. Always telling you not to have any fun, and that it's for your own good."

"You got that right." He leaned over conspiratorially. "Two glasses of wine, but they didn't say anything about grappa. I have a little slug of that at closing. Helps me sleep better. And I figure that what the doctors don't know doesn't hurt them."

"Always been my philosophy," Peter said.

Bruno walked back to his stool, took a small sip of wine and looked morosely at his glass.

"You're not very loyal to your profession," Gordon said.

"But it's true. I can't do half the stuff I tell my patients to do. Most of us can't."

Elke Sundstrom walked through the front door. She was dressed as she had been in the office that morning, but had removed the baseball cap, allowing her hair to reach her shoulders, and had added a pair of teardrop turquoise earrings. Bruno stood to greet her, gave her a hug, and sent her to the booth with a pat on the butt. Gordon stood up to let her move in next to him and introduced Peter as Dr. Peter Delaney.

"Oh, what kind of doctor," she said, sliding into the booth.

"General surgeon now. Before that, I worked emergency room for quite a while."

"You must have all kinds of stories to tell."

"Only to people I know well."

Another woman came through the front door. She was in her early fifties, a bit plump with a kind face and short, straight hair, and was wearing a pale blue blouse and a peasant-style skirt with a blue, black and brown print, reaching to mid-calf. She began walking toward their booth, and Gordon, guessing the party was now complete, rose to greet her. Peter did the same. She introduced herself as Gina Lindsay, and Gordon and Peter introduced themselves.

"I guess you're sitting here with me," Peter said.

She gave him a quick, appraising glance.

"I've done worse." And with that she scooted into the inside spot on Peter's side.

"Dr. Delaney is a surgeon in San Francisco," El said.

"A good-hands man, eh? Just to clear the air, are you married?"

"Any particular reason for asking?"

"I just want to know what I might have to climb over if I have to get out of a tight spot."

"Not at the moment," Peter said.

"But you have been?"

"Five times."

Gina considered that for a moment. "That's impressive. You don't see too many men these days who are willing to make a commitment."

The conversation was fortunately diverted by the appearance of a middle-aged waitress wearing a bright-white blouse and black pants, who took their drink orders. Gina had a glass of Bruno's special Chianti, El ordered a Pinot Grigio, Peter (who had been three months without alcohol) a ginger ale, and Gordon a club soda with a twist. Gina looked at Gordon after the waitress left.

"You're having a Lenny Briscoe," she said.

"A what?"

"Lenny Briscoe's the detective on *Law & Order*, played by Jerry Orbach. He's a recovering alcoholic, so every time he goes into a bar on an investigation, he orders a club soda with a twist."

Gordon wasn't sure how to answer that. El pulled up her shoulder bag, opened the flap, and took out the manuscript Gordon had given her that morning.

"Now that we've dispensed with the preliminaries," she said, "let's get down to the business at hand. Gordon came to the newspaper office this morning with quite a story." She turned to him. "Why don't you tell it yourself?"

He was beginning to tire of the story, but told it again anyway. He must have sped through it, because he finished as the waitress arrived with drinks.

"What do you think, Gina?" said El, when he was done.

"I don't *think* anything," she said. "I *know*. They're saying a pile of oily rags spontaneously combusted in her service porch. Baloney! Baloney on two counts! First of all, Charlotte was utterly hopeless with machinery of any kind. At school, we ran for cover when she tried to use the photocopier. There's no way she would have been doing anything that would have gotten a rag oily to begin with. And second, if for some mysterious reason she had, there's no way she would have left a pile of dirty, smelly rags on the floor for more than 30 seconds. God bless her, she was the biggest neat freak I've ever known. I don't know anything else about it, but I know that fire was no accident, and somebody must have gone to a lot of trouble to make it look like one."

A brief silence followed her outburst, then Peter spoke.

"We seem to have a consensus. The question is what do we do about it."

"I think Gordon, or maybe Judge Fletcher had the right idea about that," El said. "People come to the newspaper because they hope we can do a story that will drive people in power to take action. We need to get as much information as we can and have a story in next week's paper that raises these questions. Maybe that'll get our sheriff off his ass."

She looked around and saw shrugs and nods of approval.

"The problem is, I can't do it all by myself. One reporter and I have to get all the stories for each week's paper, and that's a full-time job and then some. I can write the story when the time comes, but I need all of you to help me run down the information in the next few days. Can you do it?"

"I'm in," said Gordon.

"Absolutely," said Gina.

Everyone turned to Peter, who seemed to be looking at something over Gordon's shoulder. Finally, he sighed.

"Sure. Why not? It's not like I'm going to be going fishing or anything."

"All right, then," said El. "We have a team."

Peter lifted his ginger ale glass. None of them had touched the drinks yet.

"Then a toast: To our investigation. May it see justice done."

They clinked glasses all around. The waitress reappeared.

"How are you doing on drinks?" she asked. "Could I bring you a menu?"

Gordon looked around the table.

"You'd better bring some menus," he said. "I think we're going to be here awhile."

A TUREEN OF MINESTRONE arrived, and the waitress ladled out bowls for all of them. After a few minutes of eating in silence, Gordon turned to El and said:

"The soup's good. I take it you come here often."

"Often enough. Have been ever since we got here."

"And when was that? I'm guessing the two of you (he looked at Gina) have been here awhile. I'd like to hear your stories."

He looked back and forth between the two women.

"You first," said Gina.

El sighed and set her spoon down in the soup bowl.

"It was a long time ago, but it seems like yesterday. I think I told you (she turned to Gordon) that in 1970, I was hanging out with a group of people who would have been called hippies, though we never used the word ourselves. Several of us lived in a townhouse on Judah Street in San Francisco, near Kezar Stadium, if you know where that is. It wasn't too far from the Haight, but of course the Haight had changed by then. The drugs and crime were worse.

"There were about eight of us in the core group and usually about as many more around the edges, though they came and went. In November of 1970 (and I remember, because I decided I was *not* going to go home to my parents for Thanksgiving), Andre Franklin moved in. Oh my God, he was gorgeous! Tall, thin, curly brown hair over his ears and down to his shoulders. The first time I saw him I thought I'd die if he didn't ask me to go to bed with him.

"And with a little encouragement on my part, he did. It was on Thanksgiving Day, actually. Those of us who stayed in the house, including Andre, cooked Swanson frozen turkey dinners. Afterwards, he invited me to his room and played the guitar for me. He had a gift with music. And afterwards … well, we were a couple from then on. Soul mates, really, or so I thought at the time. And not a Thanksgiving has gone by since that I don't think about what happened in his room that night.

"Andre worked for a health food store, and because he was stoned less often than the other staff, they trained him to keep the books. I'd taken journalism classes at Cal and was working for the *Bay Guardian*, as a copy editor at first, because nobody wanted to do that, then they let me do a couple of stories. That worked pretty well, and I started to move up. It didn't pay much, but you could still live fairly cheap in San Francisco then. Not like now. At the end of 1972, I got pregnant. Our daughter, Anna, was born in late July of 1973. Andre and I talked about getting married, but decided a marriage certificate was just a piece of paper." She took a sip of wine. "My father was *not* happy.

"The year after Anna was born, Andre's aunt died. She'd married a well-off businessman, and they lived in Hillsborough, but they never had any kids. She was very fond of Andre and left him a quarter of a million dollars, saying she hoped he'd buy or start a business with it. That changed everything.

"It was getting more expensive to live in San Francisco, and we weren't sure we wanted to raise our daughter there. A lot of people we knew had moved to the country or to small towns and tried to live a simpler life. We thought maybe we'd do the same. So in the fall of 1974 we drove around Northern California in our VW bus, sleeping in it most nights, and looking for a town we might move to. We got to Arthur in mid-October, and the weather was nicer than usual, warm and clear, though the nights were chilly. Then one morning we were in the Shotgun Café, and we heard someone at the next table say the newspaper was up for sale."

The waitress cleared the soup bowls and set salads in front of them. Garbini's was one of the few places left that served both soup and salad before dinner. El took a bite of salad and continued.

"We took a drive all the way around the lake after breakfast and talked about it. Andre could run the business side and I could be the editor. By the time we got back to town, we knew we were going to go for it. We offered ten percent under the asking price, and the owner accepted. Later, we realized we probably paid 20 percent too much, but to us it was a dream, not an investment.

"The old owner wanted to work until July of the next year when he'd be 65 and could collect Social Security. That was fine with us. It gave us a chance to make plans.

"When we got back to The City, Andre proposed to me. He said if we were going to move to a small town, we had to be respectable. We also had to give up marijuana. That was fine by me. I'd pretty much been leaving it alone since I got pregnant with Anna, anyway. But he said we could drink, since that was legal and everybody in town did it. If only I'd known then."

She stopped to swallow the last of the Pinot Grigio.

"We took over the paper in the summer of '75, and I went real slow about making any changes. We had to become accepted in the community first. And I'll have to say, after writing about police brutality and social problems at Hunters Point, it took some doing to get used to writing about ribbon cuttings and school bake sales. That winter, the high school basketball team won the league championship and three games in the state playoffs. We covered the hell out of it and basked in the glow of their achievement.

"But something else happened that winter. First of all, there was the winter. It didn't snow much that year, but it was cold and dark, and we weren't used to it. Andre took it harder than I did. And the other thing was that he'd started drinking regularly, and it was a problem. Pot he could handle. Smoked a bit and got mellow and horny. But it turned out he couldn't handle alcohol at all. If he took one drink, you never knew when he was going to stop, and it was almost never early. By next April he was drinking every night, and I was feeling like a grass widow.

"It didn't help that the paper was having cash-flow problems. We had great accounts receivable, and that was what we were looking at when we bought it. The problem was, a lot of them took their time paying, and Andre wouldn't lean on them. After a while, he didn't even care.

"One night in December of 1976, we had a huge fight just before dinner and he stomped out. It had happened before, and I figured we'd make it up later. I waited up for him, then finally went to bed. I was fast asleep when the doorbell rang, and the clock on the nightstand said 2:30. I thought Andre had locked himself out, so I ran to the door, flipped on the porch light, and opened it.

"It wasn't Andre. It was a Highway Patrol officer, who'd come to tell me Andre had run off the road and into a tree and been killed. He'd clearly been drinking. Thank God, he didn't hurt anybody else. And now, 20 years later, I'm still here."

The table was silent for a moment.

"I never knew that — about your husband, I mean. I'm sorry," Gina said. "That was before we got here."

"And when was that?" Peter murmured.

"My story isn't nearly as interesting, but I'll give you the short version. I grew up in Southern California, normal family, suburbs, all that. Went to school at San Jose State, got my teaching credential, and got hired in Sacramento. One night in a bar (I had to clean the story up for our kids), I met a cute guy who worked for Crocker Bank. One thing led to another, and Ken and I got married. We had two kids, Jason and Jennifer, and I quit teaching to take care of them.

"Ken was getting tired of Sacramento and talking about moving somewhere more quiet for the kids' sake. One day he saw an ad that Cascade Pacific Bank needed a branch manager in Arthur and applied. He got the job, and we moved here in the fall of 1979. A year later, I felt the kids were old enough that I could go back to work.

"I didn't realize how much of a strain it would be. I was out of the groove on doing lesson plans and grading papers and tests, so I was putting in long hours. Ken started working late, too, but I wasn't paying much attention. I guess I was the last one in town to find out that 'working late' meant doing a little double entry with one of the tellers. It blew up, finally. I got the house and they left town. And now the kids are gone, and I'm still here."

"What are the kids doing?" Peter asked.

"Jennifer just graduated from police academy and will be going to work at the Roseville Police Department, just outside Sacramento. Jason is getting his teaching credential at San Francisco State."

"How about Anna?" Gordon asked El.

"She just finished her first year at USC law school. She'll be home a week from Sunday."

"So all the kids did well," he said.

"Since you were so bold as to ask me," Peter looked at Gina as she said this, "are either of you attached now?"

Both women laughed. Peter gave Gordon a "What's the joke?" look.

"Do you want to explain?" El said.

"This is probably the worst place in the world to be a single woman," Gina said. "There are two kinds of people in a town like this. The ones who get married straight out of high school and never leave, and the ones who leave after high school and never come back. And the ones who get married tend to stay married, so there aren't a lot of eligible bachelors around here."

"To give you an idea how bad it is," El continued, "I belong to the Rotary Club. I was the first woman they let in when they had to. Every Thursday I go to that meeting, and there are 47 men in the room. Forty six of them are married."

"At least there's one prospect," Peter said.

"That 'prospect' would be Len Iverson, the former football coach. He's 88 and comes to the meetings with a cane. Just between us, I think he's hanging on for one more football season before he goes to the great stadium in the sky. No, I'm not even looking anymore. I figure my only chance is to wait another ten years until one of the wives dies, and pounce."

"You've thought it out better than I have," Gina said. "I'm just going to wait for the perfect man, and you know what they say?"

"I'm afraid I don't," murmured Peter.

She looked at him. "The perfect man doesn't drink, doesn't cheat and doesn't exist."

Both women laughed louder and longer than would have been expected given the single glass of wine they'd each consumed. Peter and Gordon exchanged a silent glance. The waitress showed up with their dinners, once again saving the day.

AS HE ATE HIS SPAGHETTI, Gordon could see why the workers who built Año Nuevo Dam had liked it so much.

It was hearty, with a rich tomato flavor, but the herbs and spices kept the tomato from overpowering and made the sauce feel almost creamy. He remembered eating spaghetti like this at restaurants his parents had taken the family to when he was a child, and realized that this sort of comfort-food spaghetti had all but vanished from the menus of Italian restaurants in the Bay Area.

After a few minutes he set his fork down and looked at Gina.

"Now that we've decided to follow up on what Charlotte gave me, I'd like to know a bit more about her. I take it you met at the high school."

Gina nodded. "She helped me out quite a bit my first year there, but that was Charlotte. She made a point of being accessible to the new faculty, and what she did for me, which helped a lot, wasn't unusual. We didn't really become good friends until my marriage blew up."

"You confided in her?" said El.

"She was easy to talk to, and I needed someone. We hadn't been here that long, you know, and almost everyone we knew, we knew as a couple. That made it awkward. She just knew me, so I could vent with her." She laughed. "God, I'd forgotten how tiresome I must have been back then. But we ended up getting together a lot after school that year, and it grew into a friendship. I never thought of it until just now, but being single in a town where almost everybody's married, well, she must have needed a friend, too."

"Is there anything you particularly remember her saying?" interjected Peter. "Anything that made an impression on you and really helped?"

"Early on, when I was really angry and having revenge fantasies, she told me to remember what we try to impress on our students as English teachers: That everyone is flawed, that everyone has his reasons, and we need to keep that in mind, even as we judge. There was one other thing she said that I've never forgotten. I was crying in my wine one night, and wailing about how could he do this to me. She leaned across the table, put a hand on my forearm, and said:

" 'Gina, darling. There's something you need to remember. It's very seldom that people are doing something *to* you. They are usually doing it *for* themselves, and if you get hurt along the way, you're just collateral damage.' I really didn't want to hear those things at the time, but after a while I processed them, and it helped me let go."

"And that was the beginning of a beautiful friendship," Gordon said.

"We had a lot in common, and we were both single. Most of the other teachers were married or moved on after a couple of years. So we started doing more and more things together. Every Monday night, we'd get together, usually at her house, for a glass of sherry and conversation. I was on my way over this past Monday night when I saw the fire. Actually, I called first, but she didn't answer, so I left a message and started over. Oh, God. I wonder if she was trapped in the fire when I called?"

Her lip began to quiver, and a tear rolled from the corner of her left eye down her cheek. She dabbed at it with her napkin.

"There was nothing you could have done," said El. "Why don't you try to remember some more?"

Gina collected herself after a moment.

"A lot of great memories. Charlotte was mad about books, and every other month, we'd leave first thing on a Saturday morning and drive to Sacramento. We'd go to Time Tested Books and spend a couple of hours there. Sometimes Charlotte bought $500 worth of books. Money wasn't an issue for her, you know. We'd have lunch, maybe do some other shopping, and drive back. Sometimes in the winter, if a storm was moving in, we'd stay overnight. What I really remember, though, was the conversations we had on those long drives, when it was just us in the car and we didn't have to worry about being overheard.

"And every summer for the past ten years, we've gone to one of the Shakespeare festivals — usually at Tahoe or Ashland, Oregon. In fact, we had tickets for Ashland next month. They're doing *Coriolanus*, and Charlotte was really looking forward to it. It's a wonderful play, and one that doesn't get produced terribly often."

"It sounds," Gordon said, "as if she lived what she taught. I'd like to know what kind of a teacher she was. In your opinion."

"She was the best, and that's not my opinion — it's everybody's. When she retired a year ago, she was irreplaceable. They don't make teachers like her any more. Smart young women can make so much more money in business now, but that wasn't an option for Charlotte when she graduated from college in 1957. The choices were nurse, librarian and teacher. This town has no idea how lucky it is that she picked the last one."

"I still remember the good teachers, from early on all the way through medical school," said Peter. "It's a gift. What do you think made her good?"

"She loved language, and she loved literature, and she had a real ability to convey that love to students and get them caught up in it. Not all of them, of course. That never happens. But a surprisingly high number. She treated them like adults, and challenged them, and they fed off her enthusiasm. Charlotte believed that being able to think and write well were part of the same package, and that they were skills that helped immeasurably in life. Her students wrote a lot, and she spent a lot of time grading their papers and commenting on them.

"And she also had a way of conveying literature. She could show the students — well, some of them, anyway — that it was a way of understanding your feelings and understanding other people. And again, that those were skills that definitely served you well as you went through life.

"Her senior Advanced English class was legendary. Over the course of a year, she taught *Oedipus Rex*, the Book of Job, a bit of Chaucer and Milton, *Macbeth*, Wordsworth, Coleridge, Byron, Shelley, Keats, the Brownings, the Rossettis, and *Great Expectations*."

"That's impressive," said Gordon. "I thought the nuns at my high school made us read a lot, but it wasn't that much."

"Hmm," said El. "A Catholic boy. My father always told me to watch out for Catholic boys. He said they'd have their way with you, and figure all they had to do to make it OK was confess to the priest."

"Did that keep you away from Catholic boys?" Gina asked.

"It didn't keep me away from *any* boys, but we're getting off subject."

Gina continued. "There was one decision about that advanced class that Charlotte put off until Christmas each year. Between Coleridge and the other poets, the students would read another novel, and she wanted to see how good a class she had before deciding which one. If it was a really good class, they read *Pride and Prejudice*. If it wasn't quite so good, they read *Jane Eyre*."

She looked around the table to see if that had sunk in.

"That makes some sense," Peter said. "Bronte's a very good writer, but you don't get from her what you get from Austen. And Austen takes more teaching than Bronte."

"Exactly." She put a hand on his arm. "You understand. And *Pride and Prejudice*, though some people might not think so, is a relevant book here. So much of it is about making a good match, and we see so many students who get married straight out of high school — just because. Charlotte felt that reading and understanding that book would make at least some of them think more broadly and deeply about what, after all, is one of the most important decisions they'll ever make."

"I'd be curious to know," Gordon said, "if there were any books Charlotte wanted to teach but didn't."

Gina nodded. "We actually talked about that several times on the way to Sacramento and the Shakespeare festivals. She said the regret she'd die with was that she couldn't teach George Eliot and Tolstoy; she really loved *Middlemarch* and *Anna Karenina*. But she just didn't feel that even the best high school class, as a group, could handle the length and complexity. She gave copies to a few special students, but she was afraid an entire class would get lost."

"She's probably right," Gordon said. "I finally got around to *Middlemarch* a couple of years ago, when I was recuperating from a hernia surgery. Peter did it, actually; that's how we met. It's a wonderful book, but I wouldn't have gotten it in high school. And I doubt I would have taken it on at all if I hadn't been facing a week at home, barely able to move, during a rainy winter."

"I haven't read either of those," Peter said. "I'm more of a poetry man. 'O wild west wind, thou breath of autumn's being …' Keats, right?"

"Shelley," Gina said, "but I'm impressed nonetheless."

"Could we interrupt the book circle and get back to something else?" said El. "You mentioned how Charlotte helped you when you were going through the other woman and the divorce, and I was interested in what she said. We know she never married, but do you think she had any experience in love that she might have drawn on? It sounds as if she might have."

"That's a very good question. And one I wondered about a number of times. Charlotte was so forthcoming about a lot of things, but she very much gave the impression that her love life was off limits, and there was something about her that, well, I wouldn't have dreamed of asking. But just once, something slipped out.

"It was when the divorce became final. It hit me like a ton of bricks, and I went over to her place to cry on her shoulder. And at one point she said, 'I know how you feel. I've loved someone myself, and it didn't end well.' The she seemed to catch herself and turned the conversation back to me and my problems. That was more than ten years ago, and she never brought it up again."

It was 8:30, and they had finished their dinners. The waitress came to clear the table and asked about dessert. Gordon looked around.

"We still haven't discussed what we're going to do next," he said. "We might as well have dessert while we do that."

"I'm easy," said El.

"But we knew that already," muttered Gina.

"THE FIRST ORDER OF BUSINESS," Gordon said, after they ordered dessert, "Is to figure out what needs to be done and who's going to do it."

"A lot of it's going to fall on me," El said. "For no other reason than the newspaper would be expected to be asking questions."

"It may not be as bad as that," Gordon said. "As it turns out, I have an excellent reason for asking questions and talking to people as well." All eyes turned to him. "This morning I got a call from Cameron Winters, Charlotte's attorney. It turns out that the day she died she added a handwritten codicil to her will appointing me as her literary executor."

"What?" said Gina.

"I don't understand it, either. I'd have thought if she were doing something like that, she would have named someone she knew. You, for instance. Or her brother."

Gina sat silently for a moment before answering.

"Not her brother. He's a decent man, at least as far as I know, and reasonably smart in a business sense. But he doesn't have a literary bone in his body. Still, that's the sort of thing she could have asked me to do, and I would have said yes gladly."

"I'm in over my head on this," Gordon said. "I'm probably going to have to lean on you for help, Gina."

"Anything I can do, but … Well, if she picked you, she had a reason and probably a good one. We just don't know what it is yet."

"Just looking at the family history," Gordon said, "there are three things that jump out right away. The first is the A.D. she had in her notes to talk to about her father's accident. Anybody have any ideas who A.D. might be?"

Nobody did.

"We'll leave that for the time being. The second thing is to talk to Bart Sturges about what happened when he changed his mind and voted for The Peninsulas."

"I can set that up," said El. "He's in Sacramento but he usually comes up weekends."

"The weekend would be good. That gives us a little more time to pull together some background information on what happened back then. How are the newspaper's clip files?"

"For 1970-71? A disaster area. The guy we bought the paper from never did any indexing or clipping. He figured he could remember anything he needed, so he held on to back issues for two years, then threw them out. By the time we took over, 1970-71 were turning into organic matter at the landfill."

"Wait a minute," said Gina. "Alice could help with that. Alice Laszlo."

"The librarian?" El said.

"Sure. They have a microfilm machine that makes copies. She could probably have someone on her staff go through the six months before the vote and print out all the articles. That's only 26 issues of the paper to wade through."

"If she can't do that, I can," Peter said. "I need to contribute something."

"I'll call her in the morning. Do you have a phone number where I can reach you if she says no?"

Peter took a business card from his wallet, circled his cell phone number and handed it to her. "If you can't reach me on that, leave a message at Stanhope House." A flicker of a smile crossed her face as she slipped the card into her purse.

"The other thing, at least for right now," Gordon said, "is to talk to Charlotte's brother and the Paris family. They were the ones who worked with her father on The Peninsulas, and I'd like to hear the story from them."

"I can talk to Greg," Gina said. "I know him a bit, and the fact we're both mourning Charlotte is reason enough for asking."

"Good. But wait a day to see what we find out tomorrow." He turned to El. "How do I go about setting up a meeting with the Paris family?"

"Tomorrow's your lucky day. What are you doing at noon?"

"Well, we were going fishing in the morning, but if you had something else in mind …"

"Skip the fishing or cut it short. The Rotary Club meets at noon tomorrow at the North Woods Inn, and you're going to be my guest. Roger, Robert and Ronald Paris should be there. I'll introduce you and tell them your connection to Charlotte. I'm sure they'd talk to you."

"Deal."

Dessert arrived, and the waitress set the check on the table halfway between Gordon and Peter, who pushed the check across to his friend.

"This is on Gordon," Peter said. "He's opening a detective agency, so it's a tax-deductible business expense."

The women laughed and thanked Gordon, who quickly added up the bill in his head and slipped a credit card over it on the tray.

"We need to meet again tomorrow," El said. "Is everybody free at the end of the day?

"I'm in," said Gina.

"So are we," Gordon said.

"How about six o'clock at the newspaper office? The rest of the staff should be gone by then."

It was settled, and they parted after finishing dessert. Although it was after nine and mostly dark when they stepped outside, there was still a hint of light in the western sky. The wind that had been blowing all day had finally died down, but it was cooler than the last two nights. Gordon and Peter walked the short distance back to Stanhope House and crossed the deserted state highway at a leisurely pace.

As they got to the gate, Gordon turned to Peter.

"I think I'm going to sit in the gazebo for a few minutes and clear my head."

"You want company, or would you rather be alone?"

"If you're the company, that's fine."

They walked across the broad, well kept lawn to the gazebo. There was little moon, and they could look upward to the entire nighttime constellation — something they never saw in the city. An owl hooted, a dog barked in the distance, and a car drove past on the highway as they reached the gazebo. Otherwise it was silent. Two cushioned rattan chairs were placed at angles, and they sat in them. They could see Stanhope House across the lawn, most of its windows dark. Neither said a word for minutes.

Peter broke the silence.

"Well, it's not our vacation any more. It's Miss London's."

Gordon nodded. Peter continued.

"And between looking into what she left you and dealing with the Merry Wives of Windsor, I'd say we're going to have our hands full."

Gordon laughed. "I'd say the second part is more your concern than mine." He gently jabbed a finger into Peter's paunch. "Though come to think of it, I'm seeing a bit of a resemblance to Falstaff."

"I wouldn't be too confident of that if I were you. I was sitting across from you and madam editor, and I saw some things you didn't. Watch your back around her, Gordon." A breeze came up and rattled the aspen leaves. "She's the end of a symphony, waiting to happen."

Part II: Knowledge and Love

" 'I was in love in my young days with a deacon,' said Princess Myakaya. 'I don't know that it did me any good.' "

— **TOLSTOY**, *Anna Karenina*

Thursday June 20

BEFORE THE NOON ROTARY CLUB MEETING, Gordon tended to business. Peter had said he was going his separate way that morning, and left Gordon on his own. Shortly before ten, Gordon drove to a small, locally owned stationery and copy shop. With the help of a tattooed young shop assistant in a tank top, he made six copies of the London family history, at a nickel per page. To the cost of this, he added a 9-by-12 manila envelope, paid with a credit card, and requested a receipt to satisfy Miss London's executor, if necessary. The transaction took 35 minutes, and he was the only customer during that time.

Four of the six copies were for members of the investigation team (himself, Peter, Gina, and Alice Laszlo, bearing in mind that Elke Sundstrom had been given a copy the previous morning.) A fifth copy was for contingency purposes, and the sixth he put in the manila envelope, addressed to himself at his San Francisco P.O. Box, and patiently waited in line at the one open window at the Arthur post office until he could mail it. He thought of including a "to whom it may concern" note in the event he didn't live to receive the envelope himself, but decided against it on the grounds of excessive melodrama.

That left him time for one more task before Rotary. He wanted to see Charlotte London's house.

It was a beautiful morning, with a slight breeze and a congregation of clouds forming over the mountains to the west. With the help of a visitor guide, which had detailed street maps of Arthur and the Peninsulas, and that morning's *Forest Clarion*, which gave the address in its top-of-the-front-page story, he found the house, or what was left of it, with no difficulty. It was on the west side of the East Peninsula, in a development called Sunset Vista Estates, on Hawk View Drive, which dead-ended at a turnaround 250 feet beyond the London residence. The development had been carefully designed so that the houses on the lake side of the road were offset from the houses across the street on slightly higher ground. Every house had a clear view of the lake, and no homeowner was looking directly up or down at a neighbor. Año Nuevo Lake was glistening in the bright morning sun, and when Gordon parked in a slight turnout and got out of the Cherokee, he could hear the sounds of boats roaring or purring to and from Woodward's Marina.

From what he'd seen of the fire Monday night, Gordon was surprised at how much of the skeleton of the house remained. It looked like a total loss, but the firefighters had arrived in time to prevent it from collapsing into a heap of rubble. It was not an excessively large house — probably 1,700 to 1,800 square feet — and the massive stone chimney on the water side of the dwelling had survived the fire intact. A two-car carport, badly singed, stood to the right of the house itself, connected by a protected walkway, also badly burned. A Honda Accord that looked as if it had been white before it was charred was parked in the carport. The license plate number indicated it had been bought in late 1993 or early 1994. Yellow tape ran across the front of the property, and several standing signs warned people to keep out by order of Peninsulas Volunteer Fire Department.

"Looking for something?"

Gordon started. He hadn't heard anyone approaching, and the voice sounded enough like Charlotte London's to spook him. When he turned, he saw a woman in her mid-seventies, five-five and of average build, with short white hair under a San Francisco Giants baseball cap. She was holding a leash, connected to one of the ugliest little dogs Gordon had ever seen. It was a dirty off-white, with an uneven coat, bangs over its eyes, and spindly legs that looked as if they had been shaved.

"This is Roscoe," she said. "I'm Amanda. Amanda Blake."

"Quill Gordon. I'm a friend of Miss London's — Charlotte's — from San Francisco. I came here to … well,

I suppose to pay respects and come to terms with what happened."

"Former student?"

"No, just a friend."

They both turned and looked at the remains of the house.

"It was terrible," she said. "I was here that night. In fact, I called it in to the fire department."

"So you live nearby?"

"Two houses down that way." She gestured in the direction by which he had come in.

Gordon looked up and down the street. "That's a ways off, and there are a lot of trees in between. Didn't one of the closer neighbors see it?"

"Uh-uh. Miss London is the only year-round resident between our house and the Perrys at the end of the road. The others are all second homes. A couple were occupied this weekend, but everybody was gone by Monday morning."

"How about the Perrys?"

"In Europe until the end of the month. No, I walked Roscoe to the end of the road and back about 7:45 that night, and there was nobody here but Miss London. Harvey used to come with me on the after dinner walks, but he doesn't get around so good now."

Gordon wondered whether Harvey was her husband or another dog.

"It's his hip. The doctor recommended a replacement, but it's taking Medicare forever to process it. Glad we've got it, even so."

"So at 7:45 there was nobody here. What time did you call in the fire?"

"An hour or so later. I looked outside, and it was almost dark, but there seemed to be a glow somewhere. I got up from the couch and walked to the window. That was when I saw it."

Gordon surveyed the scene. If someone had, indeed, called on Charlotte London that night, he (or she) could have done it without being observed. The way the houses were situated, and with all the trees, it would have been hard to see that anyone was there. Someone could have parked in the turnout where Gordon did, or even in the

London carport, and absent the worst kind of bad luck, gone undetected.

"I'm still wondering about the car, though."

Gordon turned and looked at Mrs. Blake again.

"There was no one down here at 7:45, but later, probably about 8:30, I was making tea in the kitchen and I heard a car go by. I looked out the window and saw two headlights and what looked like a normal-sized car driving away from the end of the road."

"Away from where Miss London's house was?" She nodded. "Did you get a good look at it?"

"It was getting dark, and I only took a quick look. Normal-sized car and probably a dark color is about all I could say for sure."

"What did the fire department say when you told them about that?"

"They didn't say anything, because I didn't tell them."

Gordon looked at her quizzically.

"They didn't ask," she said.

THE ROTARY CLUB OF ARTHUR/AÑO NUEVO meets Thursdays at the North Woods Inn, which opened in 1939 and holds the distinction of being the longest continuously operating restaurant in the area. The building is a large log cabin, made from local timber, with a fireplace framed by river rock in the main dining room. Murals of mountain scenes, some including Paul Bunyan and Babe the ox, cover the walls, and sawdust covers the hardwood floors. (In the bar, peanut shells tossed by customers add to the floor decoration.) Behind the main dining area is a banquet room where the Rotary Club holds court.

Gordon pulled into the parking lot at five minutes to noon, and as he got out of the Cherokee, Judge Fletcher pulled into the space to his right. Must have been a short calendar that morning, Gordon thought. They greeted each other, and on the way into the building, Gordon explained that he was Elke Sundstrom's guest.

At the entrance to the back room, a silver-haired man in his late sixties or early seventies was sitting behind a folding table, with a cash box to his left and two rolls of tickets (one for the meal and one for the drawing) to his right. He stood and extended a hand to Gordon as he came in.

"Claude Brown," he said. "Visiting Rotarian?"

"No, actually I'm Elke Sundstrom's guest today. Quill Gordon."

"Not from around here, I take it."

"San Francisco. I'm here on a fishing trip."

"Ah, and what do you do in San Francisco?"

"I used to work for a family-owned stock brokerage. Now, I'm doing a bit of financial consulting."

Brown looked at him knowingly. "In other words, you're unemployed." He laughed at his own line and slapped his right thigh once.

"He went to Cal, like you did," said Judge Fletcher. "That's what happens to Cal graduates after they leave school."

"At least we're not living off the taxpayers, like some Stanford men I could mention." They both laughed at this, and the ice was broken.

By the time El arrived five minutes later, the judge had already introduced Gordon to District Attorney Cy Southworth; Walter Williams, the high school principal; and Paul James, the fire chief. Gordon exchanged a few polite words with each. He was talking to the fire chief when El walked up, and the chief turned to her.

"No comment, as usual," he said. They both laughed.

"I must say, El," said Judge Fletcher, "your men are getting younger all the time. But lovely as you are, I suppose you can pull it off."

"I can pull off anything for your honor," she purred insinuatingly. The fire chief, the judge and El all laughed at that, while Gordon maintained a straight face. "Guys, can you excuse us? I need to introduce Gordon to someone." She took him by the arm and pulled him aside, gesturing toward two men on the other side of the room.

One was in his early eighties, tall, heavy-set and red faced, with silver hair and a glass of white wine in his hand. The other was in his mid fifties, just under six feet, with a lean-to-average build and short brownish-gray hair. The older man wore khakis, a blue shirt with no tie, and a camel-hair blazer. The younger man was well dressed in a dark gray suit, white button-down shirt and blue stripe tie.

"That's Roger and Ron Paris. Roger was Ned London's partner in The Peninsulas, but Ron and his brother Bobby run the company now. Ron's the brains of the operation."

They walked over, and El did the introductions.

"Gordon particularly wanted to meet you," she said. "Charlotte London named him her literary executor, and he's going to be responsible for seeing that her family history is completed and published."

Roger Paris blinked at the news, but quickly reverted to hail-fellow-well-met mode. Ron didn't bat an eye.

"Glad to hear it," Roger said a bit too loud, the wine and partial hearing loss amplifying his voice. "Ned London was a dear friend; the whole London family, actually. We went through so much together. If there's anything at all that I — that any of us — can do to help, just say the word."

"Do you really mean that?" Gordon said. "Because I'd love to sit down with you some time and talk about The Peninsulas. It'll be an important part of the book."

"As it should be," said Ron. "How long are you going to be in town?"

"My friend and I are here until next Wednesday."

"Then there's no time to lose," said Roger. He turned to his son. "Let's ask Mr. Gordon to join us at our lunch tomorrow. My sons and I have lunch at Ike's Lakeside every Friday at one o'clock sharp. Can you be our guest tomorrow?"

"I wouldn't want to interrupt a family tradition …"

"Nonsense. Talking about The Peninsulas is talking about family. We insist. That way, you can meet Bobby, too. He had to look at a property in Crenshaw [a small town 20 miles to the east] today, but he'll be there tomorrow.

"That would be wonderful," said Gordon. "Thank you so much."

A loud bell clanged, and everyone in the room stopped talking and turned to the front, where a middle-aged man in a checked sport coat, striped tie and bad comb-over stood at the lectern.

"Welcome to the Rotary Club of Arthur/Año Nuevo," he said. "Please join me in the pledge of allegiance." The whole room said it as one, and Gordon realized it was the first time he'd said the pledge since high school.

"Our invocation today will be given by the Reverend Timothy Blood of St. Luke's Episcopal Church."

A slight man in his early thirties, with thinning hair, tortoise-shell glasses and a clerical collar came to the lectern. It was clearly his minute of glory, and he made it last for three, invoking a long list of blessings The Lord had bestowed upon those in the room. Several people were fidgeting by the time he finally said, "We thank thee in Jesus' name, amen."

The club president recaptured the lectern and said, "We will now get our food and enjoy fellowship before beginning the business part of the meeting in 20 minutes." He hit the bell again.

Lunch was a buffet. There were macaroni and lime-Jell-O-with-marshmallow salads for starters, and the entrée was chunks of beef in a sauce that couldn't seem to make up its mind if it wanted to be beef burgundy or beef stroganoff. It could be eaten over or next to mashed potatoes or noodles and accompanied by a broccoli-carrot-string bean medley dripping with butter. Gordon tried to control the damage by taking small portions, and he found himself wondering if Rotarians 50 years ago had faced the same buffet. Probably so. He saw Bruno Garbini behind him in line and found himself wishing for the comparative healthfulness of Garbini's spaghetti and meatballs.

Two long tables covered with white tablecloths, with ten chairs on either side, were set perpendicular to the lectern and head table. All but three chairs were eventually filled. Gordon and El sat on the outside part of the table to the left of the lectern, with Roger Paris across from El. Gordon was to her left, directly across from Ron

Paris. To Gordon's left was a distinguished-looking man in his late forties, who introduced himself as Harold Hansen, owner of the town's State Farm agency. Across from Hansen was a man in his eighties, walking with the aid of a cane, who was one of the last to be seated. He turned out to be Len Iverson, the former football coach for whom the high school field was named. Ron Paris introduced Iverson and Gordon, mentioning that Gordon was working on Charlotte London's family history.

"Miss London?" Iverson said. "By gad, what a woman."

"You must have worked with her," Gordon said.

"Not directly, but all the teachers knew each other. She was one of the best." He paused and took a sip of iced tea. "Tragedy what happened. Never thought I'd outlive her.But then I've outlived a lot of people."

"I had her for senior English," said Hansen. "My daughter had her four years ago. Not my son, though. He wasn't a good enough student."

"What was she like as a teacher?" Gordon said.

"It was almost 30 years ago. I don't remember much. To be honest, English was never my favorite subject, and I haven't read a book in years. I read *The Wall Street Journal, The Forest Clarion*, and reports I have to do for work. But I got more from her English class than I did from the others. I don't remember the books as much as what she said about them, and some of the ways they helped you look at people. Actually, understanding people comes in handy in the insurance business. It's about helping people, after all."

"She taught character," Iverson said. "We used to think as coaches that we were responsible for building character, but for a long time, there weren't any sports for girls. Miss London's English classes were part of their character-building. Some of the boys, too."

The conversation sagged for a moment. Gordon turned to El, but she was speaking to Cameron Winters, who had sat down to her right. Ronald Paris moved to pick things up again.

"So where have you been fishing?" he asked Gordon.

"We were on the lake Monday afternoon and evening; Copper Creek Tuesday morning; the Middle Fork of the Hawk River yesterday afternoon."

"Wasn't it running high and fast?"

Gordon nodded. "We caught a few, but it'll probably be better in a month. We thought we'd try the North Fork above the lake this afternoon."

"It's a good spot early season. Good luck."

The meeting was called to order. After announcements (a couple of which were on the long-winded side), Rotarian and dentist, Dr. Jerry Mack, stepped up as the "Sheriff" and imposed fines on members of the club to raise money for the scholarship fund. The cause was good, but the extraction process was painful: Dr. Mack tried to be funny, but most of his jokes fell flat and were greeted by polite titters. Roger Paris chuckled several times, probably as loudly as anyone, but Ron Paris barely cracked a smile. At the end of the performance, he leaned across the table and said to Gordon and El, *sotto voce*:

"They say in comedy, timing is everything. I think Jerry needs a new watch."

The speaker was Captain Ben Vestal of the California Department of Forestry, who spoke about the prospects for the upcoming forest fire season and managed to be reasonably interesting and occasionally funny. His presentation benefited greatly from the act it followed, and he received a genuinely warm round of applause when he finished just before the meeting ended.

"I don't see how you can stand this," Gordon said to El as they left.

"Duty calls. Actually, it grows on you after a while. See you at six."

After she drove off, Gordon looked around the parking lot. There were several groups of people talking after the meeting, including a foursome that included District Attorney Southworth, Judge Fletcher, Cameron Winters, and Sheriff Ballou. Gordon was beginning to see why Charlotte London might have trusted him, an outsider, with her family history. He still had no idea what was in it that could have gotten her killed, but after the meeting today he didn't see how anyone prominent in town would have the inclination to press forward on anything that could have been unpleasant for one of his peers. The people here are too close to each other, he thought. They hang together. Everything that happens is a hometown verdict.

'THAT BAD?" said Peter, as they pulled out of the driveway at Stanhope House.

"I'm probably overreacting," Gordon said. "But it was definitely a good ol' boy fest"

"Speaking of which, what was your impression of the Paris end of London & Paris?"

"Roger — he's the old man — is a character straight out of Sinclair Lewis. Thinks the Chamber of Commerce can do no wrong, accepts all the conventional pieties. Ron — the second son — seems to be a bit sharper and more well-rounded. You might even find some irony in him if you dug deep enough."

"So it was just the father and son?"

"Two other sons, but they were absent. Robert, the oldest, was apparently out looking at some property today, but I should meet him tomorrow. The youngest, Richard, has been living in San Francisco for years, so he's probably out of the picture as far as what we're looking into."

"Not surprised he had to leave town," Peter said. Gordon shot him a look. "He has the wrong vowel after his R."

Midway into Arthur they turned right on County Road 27, which crosses the North Fork of Hawk River a mile out of town and follows it upstream for about ten miles before looping back to the east-west state highway. Several dirt roads lead from the county road to mountain lakes and meadows, and in one instance to an old hotel and hot springs developed as a resort early in the century.

"How about you?" Gordon asked. "What were you up to this morning?"

"Satisfying my curiosity. Actually, I discovered something interesting."

"Spill."

"No dice. I'm saving it for the group tonight. It's not just you and me, Gordon. We have a team now."

Two miles out of town, the county road had changed from badly paved to densely packed dirt that nonetheless kicked up dust behind them. They saw two cars parked in turnouts, the owners presumably fishing. A bit farther, the road moved away from the river, with forest in between and logging roads, marked by numbers spray-painted on trees, leading toward the water.

"We're looking for 148," Gordon said. "We've passed 128 and 138, so we should be getting close."

"I hesitate to say anything, but it seems to me the same car has been behind us for quite a while now. Does that affect our plans?"

Gordon looked in the mirror. "Hard to see much through the dust. Dark sedan is about all I can say for sure. Here's our turnoff. Let's see what happens."

He turned left on the logging road and pulled as far to the right as he could on it, stopping the Cherokee so the other car could pass, if it, too, made the turn. But it sped past the logging road in a cloud of dust and kept going.

"Guess we were just going too slow for him," Gordon said.

He started forward again, and drove a half-mile to an intersecting dirt road, on which he turned left. A hundred yards down the road an old, one-lane wooden bridge with no railings crossed the river. Just before the bridge was a turnout, big enough for four or five cars but empty at the moment. From it they could look down on a broad meadow below, with the river — more like a wide stream at this point — running through it.

"There will be fish in there, if I'm not mistaken," Gordon said. "Let's try to make their acquaintance."

They put on their waders and vests and followed a well-worn path to the river. When they reached it, Gordon knelt and stuck his hand in the water.

"Feels like 55 to 60 degrees," he said. "We may have gotten here at the right time. Let's go upstream a ways and identify the good spots, then work them on the way back."

Gordon stopped from time to time to check out likely places: riffles, deep pools, overhanging banks, logs and boulders in the stream that would provide protection against predators. They began by fishing dry flies but caught only two or three trout six inches or smaller. They switched to nymphs, which imitate insects emerging from the larval stage beneath the water, and had more success, catching and releasing three Rainbow Trout 12 to 14 inches and several more Rainbow and Brook Trout 9 to 11 inches. The clouds that had been bunching up in the west that morning had become thicker; they blocked the hot afternoon sun but didn't appear to threaten rain. At four o'clock there was a caddis fly hatch, the fish began feeding on the surface, and the men switched to dry flies, catching several more good fish in the 10 to 14-inch range. At 4:45, Gordon looked at his watch and declared it was time to head back. He hadn't thought about Charlotte London or her family history for more than two hours and felt mentally refreshed.

As they approached the Cherokee from a distance, Gordon thought something wasn't quite right, and as they drew closer, he could see that both doors on the driver's side were open. He was certain he'd locked the car before they started down to the meadow, and he broke into a jog. Then he realized that the driver's window had been smashed. He could see shards of window glass on the dirt next to the car and on the seat and floor inside. He swore.

His backup fly rod, worth $400, was still in its case on the back seat, and his bag with hundreds of dollars of equipment was next to it. A number of objects in the back seat and the rear storage area seemed to have been moved, but, as far as he could tell, nothing had been taken.

"Let's get the glass off the seats and head back," he said. "I saw an auto-glass shop in town, and maybe they can deal with this.

"Another burglary with nothing taken," Peter said. "I don't think what our man was looking for was in the car at any rate. Damn, Gordon. I feel bad about this. I should have told you earlier instead of being cute about it."

"Told me what?"

"When you were sampling the cultural amenities of the Rotary Club, I walked around to the motels in town and asked if any of them had gotten a call Tuesday morning from someone asking for a Quill Gordon. Good that you have a memorable name. Three of the five said yes, and the other two couldn't rule it out altogether."

Gordon sat in the driver's seat and slumped forward.

"Somebody has been looking for you since Tuesday, the day after Charlotte London died."

"I REALLY TRIED TO GET IT ALL DONE, but it was just impossible today. Our summer reading program is going full swing, and Nancy, who is supposed to read to the under-7 group, called in with morning sickness. She's missed so many days she might as well resign right now, but of course she won't, so not only did I have to read to the little nippers — who, by the way, must have been fed amphetamines before they came in — but we were one librarian short all day. And then Mrs. Marshall came in with two overdue books totaling $2.35 in fines and insisted, positively *insisted*, that there must have been some mistake and she wasn't going to pay. She practically threatened to take the matter to the Supreme Court, and tied up the front desk for 20 minutes arguing. Not only did I think we'd have to call the sheriff to escort her out, but guess who was waiting in line behind her? None other than Olga Menke, whose husband, as you know, is president of the Forest County Taxpayers Association, and who will no doubt be getting a full report over dinner tonight about the waste and inefficiency of the public libraries. And I still don't know if Nancy will be back tomorrow to handle the under-7 reading, plus Naomi is off tomorrow so she can work Saturday, and we may be doubly short-handed. Oh, El," said Alice Laszlo, "while I'm on the subject, you *will* do another piece on the summer reading program, won't you?"

"Anything that happens at the library is news, as far as the *Forest Clarion* is concerned," said El.

111

"So at two in the afternoon, I realized it was hopeless, and then I thought of Karl Bjornstad." She gestured to the tall, stocky man next to her, in his late sixties with white-blond hair and a stubborn-looking face, "and I thought, of course, we should bring Karl in on this. As you know, El, Karl is working on the definitive history of Forest County ..."

"Probably the *only* history, I'm guessing," Peter whispered to Gordon.

" ... And there really isn't anything he doesn't know about this community, plus he knew Charlotte well and had been talking with her about her family history, and I thought, this is someone who's smart and knowledgeable and could be an asset to our investigation, so I invited him to come along. I hope that was all right."

Karl coughed. "Aaah," he growled. "I'm not so smart. I'm just a plodder who can look through boxes and boxes of files and documents without getting tired or bored. You don't have to be smart to do that."

No one had an immediate response to that remark. Gordon looked at Alice — trim, handsome, with gray-white shoulder-length hair, wearing a print dress and sandals — and sensed she was about to speak again, so he jumped in.

"Thank you, Alice, Karl. We're glad to have you on board. Did Gina explain what our little group is trying to do?" They both nodded. "And you're willing to help?" They both nodded again. "And you can be quiet and discreet, and talk to no one outside this room about it?" Karl nodded, and Alice made a cross-my-heart sign. "Good. Well, then, welcome."

The six of them were tightly packed around the table in the newspaper's small conference room. El and Gordon sat at either end, with Gina and Peter on one side and Alice and Karl on the other. It was 6:15, and no one else was in the building.

"I guess the first question," said El, "is whether we have any news stories from 1970 to look at."

"I didn't get to the library until 4:30, so I only worked on it for a bit over an hour," Karl said. "You can't just look at the front page; you have to check every single article in the paper, or you might miss something, so it doesn't go fast. Per instructions, I began with the first issue of August, 1970, and these are all the stories I found through the end of September." He took a manila folder about three quarters of an inch thick, and, though El was sitting directly to his left, slid it down the table to his right toward Gordon. "It doesn't look like they got to the juicy stuff yet, but maybe you'll see something."

"Thank you, Karl," said Gordon. "That's a good start."

"I should be able to get all the way through January tomorrow. But before you start reading it, you should probably know something about the history of this town and how The Peninsulas fit in."

Gordon must have registered some dismay, because Alice jumped in."

"Karl, darling, I don't know if we really have time for that."

"I can give you the five-minute version. Well, seven minutes anyway."

"All right, then, but cut to the chase."

Gordon nodded at Karl, and he began.

"When California became a state, Forest County was a remote part of it. A few prospectors and cattle ranchers, and they were outnumbered by the Native Americans. It stayed that way for almost 30 years, and then Union Pacific decided to build another rail line through the mountains. Hawk River Gorge was where they decided to do it. They'd be needing a lot of lumber for railroad ties, sluices, water towers, winter dwellings for the workers — all that. So they contracted with an outfit called the Empire Lumber Company to provide the wood. Empire scouted the territory and decided this little valley would be a good place to build a mill."

Peter, who was sitting to Gordon's right, picked up the manila folder, pulled it to himself, and began looking at clippings as Karl continued.

"They built the mill in 1879, and two years later a small town had grown up around it. The citizens started thinking about naming it, and, most of them being Republicans, they chose Arthur, after President Chester A. Arthur, who took over when James Garfield was assassinated. There was a splinter group of Democrats who objected, and a lot of them lived in a small settlement a couple of miles south. They named their town, if you could call it that, Conkling, after the Tammany Hall boss Roscoe Conkling. President Arthur was rumored to be his puppet."

"The point, Karl. The point," said Alice.

"The railroad provided a market for the local lumber for several years, and when the track was being laid through the gorge, they added a spur line to Arthur. That made it cheap and easy to transport the lumber cut in these mountains to Sacramento, Oakland and San Francisco, so the lumber business kept going strong and the town kept growing. When San Francisco burned after the earthquake, half the lumber to rebuild it came from this area. A few of our old-time families have been living high for almost a century on what the locals call 'San Francisco money.' And until about 25 years ago, any kid in this town could go straight from high school, whether he graduated or not, to a job in the lumber business and do pretty well for himself.

"After the war, Pacific Crest Hydro decided to dam the Hawk River to produce electricity for the Bay Area. Between that project and all the housing that was being built in Northern California, Arthur was a real boomtown from the late forties to the early sixties. Lake Año Nuevo started getting a bit of a name as a low-key resort and vacation area, and the Hawk River Highway, which was re-built in the late forties, made it easy for people to drive here."

"Excuse me for interrupting," Gordon said, "but I always wondered about the name of the lake. I assumed it was because the dam was built near Año Nuevo Creek, but where did that name come from?"

"Keep it short, Karl," muttered Alice.

"I'm glad you asked. When gold was first discovered, a lot of people headed into the mountains, following the rivers and streams, looking for more. One of them was a fellow named Francisco Juarez, second son of an old land-grant family, and he led a small group of men up Hawk River late one fall. The exact year is in dispute, but it was in the early 1850s, and the weather stayed mild so they kept going. On New Year's Day they camped at the junction of a creek that runs into Hawk River and named it Año Nuevo Creek — Spanish for New Year's."

"You said Arthur was a boomtown until the early sixties," Gina said. "It certainly isn't now. What happened?"

"Several things. The forests had been logged for so long that there were fewer good stands left. The Forest Service started getting pickier and stingier with permits. The state growth rate was beginning to slow down. The environmental movement was gaining steam. All those things combined were putting pressure on the industry. In 1968, one of the three big mills in town, Republic Lumber, closed up and consolidated its efforts in other parts of the state. Three hundred people lost their jobs in one day."

"That's quite a few in a town this size," Gordon said.

"A lot of them moved away for good, which dumped a lot of houses on the real estate market in a short time. The town leaders were looking for something to take up the slack, and tourism seemed like the best thing. That's when Pacific Crest Hydro put the peninsulas up for bid, and that's the context in which the debate over their development took place." He looked around the table. "Any questions?"

"Not a question, but a comment," Alice said. "Six minutes. That was very good, and it does give some perspective."

"Yes, it does," Gordon said. "Thank you, Karl. The problem now is where we go from here. It seems to me that we're trying to put together a jigsaw puzzle without any idea of what it's eventually supposed to look like. When we have a blue piece, we don't know if it's the sky above or the water below."

"Speaking as a historian," said Karl, "the best thing to do is just keep digging. Usually, connections start to be made and the picture begins to form."

"Along those lines," Gina said, "the logical starting point would be the two questions in Charlotte's book draft. Talk to Bart Sturges about what happened and why he changed his vote, and find out more about the accident that killed Ned London."

"The first one is already set up," El said. "I got hold of Sturges' aide and set up an appointment for the Senator too talk to my intern and me at his house on The Peninsulas Sunday morning."

"Intern?" said Alice. "You have an intern?"

"That's what I'm calling Gordon for now." Everyone laughed. "Hey, President Clinton probably has interns, though you never hear anything about them. Why can't I?"

"Whatever," Gordon said. "But you'll have to ask most of the questions."

"Something else occurred to me," Peter said. "I've been flipping through this first batch of clippings, and I notice most of the stories were written by the same reporter — Adam Beckstein. I don't suppose anybody knows where he is now?"

Nobody did, but Alice flipped open a small notebook she had brought.

"Spell his name for me. If he's anywhere in California, I'll find him."

"You can do that?" said Gina.

"Old librarian tricks."

Peter carefully spelled the name for her. "And we need to be careful and discreet about all of this. Gordon is being stalked already." He briefly filled them in on the ransacking of the room and the vandalism of the Cherokee. The group went silent.

"Alice," said El. "If you find Beckstein's name, and better yet a phone number, get it to me right away, and I'll call him. If the call's from somebody at the *Clarion*, he's more likely to talk or call back. And one other thing. Since the group's getting bigger and we'll be meeting through the weekend, I'd like to offer my house as the meeting place, starting tomorrow."

"That would be great," said Alice.

"I've always wanted to see it," said Karl.

"All right," said Gordon. "What am I missing here?"

"It's the most — what's the word I'm looking for — distinctive house in the county," Gina said. "See for yourself tomorrow. We won't spoil things by building it up."

116

"I look forward to it," Gordon said. "What else is there to do or report?"

"I connected with Gregory London, Charlotte's brother," Gina said. "I'll be meeting him Saturday afternoon. Oh, and he said that because so many people from the school are out of town now, there won't be a funeral right away. They'll be doing a memorial service right after Labor Day."

"Thank you, Gina. Anything else?"

"Ned London's accident," Karl said. "That's probably one I can handle. The news story will be in the papers I'm looking at, and I'll stop at the Highway Patrol office first thing tomorrow morning to get a copy of the accident report."

"They'd still have it?" said Peter.

Karl smiled. "In the past 30 years, there have been only two commanders of the county's Highway Patrol office. Neither of them ever threw anything away, and the office is blessed with ample storage space. Pack rats with storage space are the historian's best friend."

"I didn't know you were on such good terms with the Highway Patrol," Alice said.

"Well," he said, "I *am* working on a history of the county. And you'd be surprised, if you looked into it, how many of the leading citizens of Forest County have died in automobile accidents over the years."

SINATRA WAS SINGING "Strangers in the Night" when Gordon, Peter, Gina and El walked into Garbini's. After the previous night, it seemed as if they were coming home.

"First of all," said Gina, when they had been seated, "I apologize about Karl. I had no idea Alice was simply going to bring him in."

"He might be an asset," Gordon said. "He obviously knows a lot, and he's getting things done."

"What worries me," Peter said, "is the way this group is growing. Somebody's after Gordon, or something they think he has, and if we invite the whole town into the group, sooner or later, somebody's going to be connected to our stalker."

"But Peter," said Gina, "You did a really good job of pointing out the threat."

"And El," Gordon said, "made it very clear tonight that we have to keep this to ourselves."

"Self-preservation," said El. "Whatever story we come up with, I want the paper to have it before the whole town knows. I think we're all right for now."

After drink orders were taken, Gordon turned to Gina.

"It occurs to me," he said, "that with the family history at the center of all this, Charlotte's attitude toward her family is worth exploring. She cared enough to write the history, but did she ever talk about them to you? In a personal way, I mean."

Gina paused to sort out her answer.

"Not on an ongoing basis, but over the years, I suppose I picked up some things. Did you have anything specifically in mind?"

"For starters, how did she feel about her parents?"

"She adored her father. She said a number of times that he really encouraged her to be her own person and have her own life. And she told me that when he died so suddenly, she almost had a nervous breakdown. 'The winter of 70 and 71 nearly did me in,' was the way she once put it."

"What else did she say?"

"I think she felt he was a warm and generous person, but also strictly moralistic. I know she once told me he was the son of a sheriff and had a very black-and-white sense of right and wrong. Charlotte was more a shades-of-gray person herself. I think that's part of what she got from literature and tried to convey to her students. But she also said it helped being raised with a strict sense of right and wrong because it helped you draw the lines in the gray areas. If that makes any sense."

"It makes a lot of sense," Peter said.

Drinks arrived, same as the night before. Gina looked at Peter's ginger ale.

"So are you a teetotaler?"

"I have been lately. Nothing against alcohol, but lately it's felt like it was slowing me down. I have to be at my best in what I do, so I'm laying off. Sign of age, I guess, but I don't miss it at all."

"Age!" snorted Gina. "You're younger than I am."

"Ah, but you're younger at heart."

"Getting back to Charlotte," said Gordon, "how did she get along with her mother?"

"Now that was a pricklier relationship, I gather. Her mother had a nervous disposition and wasn't physically well by the time Ned died. I get the sense that some of it was real, and some of it was hypochondria, but it all came down on Charlotte. Her mother was gone by the time I came along, but Charlotte took care of her the last years of her life. That took her well into her forties and probably wiped out any chance she had of getting married."

"Was she bitter about that?" Gordon asked.

"Not as far as I can tell. She seemed to feel it was one of those things that had to be done, so she did it. Still, it can't have been easy."

"How about her brother?"

"A nice guy, but a bit of a stick. He managed to get his father's business sense without any larger world view. I gather Ned London was universally liked and respected, and that people felt his integrity was solid. Greg is honest and competent as far as I can tell, but he doesn't have that sense of completeness that his father did. He went off to college and came back and married his high school sweetheart."

"Gave Charlotte a niece and a nephew, didn't he?"

"And Charlotte adored them. They were the kids she never had, and she loved having them over to her house when the parents were away or having a date night. She and Greg got along all right, but they weren't really tight. She made a point of having lunch with him once a month after church as a way of staying in touch without getting too close."

"Which church?"

"St. Luke's Episcopal. I wouldn't say she was terribly devout, but she felt it was important to formally incorporate some sense of a God in her life, and her father's church was as good a way as any of doing that. I'll tell you one thing, though. Lately, she only went twice a month. She said the new minister's sermons lacked structure and intellectual rigor."

Gordon and El looked at each other and broke out laughing. Gina arched an eyebrow.

"He gave the invocation today at Rotary," El said. "I think we can appreciate what she meant."

"Knowing how she felt about structure and intellectual rigor, it must have taken some effort on her part to go twice a month," Gina said. "But Charlotte was nothing if not disciplined."

They decided to stay for dinner, and when it arrived, El raised another point.

"We've been looking at this from the family history angle," she said, "but there's another point we shouldn't overlook. Who benefits from her death? We need to find out what's in her will as soon as we can."

"I can answer that," Gordon said. "Winters said it was all right to tell me since I'm the literary executor and it'll be public pretty soon when he files for probate. But I don't think it gets us very far."

Everyone had stopped eating.

"The short version is that the niece and nephew get the house. Not much of it left, but the land's valuable and they can rebuild. After a few bequests, the residue of the estate goes to Planned Parenthood of Northern California, with the directive that the money be used to expand services in Forest County."

"Well, I'll be," said Gina.

"You're surprised?"

"Not really. I mean, I wouldn't have thought of it myself, but as soon as you said it, I thought, that's Charlotte. We talked quite a bit about the bright girls in the school who got pregnant and either married too early, and often unsuitably, or ended up being single moms. Charlotte felt very strongly — we both did — that it was a waste of human potential. And some of the girls would go to Charlotte about it because they didn't feel they could talk to their parents. So she understood at a deep, emotional level."

"I take it, then," said Peter, "that there's no Planned Parenthood in this county?"

"I'm afraid reproductive health here is pretty medieval. It amounts to one doctor who will prescribe contraception for a teenage girl, but only with the written consent of both parents. He doesn't get much business in that line."

"Oh my God," said El. "Doc Blanchard. I'd almost forgotten about him."

Everyone turned to her.

"I was one of the few customers," she said. "Anna and me. "When Anna turned 15, I took her in and got a prescription for the pill. Whatever else happened, I didn't want her getting pregnant until she was good and ready."

"Good for you," said Gina. "That's why she's in law school."

"You know what, though? When I was her age, I would have given anything for that, but I don't think she appreciated it. I don't even think she used it. I have a sneaking suspicion she was still a virgin when she graduated from high school."

"Speaking as a medical man," Peter said, "I think that was a good practical decision. Putting her on the pill, I mean. But why at 15?"

"That's how old I was when I was ready to have sex, and I can guarantee you *my* father would never have signed the consent form. It still amazes me that she didn't take advantage of it, but I suppose being a parent means your kids don't appreciate you."

"Fifteen," said Gina thoughtfully. "You lost it at 15?"

"Actually, not until I was 16." She took a sip of wine. 'The wait just about killed me."

Friday June 21

THE NIGHT BEFORE, Gordon and Peter had caught the auto-glass shop owner as he was closing up. With a quick phone call, he ordered a replacement window due in around 1 p.m., and said he could make Gordon's Cherokee the first order of business after lunch. Accordingly, they decided to rent a boat for the morning and get back in time for Gordon's lunch with the Paris family, during which Peter would take care of business at the glass shop.

The morning air that streamed in where the window had been suggested they would get a hot day, perhaps with a late afternoon thunderstorm. Everything but the gear for the morning's fishing had been cleared out of the Cherokee, and Gordon decided to leave it unlocked in the marina parking lot and take his chances.

The boat eased out of the marina and onto the lake under a cloudless blue sky. A lone hawk coasted lazily overhead. It was early for the water-and jet-skiers, and aside from the thrum of the boat's motor, it was agreeably silent.

"Can you humor me today?" asked Peter.

"Depends on how much it would put me out."

"I'd like to try fishing Trout Creek."

Gordon thought for several seconds. "All right," he said. "I don't really know anything about it, but we could try the usual small-stream techniques and see what happens." He paused several more seconds. "I doubt the fish are very big."

"It's not all about size, Gordon. Catching an eight or nine incher in a small creek can be a lot of fun."

"Let's try it." Gordon was feeling a bit of guilt over the way his charge from Charlotte London had interfered with their fishing; he figured he owed Peter agreement on a request so reasonable.

Half an hour later, he eased the front of the boat onto a small gravel beach were Trout Creek entered the reservoir. Peter jumped out and helped Gordon get the anchor, a block of cement, down on the sand. Gordon studied the creek. It was ten feet wide where it entered the lake, and it cascaded down a steep hillside, stopping for a series of small pools before continuing its descent. The creek was running full now, but by August, he guessed, it would be reduced to a trickle, and the fish in it would have moved into the lake.

They put on waders and tied on dry flies that mimicked no particular insect but looked good to most trout. The creek was closely flanked by aspens, pines, and shrubs. Gordon had expected it to be tight fishing, but as they moved upstream, it proved worse than he imagined. There was almost no room to cast and none at all for error. Many of their casts hooked the brush along the stream or the overhanging branches. They tried to fish the small pools from downstream, but even when they were able to make a decent cast, no fish rose to it. The climb upstream became steadily more difficult. In many places, brush, trees and boulders blocked them from getting out of the stream, and they had to grab hold of rocks and scoot up to the next pool. On three occasions one of them was about to put a hand on a rock for support but saw a snake on it. They were harmless garter snakes, but unsettling nonetheless.

The water cooled their feet and lower legs through the waders, and the canopy of trees kept the sun from beating down directly on them. Nevertheless, it was getting steadily hotter, and their exertions had them sweating. At ten o'clock, mosquitoes began to appear. Gordon had insect repellent in his vest pockets, and it kept them from being bitten for the most part, but the insects still swarmed annoyingly close. Half an hour later, sitting on a rock at the edge of the creek, swatting away mosquitoes, Peter raised the white flag.

"Maybe this wasn't such a good idea after all," he said. "I vote we turn back."

Gordon looked upstream and down. "I don't see any reason to believe it's going to get better. I make it unanimous."

Peter stood up.

"Did you ever read Richard Brautigan's *Trout Fishing in America*?" he asked.

"A long time ago."

"There was a section where he wrote about fishing a small, overgrown creek like this one, with about as much success as we've had. At the end, he said, something to the effect that only a plumber could fish that creek. That pretty well describes our morning."

They worked their way back downstream, trying one or two likely spots with no success. It was 11:15 when they returned to the area where they had beached the boat. Peter loaded his gear in, while Gordon looked at the creek running into the lake.

"I want to try one more thing," Gordon said. He snipped off the dry fly that had been on his leader and tied on a #14 Hare's Ear Nymph, adding a floating indicator seven feet up the line from it. "This creek is probably washing insect larva into the lake. Let's see if there are any fish waiting for it."

He lobbed the fly and indicator into the lake a few feet from where the creek emptied in, then began stripping out line to let the fly drift into the lake following the stream's current. Forty feet from shore, the indicator jerked under water, and several minutes later Gordon landed the 15-inch Rainbow Trout, that had taken the nymph.

"It would appear," Peter said sardonically, "that we were fishing in the wrong direction."

AFTER CATCHING TWO MORE FISH apiece where the creek entered the lake, they motored back to the marina. Gordon cleaned up at a public pay-shower at the marina, changed into khakis and an olive-checked shirt he had brought in a gym bag, and was presentable for the lunch appointment at Ike's Lakeside.

Ike's had the look and feel of a building of mid-70s design. The interior featured an extensive bar on the left as one entered, opening up to an expansive dining area featuring tables with white linen tablecloths flanked by blond wood chairs, with a large circular stone fireplace in the center of the room. Across from the bar, the wall consisted of a solid row of double-paned windows, and at either end of the windows was a door leading down a short flight of steps to a capacious outdoor deck. On this warm day, the deck was nearly full and the fireplace was in disuse.

Roger Paris and his sons were seated at an indoor window table, with a commanding view of the lake and East Peninsula. If you knew where to look, you could barely make out the charred remains of Charlotte London's house across the water in the distance. Gordon spotted them at the same time Roger, seated with his back to the window, saw him and raised a hand.

"We saved a seat with a view for you," he said as Gordon reached the table.

Gordon shook hands all around and sat down. Roger was to his right, Ronald to his left, and Bobby directly across from him. Bobby had thinning, sandy-colored hair, blue eyes, and a round, soft face that suggested decency and vulnerability.

"Just so there's no misunderstanding," Roger said, "we're buying lunch. The London family and ours have been close friends for years. If not for Ned London, this restaurant wouldn't be here, and we couldn't afford to have lunch here every Friday. We're grieving over what happened to Charlotte on Monday, but if you're carrying on with her family project, you're a friend of ours. Automatically."

He lifted the glass holding his vodka martini in a toasting gesture, and Gordon raised his water glass in return.

"Thank you," he said.

"And if you've never been here before, the trout is excellent, and the salmon left the docks in San Francisco this morning. Everything else on the menu is pretty good to excellent, so whatever you want."

Gordon studied the menu, settled on the salmon, blackened Cajun-style, and after the waitress took their orders, leaned forward toward Bobby.

"You missed a good Rotary Club meeting yesterday," he said. "I gather you were looking at property somewhere?"

"Come on, Gordon," said Ron. "You're being far too polite. I regard those meetings as my weekly dose of Babbitry, and I suspect your impression was along the same lines."

126

"Now, Ron," said Roger. "You know how much good the club does in our town. Think of the Little League fields, the Town Hall restoration …"

"I'm not denying that, father. I wouldn't keep up my membership if I didn't think it was doing some good. All I'm saying is that to someone coming into it cold, it probably looks as bizarre as the jungle rite of a South Pacific tribe."

"It held my interest," Gordon said.

"Talking about the London family," Roger said, "that reminds me of when I joined Rotary in 1964. I was in real estate, but Ned London already had that classification, and back then you could only have one person from each profession in the club. Ned thought I should belong, so he proposed me as a member under the classification Land Management. That's the kind of man he was."

"I understand the whole Peninsulas project was his brainstorm."

Roger took a small sip of his martini.

"Ned was a visionary. You don't see too many in a town this size. When the first lumber mill closed, most of the people in Arthur were trying to figure out how to attract another lumber company here. Ned grasped that it was the beginning of a long and possibly fatal decline for the whole industry and that we had to find something else to take its place."

"You have to remember," said Ron, "that a lot of people who lived here at the time grew up before the dam was built. They weren't thinking of the lake as an asset to be capitalized. Ned understood it was the town's best hope. When the Peninsulas came on the market, he realized it was a once-in-a-lifetime opportunity."

"A great business venture, certainly," Gordon said.

"By all means," Roger said, "but good for the town, too. Ned really believed that. We all did. And I think we've been proven right. The local economy is pretty tough, but without The Peninsulas, this would be a ghost town now."

"How, exactly, did it work? Ned London brought you in and formed a partnership. Who did what?"

"Dad and Ned oversaw the whole project," said Ron. "They hired local people to do the surveying, the subdivision design, the legal work. They also represented the plan in the community. That's where Ned was so valuable. He was one of the most respected men in the county, and even people who were against the project felt they had to be civil about it. I, being the MBA, ran the finances, which at times was an exercise in creativity, tended to the paperwork and details, and tried to keep Ned and my father from getting too carried away."

"How about you, Bobby?" Gordon asked.

"Bobby ran the Paris real estate office and kept it profitable when we were working on the project," Roger said. "I can't tell you how valuable that was. We were stretched pretty thin, financially, so what he brought in was critical. Absolutely critical."

After a few more minutes of small talk, lunch arrived. The salmon was excellent, and as Gordon was chewing his second bite, Ron turned to him.

"You were quite a basketball player back in the day, weren't you?"

"How did you know?"

"Judge Fletcher mentioned it yesterday, and it jogged a memory. Didn't you make two free throws with almost no time left to beat USC in Los Angeles? I was working late and listening to the game on the radio."

"You a Cal fan?"

"Divided loyalties. I graduated from Cal in '61, did my two years in the Army, then went to USC for my MBA. I'd like to hear the story from your end."

"It wasn't much of a foul, if the truth be told, but I beat him to the spot, and he was out of position. That's what the ref saw. We were big underdogs, but the coach put us into a zone instead of man-to-man, and their shooting was a bit off, so we hung with them. We had the ball with a tie score and five seconds left when I made a back-door cut into the key and caught a bounce pass from Clarence Washington. Stevens, their small forward, left his man to cover me, but had to hurry to get there. When I made a head fake, he left his feet, so I went up, too, holding the ball away from him. He really only brushed against me, but, as I said, I had position and threw up a prayer. It rimmed out, but they called the foul."

"Two free throws. Seconds left. On the road, with the crowd screaming. How do you tune that out?"

"Every day at practice, we shot a hundred free throws. Everyone on the team did. If I made fewer than 90, I stayed after and shot another hundred. The reason you do it over and over in practice is so when you get into a situation like that, game on the line, you can tell yourself, 'Just like practice.' Same routine. Take two deep breaths, dribble the ball twice, bend the knees and back just so, put the middle finger of the right hand on the manufacturer's logo, then just do what you've done thousands of times before."

"You make it sound easy," said Roger, "yet a lot of players can't do it."

"They start to think," said Bobby. Everyone turned to him. "You can't think, or you're dead."

"Bobby was a starter on the high school team," Ron said.

"You're right, Bobby," Gordon said. "Thinking is fatal. You have to tune out everything but the routine you've been practicing. Just focus on doing what you always do. I'm sure that's what your coach told you."

Bobby nodded.

"There's one thing I've been meaning to ask you, Gordon," said Ron. "You're now Charlotte London's literary executor. What, exactly, does that mean?"

"I'm still learning on the job. From what her attorney tells me, I'm responsible for the manuscript of the family history and her personal papers. Unfortunately, the personal papers were all destroyed in the fire."

"But the manuscript exists?"

"She did get a copy to me, yes."

"Is it in any kind of usable condition?" asked Roger.

"It seems fairly complete to me, but then I don't know what else she might have been looking into."

"And have you thought about what you're going to do about it?"

"Only in general terms. My old college roommate works for the *San Francisco Chronicle*, and I was going to ask him if he knows a former reporter who might be willing to try to finish it on a freelance basis. I gather it was important to Charlotte, so I'll get it as good as I can and do a small publication run. Her estate will pay for it."

"I think I speak for all of us," said Roger, "in saying that we'll be happy to help out in any way we can. If your writer needs more information, we'll be happy to cooperate."

"Glad to know that."

"Our families have been very close since we worked together on The Peninsulas a quarter of a century ago. I've felt as though Charlotte was the daughter I never had."

"Tell him about her house," said Ron.

"Ah, yes. When we had the plan put together, all of us sat down around the subdivision map one Saturday afternoon and picked out the lots we wanted for our own homes. It was a way of making it personal and committing to the future. Ned picked out a lot for Charlotte, and after the county approved it, I personally took charge of the design and building of her house. She was most appreciative, but it was the least I could do. She was like family."

They fell back to eating for a moment, then Gordon raised the point he had been working up to.

"You said Ned London was the public face of the project, the one who gave it credibility in the community. It must have been a terrible blow when he died before the county board voted on the project."

"A terrible blow to the project and a blow to us as friends," Roger said.

"I don't know if Charlotte mentioned it in her manuscript," said Ron, "but he was headed home from our house when the accident happened. We were meeting almost every night trying to make sure everything was in place for the public hearing."

"There was some malicious gossip that Ned was drunk when he ran off the road," Roger said with feeling. "Nonsense! He had two weak whisky-sodas in two hours and was fine when he left. He hit a patch of ice, and ran off the road. That's all there was to it. It was a tragedy."

130

After a moment of silence, Gordon said, "And he wasn't there when the project was approved. One thing I wasn't clear on from the manuscript: The way Charlotte told it, a lot of people were surprised when Bart Sturges voted in favor. It had been widely assumed he was against it."

"We weren't surprised," said Roger, "because we'd been talking to him, and it was clear he could see our side and appreciate what the business community was saying. We didn't know whether we'd carry the day, but we knew we at least had a chance."

"There's one other thing that should go in the book," said Ron. "It's the truth, and I'm sure Sturges will confirm it after all this time. I mean, it's ancient history now. He came to that meeting with two speeches in his briefcase. One was to read if he decided to vote in favor of it, and the other was if he voted no. That's how close it was."

"Wow," said Gordon. "So what would have happened if Sturges had read the second speech and voted no?"

"We'd have been back," said Roger.

"That's right," said Ron. "The people who thought they could stop anything from happening were delusional. We would have been back in a few months with a downsized plan, and the county board would know it was facing a lawsuit if it rejected that one. It would have been a smaller project, but we could have come back over the next few years with additions to it and ended up with pretty much what there is now. More bother and less profit, but still well worth the effort.

"You see, Gordon, on something this big, the land owners can wait. We'll always make money in the end."

WHEN GORDON EMERGED from Ike's, the temperature was in the high 80s, and the sun was beating down mercilessly through a cloudless sky. It was dry heat, but still getting uncomfortable. He sat on a bench in the shade of the restaurant and ruminated. Were the Parises being genuinely helpful, or were they overdoing the sincerity just a bit? He didn't know them well enough to make a definitive reading.

He called Peter, who said the Cherokee would be ready at 3:30, and that he'd head over to Ike's immediately afterward. Gordon was wondering how he would kill the next hour and a quarter, when his pager beeped. It was an unfamiliar number from the local area code, and a man's voice answered when he called.

"Hello."

"Hello. This is Quill Gordon. Is that you, Karl?"

"Speaking."

"You just paged me."

"You're a smart guy. Actually, I tried Elke first, but she was out of the office, and I thought this might be something that someone would want to get on to right away."

"I'm listening."

"I went to the Highway Patrol office this morning, and as I thought, they had the report on Ned London's accident in storage on site."

"Good work."

"It gets better. When Sergeant Hancock came back with it, would you care to guess what he said?"

"I'm not good at guessing."

"He said, 'This thing sure seems to be popular. Second time this month I've been sent to get it.' I asked him who else had requested it, and it turned out to be none other than our Charlotte. She picked up a copy Tuesday of last week."

Gordon whistled.

"But wait, it gets even better. Would you care to guess the name of the patrolman who wrote the report?"

"Just tell me."

"His name was Alvin Davies." Karl paused for dramatic effect.

"A.D.," said Gordon. "In Charlotte's manuscript, there was a notation to check with A.D. in the section describing the accident."

"Has to be, don't you think?"

"I don't suppose this is our lucky day and Davies is still working there."

"Nope. Left ten years ago."

"I wonder where he is now."

"I thought the same thing, so I did what any competent historian would do. I asked Hancock."

"And?"

"Turns out he's now the chief of police in Cabrillo."

"Cabrillo. That's southeast of here, in the next county."

"Easy drive, no traffic. I thought Elke might want to call him and make an appointment for an interview tomorrow."

"I'll do that. When we meet tonight, we can sort out who actually goes."

"That's the way to do it. I even got the number. You have something to write with?"

Gordon realized, to his irritation, that he didn't. He had deliberately gone into the meeting with the Paris family with no notebook, wanting to keep the session informal and them off guard. He didn't even have a pen in his shirt pocket — everything was in the Cherokee ten miles away in an auto-glass shop.

"I don't," he said. "Stupid of me. Can you hold on for a minute while I go back into the restaurant and cadge a pen and a piece of paper?"

"Take your time. I got nothing to do but act like a historian, which means moving piles of paper around."

Gordon went back into Ike's. In the middle of the afternoon it was nearly empty. An older man and woman, having late lunch or early dinner, were the only occupants of the dining room. Three regulars were hunched over the bar, staring into their drinks rather than looking at the lake behind them. At the reception table, the hostess was talking to a man in his early thirties, dressed in khakis, a short-sleeved, button-down white shirt and plain black tie. Guessing it was the uniform of the manager, Gordon walked up to them.

"Can I help you?" the man said.

"I just got a phone call and don't have anything to write with. Could I possibly borrow a pen and a piece of paper?"

"No problem." He reached into the hostess stand and took out a 5-by-8 pad of note paper and a cheap ballpoint pen, both emblazoned with the restaurant's logo. Gordon thanked him and sat down on a bench in the deserted waiting area.

"OK. Shoot."

Karl gave him the number. "It's the direct line to his office. Hancock says he's a nice guy, so hopefully he'll cooperate."

"Thanks, Karl. This is great. Anything else?"

"I finished copying all the newspaper articles, and things did get more interesting as the project moved forward. I'll bring those and copies of the accident report to the meeting tonight."

"Good. See you at six."

He took the pad and pen back to the manager, who waved them aside.

"If you're here with the Paris family, you're a VIP customer," the manager said. "Keep the pen and pad."

"That's very kind. I guess the Parises are regular customers."

"Lunch every Friday, dinner a couple of times a month, other lunches from time to time. Fact, they were here Monday with Miss London. You heard what happened to her?" Gordon nodded. "Awful. And there she was at lunch Monday, just like any other day, with no idea. In fact, on the way out, she made a reservation for lunch on Wednesday. Party of three."

Gordon went outside, thinking about the lunch with Charlotte that never happened. He switched to the call at hand, thought for a few minutes about how to make the approach, and dialed Davies' number. It rang three times, and Gordon was beginning to think the chief had gotten an early start on the weekend. Halfway through the fourth ring, the call was answered.

"Davies."

"Chief Davies. Glad I caught you. My name is Quill Gordon, and I'm working on a history of the London family of Forest County. You're listed as the author of the report on the accident that killed Ned London, and I was wondering if I could have a few minutes of your time to talk about it."

There was silence on the other end of the line.

"Any time that's convenient for you. It shouldn't take too long," Gordon added

"No, I'll meet with you. But it'll have to be Monday. My son's getting married in Tahoe tomorrow, and I was heading out the door to get down there for the rehearsal dinner tonight. If you'd called 30 seconds later, you'd have missed me."

"Monday's fine. You tell me when."

"Where are you now?"

"I'll be in Arthur through Tuesday. Maybe a bit longer."

"How about eleven o'clock?"

"Done. Thank you so much."

"I always wondered if somebody might come along asking about that one down the road. Didn't think there'd be two people."

"Two?"

"London's daughter called last week. We were supposed to meet Tuesday, but she never showed and never called. She'll probably turn up on Tuesday of next week."

"Actually, I don't think so."

"Oh?"

"Her house burned down Monday night, with her in it. That's why she missed the appointment."

"Geez, I'm sorry to hear that. So you're taking her place."

"You could say that."

"That makes sense, then."

"I won't keep you any longer, chief. Have a safe drive to Tahoe, and I'll see you Monday."

They rang off, and Gordon looked at his watch. It would be an hour before Peter arrived, so he walked to The Chainsaw and ordered a frosty. He sat under an umbrella at an outside table, thinking about how he seemed to be following directly in Charlotte London's footsteps. Given that she had died before her time, the prospect made him a bit uneasy, but the midafternoon heat was melting the ice cream at an alarming rate, and he turned his attention to the frosty.

PETER DROVE UP AT EXACTLY 3:48 and hopped out of the Cherokee so they could switch places. When Gordon got behind the wheel, Peter handed him an envelope. Inside was the itemized bill from the glass shop.

"Pretty reasonable," Gordon said.

"I thought so, too. I put it on my VISA, so write me a check when we get home."

As they drove back to town, Gordon filled in his friend on the lunch with the Paris family and his conversations with Karl and Alvin Davies.

"That Karl's a real woodpecker," said Peter.

"What do you mean?"

"He keeps banging his head against the tree until he's got all the grubs and worms and beetles out of it. You probably wouldn't want him writing the story because he'd insist on getting every last fact into it and make it twice as long as it should be. But we need somebody like that to dig up the raw information."

Gordon nodded. "I was annoyed when he showed up last night, but now I'm glad he's on board."

When they reached Arthur, Gordon made a point of stopping at Frank's Market, the locally owned super, to buy a bouquet of flowers for El Sundstrom. As they turned into the driveway of Stanhope House and Gordon's pager beeped again.

"This thing didn't go off half as much when I was working at the brokerage," he said. The number was from the local area code, but unfamiliar to him.

He took his mobile phone from the glove compartment and called the number.

"Sheriff's office," said a female voice on the other end.

"This is Quill Gordon," he said. "I just got paged from this number."

"Yes. Sheriff Ballou is expecting your call. Let me put you through."

Ten seconds later, Ballou picked up.

"Gordon!" he said. "Thanks for getting back so fast."

"I was raised to cooperate with the lawful authorities. What can I do for you?"

"I'm calling about that floppy disk you brought by the office on Tuesday. You still have it?"

"I sure do, but I thought you weren't interested."

There was a silence on the other end, and Gordon imagined that Ballou was carefully formulating his response.

"It's a matter of routine and just making sure we cover all the bases," he said. "I'm going to have one of our resident computer geniuses see if he can get anything usable off it."

"I might be able to save you some trouble on that score, sheriff."

"What?" He barked the word out a bit too quickly, and Gordon realized something had made him more interested.

"After I talked with you," Gordon continued, "I tried putting it into another computer and it came up nice and clear. It's her family history, all right. About a hundred pages long."

"Did you read it?"

"Of course I did. She gave it to me, after all."

Ballou was silent, and Gordon figured he was probably trying not appear too eager. The next question seemed unnaturally low key.

"Well, that makes sense now. I guess I should have expected that." Pause. "I know you're not from this area, but did anything in it seem, how shall I say this, unusual to you?"

"Not so much unusual, strictly speaking, but there were a couple of places in the manuscript where she had made a note to herself to look further into some matters. That might be something that bears further investigation — not that I want to tell you how to do your job."

"Why not? Everybody else does."

"Probably the easiest thing would be if I printed it out at Stanhope House, but unless it's really, really urgent, I couldn't do that until later tonight. Would it be OK if I brought a printout to your office first thing tomorrow morning?"

"That would be acceptable. As I said, we're just making sure we cover all the bases."

"If you don't mind my asking, has some new evidence come up? On Tuesday you were saying it was strictly a fire department case."

"I wouldn't say new evidence, exactly. The medical examiner's report came in this afternoon, and there are a couple of … " he stopped to choose the precise word, "… ambiguities is how I'd put it. Most likely doesn't mean anything, but until they're ironed out, I should probably dot all the I's and cross all the T's."

"Due diligence and all that. What time should I come by?"

"I'll be here at seven."

"I'll have it to you by eight, then. If that's all right."

"That's fine. And Gordon, one more thing."

"Yes."

"Don't repeat what I said about the medical examiner's report to anybody. It's probably nothing, so there's no reason to start people talking."

"Mum's the word."

"It better be. Because if I hear that anybody learned about it from you, I'll have your ass in a sling."

THEY LEFT STANHOPE HOUSE at 5:30, driving down the west side of the lake, a mile and a half past Año Nuevo Pines, until they came to another road marked with a small sign that read "Aspen Cove." It ran through a sparsely developed subdivision where spotting a street number was challenging. Finally, Peter said:

"That's Gina's car. Turn left here."

They turned into a gravel parking area and parked between Gina's Toyota Camry and a white 1994 Ford Ranger. Gordon got out, looked over the lip of the parking area, and whistled.

From where they stood, a flight of 16 steps led to a pier below. The pier, four feet wide with hand railings of metal cable, extended a hundred feet into the lake, reaching its terminus at a house. The house was square, 40-by-40 feet, with a front door on the left of the outside wall facing the parking area, a barely sloping roof, a deck on three sides, and floor-to-ceiling windows facing on to the deck and lake.

"So this is *her* place," Gordon said in a low voice.

"Didn't we see it from the restaurant Tuesday night?"

Gordon nodded. They went carefully down the steps and knocked on the front door. El opened it, her hair down, wearing a white blouse with the top three buttons open to desired effect, and an ankle-length skirt, brightly patterned in red, brown and gold. It suited her well.

"Come on in," she said. "Oh, flowers. How sweet! Alice and Karl are coming over together and should be here any minute."

They stepped into an entryway with a large standing coat rack and plenty of room for fishing waders or muddy winter shoes. It narrowed and went between two walls. Gordon later learned that the master bedroom was to the left and two other bedrooms plus a half-bathroom were on the right. They walked through the hallway and emerged into a large open area. To the left, adjacent to the master bedroom, was a kitchen and dining area. In the outer corner at the left was a small work area, with desk, personal computer, printer and fax machine, flanked by windows on both sides. To the right was a large, open living area, taking advantage of the lake view. Two couches, upholstered in a warm brown, formed an L, facing a river rock fireplace with a four-foot opening that sat diagonally across the corner. Gina, sitting on one, waved. Four comfortable-looking chairs rounded out the ring around the fireplace. The house was in shadow, but it was the longest day of the year, and most of the lake was still in sunlight, as were the mountains behind. The dam was clearly visible a mile and a half to the right, and it, too, was beginning to take on a golden cast.

"Wow," said Gordon.

"That's what everybody says," El replied. "I was hoping for more from you."

"It's one of a kind. You couldn't build something like this today."

"Pure luck that I ended up with it. Andre had taken out a large life insurance policy before he died, unbeknownst to me. Tom Cutter, who owned this place, was getting too old to climb up and down those steps, and the market was dead when he put it up for sale.

Sometimes you get the breaks. Anna and I have a lot of good memories."

A sharp rap on the door announced Alice and Karl. El poured glasses of Chardonnay for the women, produced a bottle of beer for Karl, and provided Gordon and Peter with ginger ale. She installed Gordon in a chair by the fireplace and took the one on the other side of it for herself. Peter and Gina sat on one couch, while Karl and Alice took the other.

Gina asked how the fishing had gone that day.

"Not too good," Peter lamented. "We boated over to Trout Creek and fished our way up it, but it didn't live up to its name. We didn't even *see* a trout, let alone catch one.

Karl cleared his throat.

"When you're a historian, you learn that names aren't always what they seem. Trout Creek, for instance, was named for an early homesteader by the name of Jacob Trout, who farmed the land where the creek runs into Hawk River — or did, before the dam. Come to think of it, I've never heard of anyone catching a fish in that creek."

Eager to change the subject, Gordon called the meeting to order and led off with a summary of his conversation with Sheriff Ballou, which caused a mild sensation. Everyone laughed when he recounted Ballou's parting threat.

"I don't think you have too much to worry about," said Alice. "You're bigger and younger than he is."

"Do you see me trembling? But it was a strange conversation. It was pretty obvious that something in the coroner's report got his attention, but how do we find out what?"

"That may not be too hard," El said. "John Brantley, the medical examiner, is cooperative with the press, and he's usually in his office Saturday morning. I'll give him a call and see what I can get out of him."

"Wouldn't Ballou have told him not to talk?"

"You're giving our sheriff too much credit. First, he'd have to think of it, and second, I doubt they've talked face to face. Brantley operates out of Adams, and he probably just faxed the report over."

"I'm not an expert on these things," Peter said, "but isn't it unusual to have the sheriff and the medical examiner in cities 35 miles apart?"

"Local politics." El looked at Karl, who had leaned forward and taken a deep breath. "You want to explain it, Karl?"

"But cut to the chase," Alice said.

"It was an interesting political story," Karl said. Back in the mid- to late 1950s, some of the people in Adams started agitating for a vote to move the county seat there from Arthur. Looking at where the population of this county was in the 1950 census, they might have been able to win, but we'll never know. The county Board of Supervisors put together a closed-room deal. There was state bond money available to build a new county hospital. The old one, which was in Arthur, was inadequate. There was also a move under way to bring a community college to the county. The deal was Adams got the new hospital and the college, while Arthur remained the county seat and kept the courthouse."

Peter turned to El. "When you call the medical examiner tomorrow, can I be there? I might hear something that a lay person wouldn't."

"Please," she said. "He usually gets in around 9. We'll call from the newspaper office and use the speaker phone."

"All right," Gordon said. "Let's move on to Karl's newspaper search. Anything interesting in the stories about the campaign for The Peninsulas project?"

"Never seen an old newspaper story that *wasn't* interesting in one way or another," Karl said, pulling out a bulging file folder. "I made a copy of every story for everybody in the group. Maybe somebody will see something I didn't."

"Good idea."

"What struck me as I read through the stories in sequence, over a short period of time, was the way the opposition changed. Reading a story once a week, then reading the next one a week later, you might not notice it, but when you read the stories one right after the other, it jumps out at you."

"You're losing me, Karl," said Gina. "What do you mean by the opposition changed? Different people got involved?"

"Not so much that as the arguments got more sophisticated. More legalistic, really. When the plan for The Peninsulas was announced in August, the opposition was more reactive and emotional. 'Keep the peninsulas wild,' that sort of thing. By late October, early November, they were more specifically attacking the plan in detail. The subdivision map is deficient; the drainage plan won't handle runoff and will cause erosion; there hasn't been a study on how much water this will use and where it will come from. You could almost see them laying the ground for a lawsuit."

"Was there a lawsuit?" said El.

"I didn't get past the Board of Supervisors voting to approve it, so I can't say. But if there was a suit, it didn't go very far because the development that occurred is pretty close to the proposed development — at least as it was described in the paper."

"I don't suppose," said Alice, "that there was a leader of the opposition who's still alive and living here today?"

"As a matter of fact, yes. Celia Strickland came up quite a bit."

"Celia," said El. "Well, it figures."

"Who is she?" asked Peter.

"She owns Shore Acres Lodge, and she always seems to have a finger in any local shit-stirring."

"Do you think she'd cooperate?" Gordon said.

"Getting her to talk won't be the problem — it'll be getting her to stop. That, and sorting out the wheat from the chaff. You'll have to listen to her whole catalog of resentments to get to the good stuff. But I guess we'll have to. I'll call her tomorrow morning and try to set something up."

"One other thing, Karl," said Peter. "How good were the stories in the paper? How much do you think we can rely on them?"

"As a historian you want to get all the facts from all the sources, but my impression is that these stories are a pretty solid basic source. I've read almost every issue of the *Clarion* over the last hundred years, and I'd say the reporting in these stories was well above average in detail and understanding."

"All the more reason to talk to the reporter if we can," said Gordon. "Alice, did you have any luck running down Adam Beckstein?"

"Luck had nothing to do with it, Gordon. I had to work on it during my lunch break, what with filling in on the circulation desk and doing not one, not two, but three children's story hours. I mean, *Green Eggs and Ham* with three different sets of children, all of whom were more interested in committing mayhem on each other than in listening to a story, even if it *is* a classic, and then of course this was the day the book club from the rest home came in to check out half the mystery and romance novels on the shelf to get them through the next two weeks. All I can say is thank God I was looking for Adam Beckstein and not Bill Johnson. It's always easier when you're looking for a name that's relatively uncommon."

"So you found him?"

"Of course I did. I told you I would. I did an internet search for him by name and came up with an Adam Beckstein in Southern California. Then I went to the Editor & Publisher newspaper yearbook and searched the listings of people working for newspapers in Southern California. He's Assistant Managing Editor-News for the *Riverside Press-Enterprise*." She took a scrap of paper from her purse and walked it to El. "Here's their phone number."

She looked at it blankly. "One more call to make tomorrow morning."

"Are you all right, El?" said Gina. "You look shell-shocked."

She shook her head. "I'm OK. I was just thinking about what it must be like to have such a big newsroom that you need more than one *assistant* managing editor."

"I think we can cross Beckstein off the list for tonight," said Gina. "I'm dying to hear about Gordon's meeting with the Paris family."

He summarized the high points of the lunch, his chance discovery about Charlotte's Monday lunch with the Paris family, and ended by saying he wasn't sure how to read his meeting with them.

"Well," said Alice when he was through, "I'd say it's more than suggestive that she had lunch with them the day she died."

"Gina," said Gordon, "do you know if Charlotte met regularly with the Paris family?"

"Not much. She didn't talk about them much either. I gathered that her relations with them were cool but cordial."

"So it *could* mean something," said El.

"It could mean something or nothing at all," said Peter. "Let me ask a question, since I don't know the Paris family first-hand. Does anybody here like them as suspects in Charlotte's death, her father's death or both deaths?"

There was a long silence, which Alice finally broke.

"They're a gang of buccaneers, but murder ... I don't know."

"What I can't figure out," said Gina, "is what Charlotte suspected about her father's death. It seemed to be an accident, but if it wasn't, what motive would the Paris family have to kill Ned London? They all had an interest in getting the project approved, and Ned was their best ambassador to the community. It doesn't add up."

"Good point," said Peter. "But if Charlotte had dug up something dirty about that project, they might have a lot of reasons for wanting to keep it quiet. Maybe they had something to do with Charlotte's death, but not her father's."

"It's sounding to me," said Gordon, "like we still don't know much at this point, including what we need to know. And that brings up another question." He looked around at the group. "Given the call from the sheriff this afternoon, it looks as if he may be moving toward treating Charlotte's death as suspicious. If the authorities are investigating it, should we be duplicating their efforts, or should we turn over what we have to the sheriff and let the professionals do the job?"

The reaction was silence, with a lot of awkward looking back and forth. Karl spoke first.

"Ordinarily," he said slowly, "what Gordon is saying makes sense and would be the way to go. But …"

"Look who the sheriff is," said Alice.

"And Charlotte was my best friend," said Gina. "I want to feel I personally did everything I could for her. Besides, the sheriff hasn't even told you there's a criminal investigation under way, so your only obligation is to give him what he specifically asks for."

"The problem with handing the whole thing over to the sheriff," El said, "is that he can then do anything he wants, including filing it and forgetting it. At the very least, I think we have a responsibility to light a fire under him and keep the heat on. If we move forward and run a big front-page story in next Thursday's paper, he isn't going to be able to let it drop."

"I think you're outvoted, Gordon," Peter said, "and El makes a good point. Gordon and I are here through Tuesday and we could stay another day if we have to. Let's get everything we can for next week's paper, then decide how to deal with the sheriff."

All heads, including Gordon's, were nodding in agreement.

"I think that's settled," Gordon said. "So that leaves one more item on the agenda. Ned London's accident. Karl dug up the accident report and the news stories, which we'll all get copies of. But there was something else interesting. In her manuscript, Charlotte had made a note, in the section about the accident, to check with 'A.D.' It turns out the officer who wrote the report was named Alvin Davies, and Karl tracked him down. He's the chief of police in Cabrillo, and I made an appointment to interview him next Monday morning."

"El!" said Alice. "Are you all right? You look pale as a ghost.

El had half a glass of wine left, and she took two large gulps, her hand shaking as she lifted the glass to her lips. When she spoke, her voice was almost a croak.

"I wasn't expecting that one. Al Davies was the Highway Patrol officer who showed up at my front door late one night to tell me that Andre had been killed in a car wreck."

145

"I AM SO SORRY ABOUT THAT," Gordon said.

"Let it go, Gordon," said El. "You had no way of knowing."

"I should have thought of it. You told us two nights ago about the Highway Patrolman coming to your door, and I should have put two and two together."

"Nobody would have. And it was the surprise that got me more than anything else. I'm fine now."

Peter, Gina, Gordon and El were back in the same booth at Garbini's. It was Friday night and busier than the previous two nights. Two more waitresses were on duty; Bruno was walking the floor with a proprietary air; and Vic Damone was singing "An Affair to Remember" on the sound system.

"All right," Gordon said. "But I'll talk to Davies myself, or with Peter (looking at him) if you want to come along."

"I might as well," said Peter. "It looks like we're about done fishing on this trip."

"Martyrdom doesn't become you, Peter."

"Speaking of coming along," Gina said, "I wouldn't mind if someone came with me tomorrow when I talk to Greg London. I've known him for so long I might not pick up on everything he's saying, just because I've heard it before. Could anybody join me?"

She looked quickly at Gordon and El, then longer at Peter.

"Peter?"

"I suppose so," he said slowly. "When is it?"

"Three thirty. The group's meeting at two because Alice and her husband have plans tomorrow night. We could drive over together and I could drop you off at Stanhope House afterwards."

"I'll come.

Drinks arrived: Merlot for Gina, a white wine for El, ginger ale for Peter and the usual Lenny Briscoe for Gordon. Peter followed the Merlot with his eyes as the waitress leaned across the table to put it in front of Gina. His gaze lingered on it for several seconds before he snapped back to his own drink."

Gordon noticed, and remembered that Peter was partial to red wine — when he was drinking wine, at any rate. He picked up the thread of the conversation.

"Tomorrow should be a busy day," he said. "I'll be dropping off a copy of the manuscript at the sheriff's office at eight … "

"And pumping him about the investigation," said El. "Don't forget to do that."

"I'll try, but that's more in your line than mine. Why don't you do that?"

"I want to see what I can get from the medical examiner first. The more I know, the more I can get Ballou to spill."

"When are you calling the doc?"

"Nine o'clock, or whenever you get over from the sheriff's office. I'll wait for you."

"And what about Celia Strickland at Shore Acres?"

"I'll try to set something up for Saturday afternoon or Sunday.

Gordon picked up the folder of clippings and the accident report that Karl had given him. "Try to make it Sunday if you can. I need some time to go through this."

"I'll do what I can."

"Well," said Gordon, "I still don't know where we're headed, but it feels like we're moving somewhere." He raised his glass in a toast. "To the investigation."

"To the investigation!" said the other three, raising their glasses.

They sipped their drinks silently for a moment. Vic Damone had given way to Perry Como, backed by an ethereal choir, singing "Young at Heart."

AT STANHOPE HOUSE after dinner, Peter and Gordon were waiting for Emma to come back with paper for the printer so they could run off Ballou's copy of the manuscript. Peter was fidgeting.

"You all right?" asked Gordon.

"I'm fine."

"Still OK with not drinking?"

"I said I was fine."

"I know what you said, but I also saw how you were looking at Gina's Merlot tonight."

147

"For God's sake, Gordon. You're starting to sound like my third wife. I always used to tell her it's not *looking* that's the problem; it's *acting*."

"You weren't talking about drinking then, were you?"

"No, but it's the same principle. You're never going to get it off your mind entirely if you're human. I'm OK. Really."

"All right. Just asking."

A moment passed, and Gordon remembered something.

"What about Stella?" he said, remembering the nurse Peter was going with. "Wasn't she supposed to be here tonight?"

"She said she'd call Friday morning if she could switch shifts and get off Friday night. She didn't call, so I'm assuming she had to work. Maybe she can come up tomorrow, but they're really short-handed because of vacations. She might get called in on overtime tomorrow night. It's up in the air."

"Sorry it took so long," said Emma, coming around the corner with a ream of copy paper, still wrapped. "This is the last one, and I had to go to the storage closet to get it."

She paused. "Could I ask you one thing?"

Gordon nodded.

"I ran into Alice at the library today, and she told me, in the strictest confidence, of course, that some of you are looking into what happened to Charlotte London."

Gordon flinched. It was just what he had been worrying about, and he wondered how many other people Alice had told — in strictest confidence, of course.

"That's maybe overstating it a bit. We're helping El Sundstrom with the article she's working on for next week's paper."

Emma was trying to decide whether to say something.

"I know this is being really forward," she blurted out, "but could I join your group?"

Gordon and Peter looked at each other.

"This may sound silly," she continued, "but when we moved here from Colorado, our daughter, Michelle, was really worried about making friends at a new high school. Miss London picked up on that, and made a point of putting her with another girl on a team project the first week of classes. The other girl became her best friend, and that English class changed her life. It made her decide to be a teacher. I feel our family owes Miss London a huge debt, and if there's anything unsettled about what happened to her, I'd like to help. I'd gladly do any task that needs doing."

She looked at them with pleading eyes. Gordon glanced quickly at Peter, who shrugged, unhelpfully.

"All right," said Gordon after a pause. "I don't see how I can say no to that. But please, please don't tell anybody — not even your husband."

"Word of honor," she said. "If there's one thing innkeepers know how to do, it's keep a secret."

Gordon smiled.

"Do you know where El Sundstrom's house is at Aspen Cove? We're meeting there at two o'clock tomorrow afternoon."

She nodded vigorously.

"Thank you, thank you. This means a lot to me."

"Welcome to our team," said Peter, putting out his hand.

"Welcome," said Gordon, doing the same.

Saturday June 22

SHERIFF BALLOU came out quickly when Gordon was announced. He was dressed in jeans and a long-sleeved shirt in navy check and wore an olive Stetson with a feather in the band on its left side.

"Thank you for coming by," he said with forced cheerfulness, once they were in his office. "Appreciated your coming by the other day, even though it didn't look like you had much at the time. But at least we knew it was out there when we wanted to have a look at it later."

"Something's changed?"

"Well, now, it's too early to say that yet. Let's just say a couple of things have turned up that have made us feel we need to look at this sad situation more carefully — just to be sure."

Gordon played along. "I understand. From what little I know about law enforcement, there's a lot of following dead ends, just to rule things out."

"Exactly. What you have here," he lifted the manuscript and dropped it on his desk, "may be something really important or it may be nothing at all. Probably nothing, but we won't know until we take a good look at it."

"Of course. And since I'm now legally responsible for the manuscript, I hope you'll let me know if you do find something in it."

Ballou's eyes narrowed.

"What do you mean 'legally responsible,' Gordon?"

"In her will, Charlotte London named me her literary executor." He paused for effect, and Ballou bit.

"What the hell is a literary executor? I never heard of such a thing."

"That means I'm responsible for her family history and all related papers — not that there are many of those, what with the fire and all. So I do have an interest in knowing if there's any more to her death than a tragic accident."

"Any idea how you got that job?"

"I must have aced the interview."

Ballou drummed his fingers on the desk.

"You said before that when she walked up to you at the Shotgun Café and gave you that family history, you'd never met her?"

"Never."

"You're sure?"

"She's not someone you'd forget."

"And did she say why she wanted you to hold on to that computer disk, when she presumably had dozens of people in town she could have asked?"

"I've wondered about that myself. All she said was that I had an honest face."

Ballou looked at the face.

"Yeah," he finally said, "You're the type old ladies take a liking to. Probably be a good confidence man if you put your mind to it."

"Not for me, thanks."

"It *is* strange. You have to admit that, Gordon."

"A big part of me wishes she'd chosen someone else, but ... "

"But she didn't. You still think your hotel room being broken into had anything to do with all this?"

"More than ever." Gordon told him about the Cherokee Thursday afternoon.

"Did you file a report?"

"No, and I'm not telling my insurance company either. What are the odds of catching someone on a smash-and-grab in the middle of nowhere?"

"Not good, though you said nothing was grabbed."

"You know what I mean."

"How long are you going to be here, now?"

"Through Wednesday morning, then back to San Francisco."

"All right. I'll get in touch with you if I need to, and you might want to give me a call Tuesday afternoon, just in case."

"Fine," said Gordon, standing to go. "And if you need to reach me later on, you know how to get hold of me in the City."

Ballou shook his hand.

"Enjoy the rest of your fishing trip. I hear they're biting pretty good near the dam."

"THAT'S ALL YOU GOT?" she said.

"Sorry. I may be your intern, but I never took a journalism class."

El looked askance at Gordon, while Peter pretended to be studying the ceiling tiles.

"All right," she finally said. "Let's see if we can get anything out of the medical examiner."

She picked up the phone from her desk, took a phone list from a stacking tray and studied it for a moment before dialing. This morning, she was wearing a snug, low-cut light-blue top over her jeans, and Gordon couldn't help noticing the way her breasts rose as she breathed. When the connection was made, she hit the "speaker" button on the phone.

"Brantley," said a voice on the other end.

"Sorry, I was looking for Doogie Howser, M.D."

"Now why did I think I might be hearing from you today, El?"

"If you weren't so rational, I'd say you were psychic. Do you have the report there?"

"As a matter of fact, I do."

"Good. Well, I happen to have my own medical expert here …"

"Advertising must be good this summer."

"Let's not go there. I want you to meet Dr. Peter Delaney, a surgeon and emergency room doctor from San Francisco. Say hello, Peter."

"Good to make your acquaintance, doctor."

"And in the spirit of full disclosure, my summer intern, Quill Gordon is also here."

"Quill Gordon? Like the trout fly?"

"I get that a lot," Gordon said.

"I'll bet. Well, where did you want to start, El? Did Ballou show you the report?"

"He told me what he thought was in it," she lied. "Now I'd like to hear it from someone who knows what he's talking about."

"Never a bad idea. Well, what we have here is a white female, age approximately 60 years, good health overall, probably would have lived to 90 if this hadn't happened … "

"Excuse me, doctor," said Peter. "But I haven't seen the report. Could you briefly tell us what condition the body was in when you got it?"

"Oh, sorry. So, to put it in layman's terms for the fourth estate, she was a bit crispy on the outside," El and Gordon cringed while Peter listened impassively, "but overall the corpse and internal organs were well preserved. Just between us, the firefighters did a helluva job. If they'd gotten there just a couple of minutes later or been any less effective when they did arrive, I probably would have been looking at a charred skeleton."

"So you were able to do a thorough autopsy, then?" Peter asked.

"As thorough as the body and my facilities allow."

"And you were able to check for smoke in her lungs?"

"You're getting ahead of me, doctor, but that's the question I'd expect. The answer is yes I was, and no I didn't find any."

Peter tapped the desktop three times with the pencil he was holding.

"So that means … "

"I think you know the answer. Either she was dead before the fire broke out, or we have a set of highly unusual circumstances. I'd say the odds are 99.9 percent it's the first scenario."

The three of them looked at each other.

"I don't suppose," said Gordon quietly, "that there was any indication as to what the cause of death might have been?"

"I can't be absolutely certain about it, but there was a severe wound to the back of her head. To use layman's terms again, it was cracked like an eggshell. It would have been enough to kill her."

"Did you run a tox screen?" Peter said.

"Came back negative."

"Is there any chance that wound could have been the result of an accident — a fall, for instance?"

"There's always a chance, but I'd say it's pretty slim. The skull was shattered near its base, just below her left ear. That isn't normally where someone's head lands in a fall, but stranger things have happened. If a defense attorney asked that question, I wouldn't be able to absolutely, positively rule it out."

"Is it possible," said Gordon, "that the roof of the house could have collapsed from the fire and struck her on the head?"

"Possible, but it didn't happen. I had the same question and checked with the fire department. They were able to get the fire out before the roof caved. Whatever coshed her, it wasn't the roof."

"And no signs of any other trauma?" said Peter.

"Nothing that would have killed her. No gunshots or stab wounds, if that's what you mean. No other serious skeletal trauma."

"So, John," said El. "You mentioned defense attorneys asking questions. Is that what you're expecting? That this will be a criminal case?"

He didn't answer for 15 seconds.

"Shit. I shouldn't talk to you over the phone, El. You get me off guard, and I say things I don't mean to say."

"Don't get a swelled head over it. You're not the only one."

"All right, can I talk on background? You don't quote me or tell anyone I was the source for this?"

"You're on."

He spoke slowly, choosing his words carefully.

"I think the medical evidence points very strongly in one direction: That someone killed Charlotte London with a blow to the head and set her house on fire to cover it up. I think we're dealing with an unlucky killer."

"You mean," said Gordon, "if the house and body had burned more completely, someone could have gotten away with murder?"

"Someone still could. None of this gets us any closer to figuring out who did this. But someone very nearly committed an undetected murder. At least now the sheriff should be looking into it aggressively. And, El, put the heat on him to do that. If what the evidence points to is true, this was a horrible crime, and I hope our killer's luck stays bad."

After a few pleasantries, they concluded the conversation. As soon as the phone was off, Gordon turned to El.

"Are you going to go after Ballou about this?"

She raised a hand. "Not so fast. He just got the report yesterday, so let's give him a chance to come clean first. And let's keep digging ourselves. Then on Tuesday afternoon, I'll call our sheriff and put the screws on him."

"All right. I think, though, that we have the top agenda item for this afternoon's meeting."

"What I can't figure out," said Peter, "Is why the medical examiner was so forthcoming. In the Bay Area they don't talk to the media that much and they're really careful about what they say."

"You could call it a Forest County tradition," said El with a smile. "When I got here 20 years ago, the county had a medical examiner by the name of Roy Cahoon. Now there was a man who loved his work. He'd call me after an accident or violent death to give me all the details. He said the taxpayers were paying for his reports and they had a right to know what was in them. Of course, he got off on seeing his name in the newspaper, but he did things that way for so many years that his successor felt obliged to be open, too."

"Still," Gordon said, "I'm surprised Ballou didn't coordinate with him better. He's going to be furious when he hears what you got out of Brantley."

"What you have to remember," she said, "is how unusual this is. Ballou's had two murders in his 12 years as sheriff. One was a domestic violence case and the other was a bar fight — both open and shut. This is the first case he's ever had where the medical examiner could trip him up, and it probably never occurred to him to head that off. We won't be so lucky if it ever happens again, but for now … "

"Thank you, Roy Cahoon," said Peter.

THEY CHEWED OVER THE CASE some more, and El made an appointment to meet with Celia Strickland at Shore Acres Lodge Sunday at two o'clock. Gordon and Peter emerged into the growing heat of the bright late-morning sunshine. Thunderheads forming over the western mountains held out hope for a cooling storm later in the day.

"I'm hungry," Gordon said. "All I've had is a croissant."

"If you'd stayed for breakfast," Peter said, "You'd have had an omelet with sausage, basil and white cheddar cheese."

"Don't rub it in. Can you do an early lunch?"

"I suppose so. The Shotgun?"

"I was thinking of giving the coffee shop by the airport a try."

"Go for it."

They drove to the airport and turned in at the main entrance, pulling up in front of The Barnstormer Café, a 1950s-vintage wood building with several hard-used pickup trucks parked in front. As they were getting out of the Cherokee, Gordon's pager beeped.

"Local number," he said. "Looks familiar. I'd better call."

He punched the number into his cell phone, and on the second ring, Cameron Winters answered.

"Law offices."

"Winters!" said Gordon. "What can I do for you?"

"Well, if you can get to my office by noon, you can pick up a package that arrived for you this morning. If not, I'll put it in my safe, and you can come for it on Monday."

Gordon hesitated, and before he could say anything, Winters continued:

"It's from Charlotte London."

"I'll be there in five minutes."

He told Peter about it as they drove back and parked under the shady tree across the street from the law office. Peter waited while Gordon went in. Winters stepped out of his office, wearing jeans and a burgundy polo shirt.

"No court today," he said. "Come in and have a seat."

On the desk blotter in front of Winters was a book-sized parcel, wrapped in plain brown paper and sealed with tape. Gordon couldn't take his eyes off it.

"All I can say is this was quite a surprise," Winters said. "When I went to my PO box at 11, there was a card that I had a package. It was addressed to me, but when I unwrapped it, I found this," he gestured to the parcel in front of him, "It came with a handwritten note from Charlotte London. A very peculiar note, I might add."

Gordon nodded for him to keep going. Winters opened a sheet of plain white copy paper that had been folded once.

"It says, 'Dear Cameron, Please hold the enclosed parcel, unopened, in your safe until further notice. In the event anything should happen to me before I claim it, please deliver it, also unopened, to my literary executor, Mr. Gordon. Thank you. Sincerely, Charlotte London.' That's it."

Gordon exhaled sharply. Winters pushed the parcel across the desk toward him.

"All yours," he said. "You're under no obligation to tell me anything about it, but to be frank, I've never had something like this happen before. If you do feel you can give me an explanation later, I'd be most grateful."

Gordon picked it up. It was heavily taped and bound with string. On the brown wrapping paper, in Charlotte's unmistakable hand, were the words:

"To: Mr. Quill Gordon
"From: Charlotte London"

He shook his head.

"I don't understand," he said slowly. "She died on Monday, but this just arrived today?"

"That, I can probably explain." Winters opened a desk drawer and took a large piece of brown paper from it. He set it on the desk facing Gordon. "This was the outer wrapping. As you can see, the postage is covered by a bazillion stamps — probably twice as many as were needed. The postmark is Tuesday. I'm guessing it was mailed after hours on Monday night. There's a postal substation not too far from Miss London's house on the Peninsula, and she could have simply loaded it up with stamps and pushed it through the mail slot."

"And it took nearly a week to get a few miles to you?"

"Not without reason." He pointed to the address. "The last two digits of the zip code were transposed. You can see here where it went to the other zip code and was postmarked there before being sent back here. If it had been handled by a careless or stupid postal clerk, we might never have seen this." He paused. "I guess you were meant to get it."

"Thank you, Winters. I'll handle it with care."

"You've been to Rotary, so you can call me Cam. You can also call me bothered. Can I tell you what I've been thinking ever since I picked this up?"

"Please do."

"I've been thinking about what a remarkable woman Charlotte London was. I'll miss her, and not just as a client. And I've been thinking how it's funny what troubles you about someone's behavior.

"When she came into the office Monday morning and wrote a holographic codicil to her will, naming you, a total stranger, as her literary executor — something she's never discussed with me in all the years I've represented her — I didn't bat an eye. After all, she had a confidence, bordering on hubris, about her ability to size people up. Strange as it might look to someone who didn't know her, it was the sort of thing she *would* do.

"This parcel, on the other hand, disturbs me very much. Miss London had two qualities that were fixed and immovable. One was thriftiness. She'd spend money on something that was important to her, but she hated to pay too much for anything. The second was that she was absolutely meticulous and intolerant of carelessness. So when I received a parcel from her with way too much postage on it, and a mistake in the address ... well, I can only conclude that something was terribly wrong."

"You may be right," Gordon said softly.

"I would hope that if you see anything in here," gesturing to the parcel, "that strikes you as being suspicious, you'll go straight to the authorities with it."

"I've already given the sheriff a copy of her family history."

"All right, then. You know what I mean." He paused. "Is there anything else I can do?"

"No, I don't think so," said Gordon, rising. "Thank you. Cam."

"Thank you for coming by. And Gordon: Be careful."

The package felt as if it weighed a hundred pounds as he carried it back to the Cherokee. Gordon filled Peter in as they drove back to the Barnstormer, which was down to one truck parked in front when they arrived. Clouds were beginning to bunch up over the mountains, and an afternoon thunderstorm seemed like an increasing possibility. When they got out to go into the café, Peter froze Gordon with a look.

"You're not going to leave that thing in the car, are you?"

"What?"

Peter moved closer and lowered his voice.

"Hasn't it occurred to you that this might be what your stalker has been looking for?"

"Sorry. So much is happening that my brain's turning into oatmeal."

He fished the package out of the car and took it into the coffee shop. Two men were at a table at one end, so they took a corner table at the other end, where they could have relative privacy. The place was decorated with old photos and aviation documents that covered all the wall space, but Gordon hardly noticed. A clock-watching waitress brusquely took their order and left.

"Well?" said Peter.

"I guess I should open it."

He took a small folding knife from his pocket and slowly and carefully began unwrapping the parcel by gently prying apart the tape where it was sealed. Peter drummed his fingers nervously on the tabletop.

"You must have driven your sisters nuts on Christmas morning," he said. "Can't you go any faster?"

"This could be evidence. I'm almost there."

He broke the last piece of tape and opened the wrapping to unveil a book, morocco-bound with a maroon cover and no legend. Flipping quickly through the pages he recognized Charlotte London's distinctive, crisp handwriting, essayed with a fountain pen or pens with blue ink. He stopped at the last page and looked up at Peter.

"It's her journal," he said. "From September 1, 1970 to February 28, 1971. The time The Peninsulas were being debated and approved."

A GROWL OF DISTANT THUNDER was heard as Gordon convened the meeting. The heat had been withering until a half-hour earlier, but the temperature was cooling as the storm moved in from the west. Its advance clouds were scudding in front of the sun from time to time, creating alternating intervals of shadow and bright light, but as the meeting progressed, the sound of thunder drew closer and the periods of darkness longer.

Gordon introduced Emma as the newest (and final, he hoped) member of the investigating team. She was known to all, was greeted warmly, and said that as this was her first meeting, she planned to listen and do no more than ask a question or two.

After that, Gordon turned the meeting over to El and Peter for a report on the interview with Medical Examiner Brantley. Their summary caused a sensation.

"I knew it!" said Gina. "I knew this was no accident. Is there any chance at all he was wrong?"

"Unlikely," said Peter. "Those guys know their stuff, and he struck me as being sharp on the details."

Her face clouded over. "Poor Charlotte. I hope she didn't suffer."

"From the way he described the trauma to the skull, she had to have been either killed instantly or totally unconscious from the time she was hit until the time she died. For whatever the sentiment is worth, it could have been worse."

"No question it's a big development," Gordon said, "but at the end of the day it only tells us we're on the right track. We're no closer to knowing who did it or why."

"And," said El, "it's far from being provable that it was a murder. That's what it looks like, but Brantley said he couldn't swear to it, and a defense attorney could poke holes in the theory."

"I say worry about the defense attorney later," Karl said. "We need to concentrate on who and why."

"I agree," Gordon said, "and toward that end, something else has dropped into our laps." He took Charlotte's journal out of his bag and summarized his meeting with Winters that morning.

"I just got it a couple of hours ago, and haven't done anything with it aside from quickly flipping through it to confirm it is what it is. I'd appreciate some guidance from the group as to how we should handle this."

"Well, I know what I think," said Alice, "but I'd like to hear what Gina has to say. After all, she was Charlotte's best friend."

Gina stirred restlessly, and it was clear she was agitated.

"I think you should read it," she finally blurted out. "One of the last things she did in her life was to make sure you got it if anything happened. So I don't see there's anything to argue about, Gordon."

"I agree," said Alice, "but given that it's a personal journal and we all know Charlotte, I think Gordon should read it and report back to us tomorrow on only what he thinks is relevant to the investigation."

There were nods all around.

"If that's what you all want, I'll do it," Gordon said. "But it's a heavy load for me to carry, trying to decide what's relevant and what isn't. If anyone else wants to look, we could make a copy … Gina?"

"No, she left it for you, and you should look at it, but … "

"But what?"

"All right, I know this is going to sound petty, but I have to get it off my chest. Charlotte has been my best friend for nearly 15 years. I thought we confided everything to each other. Smart as she was, she must have had her reasons, but I just don't understand why she turned her journal over to a complete stranger instead of to me."

The awkward silence that followed was finally broken by Karl.

"There's probably something in it she didn't want you to see. You wouldn't believe what people put in their journals."

"Karl!" snapped Alice.

The room was as charged with tension as the outdoors was with the approaching storm, which produced a rumble of thunder at that point.

"You may be right, Karl," Gina said softly.

"I'd bet money on it," said Peter. "The whole question of why Miss London landed on Gordon has been gnawing on me, but now we might have two answers: a) she didn't feel she could trust anyone in town to follow up aggressively, and b) she had to share something personal and didn't want to do it with someone she knew. I doubt she imagined, Gina, that you and Gordon would get together so quickly."

Gordon sighed. "All right, then. I'll do it myself, but I'd still like a little help. Who was here in 1970, in case I have a question?"

Gina, El and Alice shook their heads.

"I was," Karl said, "but I can hardly remember what I had for lunch yesterday, never mind 25 years ago. Happy to look something up if you need that, though."

"All right."

"Are we done?" asked Karl.

"I think so," said Gordon, and hearing no dissent, continued, "What time tomorrow?"

"We're meeting Celia Strickland at Shore Acres at two," said El. "It could take a while. Shall we say 4:30?"

Everyone agreed to that and stood to go. Peter looked at Gina, then at Gordon.

"How are we going to handle the logistics of this?" he asked.

"I know the way to Greg London's place," Gina said. "Why don't you come with me, and I'll drop you off at Stanhope House on the way back?"

Peter glanced at Gordon, who nodded. Gina and Peter started out the door.

"Gordon," said El.

"Yes."

She waited until the door was closed.

"If you don't want to read that in a small room all by yourself, you're welcome to stay here for a while. Comfortable chairs, lake view."

"Are you sure that would be all right?" he said.

"I'm sure."

LOOKING BACK ON IT LATER, Gordon realized that he had come to Charlotte London's journal with preconceived notions, and that she would not have approved. He had expected it to contain significant and previously unknown details of what her father and brother were going through in their effort to get the plan for The Peninsulas approved. It held nothing of the sort. Charlotte had been indifferent to the point of obliviousness about the project that was consuming the rest of the family. Instead, she was caught up in the details of her own life, and not entirely without reason.

She had fallen in love.

The first few entries in the journal were routine descriptions of the details involving the beginning of another school year — one of 36 such beginnings in her professional career. But the tone changed with the entry for Thursday September 10:

Annual Rotary Club new teacher luncheon today. School let out early at 12:30, and at one o'clock hundreds of people gathered in the cafeteria for the grand occasion. Old hat for me now, but I remember how thrilling it was that first year to see so many people in town turn out to recognize us — making us feel that what we were doing for their children was important. The lunch may be more routine now, but I still believe what we are doing is important. I couldn't go on otherwise. Something unusual this year, though. The gentleman sitting next to me (not saying who because I don't want to make too much of it) was unusually attentive, to the point where, by the end of the luncheon, I was beginning to wonder if I have a secret admirer. He asked a great many questions about the books I would be teaching in Senior English this year. They were good questions, and I found myself wishing the parents of my students took such an interest. We carried on a free and easy conversation for some time, and to such an extent that I've quite forgotten everything else about the event. No doubt there was nothing to it, and I am being carried away by an excess of maidenly imagination, but the flutter was nevertheless enjoyable.

The matter seemed to drop there, and for the next week and a half there was no follow up. Then, an entry for Saturday September 19.

Quite a surprise this afternoon. I had just returned from the store and was looking forward to an early dinner, some reading, and watching the first episode of the new "Mary Tyler Moore Show." She was so good in "The Dick Van Dyke Show," and the premise of a modern career woman is intriguing. I had set down my bags when the phone rang, and I was surprised to find that the caller was my Secret Admirer from the new-teacher luncheon. SA (as I'll call him) said he wanted to tell me how much he had enjoyed our conversation, and after some hemming and hawing said he'd like to talk to me again and asked if I would have lunch with him at Grouse Lake Resort next Saturday. I said yes more quickly than I ought to have, and spent much of the evening wondering why I agreed, when I really shouldn't have. I finally concluded it was because I wanted to, and for now, I can comfort myself with the assurance that it's only lunch, after all. "The Mary Tyler Moore Show" was quite promising; I plan to keep watching it and hope they develop some of the possibilities.

He called in the middle of the week to make arrangements, and the Friday entry reflected some concern on her part about how to dress and approach the occasion. As Gordon reached Saturday the 26th, the first drops of rain began to fall outside, and a bolt of lightning struck somewhere to the south.

A beautiful day, warm, sunny, hardly a cloud in the sky. The calendar says autumn, but today it felt more like midsummer. SA picked me up at nine and seemed a bit preoccupied on the 40-mile drive to Grouse Lake. I allowed him his thoughts and concentrated on the scenery. Father used to take us to Grouse Lake when we were children, but I haven't been there for years and had forgotten what a lovely drive it is. When we got to the lake, we stopped at a picnic area, nearly deserted this time of year. We shared pastries and a thermos of coffee and talked. He is a good talker (something I like in a man) and at one point he even quoted from "The Lady of the Lake:" "Boon nature scattered, free and wild …" I wondered if he had looked it up for the occasion, but decided that he is the kind of man who would like Scott, so it was all right in any case. At least it wasn't "Lochinvar." At one o'clock we went to the lodge. It was half full and no children, just groups of men there for a last fishing trip of the season, along with a few wives. I was afraid we would run into someone we knew, but we didn't, and I was finally able to relax and enjoy our conversation. He was considerably more animated on the drive back to Arthur. I felt positively vibrant the rest of the day and was glad I had done this. "The Mary Tyler Moore Show" was very good again. I think it may turn out to be something.

Her journal for the next couple of weeks recorded several evening phone calls from the Secret Admirer and a Saturday lunch trip to Adams with him on October 10, in which they again avoided encountering anyone they knew. The tone of the journal entries was taking on an additional urgency and tension. Gordon had reached the slightly longer entry for Friday October 16 when El came up behind him and put a hand on his shoulder, startling him.

"Doing all right?"

Huh? Yeah. I'm fine."

"I just made a pot of tea. Earl Grey. Would you like a cup?"

"That would be nice."

Gordon realized that it was pouring rain outside, the large drops bouncing sharply off the deck outside like basketballs on a fast-break dribble. He'd been so focused on the journal he noticed nothing else. El brought a large mug of tea, which he accepted and continued reading.

Homecoming night, and nearly everyone in town is at the football game. I believe mine was the only house on the street with lights on between six and ten o'clock. SA called at six and asked if he could come over. I thought that just for tonight it would be all right. He was tense and agitated when he arrived, and finally blurted out that he loves me. It was not unexpected, and from that declaration, one thing led to another, ending in the bedroom. To be honest, it was more a relief than a pleasure. The unspoken tension that had been building between us for weeks was finally broken, and we now know where we stand. That, at least, is something, and with any luck, there is greater pleasure ahead. One thing quickly became clear, however. We cannot continue to meet at my house. We lost track of time, as people do in such situations, and he barely got back to his car before the neighbors started returning from the football game. I shall have to insist that if we are to continue meeting, we need to find another place.

Over the next couple of weeks, they went back and forth over that issue and did not meet in person. Finally, in a way that was never explained, SA found a cabin they could use as a love nest, and on the afternoon of October 30, after school was out, they met there for the first time.

The place is three-quarters of a mile from the state highway on a well maintained dirt road. Turning into the driveway, I looped behind some concealing shrubbery and trees, where my car would be out of sight. I arrived first, got the key from under the doormat, and let myself in. It is a small, one-bedroom cabin with a loft for children, and it was chilly. But the heating system worked very well, and once I turned it on, the place quickly became comfortable. SA arrived 20 minutes later, and we wasted little time on conversation. Like Napoleon returning to Josephine, he was not there to talk. I am not as innocent as my father would like to believe, but neither am I greatly experienced. I can't offer a measured judgment — merely my own sense of things. And that sense is that there was a level of passion and pleasure in our coupling today that was more than I have ever known. We did talk afterwards, and the conversation was good, for whatever that's worth. I don't want this to end!

The cabin was well used over the next week and a half. Veterans Day that year was on a Wednesday.

A rare mid-week day off during the school year, and we made the most of it. The Guv picked me up shortly after 9, and we set out for Spirit Lake, 15 miles outside of Adams. I have decided to start calling him The Guv because his admiration is no longer a secret (at least to me) and, besides, it suits him well and sounds like something out of a Victorian novel. It was a clear, sunny day that was trying to be Indian summer, but the sun is so far away it couldn't properly warm things up. Still, it was cool and pleasant, in a crisp, autumnal sort of way. As we hoped, there was no one at Spirit Lake. The Forest Service had closed the picnic area for the winter, but we parked outside and walked in with the picnic lunch The Guv picked up at the store.

I am normally a light eater, but the mountain air and the setting made me ravenous, and I think he enjoyed watching me overdo it. Later, we went for a walk on the trail around the lake. The erotic tension from just holding hands became so powerful that we ended up making love standing against a tree. A Ponderosa Pine, actually, and in full view of anyone across the lake — if there had been anyone. I have never experienced anything so passionately intense and will probably remember it as I lay dying. Our feelings and desire for each other have become so strong that we are utterly unfettered by propriety, convention, or any other form of restraint. Part of me recognizes this and wants to hit the brake, but an even larger part of me is pushing the accelerator to the floor.

Six days later, back in the cabin after school:

After a pleasant interlude this afternoon, The Guv said we needed to talk about his wife. I had been wondering when that would happen. He said he doesn't love her; that their marriage was a mistake; that he wants out, but doesn't know what to do. I felt a considerable sympathy for his position, but I do hate to see a man mope, and it was clear the matter wasn't going to be settled today. So I told him he needed to take his time and think it over and do what he feels he has to do. And I added that in the meantime, we should enjoy the moment. That, in turn, led to yet another enjoyable moment, and the rendezvous ended on a positive note. Back home, I got out Anna Karenina *and tried to look up a quote. I finally found it in Part II, Chapter 7: "You and I are one to me. And I see no chance before us of peace for me or for you. I see a chance of despair or wretchedness … or I see a chance of bliss, what bliss!" Then a couple of paragraphs later, "Friends we shall never be, you know that yourself. Whether we shall be the happiest or the wretchedest of people — that's in your hands." Of course, Vronsky was saying those things to Anna, not the other way around, but I suppose in this affair, I'm partly Vronsky. I must force myself to concentrate on now, rather than worrying about a future I can't control.*

Gordon had finished his cup of tea and set it down on the floor by the chair. It was still raining steadily, but the storm was beginning to wind down. He tried to remember something Peter had said when they met

Charlotte London for the first and only time. Finally, it came to him:

"It wouldn't surprise me at all if our Miss London turned out to have a reservoir of passion inside her that makes Lake Año Nuevo look like a backyard fish pond by comparison."

How did Peter know? In any event, it was obvious why Charlotte hadn't turned the journal over to Gina, who had lost her husband to another woman. Gordon himself was beginning to feel like an intruder in Charlotte's life, but he was far enough in now that he couldn't stop. Thanksgiving that year was Thursday November 26.

Up early this morning and over to mother and father's house to pitch in on Thanksgiving dinner. Very cold day, with the first snow of the season supposed to be moving in tomorrow. An uneasy holiday this year. For the first time, I would rather have been with someone else, yet that's impossible. Mother was overbearing and difficult, as usual, but I find that as the years go by, I can let it go more easily. Most of the time, anyway. Greg's son, Michael, is a year and a half and cute as a bug. Pam is clearly showing child number two, and they seem so happy. Because of everything else, this is the first time in a couple of months that I've been with father for an extended period, and he is clearly worried. This Peninsulas land deal of his is clearly taking a toll. I don't understand business at all, but it seemed that when he started in on it, he was much more optimistic. Greg hasn't been as involved in it as dad, but even he seems worried, though he's so solid, it's hard to tell. I'm sure it will all work out.

That was almost the only reference to the project in the journal. Then it was back to talk of school and the affair, which continued in its set path. On Friday December 11, it headed for a new level.

Our first meeting since Monday, and we seemed to be making up for lost passion. Which is not a bad thing. During a break, The Guv dropped a surprise on me. He said he has to tend to some business in San Francisco right before Christmas, and he wants me to come with him. I'd like to know how he talked his wife out of coming, but won't worry a good thing to death. Just two weeks ago, I was thinking about how I'd like to spend Christmas with him. This won't exactly be Christmas, but it will be a special holiday occasion, of sorts. When I was in college at Berkeley, I enjoyed going to San Francisco, but always had to come home right at the beginning of Christmas season, so this will be my first chance to enjoy the city at that special time of year. We'll be staying three nights at the Mark Hopkins, and the best part is that we'll leave Sunday morning. That means I can watch "The Mary Tyler Moore Show" Saturday night. I have become hopelessly addicted to it.

GREGORY LONDON LIVED on the east side of the West Peninsula in a house twice the size of his sister's. In fact, it faced across the cove between the two peninsulas toward Charlotte's house — or rather where it used to be. The rain was falling steadily and heavily as Peter and Gina pulled up in her blue 1990 Camry.

London answered the door himself. He was 58 (three years younger than Charlotte), but looked almost 70, with bags under his eyes, sagging jowls, and thinning hair that aligned itself in such a way it would always give the impression he had just gotten out of bed in the morning. He had the resigned look of a man who had endured, rather than embraced, his life. He showed Gina and Peter to a couch in a living room that opened onto a deck with a sweeping panorama east to the cove and rising sun, and south to the lake itself. Gina introduced Peter as a representative of Charlotte's literary executor, which drew a frown and puzzled look.

"Literary executor?" he snorted. "What's that?"

"A literary executor," Gina said brightly, "is a person who assumes the stewardship of someone's writings and literary output after their death. Because she was working on a family history, she appointed a man from San Francisco to carry on if something happened to her before she finished."

He took a few seconds to digest this.

"Sounds like Charlotte," he finally said. "Hope she's paying him for it. Can't imagine anyone would be interested in that book of hers."

"I gather books were very important in her life," Peter said gently.

"Oh, sure. Ever since I can remember, she always had her nose in a book. Made it hard to follow her in school. I guess it was only a matter of time till she tried to write one herself."

"Did she ever talk to you about it?" asked Gina.

"All the time. I tried not to listen too hard. I'm more interested in now than then."

"A common sentiment," said Peter. "My friend was wondering — and there's no urgency or pressure about this — if you have any family documents in your possession that might help in completing the family history."

"Nah. Gave all that to Charlotte two years ago. Good riddance. Saved me the trouble of burning it."

"All right. That was easy. We also were wondering what you remember about the development of The Peninsulas and the controversy that surrounded it. Do you think you might be willing to talk to my friend later, if he needs more information for the book?"

"I guess it wouldn't hurt to talk to him, but I'm not sure what I could say. Dad really did most of that. I helped by running the office so he could work on his project, and since I was doing the work both of us used to do together, I was pretty busy. Sometimes I'd go with him to one of his meetings with the Paris family, but I didn't understand half of what they were talking about."

"We'll keep that in mind. Just one more question, then. Do you remember anything about how your father felt about it? Did he say anything that sticks in your mind?"

Gregory London digested the question slowly.

"No one thing that I can recall. What I do remember is that in the last month before it was approved, he was worried. More worried than I've ever seen him. He had a lot riding on it, I guess, but it somehow seemed more than that." He paused. "It's always bothered me to think he died worried and never lived to see that it turned out OK."

"You've been very helpful, Greg," said Gina. "Could I ask you a thing or two about Charlotte. You've mentioned she always had her nose in a book when she was young and that she did well in school. Is there anything else you remember about her when you were growing up?"

"No."

"Did she have boyfriends when she was in high school?"

"No."

"Come on," said Peter, his irritation barely suppressed. "She must have gone to the senior prom."

"I don't remember if she did or didn't, but if she did, whoever took her never came back. She was so smart she scared most of the boys around here. There may have been someone when she was in college, but I'm sure she never had a boyfriend when she was living in this town. It wouldn't surprise me if she died a virgin."

Gina and Peter agreed with a glance that the interview was over. To be polite, however, she and Gregory traded reminiscences of Charlotte for another five minutes, but Gina had to do most of the work.

Outside, the rain had eased to a drizzle, and the crackles of thunder had become less frequent and more distant. They got into her car and sat quietly for a minute.

"Well," she said, "in the books and TV shows, the police are always saying they have to eliminate possibilities. I think we've eliminated this one. He's known her longer than anyone else and he seems to know nothing."

"It's worse than that," said Peter. "He knows things for a fact that just aren't so. You'd think siblings who grew up together would know each other better than anyone else, and sometimes that's the case. But a lot of times they form a first impression, then try to make everything else conform to that impression, so they know less and less as time goes by."

"All right. What do you think he knows that's wrong."

"For starters, he thinks his sister died a virgin. I'd bet anything she didn't. I only met Charlotte London that one time, but even on short acquaintance, she struck me as a woman who had a feeling for life. It's almost impossible to acquire that feeling unless you've been deeply in love and intensely sexually involved at least once."

After a pause, Gina said, "That's very perceptive, Peter. I suppose I've kind of thought the same thing, but I never articulated it that well."

She started the engine.

"Back to Stanhope House?"

"Actually," he said, "It's almost five o'clock. Are you hungry yet?"

"Famished. I skipped lunch today."

"Well, I've been trying to get to Ike's Lakeside since we got here. Would you like to have dinner?"

"I'd like that very much," she said.

CHARLOTTE AND HER LOVER drove to San Francisco Sunday December 20, 1970, and returned on Wednesday December 23. Their getaway was described in two long passages in the journal. The first, dated Monday December 21, was most likely written late that afternoon, before dinner.

Have been out all day taking in the spectacle of The City at Christmas. A cool, breezy, overcast day with showers from time to time, and nearly everyone on the street with a raincoat and umbrella. The crowds and bustle here bring Arthur into relief as the sleepy little town it is. The Guv has been tending to business (or so he says), and I had the day and the city to myself. It was like being a child in the toy store. In this morning's San Francisco Chronicle, there was an ad that Ransohoff's was having a sale on shoes (Regular, $18-55; sale prices, $12.90 to $28.90). I was there when the doors opened at 10, and bought a sturdy but stylish pair of pumps for work for $19.90. From there, I strolled to City of Paris, where I bought nothing, but goggled, like everyone else, at the enormous Christmas tree, several stories high, in the rotunda. Dipping in and out of stores, I found myself unable to resist an apricot-colored scarf at Gump's. I'm being extravagant, I know, but I have been living frugally and exercising thrift in all matters for years, so I tell myself I'm allowed a little indulgence. Just this once. At noon, I noticed there was a choir gathered outside First Western Bank at Bush and Montgomery, and stopped to listen as they sang Christmas carols. They were from one of the *local churches, sang with ethereal beauty, and didn't miss a note, even when a sudden downpour caught them, unsheltered. I was hoping they would sing "O Come, All Ye Faithful," which is my favorite, and they concluded with it. Funny I should like that song so much. I am not particularly devout. Really, I am the epitome of a modern churchgoer. I feel the need to acknowledge that there's something bigger than me, even if I don't know what it is; I get comfort from the fellowship of the spirit; and I don't in the least feel I have to believe everything Father Michael says. I can easily imagine what he would say about my love affair, but I would like to believe that a just and loving God, who made this world such a trial at times, would be understanding and forgiving about human passion and frailty.*

I enjoyed a cup of tea and a sandwich at some small café near Union Square. Everyone around me was talking about how the San Francisco football team won yesterday and is going to the playoffs. Big city or no, it was like one of our local cafes the morning after the high school team played. Afterward, I hailed a taxi to the Opera House. I had seen in the Chronicle that the San Francisco Ballet would be doing a matinee of The Nutcracker tomorrow afternoon and was hoping there might still be seats available. As fate would have it, someone had just returned two orchestra tickets, and I unhesitatingly bought them. (The extravagances are piling up!) I'm not so sure ballet is The Guv's cup of tea, but how he reacts to my plans for us should provide an added measure of the man. Returning downtown, I stopped at Roos/Atkins and bought him a tie for Christmas — navy with thin stripes of gray and light green. If his wife asks, he can say he got it himself, but when he wears it, he will think of me. Then, the cable car back to the hotel and a little quiet time before dinner.

The second entry was dated Wednesday December 23, apparently written back in Arthur.

All too soon, the trip is over, but no matter what, I'll have the memory of it. The Guv came through splendidly on the ballet. When I told him I had bought tickets, I could see he was slightly taken aback, but he looked at me calmly for several seconds and finally said, "I can see you really want to go, so of course I'll come. And I'll enjoy myself, if for no other reason than I'm with you." It speaks well for him that he was willing to bend a bit for someone else. And he seemed not only to enjoy it, but also to be able to talk about it with understanding at dinner afterwards. Our dinner conversations during this trip were relaxed and spirited. We are well matched, I think, and the age difference does not seem to be important. It was such a pleasure to be able to eat and talk without constantly looking over one's shoulder to see if someone familiar had just walked into the room. I did have one brush with getting caught out, though. On Market Street on Tuesday, I was stopped by the Chronicle's Question Man (who, actually, is a woman) wanting to take my picture and print my answer to the question, "What would you buy a hippie for Christmas?" I told her I was sure I wouldn't know, and kept walking. Imagine the reaction in Arthur if that had gotten into the paper!

This morning, before we left, I gave The Guv his tie, and to my surprise, he gave me something as well: A pendant on a gold chain, with a single pearl framed by a diamond of gold. It is simple, elegant and beautiful and will go with almost anything. He has excellent taste! The drive home was subdued. I think we had invested so much emotional energy in this trip (and not just the lovemaking) that we were spent. It was a cold, gray drive, but aside from a couple of brief flurries, there was no snow and it was a smooth trip.

The City was so exhilarating and lively that I found myself thinking about what it would be like living there, instead of in my small town. But there was an item in Herb Caen's column to the effect that Lillian Hellman would be teaching at Berkeley this winter, and had rented an apartment on Telegraph Hill for $800 a month. Eight hundred dollars for an apartment — hard to believe, when I am paying $110 for a two-bedroom house on a small lot in Arthur.

It is late now, and I find myself postponing going to bed. For three nights, I was able to lay with my man all through the night — the first time we have been able to do that — and I can't bear the thought of sleeping alone. Perhaps the day will come when sleeping together will be a normal occurrence, but the decision must be his, and I can apply no pressure. What a change 24 hours has made: from bliss to melancholy.

Enough! I am going to bed now, whether I sleep a wink or not.

From Christmas to New Year, there was not much of interest in the journal. Charlotte and her lover met twice at the cabin, and she noted, in one passing line, that her father seemed even more worried and haggard at Christmas than he had at Thanksgiving. On January 1, Charlotte reflected:

New Year's Day — a time for taking inventory and making resolutions. Afraid I haven't yet gotten to the second part, being occupied, today, with taking a hard look at my situation. How did I get into it? If asked, as a general proposition, whether adultery is either acceptable or permissible, I would say no. Most women would. Yet I have followed the path of Anna Karenina, Emma Bovary, Hester Prynne, and millions of real women whose names will never become household words. The best explanation I can come up with (and I hope I'm explaining, not rationalizing) is that women, as a whole, are more emotional than men and more trusting of their emotions. When we fall in love with a man, that love becomes the guiding truth, the thing that drives out all other considerations. We tell ourselves that because our love is true, our circumstance is somehow different. Re-reading those last three sentences, I am struck by how lame they seem. But the whole point is that it's not a rational argument — rather, an emotional one. At this moment I am profoundly grateful not to be a Catholic. Having to confess this to some unctuous priest every week would drive me positively batty.

The school year resumed Monday January 4, 1971:

I have decided this year's senior English class can handle Pride and Prejudice, *so today I passed out the paperback copies I had ordered and gave my brief lecture on the importance of understanding character. Time will tell if they get it, but I hope they do, because it is one of life's most important lessons. The dire consequences of making a bad match and the blessed consequences of making a good one have been much on my mind lately. Darcy and Elizabeth are both complex characters, and theirs is an excellent match. Bingley and Jane are both simple characters, but good, and their match is likewise good. Wickham and Lydia would be an atrocious match, even if he were not so morally flawed, because he is a complex character*

176

and Lydia is frightfully simple. The Guv is a complex man who married a simple woman — a caricature, almost — and it has caused him no end of unhappiness.

Two days later, Wednesday January 6:

I told The Guv I couldn't meet him at the cabin after school today because I was temporarily indisposed, but that was a lie. My monthly visitor is running a bit late. It's true that we got carried away that last night in San Francisco, and took no precautions. But by then, I should have been safe. I've been late before, so I'm not going to worry too much at this point. The whole concept of worrying about it at all is so new to me. Probably it's nothing.

A week later, on Wednesday January 13, she wrote:

Still nothing, so after school yesterday I called the gynecologist in Adams, where I am not known, and asked if I could make an appointment for late afternoon. The receptionist seemed to understand and got me in today. I think my body was already telling me the answer, and the doctor only confirmed it. He was understanding, and said he could refer me to a doctor in Redding, who is known to take care of the problem for women in my situation. I hope that isn't necessary, but no matter what happens now, my life has changed. And what I am thinking of most now, is how I am going to break the news to The Guv. I shall take my time on that question. It is important that I tell him in the right way and not give the impression that I am pressuring him.

Then, the following day:

After crying myself to sleep last night, and feeling bad about being so weak, I was awakened by the ringing phone shortly after two o'clock. It was my mother, and she was hysterical — only this time she had a good reason: Father's car had run off the road, and over an embankment, killing him. I can't imagine why he would have been out so late at night, and he is normally such a careful driver. But then I thought about how worried he'd been lately, and immediately I felt guilty for being so absorbed in myself that I hadn't given him more attention, tried to talk to him about what was going on with him. I will never forgive myself for not thinking more of him at a time when he needed my support. After sitting up with mother (and Greg) for four hours, I dragged myself to the high school and sleepwalked my way through the classes. I have arranged for a substitute teacher to cover for me tomorrow. At the moment, I feel simultaneously numb and overwhelmed. It's as if I'm standing outside my body watching all these things happen to someone else. I have heard of people having nervous breakdowns and never thought it could happen to me, but maybe this is what it is. Off to mother's now. Perhaps comforting her will do me some good.

The Peninsulas came up again in the journal Wednesday January 20.

Father's project was approved by the County Board early this morning. I had not been following it as closely as I should have, and there was talk today at the school that the vote was very close and the outcome something of a surprise. I suppose I had been assuming all along that because it was father's project, it would turn out all right. What I heard today at least explains why he had been so worried the past two months. How sad that he couldn't know it all turned out well. I miss him terribly. It has been a long time since I was his little girl, but I always felt he was there for me and I could count on him. I wouldn't want to tell either of my parents about my current predicament, but forced to choose between them, I would have gone to father. Mother is becoming more demanding by the day, and I struggle to remind myself that she needs compassion now. There is too much going on!

Saturday January 23, Charlotte and her lover met for the first time since the first weekend in January.

Rendezvous at the cabin this morning, and I broke the news of my condition to The Guv. I had anticipated the possibility that he would not take it well, but was shocked at how badly it went. His face clouded over, and the first words out of his mouth were, "If you think I'm going to leave her because of this, you're mistaken." I felt as if he had run a spear through me. Could he really believe I had done this on purpose? Can he have forgotten that he was the one so caught up in passion that Tuesday night in San Francisco that he didn't want to break for precautions? (Although, to be fair, I didn't insist.) I tried, in vain, to reassure him that I was putting no pressure on him and that it had been a mistake, but it was as if, the moment I broke the news, we were on opposite sides of a door that had closed between us. I tried to make a dialogue of it, but to no avail, and finally he said, "It's over between us, Charlotte. I'll pay to get rid of it, but then that's it." At that point, I summoned what dignity I could muster and left. I went home and have no idea what I did the next four hours, but finally decided to try grading my students' papers on Pride and Prejudice. *As I was reading the first one, it dawned on me: The man I thought would be my Darcy turned out to be Wickham instead. I have always prided myself on being a good judge of people, yet when it mattered most, my judgment was spectacularly wrong. What a cruel lesson in humility!*

By Tuesday January 26, she had reached a decision.

After thinking of almost nothing else for three days, I have decided to end the pregnancy. I couldn't bear to have a child and give it away, and if I tried to raise it myself, without a husband, I would lose my job and become an object of scorn in the community. In teaching I have found something I know I am good at, something that allows me to make use of my God-given talents. With that to hold on to, I can have a life worth living. I got the referral to the doctor in Redding, and was able to make an appointment for the morning of Lincoln's Birthday, Friday February 12th, when we have a school holiday. The appointment is for 9:30, but I will not be able to drive afterwards and will have to go with someone. The question is with whom? I don't have a close friend to lean on, so will have to ask someone for a favor I may never be able to repay, and trust that person with the greatest secret of my life. Ordinarily, I would feel up to that, but after misjudging The Guv so badly, I am skittish — to put it mildly. Yet it must be done. And whatever it costs, I will find a way to pay for it myself. I will not allow myself to be obligated to The Guv in any way.

Wednesday February 3:

I made a decision yesterday about who to ask, and this afternoon invited Julia Baker over to my house after school. She is a second-year science teacher, probably eight or nine years younger than me, who has always struck me as being level-headed and fair-minded. Also, she is getting married in June and moving to Southern California, so if she can keep quiet for four months, my secret would leave town with her. Finally, when I had poured the tea and told her what I wanted to ask of her, she leaned across the table, put her hand on my arm, and said, "Of course I'll do it, Charlotte. I did this for my college roommate a few years ago, and I know how much it meant to her." I had been terribly apprehensive about asking, fearing rejection or condemnation. Instead I got compassion and the gift of a reminder that I am far from the only woman to have gone through this. We worked out the details today, and by the time she left, all was set.

Friday February 12:

Awake at three this morning and couldn't get back to sleep. Was it any wonder? Since four o'clock, I have been sitting at the kitchen table, drinking tea and looking out at the darkness. It is now 6:30, and Julia should be here any minute now. I am dressed and ready, and the first light is in the eastern sky. I am wearing the pearl pendant and apricot scarf and wonder if I am being sentimental or perverse. Whichever it is, I feel that going into this event, I need tangible reminders of what got me there, and perhaps, with the pendant, a way of having The Guv present in some symbolic fashion. I see headlights up the street. Time to go.

Saturday February 13:

Back home and a bit woozy; I am putting mother off by telling her I have a touch of the flu. The doctor was professional and very kind. When he did his follow-up check on me, he said he hoped some day he would be able to assist at the delivery of a baby I wanted. It was a lovely sentiment, and I'm sure he says that to all his patients, but it has no bearing on me. Already, I can feel mother's demands irrevocably sucking me into living with her and taking care of her, and, once in that position, any slight hope there might have been of love and marriage is over. At least I will have my work, and can get back to it Monday — or Tuesday at the latest.

"WELL," SAID EL, "Anything interesting in there?"

"Too much," Gordon replied. "I wouldn't know where to start.

"You want to tell me about it?"

"I think I should hold off. It wasn't what I expected, and I need some time to digest it."

"Fair enough. She gave it to you, after all."

Gordon looked at his watch. It was five minutes past five. The rain had stopped, and while it was still cloudy, with rumbles of thunder in the distance, the storm appeared to have passed, and the clouds were letting more light through.

"You have any plans for dinner?" he asked.

"I don't know. It's my birthday, so I guess I should do something special."

"No kidding? Well, happy birthday."

She gave him a long look. "You're dying to ask, I can tell, but you're too much of a gentleman. I'm 49 today. I don't know why women make such a big deal about age. It's just a fact."

Gordon nodded his head slightly.

"You know what I'd really like for birthday dinner?"

"Tell me."

"You're a fisherman, right? I'd like you to catch me a trout for dinner."

"Well, where would I go to catch it?"

"Right here, silly. Just fish from the deck. There are fish rising out there almost every night."

"All right … sorry to be a spoilsport, but I just realized my rod and gear are back at Stanhope House."

"I have a rod. Let me go get it."

She disappeared into the bedroom and returned shortly with a gear bag and a rod inside a case. Gordon took the rod out and examined it.

"Very nice," he said. "This was hand-made by a guy in Sacramento who had quite a reputation. Don't know if he's still doing it or not."

"Andre bought it when we decided to move here. Think you can catch a fish with it?"

"I can try."

He put the two halves of the rod together, attached a reel from the gear bag, threaded the line through the rod ferrules and added a leader from the bag. In the bag was a small box of flies that had seen better days. He finally found a size 14 Yellow Humpy that might pass for a terrestrial insect to an undiscriminating trout.

"Can I watch?" she said.

"Only if you promise not to laugh."

They stepped onto the deck. The air had that clean, hyper-charged freshness that follows a big storm, and Gordon breathed it deeply. He went to the right corner of the deck, where he could back-cast without hitting the house. Working the rod carefully, getting to know its flex and feel, he finally shot a cast 80 feet out into the lake. The fly landed on the water, sat there untouched for several minutes, and slowly drifted back toward the deck. Gordon picked up the line, made another cast to a point 30 degrees left of the first one. As the fly began drifting back to shore, a fish smacked it.

"Fish on!" he shouted. "Not much of one, though." He quickly reeled in the fish, a six-inch Rainbow, and lifted it out of the water with the rod. Taking the fish in his left hand, he quickly removed the hook with his right hand and dropped the fish in the water, where it swam off in a hurry.

"Go tell your grandpa we want to see him," Gordon said. El laughed.

"Look," said Gordon, "this could take a while, and even if I caught a good-size fish, I might not be able to horse it up to the deck like I did that little guy. I had a really nice trout dinner at Año Nuevo Pines Tuesday night. Let me take you there for your birthday dinner."

"All right. I'm easy." She looked at her watch. "If we get there before six, we should be able to get right in. Just lean the rod against the house while I get a sweater, and let's go."

Gordon carried the rod to where the deck dead-ended against the front of the house and leaned it against the corner, under the overhang. By the time he was back inside, she was ready. They took his Cherokee, and he brought Charlotte's journal with him in the messenger bag.

The restaurant was busy, so they decided to chance the weather and sit outside, where there were more open tables and fewer people. After the menus were brought, she leaned across the table.

"Would you like to split a bottle of wine?" she said.

He hesitated. "I'm driving, so I shouldn't have more than one glass."

"So you do drink. You just weren't because of Peter."

Gordon nodded. "He seems to be doing all right now, but I was worried about him, and I wasn't alone. When you're doing surgery, you can't afford to have a drinking problem — even a bit of one."

"I recognized the look in his eyes. I saw it in Andre when his drinking got bad. Let's order by the glass, then, but do have one anyway. We need to loosen you up a bit tonight."

"All right. But just one."

They ordered separate glasses of wine and dinner. El went for the trout, and Gordon chose pork medallions in a port wine sauce. When the wine arrived, they toasted each other and took a sip.

"I've been thinking more than usual this birthday," she said. "Maybe I'm getting to the point in my life where I feel I have to clean up some issues. Like reconnecting with my father. He's 75 and seems healthy, but who knows how much longer we have to set things straight."

"Dear old Dad," Gordon said. "I hear you on that one."

"You too?" Gordon nodded. "What does your father do?"

"He's a judge," Gordon said. "He was up here years ago to preside over the trial of the lawyer who shot his wife ... "

"I'd forgotten that. I covered the trial, but I didn't remember the judge's name. He did a really good job of running the trial."

"He would, of course. Everybody says he's a terrific judge. He sets high expectations for the trial lawyers, just as he does for everybody else, including his family."

"Surely you've met those expectations."

"Not entirely. It probably isn't possible. You know, I still remember when I was in high school, playing for the basketball team. It was the second to the last game of the season, and we were playing a team that was tied with us in the standings. Whoever won would be league champion and go to the playoffs. I was on fire that game. Scored 42 points, which was a school record, and we won the game by eight points. But I fouled out with 45 seconds left, and that's all he talked about on the way home. Never good enough. It's the story of our relationship. He still thinks I'm a failure because I didn't go to law school."

"You don't believe that, do you?"

"That I'm a failure? No. I was very good at what I did, and I certainly made good money at it. But at a certain level, it wasn't satisfying."

"In what way?"

"What I was good at was looking at numbers and guessing whether they'd go up or down. The people who trusted me with their money appreciated that, I think, but I'm not sure what good it really did. I mean, it's not like I was creating a business or jobs or anything of value. I just had a knack for figuring the numbers."

"You're being too hard on yourself."

"Maybe. But I'll tell you something. When Charlotte London put me in charge of her papers and her family history, I wasn't very happy about it. Now, as we get deeper into it, and I see what the stakes are, I'm sort of glad this happened. I feel that I'm pushing myself to do something that's really important for someone who put a great deal of blind trust in me."

"You don't want to let Charlotte down."

"Exactly."

"And you won't tell me what was in her journal?"

"Not now. It wasn't at all what I expected, and I have to think about it. Probably bounce it off Gina, too. Maybe tomorrow you'll know more."

The storm clouds had begun to break up, and rays of bright sunlight were illuminating the mountains on the other side of the lake. They watched the play of light on the mountains for several minutes without saying a word.

"We were starting to talk about your father," Gordon said, "before we got sidetracked. Anything you want to get off your chest?"

"We didn't get along, obviously. We still don't. My older brother and younger sister always toed the line, but I was the wild one. I didn't even feel I was being rebellious at the time — just curious. But let's face it. Having a daughter who spent the Summer of Love in the Haight would try the most tolerant of fathers, never mind someone as conservative as mine."

The food arrived, and El took a bite of her trout, chewing it slowly and appreciatively.

"This is really good," she sighed.

"You've said several times your father was — is, I suppose — really conservative," Gordon said. But you've never mentioned what he did."

"He was a minister. Still is. Prince of Peace Lutheran Church in Marin County."

THEY TOOK THEIR TIME with dinner and lingered over dessert and coffee, talking comfortably, like old friends. By the time they got back to the house, there was just the faintest hint of light in the sky, and the moon, nearing the first quarter, was descending to the horizon in the west. El opened a side door and stepped out on the deck, Gordon followed her.

The temperature had cooled into the high 60s, and the air was still slightly humid from the storm. The evening sky was full of stars. Along the shore, crickets were chirping, and in the shallows of the lake, several frogs joined them in full throat. They could see lights along the shore across the lake, and also along the shore on their side, but at some distance. A sense of quiet and solitude enveloped them, and for a long time, they said nothing.

"On summer nights like this," El finally said, "I'm really glad I bought this place."

"It's probably pretty awesome in the winter, when a storm's moving in," said Gordon.

"It is. In a different way, of course. You really feel the seasons in the mountains. Growing up in Marin County it seemed as if it was always cool summer or warm winter and hard to tell which."

Gordon nodded. They were leaning against the deck railing, and somewhere in the lake, a trout rose with a loud splash.

"What do you think?" he said after another silence. "Are we making any progress on Charlotte's case?"

"We're making progress all right. There's already enough for a story that should light a fire under our sheriff. And I think that with everything we're coming up with, we may be circling the solution. We need more information and the inspiration to see it in a way that points to the answer. Also, I'm dying to know what's in her journal."

"You're too young to die, so you'll have to wait. I need to talk to Gina about how to handle it.

"You can't even give me a hint?"

"Sorry."

There was another pregnant silence.

"You know what I'd really like to do for my birthday, Gordon?"

"I'm afraid to guess."

"I was just thinking about it. I'd like to run naked through a fountain again."

The darkness, fortunately, masked Gordon's reaction.

"I haven't done that since I got married, and it would be a hoot to do it again. There are only three problems."

Gordon maintained a strategic silence.

"Number one is that I probably need at least one more glass of wine before I try it. Number two is that there aren't any fountains in this damn town. And number three is that it's beginning to dawn on me that I'm getting a bit old for that sort of thing."

"You shouldn't say that. You're a very attractive woman."

"Don't just tell me, Gordon. Show me."

He did.

.

Part III: Secrets

"No man, for any considerable period, can wear one face to himself and another to the multitude, without finally getting bewildered as to which one is the true."

—**HAWTHORNE**, *The Scarlet Letter*

Sunday June 23

WEARING A BATHROBE provided for the occasion, Gordon was sitting on a couch in the living room, a cup of coffee in one hand and Charlotte's journal in the other. The day had dawned clear, bright and cloudless. All traces of the storm had vanished, and the morning air was as clear and pure as a high-country stream.

Now, with El in the shower, he was looking through the section of the journal following Charlotte's abortion. The breakup, the pregnancy, and the death of her father seemed to have taken the starch out of Charlotte. She averaged three entries a week, rather than the previous six or seven, and these entries were typically half as long as what had come before and mostly concerned with the minutiae of her life.

He found two interesting nuggets, however. The first was an entry dated Saturday February 27, in which she reported meeting with her brother and the Paris family. They informed her that her father had picked out a lot on the Peninsulas for her and that they would see to it that a first-class house was built for her on that lot whenever she was ready. It was clear that the house that had burned down less than a week ago was the result of that meeting.

The second point was that her senior English class had apparently taken to *Pride and Prejudice*, and several students had written excellent papers on the book. Gordon took this as a sign that however demoralized Charlotte might have been, she still took pleasure in seeing her students get excited about a great book.

Reaching the end, he realized he had overlooked the last entry, dated Sunday February 28.

Really good service today. Father Michael spoke on the St. Francis prayer, and I have been reflecting on the second part of it: "Lord, grant that I may seek rather to comfort than to be comforted; to understand, than to be understood; to love than to be loved. For it is by self-forgetting that one finds. It is by forgiving that one is forgiven. It is by dying that one awakens to eternal life." Not so sure about that last one, though I think Eliot (George, not T.S.) may have put it better at the end of Middlemarch. *What those words do tell me, though, is that I need to focus on what I can offer the world, to help others, and, above all, forgive The Guv. The forgiving won't be easy, but I shall vow to work at it until it happens.*

There were several blank pages at the end; Charlotte apparently didn't like to break up months over two journals and had decided this volume didn't have enough pages left to contain her writings for March. Gordon carefully looked through all the pages — just to be diligent. When he turned the last one, reaching the inside back cover of the journal, he saw something else.

The inside cover had a diagonal flap running from upper right to lower left, providing a pocket in which stray pieces of paper could be slipped for safekeeping. It held a folded piece of pink paper, and Gordon gently pulled it out. The paper was wrapped around a faded Polaroid photograph that showed several people gathered around a bright red pickup truck, with what appeared to be Lake Año Nuevo in the background. Holding the picture up to the morning light, Gordon looked at it closely. There were two middle-aged couples, and one of the men was clearly a younger version of Roger Paris. The other man was standing with his wife (presumably) and a young man and woman. The woman looked like a younger, but still determined and confident Charlotte. Gordon guessed that he was looking at the London family, including Charlotte's brother, whom he had not yet met. Two younger men stood next to Roger Paris; they could quite plausibly be younger versions of his sons Ronald and Robert. Turning the photo over, Gordon could see, written on its back in Charlotte's unmistakable cursive, the legend, "Labor Day picnic, East Peninsula, 1970." It was in pencil, and, judging from the fading of the paper on the back of the picture, had probably been written shortly after the photograph was taken.

Gordon put it back in the flap and frowned. The first question he had to consider was whether Charlotte had deliberately placed the picture there for him to see, should he ever come into possession of the journal, or whether it had been there for years and she had forgotten about it. There was nothing to indicate an answer one way or another.

He spread the pink paper on his lap and immediately recognized it as a relic from a bygone time. Back in the days of typewriters, many offices kept double-carbon memo sheets. They were triplicate sheets of 5 ½-by-8 paper used for memoranda, which, typed or handwritten on the top page, were copied through on to the pages below. The original page was sent to the recipient of the memo and the two copies, usually on different colored paper, duly filed. Howell, Burns & Bledsoe still used them when Gordon began working there in 1981, and the pink paper before him was a copy of a typed memo that read as follows:

To: Roger Paris
From: Ned London

Re: Crocker Bank Proposal

Roger, I have been giving this matter due consideration — thinking of nothing else, really. Try as I may to see your point of view on this, I cannot bring myself to go along with it. We are going to have to find some other way. I'm sorry. Can we meet tonight at your house or mine to discuss it privately and in more detail?

There were several strikeovers and cross-outs in the brief memo, indicating London had typed it himself rather than dictating it to a secretary, and it was signed, simply, "Ned," in a way that made the three letters look like a long scrawl. It wasn't until he read it the second time, though, that Gordon spotted the most salient element of the memo.

It was dated January 13, 1971, a week before the vote on the Peninsulas project, and the day Ned London had died in the auto accident.

GORDON NOW FELT CERTAIN that Charlotte had deliberately placed the photo and the memo in the journal before mailing it, but what did they mean? There was enough opacity in both documents to confound a more knowledgeable reader than himself, and he began to get irritated. Didn't these people ever spell anything out? Why was Charlotte the one woman in ten (or more) who didn't name her man in her private journal, but left him a cipher? Why did her father say nothing revelatory about the Crocker Bank proposal? Gordon guessed it was some sort of risky financial deal to fund the development and that, coming as late in the game as it did, it must have been important. But that still left him in the dark, and he couldn't imagine what pretext he could concoct for asking the Paris family about it.

As he was thinking all this, he heard someone turn the handle of the front door from outside.

Thinking of his unknown stalker, Gordon felt a jolt of fear go through his body like an electrical current. The door was locked, but the lock was simple, and the door itself didn't look any too stout. Anyone who really wanted to get in could do so quickly, and El's house was isolated enough that there were no neighbors to take notice.

He jumped up from the couch, darted over to the kitchen area, and opened a drawer by the sink. He found several knives in it and grabbed one with a sharp, nine-inch blade. Holding it in his right hand, he moved over to the hallway facing the door just as it began to open.

The woman who came through it looked like no villain. She was, in fact, beautiful, even in worn jeans and a hoodie: in her 20s, tall, slim, with raven-black hair and almond-shaped eyes a man could look into forever. As she walked into the house, she saw Gordon, saw the knife, and stopped. She spoke first.

"You're wearing The Robe, so you must be mom's new squeeze," she said, looking him up and down. "I see she's going younger. I'm Anna, by the way."

She extended her right hand. Gordon put his left hand behind his back, transferred the knife to it, and put his right hand out to her.

"Gordon. A pleasure to meet you." He paused. "We weren't expecting you until next week."

"Is that what she said?" Anna pulled down the hoodie and tossed her head, whipping her shoulder-length hair backward. She was one of the few women Gordon had ever seen make that gesture without looking affected or juvenile. "Well, she's as hopeless about dates as she is about men, so I can't say I'm surprised. I hope there's some food here. I'm really hungry."

"Actually, we were about to go out for breakfast," he said. "I'm sure … "

El emerged from the bedroom. She was wearing a pair of well fitting jeans, but was barefoot and topless without a bra. Concentrating on pulling on a light sweater top, she began talking without really looking around.

"I hope you're ready for breakfast, Gordon. I'm starving. It's been quite a while since I had that much wholesome exercise at bedtime. I could get used to it."

Top in place, she turned to where Gordon was and saw her daughter.

"Honey. You're home early."

"I'm home when I said I'd be, mother. It's good to be here."

"It's good to have you here."

They embraced, and there seemed to be genuine warmth in the hug, which went on for a minute. When they broke off, El turned to Gordon.

"Anna, this is … "

"Don't bother, mom. We've been introduced."

There was a brief, awkward silence.

"I'm hoping Anna can join us for breakfast," Gordon said.

"I'd love to," she said.

"Then we're waiting on you, Gordon," said El. "That has to be a first: The women waiting for the man to get dressed." She laughed. Anna frowned.

"I'll be ready in a minute," he said.

It was less than ten feet to the bedroom door, which led to his clothes, but it seemed to Gordon like the longest, most self-conscious walk he had taken in his life.

"I WAS HOPING TO DRIVE all the way up yesterday," Anna said, "but by the time I got to Sacramento I was beat. Finally, I pulled over in Williams and caught a few hours' sleep at Motel 6 and headed up this morning." She looked at Gordon. "I guess it worked out all right."

They were drinking coffee at a corner table at the Shotgun, waiting for breakfast. In an hour, Gordon and El were due at Senator Bart Sturges' house, and he was grateful for the self-imposed deadline on breakfast. The unplanned get-together was making him uncomfortable.

"So has anything exciting been going on in this old town?" Anna asked.

Gordon and El looked at each other. She answered the question.

"Do you remember Miss London, from the high school?" Anna nodded. "Well, she was killed in a fire at her house this past Monday."

"Oh, no. That's awful!"

El looked around the restaurant. It was the period between the early breakfasters and the after-church crowd, and they had some speaking room if they talked quietly.

"And it looks as if it may have been deliberate." She turned to Gordon. "Shall we tell her?"

"Might as well," he said, "But you do the talking. I'm getting tired of telling that story."

El launched into it, just as the food arrived, and Gordon, as he listened, felt she was doing it justice — hitting the key points and making it coherent, without missing a critical detail or including an unnecessary one. Gordon, as he ate and listened, looked back and forth between mother and daughter. He was thinking he'd like to see Anna smile; that it would be something special. But despite a couple opportunities for her to be amused by the sheriff's bumbling, he saw no such thing. She was serious all the way through. When El finished, he cut in.

"Did you have her as a teacher?" he asked.

"Junior and senior years. Probably the best teacher I had here. A lot of the kids made fun of her and her obsession with books, called her an old bat — that sort of thing. But by the end of the year, almost everyone in her classes had fallen in love with at least one of the books she was teaching. She had a way of making you see what was there that you never would have seen by yourself."

Most people, Gordon thought, would have smiled at the old bat line, but not Anna.

"And what book did she get you to love?"

"*Great Expectations*. I identified with Pip, wanting to get out of his life, but I don't know that I would have seen through the caricatures to the moral purpose of it, if she hadn't made that come across. And taught me how to write about it."

"The writing is valuable," he said.

"It's interesting. In the first year of law school, you could really tell who had a teacher like Miss London in their background and who didn't. There are people in law school who are as bright as can be, but who really struggle to get something down on paper. Because of her, it's been easy for me."

The check arrived. They were due at Sturges' house in 20 minutes, and it was a 15-minute drive.

"So what's in the journal?" Anna said.

"I'd rather not say right now," Gordon replied. "I'm still trying to sort it out, and I'll probably ask the group for guidance this afternoon. Do you have any thoughts on that?"

"Well, you're her literary executor, aren't you?" He nodded. "That means she's put you in charge of everything she wrote and left it to your discretion how to deal with it. If you wanted to publish that journal as a book, you could do it."

That might be legally correct, Gordon thought, but recalling a couple of Charlotte's descriptions of amatory episodes, he would expect her to rise from her grave and haunt him if he did such a thing.

"It's pretty private stuff. I don't know," he said.

"At any rate, it sounds like you're doing something important here."

"We'll see how it goes," said El. "And I was thinking with your legal background you might be able to contribute something to our research." She looked at Gordon. "What do you think, Gordon? Do we want her on our team?"

Gordon was already uncomfortable about having made Anna's acquaintance wearing intimate attire. He was becoming increasingly annoyed about the fact that she seemed incapable of smiling. And the way the investigation team kept growing (partly his fault, he had to admit) had him wanting to make a sarcastic remark about how they'd have to hire a hall for their meetings if the group got any bigger. But years of working at the brokerage had taught him not to say everything he thought, so he smiled (I can if she won't, he thought) and said:

"Sure. Why not? The more the merrier."

"That's how I feel," said El. "I'm a great believer in the power of the group. I think all of us together can come up with ideas that none of us could by ourselves." She turned to Anna. "We'll be meeting at the house this afternoon at 4:30. Can you be there?"

"If you want me to, mom," Anna said. "And if I won't be interfering with anything."

Damn her, thought Gordon. She didn't even smile when she said that.

EVEN BY THE STANDARDS of The Peninsulas, Bart Sturges' house was large and impressive. It was 4,000 square feet and sat on the west side of the West Peninsula, with a sunset view, looking across the lake to Arthur. It had a modern design, with high ceilings, facades of wood and river rock, and a cantilevered deck over the lake, clearly designed by an architect infatuated with Frank Lloyd Wright.

Sturges answered the door himself. He was five-seven and in good shape, with brown eyes, a well-cut head of gray hair, and a square face with a strong jaw. Dressed in khakis and an aqua/turquoise polo shirt, he looked like a man on his way to the links. The razor-sharp part in his hair matched the razor-sharp crease in the khakis. Gordon, no slouch at dressing up when he wanted to, guessed the trousers (and shirt, too) had cost a pretty penny at one of San Francisco's fine men's stores.

The Senator led them through a large living room and sliding glass doors that opened out onto the deck, where a round table with three chairs awaited. The deck was still in shade and was strewn with fragrant pine needles, blown loose in the previous day's storm. Sturges offered coffee (which they accepted) and pastries (which they politely declined), then leaned back in his chair, waiting for his guests to begin the conversation.

"Thank you for meeting with us on such short notice," El said.

"I always have time for *The Clarion*. Have I ever told you, El, that when I'm in Sacramento, I have each week's paper flown to me overnight so I can keep up on the local news?"

"You've told me about 20 times, Bart. But I don't get tired of hearing it." They both laughed.

"Speaking of which," he said, "I was going to introduce a resolution commemorating Charlotte London when the Senate reconvenes on Tuesday. It'll be the only thing we pass unanimously all day. Can I count on your story about her for some of the facts."

"Nobody's disputed anything yet. So it's that bad in our state capital?"

"Seriously, I almost didn't make it up here this weekend," he said. "We keep wrangling over the budget. It's supposed to be approved by July first, but I don't think we're going to make it this year. After a meeting with the Republican whip yesterday morning, I concluded nothing was going to be accomplished until next week and came up. I always feel better here than I do in Sacramento."

"In two more years you won't have to worry about it any more," said El.

His facial muscles tightened. "Don't get me started on that. Term limits! What a crock. They go against the fundamental principle that the voters are smart enough to decide things for themselves. You know, if the people decide they don't want me to represent them any more, I can accept that and sleep like a baby at night. But to be told I can't run again in 1998 because I've served too many years — during which I might add, I've learned how to get things done for my constituents — that's just bullshit. But it's the law, so there you are."

Gordon interjected.

"So, senator, do you think you'll be running for another office in two years?"

"Are we on the record yet, El?"

"Not if you don't want to be."

He leaned forward and looked at both of them. "Just between us for now, I'm looking at a couple of possibilities. What I'd really like to do is run for Insurance Commissioner, but that's a statewide race and would take a lot of money. There's some talk that our seat on the State Board of Equalization may be open in two years, and all my Senate district is in that district, so it could be more manageable. And, of course, if we elect a Democratic governor in two years, I could probably snag an appointment to a state commission. One way or another, I should be all right."

"And whatever happens, will *The Clarion* be the first to know?"

He put his hand over his heart. "Swear by everything I hold sacred."

"You're touching the wrong body part for that," she said. They both laughed again. "But you need your time off, so let's get to what we're here for. The Peninsulas."

He nodded without saying anything.

"I'm afraid we dropped the ball on the 25-year anniversary of the project approval, but the silver anniversary of the groundbreaking is coming up soon, so we can do a little catch-up. That was a big issue and a big vote early in your political career, wasn't it?"

"Interesting that you missed the first date," said Sturges. "That says something, don't you think? The Peninsulas have become such an accepted part of this community that nobody remembers what all the fuss was about 25 years ago."

"It was quite a fuss at the time, though," said Gordon. "I've been reading about it, and it seems the community was pretty evenly split, with strong feelings both ways."

Sturges nodded.

"I wasn't here then," said El, "but from what I can make out, you were quite the focus of interest. Did you have a lot of dealings with the London and Paris families?"

"Everybody wanted to talk to me," Sturges said, appearing pleased by the recollection. "In the three weeks leading up to the vote, I was meeting nearly every day with either Ned London — well, before his tragic death — or one of the Parises, Roger or Ronald. The Chamber of Commerce was by to see me practically every day. So was Celia Strickland, who was leading the opposition, and Pearl Wilder of the Sierra Club, God rest her soul. There were so many people coming by my office it was hard to get to lunch some days."

"I've heard," said Gordon, "that on the day of the meeting you had two speeches with you. One to read if you voted for it, and one if you voted against. Is that true?"

"Now who told you that?" he said with a smile. "I think I can guess, but it doesn't matter now, and it'll make your story better, El. Yes, I had two speeches. I woke up that morning thinking I was going to vote for it, but I was willing to listen to all the testimony and change my mind if something new came up. It didn't. But like Eisenhower at D-Day, I was ready with a speech, however it went."

"But again, Senator, it seems as if your vote surprised a lot of people. Looking back at the news stories at the time, you were pretty definite about opposing the project beforehand."

"Your intern has obviously done his homework. You hired well, El. But let me explain a little something to you about the facts of political life, Gordon." He still had the smile, but his speech was becoming tighter and more intense.

"I know what you're talking about, but you have to remember one of the first things any candidate or elected official learns — sometimes the hard way. You always have to have an exit strategy, some way of changing your mind if it seems like the thing to do.

"If you go back and read those articles closely, and if they quoted me right, which I think they mostly did, what I said was that I couldn't support the project *as submitted*. Remember those last two words, because they're crucial. What a lot of people forget is that after the election, when it looked like the county board was going to be against the project, the London/Paris group modified it. They moved the golf course back from the lake and removed about 30 building lots to do it. Over a period of six months, I'd been gradually coming around to the position that some sort of tourist/recreation development was necessary here to offset the decline in logging. Those changes allowed me to say that with the modifications made to the plan, I could now support it."

"But were the modifications really significant?" asked El.

"They weren't just window-dressing. The golf course being too close to the lake was the biggest environmental issue, as far as I was concerned, so moving it back was the right thing to do. And those 30 lots they cut came straight off their bottom line. I suspect that was Ned London's doing. He was more willing to listen to public concerns than Roger Paris. But it gave me some cover to vote yes." He stopped to take a sip of coffee. "The reality is, and don't quote me on this, that if I'd decided the economic development issue was critical and I wanted to vote yes, they could have changed the color of the cover on the plan from red to green, and I could have said, 'It's a different plan now, and I can support this version,' and voted for it."

There was a long break in the conversation, punctuated by the background noise of power boats zipping across the lake.

"Isn't that kind of cynical?" Gordon finally said.

"You can call it cynical; you can call it anything you like," said Sturges. "I just call it smart politics."

BY THE TIME THEY ARRIVED at Shore Acres, the temperature had climbed to the low 80s. Celia Strickland was dressed for the weather, looking more like one of her customers than the proprietor. A woman of middling height and weight, with long gray hair and a frequent scowl, she was wearing shorts, running shoes, and a T-shirt that read "Año Nuevo Run for Breast Cancer, October 5, 1991." She brought Gordon and El into the fireside room in the main building, offered lemonade (which was accepted), and plunked herself down in a chair at an angle to the couch on which Gordon and El were sitting.

"So you want to talk about The Peninsulas," she said. "They're there. We lost. The good guys don't always win. What else do you want to know?"

"I'm working on a story about the anniversary," El said, "and Gordon is Charlotte London's literary executor. He's going to be responsible for the family history she's writing. Both of us thought that as one of the leading opponents of the development you might have something to say that would help both of us."

"I could talk all day if you'd let me, but that would probably be more than either of you need. Maybe ask some questions."

"I've looked at some of the newspaper stories," Gordon said after a brief pause, "and it's not clear from them how extensive the opposition was. What's your sense of what the community thought back then?"

She shifted in her chair and took a sip of lemonade.

"I'm guessing half the town was for it and half against. But it's hard to say. The committee that organized the opposition had about a dozen members, but except for me, the others are all dead, moved somewhere else, or so old they don't remember much. If I'm going to be the only source for that, I'll try to be careful."

"The stories said some of the opponents wanted the peninsula lands to become a park."

"About three-quarters of the committee wanted a park; the rest didn't want anything. Keep it wild, they said."

"And you?"

"I could have gone either way. On the record, I supported the park because I thought it was politically the best alternative. It would look better if we weren't just saying no."

"Was a park a real possibility?" asked El.

She nodded. "Those were different times. The state had money then. Not like now. If the legislators who represented this area had pressed for it, the land could have been bought for a state park. There probably would have been a couple of hundred campsites built and a boat dock, but most of the land would have been protected from development. It would have been more in keeping with the character of the community."

"What do you mean by that?" Gordon said.

"When the reservoir was built after the War, a pretty good little tourist industry grew up within a few years. Most of the places were like this. Shore Acres was built in 1952, and we bought it from the original owners in 1960. They established it as a place where working people could come for a two-week vacation they could afford. It catered to families, and there was a real mix of people who came here year after year. It was very democratic.

"A state park campground would have been a democratic place, too — something that would have attracted all sorts of people from around the state. Not like those obscene houses in The Peninsulas. The rents on those are two to three times what my cabins cost! Only doctors, lawyers and executives can afford that. It's a playground for the rich now."

"Would a state park have done as much for the local economy?" El asked.

"I'm not an economist, but I doubt it. That wasn't our argument, though. If you made the argument about money, the developers won. We were concerned about quality of life. There are a lot worse things than being a sleepy little community that's true to its own values. It resonated with a lot of people, but not enough to change the way things turned out."

"Looking at it from the family history perspective," said Gordon, "I'm curious as to how you saw the players in the development. How did the Londons and Parises relate to each other, and what did they do in the process?"

"It was Ned London's idea at first. He saw the possibilities. I'll give him that, even if his vision wasn't mine. He obviously expected to make a lot of money from it, but I think in his heart, he felt he'd be profiting by serving the community. And he was the voice of the project. Without him being involved, it wouldn't have had half the public support it did."

"And the Paris family?"

"The worst kind of business people. Nothing mattered to them but the money. If they could have made more money by selling that land for a state prison, they would have done it in a heartbeat. I had a bit of a soft spot for old Ned, but none for the rest of them."

"How about Bart Sturges?"

Her scowl deepened. "He sold out," she said. "Plain and simple. I think he was really against it, but he wanted to run for the state legislature later and needed help from the business community. They got to him and changed his vote. The last few times we talked to him, he was wavering, but I was still shocked when he cast the deciding vote in favor. I'll tell you something. I haven't voted for a Republican for any office in a quarter of a century, but there's one Democrat I've never voted for either, and that's Sturges. My little vote doesn't matter much in the great scheme of things, but I can't bear to give it to him after what he did."

"What was the opposition's overall strategy?" said El. "I mean, you wanted the county board to reject the application, but what did you think would happen after that?"

"They'd have been over a barrel," she said. "We'd been working with State Senator Don Allen, and he was ready to introduce a bill to add the peninsula lands to the state park system, but only if the county board refused the development. The London-Paris partnership would have had to take an offer from the state at that point, even if they lost money. Too bad for Ned, I suppose, but if you want to get rich, you have to take risks, and they don't always pan out."

"Really?" said Gordon. "That's not what the Parises said when I talked to them a couple of days ago. Ronald Paris said they would have come back with a smaller-scale plan and gotten that approved."

She laughed: A loud laugh that began as a hoot and descended into a cackle.

"Is that what they told you?" she said. "Is that their lie? Because that's what it is — a lie. If they came back a second time, they'd have been up against See-kwah."

"Excuse me."

"CEQA. The California Environmental Quality Act. I can see that doesn't register, so let me explain. In September of 1970, the state passed a law that required, among other things, that an environmental impact report had to be done on any significant land development project. The application for The Peninsulas had been filed just before, so the law didn't apply to it. But if the county board had rejected that first plan, any plan submitted after that would have had to go through the environmental review process. They couldn't have done it.

"It would have taken time to get an environmental report researched and written. It would have taken time to have county staff review it and make changes, especially since it would have been the staff's first time doing something like that. It would have taken even more time to put it out for public comments and rewrite the report to include those comments and responses to them. And if the county had approved the second proposal, we could have sued, claiming the environmental report was inadequate. The whole thing would have taken so much time and cost so much money, the developers would have bled out financially.

"And that's not all. I happen to know for a fact that Ned and Roger took out a loan to buy that land, and they had to make a large balloon payment in December of 1971. With a plan approved, it would have been no problem to refinance. With no plan approved, or with a plan approved but in litigation, nobody would have loaned them a dime. So you see, it was all or nothing as far as they were concerned. If they didn't get their original plan approved, they were beyond screwed."

She paused for another sip of lemonade.

"But, of course, they *did* get it approved. So it was the rest of us who got screwed."

"THE MEETING IS CALLED TO ORDER," Gordon said.

Anna had joined the group and was sitting next to her mother on one of the couches, with Emma Crisp on the other side. Peter and Gina were on the other couch, their body language showing signs of tension. Gordon wondered what that was all about, but figured he'd get an answer soon enough. Karl and Alice sat in separate chairs.

"Charlotte's journal may take some time to discuss," he continued, "so let's get the other matters out of the way first. El, you want to brief the group on our meeting with Bart Sturges this morning?"

"Well, he was charming, as always. Don't look at me like that, Gordon. He went on at great length about how he'd left himself an option to vote for The Peninsulas back in 1971 and did it because of economic development. He went on a rant about term limits and what he's thinking of running for next. He's looking to move up politically, so if there was something shady about the way The Peninsulas were approved, it could give him a motive for wanting Charlotte and her manuscript out of the way."

"But wasn't he in Sacramento Monday night?" asked Alice.

"That's the story, and if it checks out, he couldn't have done it.

Karl coughed, an "excuse-me-but-can-I-have-your-attention" cough.

"Aren't you forgetting something?" he asked. El looked at him. "It's well known that Sturges is a pilot and has his own plane. Most of the time he comes here from Sacramento, he flies up. With no control tower at our airport, it's possible he could have flown in and out that night and not been noticed."

"Good point," said Peter. "Leave him on the list for now, but I'd like to see more than a 'maybe' motive before I take him seriously as a suspect."

"Gina," said Gordon, "Can you tell us about your meeting with Gregory London?"

"Not very productive," she said. "He was out of the loop on the development; said he was mostly managing the existing property business while his dad worked on the project. Seems to have hardly known his sister, either."

Gordon looked around the room. Nobody had a comment.

"All right. Remember what he said in case some of it jibes with something else we hear. The talk with Celia Strickland yielded a bit more. El?"

"She remembers it like it was yesterday and resents it that way, too. But she had a lot of good information. What I got out of it was her saying the strategy was to get the original plan rejected, which would have put the London-Paris partnership in a financial trap. They apparently had a large balloon payment to make at the end of 1971 and couldn't have made it or refinanced it without a project that was approved and ready to go."

"Along those lines," Gordon said, "I came across something this morning. It was tucked into the back of Charlotte's journal." He took out Ned London's memo on the Crocker Bank proposal and read it aloud. "I wish we knew what that was, but I'm guessing it was some risky way of refinancing the project. I'm sure the Parises could tell us about it if they wanted to, but I'm not sure I should be letting them know I have this memo. Any thoughts?"

"Crocker Bank has never had a presence in this county," Karl said.

"You're sure of that?"

"Positive. I wrote a monograph for the historical society on the history of banking in Forest County. It's a fascinating subject."

"No doubt," said Peter, "but all that tells us is that they seemed to be looking outside the county for money and dealing with a bank that doesn't exist any more. That's going to be next to impossible to run down."

No one responded.

"If anybody has any other ideas, speak up," said Gordon. "Then I found this in the back of the journal." He took out the Polaroid of the London and Paris families at the lake and passed it around.

"Labor Day, 1970," said Karl taking the first look. "Did she say anything in the journal about it?"

"Just a throwaway sentence that they had the picnic. No details."

"Hold for more information," said Peter.

"Good idea, Peter. Is there anything else before I get to Charlotte's journal?"

"I'm dying to hear," said Alice.

"I'm afraid to," said Gina.

"First of all," Gordon began, "I'm going to tell you that there's next to nothing about The Peninsulas development. Charlotte mentioned that it was taking a toll on her father, but that seems to be the extent to which she was aware of it. Most of the journal, in fact, was taken up with a matter that was deeply personal and private, and I'm really not sure how much I should be disclosing at group level. Gina, you were her best friend. I'd value your opinion."

She shifted position on the couch.

"Charlotte gave you that journal for a reason," she finally said. "She was afraid and couldn't have imagined that you'd end up dealing with so many people who knew her, but I feel she would have wanted you to follow through on it. And that could mean getting our help." She took a deep breath. "I'd say tell us the bare facts and let us decide how much more we need to know for what we're doing."

No one contradicted her.

"All right, then," he said. "In 25 words or less, in the fall and winter of 1970 and 71, Charlotte was having a torrid affair with a married man."

The silence after he spoke was absolute. Gina put her face in her hands and shook her head.

"Charlotte!" she moaned. "You dumb bunny."

"She's hardly the only woman to do that, you know," said El.

"Who was he?" Gina asked, looking up sharply. "If the bastard's still alive, I'll kill him myself."

"I'm afraid she didn't identify him. Or provide much in the way of clues. He was married, and she said at one point that the age difference wasn't insurmountable, so I'm guessing he was older."

"Or he could have been younger than she was," said El. "That happens sometimes."

Gordon had the grace to blush. "She was 35 then, so, yeah, he could have been younger."

"How did it start?" asked Anna

"That's one clue, at least. He started flirting with her at the annual Rotary Club new teacher luncheon in

September, so it had to be someone who would go to that event."

"I hate to burst your bubble," said Gina, "but that's a really big deal around here. Everybody's there except the town drunk."

"I've never been," said Karl.

"She meant everybody who wants to be," said Alice helpfully. "But I agree; that hardly narrows the field."

"At one point, he quoted poetry to her. Sir Walter Scott."

"Not 'Lochinvar,' I hope," said Gina. "She hated that poem."

"Actually, 'The Lady of the Lake.' Who in town is poetically inclined?"

"Almost no one, judging from the traffic in the poetry section of the library," said Alice. "But he knew she was an English teacher and could have come by to look something up to impress her."

"Not that any man would do such a thing," murmured Peter.

"Well, what did she call him?" said Anna. "Or did she just say 'he?' "

"Early on she called him Secret Admirer or SA," Gordon said. "But later, she started referring to him as The Guv. British slang for governor, or lord."

"Hold it," said Gina. "Some of the teachers at our school like to refer to the principal as the governor. Drove Charlotte nuts. Maybe that's why. If we could find out who was principal at the high school then, we might have our man."

"Karl?" asked Gordon.

"I'd have to look it up," he said.

"I can do better than that," said Alice. "One of my neighbors is Virginia Bolton, who was the receptionist at the high school back then. She's retired now, but still sharp as a tack. She could not only tell me who the principal was, but give me all the dirt on him."

"Sounds like we're making progress," said El.

"But we shouldn't put all our eggs in that basket," Gordon said. "I've noticed a couple of men in town, including Judge Fletcher and Coach Iverson, who lit up a bit when they talked about Charlotte. A lot of people liked her, and one of them may have tried to take it a bit further."

"Point taken," said El, "but let's see what Alice comes up with. There's one other thing you haven't told us, Gordon. How did it end? Not well, I'm guessing."

"I don't know if I should go into that."

"This is no time to be squeamish, Gordon," said Peter. "I saw her, and she was clearly worried. Whatever she gave you may be the key to her murder. Out with it."

"I agree," said Gina. "We can handle at least the critical facts."

"OK," Gordon said, taking a deep breath. "Short version: She got pregnant and told him; he dumped her; and she had an abortion."

Again the room was utterly still. It was finally Anna who spoke.

"That was 1970 or 71? *Roe v. Wade* wasn't until 1973, so it was an illegal abortion, right?"

"Actually, no," said El. "California passed a very liberal abortion law in 1967. I know because I got pregnant that summer."

"In the Haight?" said Anna.

El nodded. "The price of free love. I didn't know what to do, but there was an Episcopalian minister who hung around the scene back then, and had a reputation for helping young women who had got in trouble. He connected me to a doctor who did abortions, and it was all up front and legal. I still feel bad about it, but I don't know what else I could have done. My father would have killed me."

"I wish that had been true a few years earlier," said Gina. "My best friend in high school got pregnant in 1962. It was against the law — abortion, I mean — but there was a doctor who was known to do it anyway. I borrowed my parents' car one day and told them we were going shopping, but instead I took her to the doctor. Thank God he knew what he was doing! Another girl at our school went to a different doctor, started bleeding afterwards, and nearly died. She could never have children."

"Let me interject," said Gordon. "What would have happened to Charlotte professionally if her pregnancy had become known?"

"They'd have fired her for moral turpitude," said Gina. "No ifs, ands or buts. She couldn't have had that baby and taught here again. When I got here in '81, an unmarried teacher got pregnant and the board refused to renew her contract."

"But that's illegal," said Anna.

"Yeah, but they figured she wouldn't sue, and they were right."

Anna shook her head. "It's hard to believe it was ever like that," she said. "There's a woman in my law school class who broke up with her boyfriend right out of college and found out she was pregnant. It would have been almost impossible to go to law school and become a mother at the same time, so she did what she felt she had to do. She's near the top of the class now."

"God," said Alice, "This takes me back. I remember when *Roe v. Wade* came down, I expected my mother to be aghast. She was such a good Catholic. When the subject came up the next time I visited her, I expected a rant, and I got one. But the rant was all about how what a woman decides to do about her pregnancy is no one else's business and she was glad the law finally caught up with that. I came away from it thinking she must have had a friend who went through that."

"Maybe she went through it herself," said Karl.

"Karl!" shrieked Gina.

"No, it's all right. I thought of that myself, actually. I'll probably never know."

"Well, since we seem to have gotten into a discussion on the subject," said Peter, "I'm wondering if Karl can give us a historical perspective."

Karl cleared his throat. "A couple of years ago, I was looking through the *Forest Clarion* for 1909 and came across a story. A prominent local woman — the wife of a banker, actually — got pregnant with what would have been their eighth child. She couldn't face the prospect of having another baby, so she went to a midwife in town who had a reputation for taking care of such things. This time, though, something went wrong, and the banker's wife died. The midwife was arrested and tried for murder, and the case went to a jury …"

"Great," said Gina. "They were all men, I suppose."

Karl nodded. "They were, and the verdict was not guilty." He looked around the room. "They deliberated only 15 minutes."

"GETTING BACK ON TOPIC," said Gordon, "Is there anything else for today, and if not, what do we have to try to find out before tomorrow's meeting?"

"I think it's really important to find out who The Guv was," said Gina. "Charlotte made a big point of getting the journal to Gordon in case anything happened to her. If the journal's almost all about her affair, the identity of her lover is critical."

"I agree," said Gordon, "and suggestions welcomed. The problem is that all we know about him is her love name for him, that he was younger or older than Charlotte, and that he had the wherewithal to look up poetry to impress her. That could fit any man who was halfway intelligent."

"Maybe this is a wild goose chase," said Alice, "but for as long as I've been here, there have been rumors that Senator Sturges has an eye for the ladies."

"They're not just rumors," said El. "I know for a fact he's capable of propositioning a woman who isn't his wife."

Gordon shot her a quizzical glance, which she caught.

"Hey," she said. "It was only once and it was more than ten years ago. Can we move on, please?"

"If he fits that part of the profile," said Peter, "maybe we should take a closer look. How old is he?"

"Fifty-five," said Alice. "Six years younger than Charlotte. I looked up his biography when I knew we'd be talking to him."

"And back then he was a young politician on the make," said Peter. "Maybe people joked he'd be governor some day, and that's where the endearment came from."

"It's possible, I suppose," Gordon said. "But meeting him today, it's hard for me to see. He's kind of full of himself, and that seems to me to be something she wouldn't like in a man."

"She wouldn't," Gina said, "but maybe he wasn't so full of himself then. It's possible."

"Everything's possible," Gordon said with exasperation. "That's the trouble with that question and this whole case. All speculation and no fact."

"But speculations often lead to facts," Karl said. "I'm just a history drone, but even I can see that the ideas are giving us something to look into. For instance, now that we're taking a look at Sturges, I'm thinking that maybe tomorrow I can go down to the airport and see what I can find out about his plane."

"Good idea, Karl," said Gordon. "No harm in trying."

"Something else," said Anna. "Isn't there a third Paris son, and didn't he move out of the area?"

"Richard Paris," said Gina. "I think he lives in San Francisco.

"I wonder if there was more to his leaving town than having the wrong vowel in his first name?" Peter said. "Maybe Gordon could call him up and ask a few questions in connection with the London family history. If we can find him, that is."

"I'll find him," said Alice, writing it down in a small notebook.

"And I'll keep after Adam Beckstein, the reporter," El said. "If he doesn't call me tomorrow morning, I'll call him again."

"And Peter and I," Gordon said, "have an appointment to meet with Chief Davies in Cabrillo tomorrow morning. Charlotte was planning to see him but was killed before she could, so he may have something important. We can hope."

"This is just like historical research," Karl said. "You think there's something there, but you don't know what. So you keep chipping away at it from different angles, and quite often you eventually get it."

"Anything else?" said Gordon. He looked around and saw Emma Crisp sitting quietly on the couch. She hadn't said a word. "You've been quiet tonight, Emma. Any thoughts for us?"

"No, no. Not really," she said. "I'm still new to this and just trying to take it all in."

"That's all right," said Gordon. "But if you have any idea at all — even if you think it's crazy or stupid — share it with us. We're lost, and we have to be open to anything."

She nodded. "I will," she said softly.

Gordon turned to El. "What time tomorrow?"

"Five o'clock work for everybody?" she said. There were several nods, and no dissents. "Five o'clock it is."

Everyone began moving and pulling things together. Anna went straight to her mother, and began talking earnestly to her. Gordon felt he had to hold back until they were done. By the time that happened, the last of the group was leaving, and Anna was headed for her room. El came over.

"Can we put it off tonight?" she said in a low voice. "I've hardly seen Anna at all today, and I really need to spend some time with her."

"Sure," said Gordon. "I understand." And he did, but wasn't happy about it.

He walked out the front door into a lovely summer evening, warm with just a hint of a breeze. He saw Peter standing next to the Cherokee at the top of the stairs and made his way there. For a full two minutes, both of them stood looking out over the lake and the house without saying a word. Peter went first.

"Bachelor dinner at Garbini's? I suspect we have some catching up to do."

"SO?" said Gordon.

"I could say the same thing," said Peter.

"You first."

"No, you. I insist."

"Toss for it?"

Peter sighed and reached into his pocket for a quarter. They were seated in the back booth at Garbini's. It was fairly busy, with more of a Sunday family crowd. Sinatra was singing "One for My Baby, and One for the Road," barely audible over the crowd noise. Peter flipped the coin.

"Tails," said Gordon.

"Tails it is." He looked at Gordon, who nodded. Peter took a deep breath.

"I suppose in a couple of years, I'll be able to laugh about last night, but at the moment, my sense of humor is in the deep freeze. It was almost five o'clock when Gina and I finished talking with Gregory London. I still hadn't heard from Stella, so I figured she got scheduled on an extra shift and couldn't make it. It's a pretty common thing with nurses. And you were over at El's reading Charlotte's journal, with no idea when you'd be out. So I asked Gina to dinner at Ike's Lakeside, and off we went.

"We were there early, got a nice table by the window, and the conversation started going really well. Mostly we talked about this case and Charlotte. Gina's really glad this group is working on it, and she said, for whatever it's worth, that she's beginning to understand what Charlotte might have seen in you. We went over all the elements of it, and she did some speculating about what might be in the journal … "

"How close was she?"

"Not even on the same continent. Anyway, we raked the ground of the investigation pretty well. And I don't say it was just my imagination, but I think a certain rapport was developing, aided by a couple of glasses of wine."

"Hold it!" said Gordon. "Who was drinking that wine?"

Peter looked sheepish. "She had a glass to start with, and when they brought dinner, she asked for another, and I decided to have just one to be sociable."

"Oh, Peter."

"It's all right, Gordon. I haven't had a drink in three months, and it was just one. I'm not having one tonight. It's OK."

Gordon shook his head, and Peter moved forward with his story.

"When dinner was over around seven, I figured you'd be calling or coming back to Stanhope House, so I suggested we go back there and wait for you. We went up to my room to settle in until you called. I unlock the door, open it for Gina, she steps inside, and screams.

"My first reaction was that whoever ransacked your room had come back, so I jump into the room, testosterone flowing, ready to face the bastard down. Instead, I see Stella sitting up in the bed."

"Oh shit."

"Wearing a beautiful, diaphanous negligee she bought two weeks ago, no less. She got off work at 6 a.m. yesterday, grabbed a few hours of sleep, then started up here to meet me. But she forgot to recharge her phone, so she couldn't call. Instead, she decided to surprise me."

"Which she clearly did. So how did you respond?"

"Under the circumstances, I couldn't see anything else to do but tell the truth. I know, it's out of character, but hard cases make for hard choices."

"I don't suppose there's any chance she took it well?"

"Let me answer your question with another question, Gordon. When your girlfriend is waiting for you in your hotel room, and you walk in with another woman, and you have alcohol on your breath, and you try to explain it by saying that you were coming to the room to discuss a murder investigation ... Well, do you have any idea how lame that sounds?"

Gordon considered the question for a full minute.

"Off the top of my head, Peter, I can't imagine anything more lame. And she could smell just one glass of wine on your breath?"

"The woman has a nose like a bloodhound. I don't know how she can stand working in a hospital. But there you have it. Gina remembered a friend she had to meet and hared it out of there, and Stella read me the riot act while she was getting dressed and stalking out. And I spent the rest of the night in my room, waiting for you, with only my imperfections for company."

"At least you weren't alone."

"And since you didn't come back, I'm assuming you got to the end of the symphony."

"Don't look so pleased with yourself, Peter. Even Watson could have figured that out."

"Anything you want to tell me about it?"

"I don't know. It just happened."

The waitress arrived with their salads, and they waited until she had gone before resuming. Peter picked up his fork, but instead of using it on his salad, he shook it at Gordon.

"Come on, Gordon. I expect better from you. Saying it just happened puts you in the same league as the people I used to treat in the emergency room. Guy comes in with three gunshot wounds, and you ask how he got shot. *I don't know. It just happened.* All right, what were you doing when it just happened? *I was enjoying myself with an attractive lady when her old man came home early and shots were fired.*

"So don't tell me it just happened. Let me rephrase the question. Did she tie you up at gunpoint and have her way with you, or did you make a decision?"

"All right, I made a decision."

"That's better. Now we're getting somewhere. And do you know why you made that decision?"

"Well, I do like her in a funny sort of way. And the chemistry was right. What does it matter, Peter? This is almost the 21st Century. You don't have to intend marriage before you sleep with someone."

"True, but you have to exercise some judgment, and I'm beginning to wonder about you in that regard. You know who El reminds me of? Susan Sarandon in *Bull Durham*. You saw that, didn't you?"

"Sure."

"Remember, how she picked out a different ball player to sleep with each year. I'm beginning to wonder if our newspaper editor picks out a different tourist to sleep with each summer."

"That's not fair."

"Plus she's the queen of overshare. I hope you didn't choose her for her discretion."

Gordon took a bite of his salad and chewed it slowly.

"You're approaching it from the wrong angle, Peter. I've come to have some respect for El in a short time. She's smart, she's tenacious, and her heart's in the right place. The way she put together this group to look into Charlotte's death shows all of those things. But she's also who she is, with no pretensions, and she doesn't care who knows it. You can call it overshare, but I call it lack of guile. I meet too many women in San Francisco who are trying hard to act perfect and maintain appearances. It's kind of a relief to find one who's unself-consciously herself. Her daughter is the kind of woman I see all the time in San Francisco, and she doesn't understand or appreciate her mother. I hope she will some day."

"When and where, exactly, did Anna come into the picture? She hasn't been here all along, has she?"

"No. Actually, she came home from college early this morning and walked in on us. Or more accurately, on me. Sitting in the living room wearing only a robe from El's closet."

Peter shook his head.

"There seems to be too much of that sort of thing going on around here."

"At least in my case, what she saw was exactly what it looked like. Unlike you, I was spared having to explain."

Monday June 24

AFTER A BRIEF STOP at the Hellwithit Bakery, Gordon and Peter left for their appointment with former Highway Patrol officer Alvin Davies. The 75-mile drive to the town of Cabrillo was designated on the maps as one of California's scenic routes, and it lived up to its name. Looping around the east side of the lake, they connected with a county road that went through a long stretch of densely forested land and descended into a valley with lush green meadows ringed by steeply forested mountains. At the other end of the valley was the town of Redman, which slowed their progress for three minutes.

Ten miles south of Redman, they came to the junction of the state highway leading to Adams. It went through the heart of town and bent south, eventually picking up the middle fork of Hawk River. Along the river were numerous turnouts where an angler could park and clamber down to the water, but neither man was thinking of fishing that morning. They passed through several small towns of a few hundred souls, some of which lacked even a gas station, and finally reached a junction with another state highway heading east toward Cabrillo, and, beyond that, Nevada.

The pine trees were beginning to thin out somewhat, with clumps of sagebrush springing up between them. As they drove toward Cabrillo, the sagebrush-to-pine ratio increased. It was starting out a fine summer day, and the drive was magnificent. Uncharacteristically, Gordon and Peter barely spoke during the hour and a half they were on the road.

Twenty miles from the junction, signs of civilization — in the form of scattered dwellings, many with discarded vehicles and appliances in the yards outside — indicated they were approaching Cabrillo. Like many western towns, it had originally been built with the railroad and the horse and buggy in mind, then adjusted to fit the automobile in the 20th Century. The original settlement, now called Old Town, was south of the highway, on the other side of the south fork of Hawk

River. At this point, close to its headwaters, it was a 20-foot-wide creek running through a weedy channel, engineered to accommodate flood waters. Along the state highway were two grocery stores, four motels (all dating back to at least 1954), three cafes, four gas stations, five bars, two frosty joints, and a smattering of other small businesses.

They crossed the river into Old Town, turned left off Railroad Avenue on to Lincoln Street, and drove up a forested hillside. At the top was a cleared area with several portable buildings. This was the civic center of Cabrillo, and the police station was the first portable on the left.

Behind the counter was an attractive, businesslike woman in her mid to late 30s, with wavy hair and large glasses. She looked up, saw Gordon, and smiled pleasantly.

"May I help you?"

"Quill Gordon and Peter Delaney," he said. "Chief Davies is expecting us."

She leaned backward and glanced into an office.

"He doesn't look too busy," she said. "Come on in."

She opened a swinging door and let them into the work area. Gordon, used to the security at the Hall of Justice in San Francisco, shook his head. They followed her to a door, where she paused and said, "Chief, your appointment is here."

The man at the desk pushed an inch-high pile of papers to the left side of his blotter and stood up. He was five-nine, in his early fifties, putting on weight, and wearing a pair of gray dress slacks and a white button-down shirt with no tie. His eyes were blue, and his grayish-black hair was cropped to within a quarter-inch of his scalp and receding in front. He gave Gordon and Peter the head-to-toe Lawman's Appraisal, then waved them in, gestured to two chairs facing his desk, and sat down. They did the same.

"How was the wedding?" asked Gordon, remembering that the chief's son was being married over the weekend.

"It was a wedding," he said, with a shrug. "They're all nice, I suppose, but it's the living afterward that's tough."

"I hear you," said Peter.

Davies was leaning back in his chair, looking at them warily. Gordon knew the chief was playing the game of letting the other fellow speak, and decided to play it himself. After a minute, Davies leaned forward.

"So you're here about Ned London," he said. "What do you know about it and what do you want from me?"

"I've read your report," said Gordon, "which was clear and thorough. And I've read the news articles that were written at the time." Davies nodded, almost imperceptibly. "On the face of it, everything seems straightforward."

He took a deep breath and tried to read Davies, knowing that what he said next could make or break the interview.

"As I think I mentioned over the phone, I'm the literary executor for Ned London's daughter, Charlotte. She was working on a family history, which I'm now trying to finish. She died in a fire a week ago today, and though nothing's been said officially, it's looking as if her death may not have been an accident. In her manuscript, she has a notation that her father's death was somehow questionable, and that she needed to talk to A.D., which I assume was you. So I'm here to do the interview she couldn't."

Davies turned his chair to the left and looked out a window at the trunks of nearby pine trees. He was still looking at the trees when he spoke.

"Did you have a specific question?"

"That's just it," said Gordon. "I don't. I don't know what Charlotte London was concerned about or suspected might have happened. But I do know that she was a tough, smart woman. If she saw smoke somewhere in that accident, I'd be inclined to believe there was fire. You're sure acting like it. When I said I'd read the report, you could have told me everything was in it and sent me on my way. Instead, you're trying to draw me out about what else I know."

Davies, his hands making a steeple at his mouth, continued to look out the window.

"Am I right?"

Davies turned back to face Gordon.

"I always wondered if somebody would come asking about this some day," he said.

"Why don't you tell us the whole story of that night, as best you can remember it," Gordon said softly.

"I don't know if it would help," he said. "At the end of the day, I don't know if there was more to it. All I know is I thought so at the time."

"Maybe you should start at the beginning," said Peter, in his best bedside voice. "What were you doing that night when you got the call, and what happened from that point on?"

"All right. Maybe it'll help me, too." He covered his face with his hands, inhaled deeply twice, and put his hands on the desk.

"I have a surprising recall of that night, considering how long ago it was. It was a Wednesday night in January, so hardly anyone was out and about. It was looking like another cold, slow winter night. At 10:45 I pulled into Grady's Market in Arthur (out of business now). They closed at 11, but I knew the regular night clerks. They always brewed a fresh pot of coffee at 10:30, and I'd come by to fill my thermos before closing."

"Did you have a partner?" asked Gordon.

"They figured I didn't need one on weeknights, and that was generally true. I filled my thermos, got into the car, and the radio came on. They'd got a call from Ned London's family that he'd been at Año Nuevo Pines, hadn't come home, and the people he was visiting said he'd left over an hour ago. Usually there's nothing to those calls, but it gave me something to do.

"I drove out of town, bright lights on, looking carefully along the roadside for a gray 1967 Buick LeSabre, which was what he was driving. I turned left on the state highway that goes down the west side of the reservoir and drove slowly to Año Nuevo Pines, but didn't see anything. I wasn't expecting to, but you never know. I turned around and started going back slowly to check it from the other direction. When you only have one job to do, you stretch it out as long as possible. About three miles from the subdivision, I came to the point where the highway climbs up and hugs the cliff about 100 feet above the lake before dropping down again.

"Don't ask me why because I couldn't tell you, but as I was going uphill, it occurred to me that this was the only place along the way that a car could run off the road and not be seen. Near the top of the rise, there's a little turnout, and I pulled into it. I got out of the car — and by the way, it was colder than snot outside —and started walking along the side of the road to see if there were any indications that something had gone over."

"Wait a minute!" said Gordon. "There's a guardrail there, and it certainly should have stopped an ordinary passenger car."

"There's a guardrail now, but not in 1971. It was pretty much a straight drop down to the water if the reservoir was full or to a rocky shore if it was down a bit. There hadn't been much rain or snow that fall and winter, so the lake was down. Anyway, I decided I'd go a hundred yards in each direction from where I'd parked, then go back into town and radio in that I'd checked and found nothing.

"Except that's not what happened. There'd been a snowstorm at the end of December, and most of it had melted off, but there were still a few small patches of snow along the edge of the road. I was running my flashlight along the edge of the dropoff, when I came to a patch of snow, about three feet by two feet. There was a fresh tire track cutting diagonally across it in a way that whatever made the track would have kept going over the edge. I looked over and saw the lights of a car that was on its side. I called out a couple of times, heard nothing, then hotfooted it back to the patrol car and the radio and called for help.

"It was a hell of an operation. Fire trucks, tow truck, ambulance, sheriff's patrol. Everybody was out there. Two firefighters went down on ropes and said there was a body inside, beyond help. Took an hour and a half to get it back to the ambulance. It was dawn before they got the car back up. One of the deputies knew the family and went to tell them. I went back to the office because the

225

commander had told me to write it up right away. I wasn't sure how to do that, because I had the distinct feeling something wasn't right."

"That can happen to people who know their business," Peter said. "Happens with doctors a lot. Why were you dissatisfied?"

Davies spoke slowly and carefully. "I'd been on the job two years at that point. I had a good feel for every stretch of road in the county. And one of the things I'd come to believe is that it isn't the tight, dangerous stretches of road that kill people. That's where drivers get cautious and slow down. It's the flat, open roads that are dangerous, because that's where they get careless and take chances. So I really don't know why I thought of an accident at that spot that night. I'd never seen anyone go off the road there. Not a tourist in the dead of summer; not a teenager going too fast; not a drunk coming home in a snowstorm. Just didn't happen. Then you get someone like Ned London, who's lived here all his life, doing it. It didn't feel right."

"Had he been drinking?" Gordon said.

"When they did the autopsy, his blood-alcohol level was .08."

"So he was legally drunk."

"Not then, he wasn't. You're probably too young to remember, but in those days the presumptive limit for intoxication was .15." Gordon whistled. "I know. It was lowered to .10 not long afterward, and then to .08 when Mothers Against Drunk Driving came along. But Ned London was careful and knew the road. He shouldn't have run off it with that amount of alcohol in him. And there was something else."

He looked at Gordon and Peter.

"When they finally got that car back to the road, it was pretty beat up, as you'd expect if it had rolled over a couple of times going down that cliff. But on the driver's side there was a different colored patch of paint, not more than six inches long and a couple of inches high. That car had collided with something else beside the side of the cliff."

"But could you say when?" Peter asked.

"That's just it. You couldn't. I noted the paint mark in the original report and went out for breakfast. When I came back, the captain wanted to see me. He pointed out what you just did — that it could have happened earlier and might have had nothing to do with the accident. And he pressed me on whether there was anything else at the scene that would indicate that Ned London's car had collided with something else before going over the edge. I had to admit there wasn't. The captain told me to take out the part about the paint. Said it could cause an uproar for no good reason, and that we were unlikely to ever find out where it had come from. I didn't like it, but I followed the order."

"That wasn't by the book, was it?" Gordon said.

"No, but back then a lot of stuff wasn't by the book. If you pulled over someone from a good family late at night and they were drunk, you'd tell them to take it slow getting home. That sort of thing. Leaving a detail out of an accident report to avoid a fuss fit right in."

"What do you think really happened?"

"What I think is that Ned London's car was sideswiped by another vehicle, and that's what sent him over the edge. I couldn't tell you if it was accidental or deliberate, and I can't prove a thing. But that's what I think."

Davies rose, stepped to a filing cabinet on the right side of his desk, removed a sheet of paper from a manila folder, and set it on the desk in front of Gordon.

"I saved the original page 3 of the report. The page where I mentioned the paint streak. You can have a copy if you'd like, but I'd appreciate if you didn't tell anybody where it came from."

Gordon thanked him and put the paper in his messenger bag. There seemed to be no more to say, and after a pause, they rose to leave. As they reached the door, Peter stopped and turned back to Davies.

"Could I ask one more thing? The guardrail that's on that stretch of road now. When did it get put in?"

"Fall of 1975. I can tell you without a doubt. It was in the budget approved that summer." He paused. "Bart Sturges was elected to the Assembly in 1974, and the appropriation for that guardrail was the first bill he introduced when he took office."

THEY ROLLED INTO ADAMS just before one o'clock and stopped for lunch. The town, tucked into a small valley, with houses hugging the surrounding hillsides, was originally built as a stop on the Hawk River Railroad and had the look of a village in the mountains of New England, especially in the fall when the trees changed color. The railroad hadn't carried passengers or mail for years, and the abandoned station had been converted into the Old Station Café and Deli.

After ordering soup and sandwiches, they sat at a table on the outdoor deck. The lunch crowd was beginning to thin out, and they felt comfortable talking.

"What do you make of it?" Gordon said.

"He seemed pretty certain," said Peter. "He could be wrong, of course, but as a general rule, I'd tend to go with the hunch of a veteran cop. The good ones have a sixth sense about that sort of thing."

Gordon nodded. "And he seemed like a good one. I wonder what Charlotte would have thought if she'd talked to him."

"She was already suspicious. He'd have just confirmed the suspicion."

"Still, it doesn't move us forward very far. It's just a hunch. Even if he's right about Ned London being run off the road, there's nothing to say who did it. Any ideas?"

"From the opportunity standpoint, you have to like the Paris family. He was leaving their house. They knew he was going to be on that stretch of road."

"All right, but we've also seen from our friend who smashed my car window how easy it is to follow someone without being noticed. And what would their motive be? They were partners; they all had the same stake in the project."

"Be that as it may, he was going to their house to express his disagreement with something involving Crocker Bank. What if the disagreement was so serious that Ned London had to go?"

"Over a question of financing? Hardly seems like a reason to kill someone, even in the heat of the moment."

"Let's put it to the group," Peter said. "Maybe someone will think of something."

The food arrived, and after a couple of bites, Peter turned the conversation in another direction.

"At the meeting last night," he said, "did you pick up on what I did? When you were talking about Charlotte's journal, every woman in the room, without being prompted, volunteered an abortion story from her own experience. It obviously struck a chord and shows how common it is."

"And how seldom we hear about it." Gordon shook his head. "A horrible situation Charlotte was in. I'm glad I didn't have to make the decision she did."

"She chose not to be a character in one of the books she taught." Gordon raised his eyebrows, and Peter continued. "*The Scarlet Letter*. Pretty obvious, really. Now all we have to do is figure out who was playing the part of Dimmesdale."

"Easier said than done. About all we know is that there was an age discrepancy." He took a bite of his sandwich and chewed it carefully. "I've been thinking about that whole age issue a lot the past few days."

"I wonder why."

"It's another reason I'm glad I'm not a woman. I mean, I hate to say it, but most of the time they're smarter and tougher than we are, and all it gets them is a disproportionate amount of grief. And some of it begins with assumptions. El is 12 years older than I am, and if we got into a serious relationship, nearly everyone would think it was 'off' somehow. Not right. But if I started going out with her daughter ... "

"Not that you would."

"Not my type. Anyway, if I started going out with Anna, who's 13 years *younger* than me, no one would bat an eye. Where's the fairness in that?"

"There isn't any. Next question."

"It's funny. You and I come up here and find ourselves charmed by El and Gina —women older than we are. The journal is ambiguous on the point, but Charlotte may have been older than her lover. And in the family history, her great-grandmother was older than her husband by a few years. This place is like the forest in

Midsummer Night's Dream, where enchantment's in the air."

"As a man of science, I'd be more inclined to ascribe it to coincidence than enchantment. And in the case of Charlotte's great-grandmother, I doubt it caused much comment," Peter said. "There weren't a lot of single women in those frontier towns. The few who chanced it held the whip hand when it came to choosing a mate."

They ate in silence for a few minutes.

"So," said Gordon, "speaking of women, just how bad off are you after Saturday night?"

"Pretty bad, I'm afraid. I called Stella this morning and left a message offering to try to patch things up. It's a long shot, I know, but I have to at least try. We'll see."

"You said you had alcohol on your breath. She might be taking that worse than she took Gina."

"Could be. A big part of the reason I didn't drink for three months was her influence. She's been good for me, and I hope she can forgive. I don't expect it, and she'd be justified if she didn't. But I can still hope."

BACK IN ARTHUR, Gordon parked at Stanhope House. Peter went in to rest, and Gordon walked to the newspaper office. El was on the phone, but waved him into her work area. He took a seat at a chair next to her desk.

"You're absolutely right, Mrs. Mooney," she was saying. "We'll do everything we can to get to the bottom of this. You can rest assured of that."

She rolled her eyes as the person on the other end replied.

"No, we won't involve the sheriff. If you're right, he's part of the conspiracy."

The reply to this went on for three minutes. El was taking no notes and made typing motions on the desk with her free hand.

"I couldn't agree with you more," she finally said. "Do you have any other information we can follow up on?"

Judging from the time that elapsed before El spoke again, the answer to the question was neither a simple yes or no.

"All right, then. Well, I have to be going if I'm going to look into this. You take care, Mrs. Mooney, and be careful."

Another long pause.

"Right. You, too. Bye now."

She hung up and shook her head. "Thelma Mooney," she said. "She calls around this time every Monday."

"So what, exactly, are you going to look into for her?"

"Nothing, actually. It was a community service call. You see, she's convinced Bart Sturges and Sheriff Ballou kidnapped and murdered her son and buried him in the lawn behind the courthouse."

Gordon blinked. "How do you know they didn't?" he finally said.

"Because I talk to her son at least once a month. Twenty-five years ago, he married a girl she didn't approve of and moved to Sacramento. Over the years, Mrs. Mooney has gradually drifted deeper and deeper into senility and woven an increasingly elaborate story about what happened to her son. Thing is, he calls her every Sunday night and a couple of times during the week. But by Monday afternoon she's forgotten and calls to ask me to do a story."

"I suppose there's no avoiding it?"

"I'm sure I could. But as I say, it's community service. A small-town newspaper is a place people can call to let off steam. It probably makes her feel better for a while to think something's being done about it." She sighed. "She hardly gets out any more, and her husband isn't doing too well. I don't know what's going to happen to her when he goes."

There was a half-cup of coffee on her desk, and she stuck a finger into it.

"Piping hot when she called and stone cold now. Did you find out anything in Cabrillo?"

"Nothing concrete, but an affirmation." He paused. "Davies thinks someone may have run Ned London off the road the night he died."

She whistled. "So Charlotte may have been onto something?"

"Possibly. The main thing is that there was a trace of paint on the driver's side of Ned's car. Davies put it in the original report, but the captain made him take it out. He said there's no evidence the paint transfer happened in connection with this accident and mentioning it could cause a fuss over nothing. Thing is, the captain was right. Not about taking the paint mark out of the report, I mean, but about there being no evidence it was connected with the crash that killed Ned. But Davies' gut tells him there was a connection. He gave me a copy of the original page of that report, as he wrote it."

"Can I see?"

As Gordon opened his messenger bag, the phone rang again. El slammed her desk in exasperation.

"Honest to God," she said. "Some days I want to take a gun and shoot this thing." She lifted the receiver, forced a smile onto her face and said, in a voice that would melt butter, "Elke Sundstrom. How can I help you? Adam! (to Gordon) It's Adam Beckstein. Thank you so much for calling. No, no. This is a really good time. Listen, I have a gentleman named Quill Gordon here who's helping me on this story … Yeah, just like the trout fly. Can I put you on speaker?"

She punched a button. A male voice with a pleasing baritone came over.

"So you want to know about The Peninsulas, eh?"

"That's the long and short of it," she said.

"Lucky for you I remember it like it was yesterday. My first really big story, and for a reporter that's like your first lover. You don't forget. But there was a lot to it. Did you have a specific question?"

El looked at Gordon and nodded.

"Gordon speaking, Adam. I guess to get right to the point, I've been wondering, after looking through the records, about Bart Sturges' voting to approve it. It seemed to take a lot of people by surprise. Do you remember how it struck you at the time?"

After a brief pause, Beckstein said, "Before I answer that, let's be clear on something. I'm talking to you on background, and you're not going to quote me or use my name in connection with any story, right?"

"No problem," said El.

"In that case, I have to tell you I thought it was pretty fishy, but I couldn't prove a thing. And six months later, I moved on to a bigger paper and left that story behind. But I still remember the look of total shock on Celia Strickland's face when Sturges started reading the speech — and he was reading from a script, no doubt about it — saying he was going to vote yes."

"Did you grill him about it?" said El.

"Oh, I tried to pin him down, all right, but he was slipperier than a wet trout. He stuck to the technicality that he'd never actually said he opposed the project, which was strictly true. But I can tell you that sure wasn't the impression the community had."

"Was there anything else that made it look fishy?" Gordon asked.

Beckstein thought about it for a minute. "It doesn't prove anything, and it's only my impression, but it seemed to me that during that public hearing, Sturges and the Paris family were exchanging glances and maybe a hand signal or two. It wasn't something you could put in an objective news story, but I don't think it was just my imagination."

Gordon and El looked at each other.

"But if you think this was suspicious," Beckstein continued, "there's one other question you should be asking."

"Shoot," said Gordon.

"In 1974, Bart Sturges came out of nowhere to win an election for State Assembly. When he announced his candidacy, he already had the best Sacramento political consultant working for him. That didn't come cheap. If it were me, I'd be asking how a cow county lawyer, whose only political experience was being on said cow county's board of supervisors, came up with that sort of money."

"Wouldn't it have been on the campaign financial statements?" said El.

"The reforms triggered by Watergate hadn't come in yet," Beckstein said. "The campaign statements back then were pretty vague. You probably wouldn't get much from them. But to start a campaign with the kind of professional help Sturges did, he'd have needed at least a hundred grand in today's money. Probably 25 to 30 thousand back then. I don't think his three-man law firm was doing enough business to rack up that kind of surplus."

"But to someone who just got a million-dollar development approved … " said Gordon.

"At least a million," Beckstein said.

"Twenty five thousand would have been petty cash," El said.

Beckstein was silent for a moment, before replying.

"You said that. Not me."

WHEN GORDON CALLED THE MEETING to order, he wanted to begin with his report of the meeting with Davies. But Alice was crawling out of her skin with something she wanted to share, and in the interest of involving the entire group, Gordon let her go first.

"It was really interesting what I found out about private planes today. Like I'm always telling people, it's hard to beat a librarian's job when it comes to being interesting. I mean, they're paying me to learn. How good is that? Anyway, I went to one of our research books and looked up California airports, and my God, I had no idea there were so many. I'd never thought about it before, but if every town our size has one, that's a lot. Anyway, after a bit of mucking around, I discovered that in Sacramento, the private pilots pretty much use Sacramento Executive Airport. So I called down there and got hold of the airport manager, who, by the way, did not seem to appreciate answering questions and was in a bit of a grouchy mood. But like my mother said, you catch more flies with honey than with vinegar, so I was just really sweet and nice to him, and kept asking questions, and finally he told me that, yes, it would be possible for a private pilot to fly out of the airport and back again without there being any record of it."

"Wait a minute," said Anna. "How, exactly, did you ask *that* question?"

"Nothing to it. When I called, I told him my name was Marie Lavoisier, and that I was a mystery writer researching a new book."

"And he fell for that?" said El.

"He totally fell for it. In fact, he even told me his wife enjoys my books, which is kind of interesting, when you consider there aren't any. Books, I mean. Marie, too."

"Old librarian trick," murmured Peter.

"Anyway, he eventually got into the spirit of the interview and was surprisingly helpful. He said Sacramento Executive doesn't have a control tower, so a pilot could fly in and out without there being any record of it, though he did say there were so many people around during the day it would be hard to do without being noticed, but after hours, a little more likely. And he said that if a pilot flew from that airport to another one, like ours, that also doesn't have a control tower, there probably wouldn't be any records of the flights at airport level. The pilot would have to record the flights in his log book, but ordinarily that wouldn't be public record and only a mechanic would see it. So I think that establishes something very important. Bart Sturges could have flown up here last Monday night without there being any record of it."

"Good job, Alice," said Gina.

"Nice work," said Gordon. "We may be on to something."

"Except for one thing," said Karl, grumpily.

Everyone looked at him.

"Bart Sturges didn't fly up here last Monday night. I'm sorry, Alice. We were working at cross-purposes. I went down to our airport this morning, and our airport manager told me the same thing. But on a hunch, I asked him if anyone had been at the airport last Monday night. Well, it turns out June 30 is the end of the airport's fiscal year, and he was there until 8:30 that night, pulling together a lot of paperwork in preparation. I told him I'd heard Sturges was still in town late last Monday, and he said no way. He saw him get in his plane and fly off at 9 that morning, and when he left his office at 8:30 that night, the plane was gone and Sturges' car was parked where it always is. The call on Charlotte London's fire came in only a few minutes after that, so it looks like Sturges is out."

"I hate it when the facts get in the way of a good story," El finally said.

"Good work by both of you, even so," Gordon said. "You've eliminated Sturges, and that's something."

"Except you forgot one thing," said Karl. "There are probably half a dozen private airstrips around here, so he *could* have landed at one of those. I don't think that's too likely because he would have needed an accomplice with a car, and it would have been really dangerous to take off again after dark. But it can't be completely discounted."

"All right," said Gordon. "Let's call the Sturges flight up here last Monday a low-probability occurrence and move on. Anything else, Alice?"

"I ran down Richard Paris in San Francisco pretty easily. He has a property management business that's unimaginatively named Richard Paris Management." She handed Gordon a piece of paper. "Here's his number."

"Thanks. I'll call him tomorrow." Gordon looked around the room.

"Should we talk about the conversation with Adam Beckstein?" said El.

"Why not?"

El related the gist of the conversation, concluding with Beckstein's question about how Sturges had raised the seed money for his first State Assembly campaign. When she finished, Peter spoke first.

"What was that line from *All the President's Men*? 'Follow the money.' Any chance of doing that here?"

"Pretty slim," said El. "Campaign finance records from back then — even if you could dig them up from storage somewhere — weren't that good. Before I start chasing that wild goose, I'd like to have something to go on."

"Still," said Gordon. "It's intriguing. Sturges' change of heart on The Peninsulas struck some people as wrong. If there was a payment involved, it would have made a lot more sense. But it's the same story here as with everything else. We have a lot of tantalizing hints without any hard evidence."

"Are we considering some sort of payment as a possibility?" asked Gina.

"I'd say so," Gordon said.

"Then let me throw out an idea. Suppose Ned London's memo about the Crocker Bank plan didn't refer to financing the project. Suppose it referred to arranging some sort of payment using Crocker Bank. Would that make sense?"

"It would totally make sense," said Anna. "Laws on reporting wire transfers were looser then than they are now."

"But again," said Gordon with some exasperation, "How do we find out? Crocker Bank doesn't even exist any more."

"No, but there is one thing. It's a long shot, but I think we should try. When zipperhead …"

"Who?" said Peter.

"Sorry, my ex-husband. When he worked at Crocker Bank in Sacramento in the 70s, the branch manager was a man named Howard Sheehan. I remember my ex saying that the Sacramento branch handled an unusually high volume of wire transfers. Howard thought it might be related to the fact it was the state capital. In fact, he was suspicious enough to have copies made for himself — he even paid for it out of pocket — of all the transfers. Thought it might help in an investigation some day. If he still has those records … "

"If he's still alive," said Karl.

"He retired in 1979, so he'd be about 80 now. I'm sure my ex could track him down. He owes me one. More than one, actually."

"But would Sheehan still have those records after all these years?" said Alice.

"Once a pack rat, always a pack rat. If he's alive, I'd bet a tidy sum he still has those records. And if there *was* some sort of payment, they wouldn't have wanted to make it through a local bank. Should I try to run it down?"

"It can't hurt," Gordon said, after a silence. "But I wouldn't expect much. As you say, it's a long shot. Anything else on this?"

"No," said Gina. "But tell us about your interview with Davies."

Gordon described that meeting, with Peter adding a fine point here and there. He concluded by saying:

"So once again we have a lot of emanations and penumbras, but nothing to hang our hat on. The key thing to me is that the officer who was first on the scene at the accident thought there was something fishy about it, and Charlotte had already made an appointment to talk to him when she was killed. There's nothing you could prove in court, but it's sure starting to look like a story line. Thoughts, anybody?"

No one responded immediately, and finally Karl spoke.

"I could stop by the Highway Patrol office tomorrow and see if I could find out who might have known Charlotte was looking into it. No promises, though."

"Worth a try," Gordon said. "If we check out everything, we just might hit upon the one thing that will open this up. Does anybody else have anything?"

No one spoke, so he continued.

"Then I'd like to end the meeting with this. The more I think about it, the more I believe the key to this investigation is in the journal. And more specifically, the question of who Charlotte's lover was. If we can find out, we might be able to talk to him, and get something we've been missing so far. So I'd like to suggest that we sit here quietly for three minutes and just focus on that issue. Who could her lover have been? Who was The Guv? If we don't have any ideas in the next few minutes, let's all think about it overnight, and see if anybody has an idea tomorrow."

The suggestion was greeted with nods of agreement.

"All right, then. Before we go, three minutes of silence. Who was The Guv?"

Three minutes is a long time to sit quietly in one place. During that period, two motorboats passed by on the lake. A gust of late afternoon wind came up and animated the tops of the pine trees. As the day wound into evening, the cooling air caused El's house to creak twice as joints contracted. Karl's heavy breathing dominated the sounds inside the house.

"This is probably a stupid question … "

All heads snapped in the direction of Emma. It was the first time since joining the group that she had spoken without being called on.

"Considering where we are now, there's no such thing as a stupid question," Gordon said. "Please, Emma, go on."

"Well, we were living in Colorado in 1970, and we really don't follow politics that much." She looked at Gordon who gave her an encouraging nod. "But I just had the idea that if she was calling her lover The Guv, maybe he had the same name as the governor of California back then. Does anybody remember who the governor was in 1970?"

With the exception of Anna, who hadn't been born then, the light came on almost simultaneously for everyone else. El spoke first.

"Oh my God," she said. "It was that bastard Reagan. *Ronald* Reagan."

"And we have a Ronald in this story," said Alice. "Ronald Paris. Who would have been perfectly placed to start up a flirtation with Charlotte."

"And if anyone chanced to see them together," said Peter, "they might not make too much of it because of the connection between the families."

"He's a smart and personable guy," said Gina. "It's plausible that Charlotte could have fallen for him."

Gordon had been looking through Charlotte's journal. "She first called him The Guv in early November of 1970, right after the election that year. When Reagan won his second term."

"Defeating Jesse Unruh, who was speaker of the California Assembly," said Karl.

"Gordon!" said El. "Do you have that Polaroid that was in Charlotte's journal?"

He nodded.

"Give it to me."

He handed it to her and turned back to the group.

"Before we get too carried away about this, we should do a quick check. Look at what we know about The Guv and see if it all matches up with Ronald Paris."

"Gordon!" El again.

"What?" he snapped.

"You said Davies saw a paint mark on Ned London's car, right?"

"Right."

"What color was it?"

"I have no idea."

"Look, dammit."

He fished around in his messenger bag and found the page Davies had given him that morning. He ran his finger slowly down it, pausing halfway.

"It was red," he said.

"Like the pickup truck in this photo?"

She passed the picture back to him, and he stared at it, speechless. When he'd read the report earlier, he'd glossed over the color.

"I remember that pickup really well," Karl said. "Everybody who was around back then would. Ronald Paris drove it everywhere before it finally gave out about 10 years ago. It was a town joke."

"That still doesn't prove anything," said Anna.

"No," said Gordon. "But the picture is beginning to take shape, isn't it?"

"Let's not go too fast," said Peter. "I'm sure Ronald Paris didn't have the only red vehicle in this area. How does he match up against the rest of what we know about The Guv?"

"For starters," Gordon said, "he could have met Charlotte at the Rotary Club's new teacher lunch."

"He's been to every one I can remember," said Gina.

"And he chatted her up by talking to her about her classes," Gordon said. "When I had lunch with the Paris family last week, Ronald tried to draw me out by asking a lot of questions about Cal basketball. Same technique. Warm up the prospect by talking to his or her passion."

"Really?" said Alice.

"Old salesman's trick," Gordon said. "And she said in the journal The Guv's wife wasn't as complex as he was. Of course, The Other Woman *would* say that, but does anyone know her? Mrs. Ronald Paris, I mean. What's she like?"

"Well," said Alice, "she's kind of …"

"I know what you're trying to say," said El. "She's sort of …"

"Christine Paris is a superficial airhead," said Gina. "Let's be real. Charlotte was rarely wrong about people. That's just who she could have been talking about."

"And Charlotte also said something about an age difference," Gordon said. "Does anybody know exactly how old Ronald Paris is?"

Karl cleared his throat.

"In 1977 he was chosen as the Arthur/Año Nuevo Chamber of Commerce Man of the Year," he said. "He was 37 then."

"So he'd have been born in 1940," Gordon said. "That would make him five years younger than Charlotte."

"Lot of that going around," muttered Gina.

"Hold on a minute here," said Peter. "If our train of thought is going in the right direction, we're talking about a man who had an adulterous affair with his business partner's daughter, got her pregnant and walked away from it, murdered his business partner, and bribed or paid off an elected official in order to get a land development approved. And he gets named Chamber of Commerce Man of the Year? What does it take to get disqualified in this town?"

Alice finally broke the brief silence that followed the question.

"On the other hand," she said, "he *is* a deacon in the Presbyterian Church."

"Aren't we forgetting something?" said Anna. "Ned London and the Paris family were partners in the development. They both had the same interest and objective. Why would Ronald Paris kill his business partner just as the project was coming up for a vote?"

"I think Gina was pointing us to the answer a few days ago," said Peter. He turned to Gordon. "Ned London's father — Charlotte's grandfather — you said he was the county sheriff, right?"

"Matt London," Gordon said with a nod.

"Well, the apple doesn't generally fall too far from the tree. If your father's the sheriff, you probably were raised with a strict sense of right and wrong. Pretty much black and white. If that's the code you live by, how are you going to react to your business partner's idea of bribing a public official to get a result? Not well, I'm guessing."

"That makes sense," said El. It would explain the Crocker Bank memo, and it would explain a falling out between London and Paris."

"And if Celia Strickland was right," Gordon said, "they were facing ruin if the project didn't get approved. That's motive enough for murder, if anything is. Especially a spontaneous one like this. If we're right, Ned London drove off, and a hot-headed Ronald Paris jumped in his truck and followed him a minute later."

"It wouldn't be more than second degree," said Anna, "and more likely voluntary manslaughter."

"Even so," said Alice, "the Paris family is proud of its position in this town. I could see them doing anything to hush that up."

"And if Charlotte was starting to get warm about her father's death …" Gordon said.

There were general nods of agreement.

"It's a great theory," said Peter. "But it needs evidence."

After five more minutes of discussion that went nowhere, Gordon called an end to the meeting. As people were getting up to leave, he sidled over to El.

"We need to talk," he said softly.

"That's supposed to be the woman's line."

"Oh, come on."

"Dinner?"

"That works. Thank you."

He stepped back and let her show her guests out, appreciating the way she moved as she did. In a little more than a minute, he was alone with her and Anna. El turned to her daughter.

"Honey," she said, "we're going out to dinner."

"Oh, good," beamed Anna. "Where are we going?"

El gave Gordon a what-can-I-do look. He responded with a resigned shrug.

PETER HAD MADE THE MISTAKE of waiting too close by the front door, and Gordon drafted him to make a fourth for dinner. They drove to Garbini's in separate vehicles, grouped by gender. As they slid into the usual booth, Tony Bennett was singing "Who Can I Turn To?"

Gordon and Peter volunteered the opinion that they were making progress in the investigation, but Anna, her young mind filled with law school ideas, dissented.

"You have the outline of a case, but no proof," she said. "There's nothing here to justify a prosecution, let alone a conviction."

"That may be true, dear," said El, "but that's the district attorney's job, not ours. All we really have to do is come up with a news story that raises questions about Charlotte's death, and that the sheriff isn't taking them seriously."

"In other words," said Gordon, "we don't have to prove the case ourselves. We just have to light a fire under the people who can, and then hope they do their job."

"But if we don't have evidence," she persisted, "why should they investigate?"

"Because," said Peter, "they have much more effective ways of collecting evidence and conducting an investigation. We're limited to make-nice conversations with people who want to talk to us. The sheriff can call someone in and read them their Miranda rights to let them know he's serious. He can go to the judge and get search warrants. The district attorney can call witnesses before the grand jury. Step up the investigation to that level, and things start coming out. That's how it works."

"Do you have enough to write a story?" Gordon said to El.

She nodded. "I can certainly write a story. I'd like more than we've got, but we have enough."

"Don't you have to worry about libel?" said Anna.

"Not if you know what you're doing. Truth is always a defense, and as long as we hint at things we can't prove instead of saying them outright — well, libel's a tough rap to prove."

"What would you ideally like to see?" Gordon asked.

"I'd like to see something connecting Sturges to improper behavior when he voted to approve The Peninsulas," El said.

"That was 25 years ago," said Anna. "The statute of limitations has run out."

"He can't be prosecuted," Gordon said, "but his political career could be brought to a halt if it could be proved. He's thinking of running for state insurance commissioner, you know."

"Insurance commissioner," said Peter. "Now there's a good job for somebody with a history of taking bribes."

"No it isn't," said Anna. "You want someone completely honest."

Peter began to reply, but Gordon stopped him with a discreet elbow to the ribs. Gordon turned to El again.

"When are you going to write the story?"

"Tomorrow night. I'll wait until about four in the afternoon, then call Ballou for a comment on whatever we've got. After the group meets at five, I'll be writing as long as it takes to finish. On Wednesday morning, Gordon, I'd appreciate it if you could give the story a once-over."

"I should look at it for libel," said Anna.

"Of course, dear," murmured El.

The food arrived, and they ate, continuing to discuss the case without resolution. After dessert, the waitress went to add up their bill. Gordon had briefed Peter on the way over that his job was to get Anna out of the way, and he gave his friend an ankle-tap to indicate that now would be a good time to proceed.

"So," said Peter, sitting up, "It's almost sunset. I was wondering, Anna, if I could interest you in coming with me to watch the submarine races?"

She frowned. "But there aren't any submarines here."

El laughed and shook her head.

"Oh, Anna," she said. "You have so much to learn about the workings of the male mind. I think Dr. Delaney was suggesting he'd like to take you home and give Gordon and me a few minutes alone."

"All right." She made to leave, and as she had the inside seat, El had to get up and let her out. Gordon likewise rose to make way for Peter, slipping him the keys to the Cherokee as he slid out.

Sinatra was singing "Summer Wind" as they walked out the front door into a perfect evening. It was twilight, and the warmth of the day lingered on. The quarter-moon, which had risen early in the afternoon, was into its descent in the southwest. Traffic on the highway had all but stopped. Gordon took El by the hand.

"Let's see if we can have the gazebo at Stanhope House to ourselves."

They crossed the road and strolled up to the inn. A boy and girl of about ten and 12 were rocking in the bench swing, but the gazebo was empty.

"A quiet place to talk," he said, as they sat down. She sat to his left and leaned into him.

"This is the best time of year here," she sighed. "When the days are long and it's warm and sunny. In a good year, we get a hundred nice days, but they make the other 265 tolerable."

"About Saturday night," he said.

"Ack!" she exclaimed.

He started and turned to her. The inn's house cat had stolen into the gazebo and jumped on her lap.

"Sorry," she said. "He startled me." She began to scratch the cat behind the ears. "Ooh, you just want a little attention, don't you? Yeah. You like this, huh?" She turned to Gordon. "I guess you'd like a little attention, too."

"I think I could stand it."

"I'm sure you could. But about Saturday. What do you think it meant?"

"I don't know. It happened pretty fast."

"It usually does, in my experience. Maybe you shouldn't read too much into it. Say it was a lovely evening. Isn't that enough?"

"Do you want it to be enough?"

He could see her smile in the fading light.

"I could live with that. Let's cut to the chase, Gordon. Do you think you could move up here? To live most of the year?"

"Probably not," he said after a pause.

"And I'm married to the paper, though polygamy is a possibility. But I'm not leaving this town any time soon. So don't say you'll call me when you get back to the city. It's not going to happen. This is a summer thing." She smiled again. "And a damn good one, too. I really like you, and this is a great story we're working on. We'll always have that, just like Rick and Ilsa in *Casablanca* will always have Paris. It's something special, and most people never get that."

"Are trying to let me down gently."

"I'll be honest with you, Gordon. If Anna hadn't come home early, I would have had you over again last night, and probably again tonight. But when she showed up and we had to call a timeout, I started to think about it. It seemed to me that we had a special moment, and we should save it as that — not keep going until we run it into a ditch."

"You may be right …"

"Well, then."

"Thanks for the memory. And how about a kiss for old time's sake?"

"Just one. After two or three, I'm not responsible for myself."

He leaned over and gave her a kiss that became more ardent and passionate as it continued. The cat rolled off her lap and grumpily skulked away. Finally they broke off.

"That brought back some memories," he said, leaning toward her again. She put up her hand and stopped his chin.

"I said just one." He backed off slightly. "Dammit."

Tuesday June 25

"SHE ISN'T ANSWERING THE PHONE," said Peter.

"Which one?"

"Stella, of course."

"How do you know she's not answering? She may be working."

Peter shook his head. "No. I can feel the freeze all the way up here."

Breakfast was over at Stanhope House. Gordon finished his coffee and stood up.

"Keep trying and good luck," he said. "I have to make a call."

It was just past nine, and Gordon figured he might catch Richard Paris at his desk in San Francisco. He walked across the broad lawn and sat down in the empty gazebo. It was a clear day, with a brisk, chilly breeze, and he wished he'd brought a light jacket with him. He called the San Francisco number, and a no-nonsense, female voice answered after one ring.

"Richard Paris Property Management. This is Judy; how may I help you?"

"My name is Quill Gordon. May I speak with Richard Paris?"

"Could I tell him what it's about?"

"Please tell him I'm calling on behalf of Charlotte London."

"Just a minute, please."

Fifteen seconds later, a man's voice came on.

"Mr. Gordon, Richard Paris here. Always good to hear from a friend of Charlotte's. How's she doing?"

Gordon cursed silently.

"I'm sorry," he said. "I thought your family must have told you."

"Oh my God! Is she all right?"

"She died unexpectedly last week. I'm sorry to break the news."

There was a silence on the other end, then:

"I'm sorry to hear it. Can you tell me what happened?"

"There was a fire at her house last Monday."

"I'll have to give her brother a call. I've been really busy the past week. A lot of our rentals are to students at San Francisco State, and with school just out, I've been dealing with the turnover. Last time I talked to my father was a week ago Sunday. He said he and my brothers were going to have lunch with Charlotte the next day."

"They did," Gordon said. "The fire was that night."

"I'm really surprised Dad or one of my brothers didn't call." A pause. "Excuse me, Mr. Gordon, this has rattled me. What's your connection with Charlotte?"

"She named me as her literary executor so I could continue the work on her family history in case something happened," Gordon said. "Neither of us expected that to be necessary, but …"

"I see. Of course her family and ours have been very close."

"Closer than I had imagined at first," Gordon said, without evident irony. "But, listen, I obviously surprised you with some bad news, so you might not want to talk about that now."

Paris thought about it for a minute.

"No," he said. "If it was important to Charlotte, the best way to honor her memory would be to help, don't you think?"

"I'm sure it would have meant a lot to her. I talked to your father and brothers a few days ago and really just had a couple of questions."

"Go ahead, then. What can I tell you?"

Gordon took a deep breath.

"Well, obviously, the connection between your families had a lot to do with The Peninsulas, which is a big piece of her history. I'd be interested in knowing what you remember about it."

"I wish I could do more for you there, but it was a long time ago. Dad and Ron handled most of it. Bobby and I were pretty much running all the other business at our office. It was a hell of a lot of work and it took a big toll on everybody."

"How did all of you get along with Ned London?"

"Really well. He was a great guy, and of course, it was his idea at first. I'm sure there were a couple of times along the way when Dad and Ron wondered if they should have gone in on it, and I sensed there was a bit of tension toward the end. But I figured that was because no one knew if it would get approved. It all Too damn bad Ned never got to see it."

"That's what everyone says. One more thing, then, and I'll let you go. After I met with your father and brothers last week, I came across a photograph Charlotte saved. It showed the Paris and London families standing in front of a red pickup truck, with the lake in the background on Labor Day, 1970. Does that ring any bells?"

"I remember that picnic. Very well. The plans had just been filed with the county, and it looked like smooth sailing then. We were almost celebrating before the fact, if you will. I guess that day marked the end of our innocence."

Gordon said nothing, waiting to see if Paris would mention anything else.

"Funny, though. That's got me thinking about Ron's truck — the one in the picture. It must have been 15 years old then, and he drove it everywhere. Right around the time of the vote on The Peninsulas, it got banged up. He said somebody hit it in a parking lot and drove off. After the project was approved, he had me follow him to Chico, where he was taking it to be fixed. I gave him a hard time about that, but he said it was an older car and he couldn't trust anyone local to do the work. But I'm rambling now. I'm sure you didn't call me to hear about Ron's car trouble."

TOO TENSE AND IRRITABLE TO FISH, Gordon and Peter drove around the lake that morning, mostly in silence. At one point, Gordon pulled into a turnout with a view looking northwest toward The Peninsulas. They gazed at them for several minutes.

"Looks a lot different when you know what went into it," Peter finally said.

"Like sausage," replied Gordon, pulling back onto the road. "You're better off not knowing."

They had a late lunch at the Shotgun. Afterward, Gordon drove back to Stanhope House, dropped Peter

249

off, and walked to the newspaper office. El was on the phone, but waved him in. He took a seat by her desk, and she finished the call a minute later.

"The week is piling up," she said. "I'm catching up with what I put off to work on the Charlotte story, and I don't have any time to socialize. So if you have anything, give it to me straight."

Gordon told her about the conversation with Richard Paris that morning. She raised her eyebrows and nodded as he finished.

"It's beginning to fit together, isn't it?" she said. "Frankly, I didn't think we'd be this far along by now."

"We got some breaks."

"Breaks are what happen when you keep going after a story from every angle you can think of. It's usually the seventh or eighth thing you try that leads to the breakthrough."

"You aren't going to quote Richard, are you?"

"Not now. I'm going to play it conservatively. I'll work out the exact language as I'm writing the story, but I'll say Charlotte was looking into the possibility that her father's death wasn't an accident, and that *The Clarion* has obtained a page redacted from the original accident report saying that there was a scrape of paint on Ned London's car. That'll leave Ron Paris sweating and wondering how much else we know. Maybe it'll get him to make a mistake."

"Makes sense, I suppose. I wouldn't tell you how to do your job."

"Now don't take it personally, but if there's nothing else, I need you to leave so I can get some writing done."

"See you at 5:30," said Gordon.

As he rose, Gina rushed breathlessly through the door.

"Bingo!" she shouted. "Looks like we have something on the Crocker Bank angle."

"Gina, darling," said El, "You don't have to scream. The newspaper will reach far more people than your voice. Sit down and tell us in a normal tone."

Gordon pulled up another chair for Gina, and they both sat down. She caught her breath, then spoke in a loud whisper.

"Howard Sheehan, the former Crocker Bank manager I told you about? He's not only alive, he's sharp as a tack, and he still has all those old records. I got his number from the ex last night, and called this morning. I asked if he could see if there was any transfer relating to companies with the names London, Paris, or Sturges in December of 1970 or January or February of 1971. He called ten minutes ago to say he thought he found something. He's walking to the Kinko's four blocks from his house to fax it over. It should be coming over any time now."

It seemed as if the entire office had gone silent, but it was simply one of those lulls that can occur in an office with only a few people in it. When the fax rang during that silence, it sounded as loud as a fire alarm. They raced over to the classified advertising space, where the machine was, and shooed away the classified receptionist. The paper was just beginning to move through as they arrived. After an inch or two of white space, there was a thick black line, followed by the image of a 1988 Dodge minivan and text marked with a pen.

It was a classified ad for a local used-car lot.

Everyone exhaled at once. Gordon leaned over the machine and put a hand against the table on either side of it.

"I don't know if I can take much more of this," he said.

They remained by the fax, fidgeting for three minutes that seemed like three hours. When the phone rang again, they moved closer, leaning into each other.

The paper that came out this time was a series of densely clustered text and code sections. One of them, two thirds of the way down the page, was circled in pen or pencil. When the page had gone through, El grabbed the paper and tore it off the roll, handing it to Gordon.

"You're the financial genius. What does it mean?"

He looked at it carefully, wanting to be sure of his answer. No one was breathing until it came.

"It would appear," he finally said, "that on January 18, 1971, a $25,000 wire transfer was made from the San Francisco Crocker Bank account of London & Paris Ltd.

to the Sacramento Crocker Bank account of Sturges Enterprises."

"January 18th," said El. "The day before the Board of Supervisors voted on The Peninsulas. Guns don't smoke any more than this."

Gordon was looking at the fax again. He slammed it down on the table, and El and Gina started.

"Son of a bitch!" he said. "When Ron Paris took Charlotte to San Francisco, he was either opening that Crocker Bank account or putting the money into it for the payoff. Charlotte had no idea what was going on right under her nose."

NEEDING QUIET TIME, Gordon drove to the Hellwithit Bakery, arriving 15 minutes before closing. He ordered a cup of coffee, and let the server talk him into an almond croissant. One other table was occupied, by two women apparently discussing romantic issues, and he sat as far from them as possible.

It appeared that his most pressing work for Charlotte was pretty much done. El would write a story for the paper, and with even minimal competence devoted to the effort, the authorities should find themselves heading down some of the same paths that Gordon and the team had followed. He paused to consider that perhaps it would be wise to go straight to Sheriff Ballou and share their findings and conclusions. He quickly rationalized himself out of that line of thought, arguing that the evidence was suggestive rather than conclusive, and that Ballou would be more inclined to pursue a case if he felt he were doing it on his own. On the other hand, the trail led to Ronald Paris, who was as prominent a citizen as the town possessed, and he wondered how far Ballou would be willing to go after such a powerful suspect. Gordon realized his father would not have approved of withholding information from the sheriff, but as his father's approval in so many other areas was elusive, he was little swayed by that consideration.

He felt a vibration in his pants pocket and reached for his pager. It was Ballou. He wolfed down his pastry and took the remaining half-cup of coffee to the Cherokee, where he would have more privacy.

"Thanks for calling so quickly," said the sheriff. "How much longer are you in town?"

"Through tomorrow night. Peter and I will be leaving for San Francisco Thursday morning."

"All right. I have your number there." Gordon waited, rather than replying. "In that manuscript you gave me Saturday, there was a notation to check with Davies. I just did, and found out from his secretary — he wasn't in — that you'd been there before me."

He paused, and again Gordon remained silent.

"I don't know that I like that," the sheriff said. "Investigating crimes is my job, and I don't appreciate amateurs getting in the way."

"So you're saying you think there was a crime," said Gordon.

"Don't jump to conclusions. Maybe I should have said investigating suspicious circumstances. Either way, it's my job, not yours."

"I wouldn't dream of trying to do your job, sheriff. But I have a job to do, too, and that's to get Charlotte London's manuscript ready for publication. If she wrote in the margins that somebody ought to be talked to — well, I wouldn't be doing my due diligence if I didn't talk to that person."

"And that person you talked to, did he say something interesting?"

"I thought so." Gordon left it hanging there.

"Don't play games with me, Gordon. I need to know what he said."

"For whatever it's worth, Davies thinks there was something suspicious about the accident that killed Ned London in 1971. He doesn't have hard evidence, and his superiors told him to back off that angle at the time. If he told me all about it, he'll certainly tell you when you get hold of him."

"Fair enough. Is there anything else you've turned up that you haven't told me?"

"There is one thing," Gordon said after a silence. "It may not be important, but it struck me as being odd."

"Out with it, Gordon. I don't have all day."

"Well, it turns out that the day after she was killed in that fire, Charlotte London had an appointment to talk to Davies herself. She died before she could make it. Of course, it could be a coincidence."

"I don't believe in coincidences. All right, Gordon. I'll look into this. If you hear anything else, let me know right away. No doing things on your own."

He rang off before there was any chance to reply. Gordon set the phone on his car seat and drank the last two swallows of his coffee, lukewarm now.

Then he smiled.

"El must have got to him," he thought. "The machinery of justice is cranking up."

BEFORE THE MEETING STARTED, El's living room had the chattering vibe of a classroom before first bell the day after Christmas vacation. Gordon got everyone quieted down and filled the group in on his conversations with Richard Paris and on the Crocker Bank information Gina had unearthed. In both cases, the reports were greeted with spontaneous applause.

"And I'm guessing," he said, turning to El, "that you got hold of Gene Ballou this afternoon and put a bug in his ear." She nodded. "He called Davies straightaway and couldn't reach him, but found out I'd been there yesterday and paged me."

"What did you tell him?" said Alice.

"I gave him the short version of our conversation and let it drop that Charlotte was going to see Davies the day after she died."

"I'll bet that put a turd in his pocket," said El. "But that's good. He has to take it seriously now, and we'll keep the heat on him. After Thursday's paper comes out, he'll be calling for help from the FBI."

"How, exactly, are you going to handle the story?" asked Karl. "It's complicated and has a lot of nuance."

"I'm going to stick to the facts and insinuate."

"How so?" asked Gina.

"We'll lead off with the medical examiner's report that Charlotte was dead before the fire started. Then I'm going to say she was working on the family history and was scheduled to meet with the officer who wrote the

254

report on her father's accident, and that a page redacted from the report suggests Ned's car was hit by another. That should plant a seed."

"How about the bank transfer?" said Gina. "Aren't you going to play that up?"

"Not right now. It isn't privileged.

"What does that mean?" said Anna.

"The report on Ned London's crash is an official public document. You can make a good argument the redacted page is, too. That means that if I quote it or report it accurately, the paper can't be sued even if the document is wrong. The fax on that bank transfer, from someone I don't even know, doesn't have the same standing. I have to figure out another way of getting that into next week's story. Worst case, I might turn it over to Ballou, or Southworth who have ways of following up on it. The point is, we don't need to have the whole story in this week's paper — just enough to show we're on to something big. And I think we have that."

"Anything else?" Gordon said, trying to wrap the meeting up.

"One other thing," said El. "I called Ron Paris this afternoon and innocently asked him about the last meeting with his family and Ned London. I said it was for the story of The Peninsulas anniversary, but I wanted to set him on edge a bit and make him wonder what I know. Just in case I have to bluff him next week."

There were nods all around, but after a pause, Gordon said:

"I don't know if that's such a good idea, El. If we're right about Ronald Paris, he's already committed two murders, plus two burglaries trying to get at the information I have. He's dangerous."

"And if he did do those things, he has a lot on his conscience. So I want to prick that conscience and maybe be able to get some blood from it later."

"Aren't you overlooking something?" said Peter.

El looked at him.

"What if he hasn't got a conscience at all?" he said.

"THANKS FOR AGREEING to come here," said Peter, as they were seated at a window table at Ike's Lakeside.

255

"Don't get me wrong about Garbini's, but if they started playing Sinatra singing 'You and Me,' I don't think I could take it."

"No word from Stella?" asked Gordon, picking up a menu. "Or did you get the word and it wasn't good?"

"No word. And I can't say that I blame her. All I can do is be persistent without racking up a restraining order."

"Do I hear the voice of experience?"

"My fourth wife got a restraining order when she filed the divorce papers. I hadn't done anything, but her attorney convinced the judge I was an 'aberrant personality.' And you don't have to comment on that."

"I wasn't going to say a word."

Peter leaned back in his chair, looking out over the lake. The afternoon wind had died down, leaving the surface placid, and the sun was still in the western sky, but descending toward the top of the mountain range.

"On a positive note," he said, "Heather called today."

"Your daughter?"

"She wants to get together for coffee next week in San Francisco. We're meeting Wednesday morning. Maybe the tradeoff for not getting a second chance as a lover is that I'm getting one as a father."

"Are you looking forward to that?"

"With some trepidation. I'd love to have her in my life, but aside from our friendship, Gordon, I don't exactly have a good track record with relationships."

Dinner arrived, and after they started on it, Gordon's pager went off.

"It's El," he said. "My phone's in the car, but I'll be right back."

He returned her call from the parking lot.

"You'll never guess who just called," she said.

"I don't have time for this."

"Ronald Paris."

Gordon felt his stomach tighten as she continued.

"He said he wanted to talk to me some more about The Peninsulas and it couldn't wait. He's coming over tonight."

"Are you out of your mind, El? If we're right about this guy," he looked around to be sure he wasn't overheard, "he's already killed two people, and you're letting him into your very isolated house, just the two of you. What were you thinking?"

"We're both in Rotary, Gordon. He won't hurt me."

"Not if I have anything to say about it. We're at Ike's, but I'll be over as soon as we're done. What time is he coming?"

"Eight thirty. Really, Gordon …"

Gordon looked at his watch.

"I can probably get there before he does."

"Gordon, please! In case you haven't noticed, I can take care of myself."

"I'll be there in 45 minutes," he said, punching the end-call button.

His expression gave him away when he returned.

"Lover's quarrel?" asked Peter.

"Worse than that. Ronald Paris is going to El's house in less than an hour, and she doesn't seem to be the least bit concerned about it."

"I'm not surprised. If this was a horror movie, she'd be the one going down into the basement when everybody else was screaming, 'Don't do it!' What's your plan?"

"I say we finish dinner and get down to her place as fast as we can, so she has a little muscle at her side. Just in case."

He began bolting his food. Peter had nearly finished his meal while Gordon was out.

"I have a better idea," said Peter after a few minutes. "Why don't you go first. Let's see if we can get Gina to pick me up, and we'll follow you over a bit later. Before we come in, we'll call, and if you don't give us the password, we call the sheriff."

"Fair enough. What's the password."

Peter thought for a moment.

"We'll ask if we can come over. If there's trouble, say, 'By all means.' If you *don't* say those three words, we figure the coast is clear."

"You're on." Gordon pushed the plate away. A third of the meal was still on it, but his appetite was gone. He called Gina, she answered right away, and he gave her the short version of the situation.

"I'll be at Ike's in 20 minutes," she said.

"Not so fast, Gina. Before you come, take a few minutes to call everyone in the group. We want the whole team to know Paris is at El's house."

"Will do."

Gordon put the phone in his pocket and looked at Peter.

"You're a wreck, Gordon. Get going. I'll pay for dinner, and Gina and I will be over as fast as we can. And remember: 'By all means,' if there's any trouble."

"By all means," said Gordon, rising to leave.

AFTER GORDON LEFT, Peter looked out at the lake, then turned his gaze inward back toward the bar. The bottles, the glassware, and the laughing customers all looked friendly and inviting.

"Can I get you anything else?" said the waitress as she cleared the plates.

Peter took a deep breath, looked out at the lake, then back at the bar again. It struck him that a little Dutch courage might be in order, and with no mental resistance, he acted on the thought.

"Bring me a double Johnnie Walker Red on the rocks and add it to the bill," he said. "That should do it."

She was back with the drink and the check in three minutes. Plenty of time to knock it down before Gina arrived. He put a credit card on top of the bill, and since he was alone, turned and lifted his glass toward the lake.

"Here's to you, Heather, and to our reconciliation."

He took a sip and savored the smoky taste as he swilled it in his mouth and the burn as he swallowed. Not until he had finished the drink did he realize that the waitress had brought the credit card stub back for him to sign.

DRIVING FAST, Gordon reached El's house at 8:25. Her pickup was the only vehicle in the gravel parking lot, he noted with relief, feeling that he would much rather be there when Ronald Paris arrived.

He donned a light windbreaker after getting out of the Cherokee and slipped his phone into its right pocket. He walked down the steps to the pier leading to her house, pausing halfway to appreciate, if only briefly, the aspect of the lake. The sun was behind the mountains, and most of the lake was in shadow. On the other side of it, the very tops of the mountains were catching the sun's last rays. Halfway out, a motorboat sped north in the direction of the marinas, the sound of its engine a distant buzz.

Gordon walked across the pier to the front door of the house, and as he reached it, looked back toward the parking area. His and El's were still the only two cars there. He knocked on the front door, then turned the knob. Stepping into the entrance hall, he was struck by how quiet it was inside. He was looking right, toward the living area, as he came into the main space, and when he turned left, toward the kitchen, he froze.

El was sitting in a chair, tied up and gagged.

Next to her stood Ronald Paris, an automatic pistol in his hand pointing toward Gordon.

"You're early," said Gordon.

"I wanted this to be a surprise. Come on in. Slowly. I'm glad you could make it. Your presence will make for an interesting tableau later in the evening."

GINA CALLED EVERYONE in five minutes and either talked to them or left a message. Grabbing her purse, she raced to the back door, closed it without locking it, and ran the few steps to her parked car. She opened the purse and began to look for her car keys, but after rifling through the contents several times, realized they weren't there.

"Damn!" she said, turning back to the house.

She went into the kitchen and looked carefully at the breakfast table and the counters. No key. She slowly and methodically checked all the surfaces in the living room, with the same result. Then she canvassed the bedroom and bathroom to no avail. She felt the passing minutes as though they were a heavy weight, slowly crushing the breath out of her.

"All right," she whispered. "Don't panic. If I were my keys, where would I be?" She stood in the bedroom, hands to her temples, and retraced her steps from the day. Finally she remembered that after returning from the group meeting, she had changed out of her slacks into the pair of jeans she was wearing. Sure enough, the keys were still in the pocket of the slacks.

Racing toward the car, she pulled up at the back door, ran back to her bedroom, and took a plastic storage container from the shelf in the closet. Setting it on the bed, she dug through seldom-worn clothing to the bottom, feeling around until her hand touched the gun she kept there. Frantic because of the delay, she rushed back to her car, set the gun on the front passenger seat, and backed out of her driveway much faster than it was safe to do.

Gina's ex-husband had given her the gun for protection when they were divorced, and she had put it in storage without giving it a second thought. She had never used it; had never read the directions; had never even given it a close look. But now she felt it would come in handy, and to the extent she thought about it at all, she figured that Peter or Gordon would know how to use it. It had never occurred to her to see if the gun was loaded.

It wasn't.

GORDON HAD BEEN CAUGHT FLAT-FOOTED, and there was no feasible way of trying to be a hero. The only consolation was that Peter and Gina would be there in 20 minutes. All he had to do was hold out that long, and remember the magic words.

By all means.

"When the deputies get here," Paris said, "It will look like a classic lovers' murder-suicide. I haven't decided yet who's going to be the murder victim and who's going to be the suicide, but there's still a little time."

"That may take care of us, Paris, but we're not the only ones who know. There's been a good little group of people looking into Charlotte's death."

As he spoke, Gordon tried to take in as much of the situation as he could by moving only his eyes and not his head. Paris was too far away to be rushed and taken down, but too close to miss if he fired the gun. El was completely out of commission. Gordon had a folding knife with a three-inch blade in his right pants pocket, but it would be useless against a man with a gun.

"There may be other people," Paris said, "but you're the only two here, and El is the only one who has the power to print a story in the newspaper. With the two of you gone, I think I can brazen through the rest of it. But first things first. Where's Charlotte's journal and the family history?"

Gordon was doing a quick calculation as to whether he should tell the truth or not.

"Talk, Gordon. I know you can do it. I'd rather not have to kill you slowly, but if that's what it takes to get the journal … "

"All right, all right." He had decided the truth wouldn't hurt. "It's in a messenger bag behind the driver's seat of my car."

"And you've read it?"

Gordon nodded.

"Then you have to die."

"Is it really that bad, Paris? I mean you're not the only married man in the history of the world who got a little on the side."

Paris tensed visibly, and for an instant, Gordon feared he might pull the trigger right there. Then Paris relaxed slightly and kept the gun pointed directly at Gordon's torso.

"Did she say anything about her father's death? Was she suspicious?"

He's talking, Gordon thought. *That's good. If I can just keep him going another 10 or 15 minutes, Peter will be here.*

"She was getting suspicious. She had an appointment to talk to Al Davies, the officer who wrote the report on Ned London's so-called accident the day after she died. You saw to it that she didn't make the appointment."

"It was better that she didn't find out."

"We did, though. My friend and I talked to Davies yesterday, and he told us about the smudge of red paint on Ned's car. Then, this morning, I talked to your brother in San Francisco, and he told me about following you to Chico while you got the body work done on your red pickup. That pretty much clinched it."

"I was afraid of that." Paris shook his head. "If you hadn't called Rich this morning, you probably would have lived beyond tonight. He called me two hours ago, and that's when I got the wind up."

"Like I said, Paris, I'm far from the only one who knows all this."

"In her journal," he said, "did she mention me by name?"

"Not by name, but there were enough hints that we figured it out."

"And did she write about our love affair?"

"In shocking detail, though I wouldn't call it a love affair. It read more like a married man's cynical fling. You came across as a stinker, Paris, but I'm sure you knew that already. She even used a literary allusion to describe it. 'I fear my Darcy has turned out to be a Wickham,' she said."

Paris frowned.

"It's a reference to *Pride and Prejudice*, one of her favorite books. Wickham was a world-class scoundrel. It's pretty damning to be compared to him."

Paris stared at Gordon for a full minute, the gun unwaveringly pointed, without saying a word. Gordon said a silent prayer that Gina would drive fast. Finally Paris shook his head.

"You don't understand, Gordon. I guess I shouldn't be surprised, but you didn't get it at all. I was ready to leave my wife and marry Charlotte after The Peninsulas got approved. And for more than 25 years now, not a day has gone by that I haven't felt a deep and profound regret it didn't turn out that way. Being apart from her all those years caused me more pain than you'll ever be able to imagine.

"No, Gordon, Charlotte wasn't just 'a little on the side,' as you so crudely put it. She was the great love of my life."

PETER FINISHED HIS DRINK and set the empty glass down on the bar, looking irritably at his watch. Where could Gina be? It had been a mistake to count on her. He should have gone with Gordon in the first place. Should they be there by now? He tried to calculate the time frame in his head, but he was thinking slowly for some reason.

Gordon was probably expecting his call by now. Maybe he should call without waiting for Gina just to be sure everything was all right. He reached for his pocket, realized it was empty and banged his fist on the bar. He'd left his cell phone under a jacket on the front seat of Gordon's Cherokee. He'd have to wait for Gina after all.

He caught the bartender's eye and motioned her over.

"Might as well have another," he said, pointing to his glass.

The bartender shifted uncomfortably.

"I don't want to be a bad sport," she said, "but this would be your fourth double, and with the drunk driving laws now, we have to be careful. Can you promise me you're not going to drive home?"

"Actually," said Peter, attempting hauteur but falling short owing to a bit of a slur, "it'll be my *fifth* double, and you can serve it with a clear conscience. The lady's driving."

The bartender shrugged and turned to make the drink.

"If she ever gets here," Peter muttered.

"I DON'T KNOW ABOUT THAT," Gordon said. "If that's how you treat someone you love, what do you do to someone who crosses you?"

"You'll find out soon enough. But before you do, you need to realize what was going on."

He wants to be understood, Gordon thought. *If I can just keep him talking a few more minutes, Peter will be here.* Gordon looked at El and could see the fear in her eyes; he felt a pang of guilt for having gotten her involved. And tied up as she was, she wouldn't be able to help in any way if things got sticky. He moved his eyes to his left and noted that the sliding glass door by the kitchen was open to cool off the house. *It's too far away now*, he thought, *but if I can get a little closer …*

"You've probably figured out about Ned London," Paris said.

"I'm pretty sure you killed him, but I don't know why."

"Ah, that's the crux of the matter. Were you aware that Ned's father was the sheriff of this county for many years?"

"It was in the family history."

"Of course. I should have known. Well, his father was a man who saw the world in black and white. Things were right or wrong with no gray shades and nothing in between. I'm afraid some of that rubbed off on Ned, and it didn't serve him well."

"He wouldn't go for bribing Sturges?"

"Please. I prefer to regard it as a campaign contribution and an investment in this area's future. But, yes. He wouldn't go along, and worse, he threatened to go public with the information. We were facing financial ruin, all of us, including him, and he was going to be a Boy Scout about it.

"When we got together that night — Ned, Dad and me — there was a hell of an argument. I'm surprised the neighbors didn't call the sheriff. Ned pounded down a couple of scotch and sodas and just stuck to the point that he wasn't going to be a part of any payment to Sturges and that he'd expose us if we tried to do it ourselves. Pig-headed bastard."

"By the way," Gordon said. "When you and Charlotte went to San Francisco before Christmas, was that so you could set up the account at Crocker Bank to transfer the money to Sturges?"

"How did you know about that? Never mind. You can't prove anything."

"Actually, we have a copy of the transfer record. If we could get it without subpoena power, I'm sure the district attorney could lay his hands on it. You're not in as strong a position as you think."

"Do you want to hear the rest of the story, or are you going to keep interrupting?"

"Keep going. Please."

"Anyway, Ned finally stormed out, and when he did, my father buried his face in his hands and said,

'That's it. We're finished.' And I said something like, 'Are you just going to sit there and take it? Well, I'm not.' I didn't have anything in mind at the time, but I decided to go after Ned. See if I could talk some sense into him.

"He only had a couple of minutes' jump on me, and between his age and the drinks, he was driving slow. I pulled up behind him just as he was starting up the grade where the road rises up above the lake. As we reached the top, I got the idea that it might get his attention if I ran into him, let him know it was serious. I was just trying to get him to stop, but I swerved into his car harder than I meant to and almost spun out myself. He went over the edge in the blink of an eye. I stopped for a second. There was no one on the road, and I was in shock. Then I realized that there was no way I could explain what happened, and at almost the same time I realized our problem had been solved. I drove home, parked the pickup in the garage with the right side facing the right wall so the dent couldn't be seen, and left it there for more than a week until it could be taken out of town to be fixed."

"Did your father know?"

"He never asked, and we've never discussed it. But he's no fool. I'm sure it's occurred to him, but he'd rather not know. Dad doesn't like unpleasantness. And of course, when Ned London ran off the road, so did any chance of my marrying Charlotte."

"Why would that stop you?"

"Come on, Gordon. I'm not a monster. What kind of marriage do you think it would be if I were carrying that kind of secret? That I killed her father? The strain would have been impossible, but you probably can't understand.

"Actually, I think I can."

"It killed me to break it off, but the other way would have been worse. I had no choice but to be a bastard and try to make Charlotte feel that she was well rid of me. I guess I succeeded. Well, for a quarter of a century anyway. And then she had to get it into her head to write that damn family history. Some things are better left undisturbed, but I figured it would be the usual boring book and nothing to worry about.

"Then last Monday we met for lunch, and I got the shock of my life. She was asking us questions about her father's accident and the night he died. She was asking if we had any idea why Sturges changed his mind and voted for the project. And she let it drop that she'd been keeping a journal during the time of our affair. It was obvious that things were getting out of hand. I hope I didn't let that show."

"You might have," Gordon said. "She mailed the journal to her attorney that night, with instructions to turn it over to me if anything happened. She'd already given me the manuscript of the history that morning. She was plenty worried."

"And she wouldn't listen to reason," Paris said. "In that regard, she was her father's daughter. And she was getting dangerously close to the truth. Now you're from San Francisco, so you might not know what it's like in a small town. The reality is that if it came out now about our contribution to Sturges, I could still walk into the Rotary Club meeting with my head held high. People would think, well, it was a quarter of a century ago, The Peninsulas are a part of the community now, and maybe he just did what a businessman had to do.

"Or if something had come out about our affair — and I don't think she would have been too eager to publicize that — I'd still be accepted. Most grown-ups get that love is powerful, irrational and ungovernable. They might not approve, but they wouldn't judge too harshly.

"But if it was so much as whispered that I had anything to do with Ned London's death, I'd be through in this town, even if I was never charged. That was the one thing that couldn't come out under any circumstances. When Charlotte told me that night that she was meeting the Highway Patrol officer the next day, I realized I had to act before it was too late. She turned her back to me, and I picked up a piece of wood from the basket by the fireplace and hit her once. It was swift and merciful. Merciful because it was a better death than most of us are going to get and because she died without knowing the truth: That she's a wealthy woman because of her father's murder and a corrupt vote. It would have devastated her to find out."

"Did it ever occur to you," Gordon asked, "that she might have wanted a say in that?"

"Not at all. When I saw her lying there, I knew it was the right thing. I loved her and had to protect her."

Gordon was now thoroughly terrified, and the terror was magnified as he realized that during Paris's monologue he had lost track of time. It was almost completely dark, and Peter and Gina should long since have called or arrived. While Paris was talking, Gordon had gradually been able to inch a couple of feet closer to the open door, but he calculated that he was still too far from it to get out without being shot.

"But we've talked far too long," Paris said. "I need you to move over this way and kneel on the floor where I tell you to.

Gordon knew he had at most a couple of seconds to decide whether to break for the door and almost surely be killed on the spot or go along and hope against hope for help in the next few minutes. Neither choice was any good.

"Now!" barked Paris, gesturing with the gun.

Without a knock or any other warning signal, the front door to the house opened.

GINA LEANED FORWARD, emitted a moan, and banged the palms of her hands on the steering wheel. The lights of the patrol car behind her were still flashing in the fading light. The worst of it was that she had no idea how fast she'd been driving; the only thought in her head had been that she was late picking up Peter.

Please, God, she thought. *Let it be one of my ex-students. At least give me that much of a chance.*

The young deputy who stopped in front of the passenger window of her car was a complete stranger. She decided to put it all out at once.

"I don't know how fast I was driving," she said, barely able to control her voice, "but this is an emergency. It could be a matter of life and death."

The deputy waited several seconds before replying in a calm, even voice.

"Yes, ma'am. That's what everybody thinks. But it usually isn't so bad."

"It *is* that bad, I'm telling you. I have a friend who may be alone with a murderer."

"I see," said the deputy, in a flat, emotionless voice. "Well, why don't you tell me where this friend with the murderer is right now."

"In a house just past Año Nuevo Pines. Can you get someone over there? This is serious."

"Yes, ma'am. I'd like to be helpful, but you're not making a lot of sense. If you're friend's in danger near Año Nuevo Pines, and you're driving 30 miles an hour over the speed limit to come to the rescue, I suppose my question is how come you're driving in the opposite direction from where your friend is?"

"Oh my God! This is unreal. I'm trying to pick up someone else so there will be two of us to help out."

She buried her face in her hands, trying to hold back tears of frustration.

"*Don't move!*" The deputy barked the words out at the top of his voice. After a few seconds, he continued, "I want you to slowly, very slowly, put your hands on the steering wheel at ten o'clock and two o'clock."

She did as told and carefully and deliberately turned her head toward the deputy. She found herself looking down the barrel of his gun, just a few feet away.

"This is insane," she croaked. "Is this how you treat everybody who's been driving too fast?"

"No, ma'am, it's not," the deputy said, his voice again level and quiet. "But it is what we're trained to do when we encounter an emotionally disturbed person driving a vehicle in a reckless manner," he looked down at the passenger seat, "with a firearm at their side."

ANNA WALKED INTO THE ROOM and stopped abruptly when she saw Paris, Gordon, and her bound mother.

"What's going on here?" she said. "Gordon?"

"I'm afraid Mr. Paris has us at a bit of a disadvantage," he said. When Paris turned to Anna as she came in, Gordon had been able to edge a bit closer to the side door, but still felt he was too far away.

"If this is some kind of joke," she said, "it's not funny. Put the gun away, now."

"It's no joke," Gordon said.

"Then put the gun away anyhow," she said. "What right do you have to come into our house and do something like this?"

"Anna," said Gordon, "They probably don't teach this in law school, but it's not a good idea to argue with a man who has a gun."

In his mind, he was thanking her. Paris was still looking at Anna, and Gordon had been able to move ever so slightly nearer the open door.

"Actually," said Paris, "this makes the decision for me. I was thinking of having her (he gestured with his head toward El) kill you, then herself. But now, it'll look like you killed the women and turned the gun on yourself. That will be very plausible."

"Can somebody please tell me what's going on?" Anna said, her voice rising in panic.

Paris looked at Gordon, then back at her.

"Certainly," he said calmly. "You're about to die."

Gordon's cell phone rang.

Thank you, God, he thought. *And thank you, Peter, but what took so long?* Paris was looking hard at him, and Gordon decided to bluff.

"Don't worry," he said. "I won't answer it."

"Then that's probably a signal," Paris said. "Take it out of your pocket real slow and tell whoever it is you're fine. But if you try to say anything else, you won't live to finish the sentence."

Gordon took the phone out slowly and began to lift it to his ear. As he did, he caught the caller's number on the display.

It wasn't Peter.

It wasn't Gina, either.

It was Gordon's sister in Marin County.

What happened next was sheer instinct. With a quick backhand motion, more wrist than arm, Gordon threw the phone at Paris's head, as if passing a basketball to an open man in the key. It glanced off the back of his skull and landed harmlessly on the floor, still ringing.

But Paris was temporarily off balance, and that provided just enough time for Gordon to get out the door and behind the wall to his right before he heard the shot.

It left a small bullet hole in the door, surrounded by a spider-web pattern of cracked glass.

Up to this point, Gordon hadn't considered what would happen if he were to make it outside. He was willing to gamble that Paris wouldn't shoot El — and now, Anna — with a witness at large outside, and he fervently hoped he was right. But taking stock of the situation, he realized his position was little improved.

He was on the left side of the house, as viewed from shore. If he tried to go back past the door, he would be in Paris's view and aim. In any event, the deck ended just a few feet beyond the door, without connecting to the front door or the pier leading back to the land. He could go into the lake, but he was at best an average swimmer and would make a big, slow target.

Gordon decided his best chance was to keep going around the deck and see if he could find anything on it — a hoe, a shovel — that he might be able to use as a defensive weapon. Only a faint light remained in the sky, and he figured that if he hugged the railing at the edge of the deck, and stayed as far from the windows as possible, Paris wouldn't get a good look at him. Or, more importantly, a good shot.

He moved quickly to the deck railing, and, crouching to provide a smaller target, began scooting around the house. When he turned the corner and began going parallel to the back of the house, he could see, through the large windows, Paris and Anna arguing with each other. She's too young to know better, he thought, but if she doesn't get herself killed, every minute she drags this out has to be bringing Peter closer. *Peter, where the hell are you?*

As he reached the corner at the right side of the deck, he saw Paris making a come-here gesture to Anna with the gun. She reluctantly took two steps toward him, and he grabbed her harshly by the neck, pulling her to his body. Then he forced her toward the door through which Gordon had left.

He's coming after me using her as a human shield. As if I have anything to shoot with.

They went through the door on the other side of the house, and Gordon stood up and moved purposefully to the end of the deck on his side, looking for anything he could use defensively. He reached the end of the deck and realized he was boxed in there, with nothing to lay his hands on but a folding chair and El's fly rod, which was still leaning against the house where he'd left it Saturday night.

Gordon turned and looked back at the corner of the house, around which Anna, Paris and his gun would be coming at any moment. The basketball player in him instinctively sized up the distance, which he figured was about 30 feet.

The fly rod.

Maybe it wouldn't work, but 30 feet is a reasonably short cast for an accomplished angler. He'd need a break and a perfect cast, but what other option was there?

He held the rod out over the lake and turned it over to see the back of the reel. He switched off the drag so he could strip line from the reel without the gears clattering loudly in the still evening, and got 30 feet of line beyond the tip of the rod, dropping into the water. Now all he had to do was make the cast of his life.

It's just like shooting a free throw, he told himself. *In front of ten thousand screaming people in a gym. You tune out everything and fall back on habits. Habits you've formed in thousands of hours of practice. You've made the shot over and over again in practice, and you're going to make it now. I've probably made as many casts with a fly rod as I've taken free throws. It's a habit. Lean on the habit, and don't think about it.*

Two people pressed against each other, one unwillingly, can't help but make noise as they move. Gordon was more or less able to follow their progress by sound. As they approached the corner, Anna cried out:

"Gordon! He's crazy. Don't try anything or you'll get us killed."

Then he saw movement at the corner and raised the rod, bringing the fly line behind him in a back cast.

Paris and Anna came around the corner, and in the dim light from the interior of the house, this is what Gordon processed in a nanosecond:

Paris was standing behind her, his left arm around her neck, and the gun in his right hand, wrapped around her torso, pointing toward Gordon. From Gordon's perspective, Paris's head was just to the right of Anna's and almost touching it. The only small target he presented was a face, about nine inches wide and a foot high.

Just another cast. Nothing you haven't done thousands of times before.

And with that, Gordon drove the rod and the line forward.

A fly line shooting forward after an effective back cast is moving at a higher speed than a Major League fastball, and doing so with a terrific amount of power behind it. Ask any angler who's been unlucky enough to step in front of one, and he'll say the shock and pain are unlike anything else he has ever experienced. Gordon was counting on that.

When Paris saw Gordon's arm moving forward, he fired, but the line was speeding toward him so fast that as he pulled the trigger, the fly at the end of the line slammed into his cheek just below his left eye, then ricocheted to the side, with the hook going all the way through his left ear lobe.

There was no conscious decision on Paris's part to drop the gun; it was an involuntary response to the pain and shock that brought him to his knees, screaming in agony and taking Anna down with him. Gordon, barely aware of the searing pain at the left edge of his torso just below his bottom rib, threw the rod on the deck and started for Paris.

For a man of his age, Paris reacted surprisingly quickly. Pushing Anna down hard, he looked for the gun, saw it, and leaned forward to get it.

Before concentrating on basketball, Gordon had played one year of junior varsity football and still remembered the techniques of tackling. Paris had just put his hand on the gun when Gordon was ten feet away. Gordon lowered his left shoulder, aimed it at Paris's right shoulder, and drove through Anna to deliver a punishing hit. Both men screamed at the impact — Paris from the shock, and Gordon from the pain that seared through him from the gunshot wound. Paris dropped back hard, banging the back of his head on the deck and letting the gun fall on the other side of Anna.

With Paris unarmed, Gordon — younger, bigger, and stronger despite his wound — held all the cards. He pinned Paris down, both of them gasping for air.

"You could have taken my eye out," Paris whimpered, the fight gone out of him. "And I think you broke my collarbone. What are you trying to do — kill me?"

Gordon shook his head in disbelief.

"And that hook in my ear hurts like hell. Can you at least take that out?"

"It has a barb in it," Gordon said, hating himself only a little for being glad about it. "It'll have to wait until you get to a doctor."

Anna began to push herself up from the deck, but stopped part way through the move to grab her side and yelp in pain.

"What in God's name is going on here?" she almost shouted. "I think you broke my rib with your knee. Did you have to come on so hard? And what the fuck went flying past my head so fast I could feel the wind from it? You're all crazy!"

Then she looked down and saw the dark stain on Gordon's shirt under his left arm.

"Oh my God, Gordon. He hit you. You're bleeding. Oh my God. Are you all right? It looks bad. I can still move. Is there anything I can do?"

Gordon looked down at Paris, then back at Anna. Holding Paris to the deck with his left hand, he reached into his pocket, took out the folding knife, and deliberately handed it to her.

"Shut up and untie your mother," he said.

Closure

 "That was a memorable day to me, for it made great changes in me. But it is the same with any life. Imagine one selected day struck out of it, and you think how different its course would have been. Pause you who read this, and think for a moment of the long chain of iron or gold, of thorns or flowers, that would never have bound you, but for the formation of the first link on one memorable day."

—**DICKENS**, *Great Expectations*

Interlude 1: Thursday November 14, 1996

(From the Forest Clarion)

Ronald Paris, scion of the family that developed The Peninsulas in the 1970s, was killed Wednesday morning in an attack at Forest County Jail, two days after pleading no contest to manslaughter in connection with the last summer's death of Charlotte London, longtime English teacher at President Arthur High School. Paris was 56.

Sheriff Gene Ballou, narrowly re-elected to a fourth term last week, said little, as usual, claiming the incident was "under investigation."

Other sources close to the incident provided *The Clarion* with additional details, however. Although there was disagreement on some facts, the general picture they painted was as follows:

Most of the 18 inmates in custody were let out into the exercise yard for the regularly scheduled 10 a.m. outdoor period. Eight of them started a basketball game, and the others watched or walked around the perimeter of the yard.

Paris was walking behind the basketball backboard when another inmate, Norman Defoe, 29, suddenly lunged at him, shouting, "You killed Miss London!" and stabbed Paris in the throat with a crude, sharp instrument, apparently made inside the jail.

A melee ensued, and additional deputies had to be called in from the courthouse to restore order. By the time the exercise area was secured, Paris had lost a significant amount of blood. He was treated by paramedics and rushed to Forest Memorial Hospital by ambulance, but was pronounced dead upon arrival.

Defoe was arraigned on a murder charge Wednesday afternoon, and Judge Louis Fletcher appointed a public defender to represent him.

According to sheriff's records, Defoe had a history of arrests, mostly on charges of minor drug possession, but had not been implicated in a violent incident until yesterday. At the time of the attack, he was serving a 60-

day sentence for marijuana possession and probation violation.

He always had a copy of *The Oxford Book of English Verse* in his possession, according to sources, and was jokingly referred to by deputies as "the jailhouse poet." School records show he took Miss London's Honors English course at President Arthur High in 1985, receiving a grade of B-plus.

Paris's unexpected death brought to an end the highest-profile criminal case in this county in nearly two decades. Miss London, who retired from teaching in June 1995, had begun working on a family history when she was found dead after a fire at her East Peninsula house the night of June 17.

Her death was initially listed as accidental, but when medical evidence indicated she had been killed before the fire broke out, both the sheriff's office and this newspaper began to investigate the matter further.

In the course of researching the family history, Miss London was looking into the approval of The Peninsulas in January 1971. Her father and brother were partners, along with the Paris family, in that enterprise. It appeared she had come across information suggesting that the deciding vote in favor of the project, cast by then-county supervisor Bart Sturges, had been improperly influenced, and that her father's death in a vehicle accident just before the vote had not been accidental.

Authorities believe that Ronald Paris was involved in both matters, and that he had killed Miss London in the heat of an argument in order to stop her research, then set the fire at her house to make her death appear accidental.

Paris maintained total silence on the matter. He was originally charged with second-degree murder, and his plea to a considerably lesser charge on Monday has been criticized in the community, given the degree of premeditation that appeared to have been involved. *(See editorial, page 8)*

District Attorney Cy Southworth said that while there was no doubt of Paris's guilt, the case would have been hard to prove to a jury, and that it was better to hold him accountable through a lesser plea than to risk acquittal.

Paris's life had crumbled since the arrest. His wife of 31 years, Christine, filed for divorce, and his father, Roger, experienced a sharp decline in health following his son's arrest. He died September 19 at the age of 83.

The prosecutor's office had also been reserving the right to proceed to trial against Paris on multiple charges of kidnapping and assault with a deadly weapon. Those charges stemmed from a June 25 incident in which Paris invaded the home of *The Clarion's* editor and held her, her daughter, and a summer intern hostage at gunpoint. The intern, after being grazed by a gunshot, was able to disarm Paris and restrain him until sheriff's deputies arrived.

Interlude 2: Monday February 24, 1997

(From the San Francisco Chronicle)

The Forest Clarion, a weekly paper with a circulation of 2,800 in Northeastern California, yesterday received the California Newspaper Editors Assn. (CNEA) award for public service in 1996.

The paper was cited for its investigation into the suspicious death of a retired high school English teacher, resulting in the arrest of a prominent local businessman, who was holding the newspaper's editor hostage at gunpoint before being subdued. He subsequently pleaded no contest to manslaughter in the teacher's death.

That investigation also turned up evidence of a bribe paid by the businessman to then-County Supervisor Bart Sturges in 1971. The statute of limitations for prosecution had expired, but Sturges, now the state senator representing the area, subsequently announced he would retire from politics when his senate term expires next year under the state's term-limits law. He also dissolved the committee he had formed in anticipation of running for California Insurance Commissioner in 1998.

The Clarion is the smallest-circulation newspaper ever to win the CNEA's public service award, which is widely regarded as California's most prestigious journalism honor.

Other awards presented yesterday by the CNEA included …

Epilogue: Friday April 18, 1997

THE MAN AT THE TABLE at the front of the room set down the laminated sheet of paper he had been reading aloud and looked around.

"Are there any visitors from outside the Arthur/Año Nuevo area?" he said.

Two men sitting against the wall at the back of the room exchanged glances. The one with the beard spoke first.

"Peter, alcoholic, San Francisco."

"Gordon, Al-Anon, San Francisco," said the other.

The man at the head of the table welcomed them, and the dozen or so people in the room applauded. After two brief announcements, the man looked at Peter and Gordon again.

"It is a tradition of the Friday noon meeting to have a member qualify for 15 minutes, sharing his or her experience, strength and hope as a starting point for group discussion on alcoholism and sobriety. As the regular members of this group have heard each others' stories to the point of depressing familiarity," *a few chuckles*, "we typically ask a visitor, if there is one, to qualify. Peter, from San Francisco, would you be willing to start our meeting today?"

Peter looked at Gordon, shrugged, walked to the head table, and sat next to the secretary — the man who was running the meeting.

"My name is Peter, and I'm an alcoholic."

"Hi, Peter," said a dozen voices in unison.

"My sobriety date is June 26, 1996; my home group is Presidio Men in Sobriety; and I have a sponsor who has a sponsor. I mention those three things because I've come to believe they're critical elements in my recovery.

"And because of where we are, I should probably say that it was up here that I had my last drunk, not quite a year ago. I'd been trying not to drink on my own for nearly three months. I wasn't court-ordered, I was girlfriend-ordered." *Laughter.* "Then, on the Saturday night before my last blowout, I said what the hell and

283

had one glass of wine. That was it. Just one. I didn't have any more that night, and I didn't drink at all on Sunday and Monday. And in the back of my mind, I was starting to think, OK, I can handle this now.

"On Tuesday night, I was having dinner with my best friend — at Ike's, actually — and something came up. He asked me to be there for him a bit later in a situation that might turn a bit sticky. After he left, the waitress asked if she could get me anything else. Without any thought or hesitation whatsoever, I told her to bring me a double scotch and add it to the check. I didn't realize it at the time, but I now know that I was utterly defenseless against the first drink. I figured I'd just have the one, but when I knocked it down, I still had some time to kill, so I moved to the bar and ordered another. And another. Before I even realized what I was doing, I'd had six doubles in an hour.

"Now I'd like to be able to tell you that I hit bottom when I got thrown out of Ike's Lakeside by a female bartender." *Laughter.* "But that wasn't my bottom. Nor was it when the woman who came to pick me up arrived a few minutes later and found me sitting on a bench outside Ike's, reeking of alcohol and barely able to sit, let alone stand. No man ever wants a woman to see him like that, but she did. No, my bottom was the next morning when I came to and found that the friend I was supposed to show up for had been in grave danger and could have been killed because I wasn't there to help. Talk about pitiful and incomprehensible demoralization! I didn't drink for the next three days, and back in San Francisco, I went to my first meeting and have been in the program ever since.

"Last month, I made a Ninth Step amends to that friend. It was probably a tougher amends than the ones to my five ex-wives are going to be," *Laughter,* "even though he reacted like a gentleman. But in looking at how I'd let down my friend, I was forced to consider how I had put other people at peril, as well. You see, I'm a doctor, a surgeon, and for years, I was strictly an after-hours drinker. But the past few years, I was starting to take a beer or a glass of wine with lunch. And I'd tell myself, 'It's all right. You're only doing *minor* surgery this afternoon ... ' "

Everyone in the room cracked up — except Gordon.

IT WAS AN EARLY SPRING DAY in the mountains. That meant that the peaks surrounding Año Nuevo Reservoir still had snow on their top thousand feet; that the sun was shining brightly, though obscured from time to time by the occasional scudding cloud; and that the temperature was in the high 50s and relatively warm in the sunshine —except when the wind kicked up. The wind, cold and cutting, was a reminder that winter had not yet entirely loosened its grip.

Gordon and Peter remained in the church were the meeting had been held for nearly 15 minutes, while everyone came up to Peter, complimented him on his talk, shared, in some instances, a drinking story, and urged him to keep coming back. It was just before 1:30 when Gordon turned the Cherokee onto Union Street. They drove 150 feet down the street before coming to a stop at the end of a long line of cars.

"There may be a bigger turnout than we thought," said Peter.

"So can I ask you something while we wait?"

"You can always ask."

"At the meeting today, when you talked about only drinking before minor surgery, why did everybody laugh?"

Peter thought for a moment.

"It probably has something to do with the alcoholic mind. I'm guessing that almost everybody in that room has rationalized their drinking with lame excuses that don't even begin to make sense. So when I said that, they recognized an element of their own past behavior. That's probably what they were laughing at."

Gordon looked at his watch. They had moved one car length in three minutes.

"It's after 1:30," he said. "They wanted me there by 1:40, even though it doesn't start until two."

"Go, then," said Peter. "I'll park this thing and meet you there."

Gordon jumped out and moved toward the sidewalk. As Peter reached the driver's door, he stopped, picked something up from the floor, and called out, holding it above his head.

"Gordon! Don't forget the book."

"Thanks," said Gordon, snatching it from Peter's hand and jogging back to the sidewalk.

Gordon trudged down the sidewalk toward President Arthur High School. As he got closer, he saw that the road had been barricaded at the block where the school began, and that the parking lot next to Gary A. Bowman Gymnasium was full. He walked past the right side of the main building into a courtyard filled with folding chairs, all facing a podium. The building behind it had a large piece of canvas over its facade. Hundreds of people were milling around, talking loudly.

"Gordon!"

It was Jack Henry, the young basketball player, walking toward him. They shook hands.

"I wasn't going to stick around for this," Jack said, "but then I saw that you were one of the speakers. That's so cool."

"I'd rather be shooting two free throws in a hostile gym with the game on the line. Public speaking scares me to death."

"Don't worry. You'll do fine."

Gordon shrugged. "How'd the team do this year?"

"League co-champions, and we made the quarterfinals in the playoffs. Then we ran into a team with a big man we couldn't stop."

"Sounds like you could have used Gary Bowman."

"If he was as good as they say, we would have won it all. It was a good year, anyway."

"Any scholarship offers?"

Jack shook his head. "None. But I've been accepted at University of the Pacific, and the coach said I can walk on there. I think that's what I'll do."

"Well, good luck to you."

Judge Fletcher had walked up to Gordon's right, and Gordon turned to shake his hand.

"Gordon, my boy. Delighted you could make it. You're looking well."

"As are you, your honor."

"I look forward to hearing how Charlotte's book is going."

"You won't have long to wait," Gordon said, looking at his watch. "Are you still going to retire next year?"

"I shall make the announcement the first week in December. On a Wednesday, so The *Clarion* will have an exclusive. Or do they still call them scoops?"

"Good question."

"And how is the judge?"

"The judge is the judge," Gordon deadpanned.

"Glad to hear it. I won't bother you any longer; you have work to do. Perhaps we can talk later." And with that, he was off.

Gordon scanned the crowd, looking for El. He saw Gina at the far side of the open area, and she waved and blew him a kiss. Robert Paris was only 20 feet from Gordon, but he averted his eyes when Gordon looked in his direction. Finally, he saw her, on the other side of the chairs, notebook in hand and camera with telephoto lens hanging from her neck. She looked good. He made his way through the crowd toward her.

She saw him when he was just a few feet away and threw her arms apart to give him a hug, then remembered the camera with the long lens and slid it over her shoulder so it hung at her side. They embraced without saying anything for seconds.

"Hey, you," he finally said.

"Hey, yourself."

He stepped back and took her left hand in his right. Feeling something rough on it, he held it up so he could see better. It was a ring with a large diamond on her fourth finger.

"It looks like you have some news," he said.

She nodded and flashed a smile that was half joyous, half rueful.

"He just popped the question last week. It's all happened very fast."

"In my experience, it usually does."

"I'm still kind of in shock. We got to talking at the Rotary Club Christmas party in December, and I invited him over for a drink afterward. The next thing you know, we were decking the halls, if you catch my drift."

Gordon exercised his right to remain silent.

"It just took off from there and went full-speed. But, you know, it feels right. I'm ready to settle down now, and he's always needed to be settled down."

"Are you going to give me a name?"

"Oh, I'm sorry. It's Cam. Cam Winters."

"Charlotte's attorney? I thought he was married."

"He was, but in August, his wife got diagnosed with Stage 4 cancer. She died the first week of October, and he was beside himself. Some men were never meant to live alone."

"Well, I wish you all the best. Both of you."

"Thanks, Gordon. That means a lot. And you know the other thing that's happened because of this?" He shook his head. "I'm reconnecting with my father. He's thrilled, and if you can believe it, he wants to officiate at the wedding. Cam's been a real sweetheart about that."

"And Anna?"

"Graduating from law school in a few weeks. She was planning to go into legal aid law, but since the standoff at the house, she's decided to be a prosecutor and has been studying criminal law."

"Ronald Paris's legacy continues. But what I meant to ask was how Anna feels about your engagement?"

"Who can tell with her? When I told her the news last week, the only thing she said was, 'Well, at least I'll know who's going to be in the house when I come home.' Go figure."

Gordon shook his head again, and turned to look at the crowd, which was steadily growing.

"Looking for anybody in particular?" she asked.

"I'd like to see Alice and Karl if they're here. And maybe Coach Iverson."

"You're too late for the coach. He died the first week of December."

"I'm sorry to hear that."

"In a way, it's probably what he would have wanted. At the last football game of the season, he was standing on the sideline as usual. It was raining when the game started and it turned to sleet before it was over. He came down with something, and the something led to pneumonia, and then …"

She snapped her fingers. "Just like that. We're all that close, when you think about it."

After a brief pause, she pointed behind Gordon and to his right. "Karl and Alice are over there with Emma.'

"Will you excuse me?"

"That's fine. I have to work, unfortunately."

It took Gordon nearly a minute for to reach the others. Emma saw him first and shouted with delight. The women hugged him, and Karl gave him a hearty handshake.

"Oh, my God," said Alice. "It's so great to see you, Gordon. And look at all these people? Can you believe it? I thought we'd be lucky to get a hundred out today, but it's several times that. Who'd have thought? I feel so overwhelmed about this. I mean when you look at all that Charlotte did to teach the importance of reading and writing, and for years everybody took her for granted, and now she's being honored as if she was an athlete or a coach. It's wonderful to see books and reading honored in the same way as athletics."

"Maybe they're honoring the money she gave," said Karl.

"Karl!" shouted the two women in joint dismay.

"I just say what I think," he said.

Gordon felt a hand on his shoulder. It was Walter Williams, the high school principal, looking harried.

"Gordon! I was afraid you might have gotten stuck in the traffic. We just realized the last couple of days that this might be bigger than we expected. But follow me. We're starting in a few minutes."

That turned out to be an optimistic assessment. After being seated in the chair at the far left of the podium, he had ample time to scan the growing crowd. It was a concentrated enough mass of humanity that he couldn't tell whether Peter was in it or not. Finally, at 2:20, Williams stepped to the lectern, tapped the microphone twice, and waited as the two staccato reports gradually silenced the crowd.

"Good afternoon, ladies and gentlemen. Thank you all for coming out today to celebrate the memory of perhaps the greatest teacher in the history of Forest County and the dedication of the Charlotte London Memorial Library."

He turned and extended an arm toward the door with the canvas over its facade. Two husky student-athletes, one at each side of the door, pulled down on the ropes they were holding, and the canvas plummeted to earth, revealing the library's new name, recently painted in school red.

The crowd burst into a roar of applause, whistling and foot-stomping.

Williams continued for a few minutes, talking about Charlotte's career and quoting from letters written by former students. He was not a particularly gifted speaker, but was talking from the heart, and he clearly had the audience on his side.

He introduced State Senator Bart Sturges, who presented a joint resolution from the California State Legislature, honoring Charlotte's career. Technically, he was a better speaker than the principal, but the feeling wasn't there. He had the sense to wrap up quickly and sit down to polite applause.

"After her retirement," Williams said, "Charlotte decided to try writing a book of her own — a family history. As many of you know, she came from a pioneer Forest County family and had deep roots in the community. Her literary executor, Mr. Quill Gordon of San Francisco, will now say a few words. Gordon stood, and took two steps toward the lectern before remembering the book Peter had given him, sitting on the floor by his chair. There were a couple of titters as he went back to get it. Finally settled at the lectern, he reached into his coat pocket, took out the single page of his prepared remarks, and looked up. The crowd seemed to have grown to 50,000, though that was clearly impossible.

It's just like shooting a free throw, he told himself, *in front of ten thousand screaming people in a gym.*

"Principal Williams, people of Forest County. Thank you all for turning out to honor Charlotte London today.

"I'm told that many of you are wondering about the book she was working on at the time of her death. It's my pleasure to report that Susan Struthers, a former reporter for the *San Francisco Chronicle*, has pulled it into shape, and the draft version is now being reviewed by a professional editor. Susan has done an excellent job of finishing the work, while holding to the style and direction Charlotte established as she was writing it. If all goes well, the book will be coming off the presses in August or September, and I will personally make sure that the first copy off the press is reserved for this library."

The audience applauded robustly.

"In the course of working on this project, I've had the good fortune to meet many of the fine people in this county. In doing so, it's become clear that the students who were lucky enough to have Charlotte London for a teacher came away with lessons they will carry with them the rest of their lives. How does anyone quantify the effect of that? One of Charlotte's favorite books was *Middlemarch* by George Eliot. She often remarked that she wished she could have taught it, but she felt it was too long and complex for a high school audience. At the end of that book, though, Eliot offers a valedictory to her principal character, Dorothea, and those closing words of the book might apply equally well to Charlotte London."

He opened the book, swallowed hard, and began reading.

" 'Her full nature, like that of the river of which Cyrus broke the strength, spent itself in channels which had no great name on the earth. But the effect of her being on those around her was incalculably diffusive: for the growing good of the world is partly dependent on unhistoric acts; and that things are not so ill with you and me as they might have been, is half owing to the number who lived faithfully a hidden life, and rest in unvisited tombs.' "

He looked up and snapped the book shut. The microphone amplified the noise, and he started slightly. Then he bowed his head and walked back to his seat. He was so wrapped up in his thoughts and emotions that he never heard the applause.

THE SUN HAD DROPPED BEHIND the western mountains as the motorboat drifted to a stop near the middle of the lake. The temperature had dropped along with the sun, and the wind lashed with a greater sting than it had during the spring afternoon. The three people in the boat drew their jackets more tightly around themselves, but it didn't help much. They sat in somber silence for a moment.

"Shall we?" said Gordon.

"The sooner the better," said Peter. "It's freezing."

"You think this will be all right?"

"I think it'll be fine," said Gina, who was sitting between the two men.

"You think Charlotte would be OK with it?"

"I think she would. But what I think doesn't matter. You're the one she trusted with this. It's your call."

Gordon didn't answer immediately. Peter, his hands in his jacket pockets, was flapping his arms in an attempt to stay warm. Gina continued.

"Charlotte was a teacher. She challenged people to push themselves and do their best. You were her last pupil, carrying out her last assignment. I think you earned an A-plus."

"I don't know about that," muttered Peter. "I think he should have had points deducted for almost killing himself and two other people."

"All right, then," said Gordon. "Let's do it."

He picked up a metal lock box that had been sitting by his feet. Two dozen small holes had been drilled into its lid.

"The journal's in there?" asked Gina.

Gordon nodded. "Along with a dozen stones I gathered along the shore of the lake this morning. And it's locked with a key. It should be secure."

Reaching over the edge of the boat, he set the box on the surface of the water, keeping a hand on either side.

"So long, Charlotte," he said, removing his hands.

The box floated for a moment, its top even with the surface. They could see the water slowly going into the holes. Abruptly, it filled to its sinking weight and plummeted into the inky darkness of the lake. It was out of sight in seconds. The wind picked up again, but none of them felt it or said anything for a full minute.

"There's one thing that still bothers me," said Gordon. "In all the commotion that night at El's, I never told Paris that Charlotte had forgiven him. And I never saw him again. I don't know if he was capable of redemption, but he shouldn't have died without knowing that."

"It's not your job to decide who's capable of redemption," Gina said. "And you're hardly the first person who wished he'd had a chance to say something before someone died. Let it go, Gordon."

"Speaking of redemption," said Peter, "I have a question for the committee. I'm still working on the whole issue of a higher power. All I know now is that it's not me, and that's progress. But suppose there really is a God up in the sky who judges us, and that there's a heaven and a hell. I have some doubts about that, but let's assume it for the moment.

"What do you think a God like that does with Charlotte? Does he look at the woman whose journal we just deep-sixed and say, 'Sorry.' Or does he weigh that against the woman who was honored at the school today and let her in? If it were my call, I'd wave her through the pearly gates, but — as I said — it's not my call."

"I think you have it right," said Gina. "And for whatever it's worth, I think that's what Charlotte believed. What do you say, Gordon?"

For several seconds, he stared silently and broodingly at the dark waters into which the box with Charlotte's journal had descended.

"I sure hope so," he finally said. "For all our sakes."

THE END

Author's Note

THIS BOOK IS DEDICATED in the spirit of two mystery writers — one British, one American — each of whom published, in 1930, a well regarded book with thematic similarities to this one.

Anthony Berkeley Cox (1893-1971) was one of the stalwarts of the Golden Age of mystery novels in Britain at the time. Along with Agatha Christie, John Dickson Carr, Freeman Wills Crofts, Ronald Knox, and others, he was a founder of the Detection Club. Writing as Francis Iles, he produced *Before the Fact* and *Malice Aforethought*, two pioneering examples of the "inverted" detective novel, in which the solution is known at the beginning and the suspense lies in how it will be unraveled. Under the name Anthony Berkeley, he wrote the 1930 Golden Age classic *The Poisoned Chocolates Case*, in which a group of amateurs, similar to the group in this book, band together, trying to solve a high-profile murder that appears to be baffling the police.

Earl Derr Biggers (1884-1933) was born in Ohio, attended Harvard, and is best known as author of the Charlie Chan detective series, currently enjoying a well deserved critical revival. His 1930 contribution to that series, *Charlie Chan Carries On*, has Inspector Duff of Scotland Yard traveling from London to Hawaii, attempting to solve a series of murders occurring on a round-the-world cruise. When the inspector is shot and wounded in Honolulu, Chan steps in for him — much as Gordon and his associates do for Charlotte London — and sees the case through to its conclusion.

Finally and unrelatedly, in case anyone is interested, the historical abortion story told by Karl Bjornstad in Chapter 7 of this book very closely follows a true story that occurred in California in the early 20th Century and was reported in local newspapers.

Acknowledgements

EVERYTHING I KNOW about land use, or pretty near, I learned from my friend, business associate, and marketing guru John Bakalian. Thanks, good buddy. The late City Council Member Scott Kennedy and late State Senator Henry Mello shared candid insights about the political mind at work. The Santa Cruz Public Library was an invaluable resource for California history, and I am indebted to SPC Nicholas Wallace for information on private pilots and small airports.

Thanks, as well, to members of the Quill Gordon team for their efforts in making this a better book than it otherwise might have been. That would include Lauren Wilkins for a stellar editing job, Deborah Karas for capturing the right visual feel in the cover design, and Greg Pio for his helpful comments as the book was being written. Kudos to Chip Scheuer and Rigo Torkos for their fine work on the book's video trailer.

About the Author

MICHAEL WALLACE published his first mystery novel, *The McHenry Inheritance*, in 2012. He is former editor-in-chief of a daily newspaper and has had a lengthy second career as a publications and public relations consultant. He lives in the Monterey Bay area of California, is a lifelong fan and voracious reader of mystery novels, and has been a fly fisherman for more than three decades. He may be contacted through his website, quillgordonmystery.com.

Photo/Greg Pio

Made in the USA
Monee, IL
28 August 2023

41779488R00175